Whispering Corner

© Marc Alexander 2014

ISBN 978-1-909473-14-0

Text prepared by Willow eBooks
Original cover artwork © Phil Biggs of
www.heritagewatercolour.co.uk

Whispering Corner

by

Marc Alexander

Published by Willow Books

Works by Marc Alexander
Available on Lulu.com

History

The Outrageous Queens
Royal Murder

Stories for Young Teenagers

The Mist Lizard
Turtle Island

Westerns

Golden Dollar
Hand of Vengeance
A Fast Gun for Judas
The Sundown Trail
The Water War

Fantasy

Ancient Dreams
Magic Casements
Shadow Realm
Enchantment's End
(Collectively known as **The Wells of Ythan**)

Horror

The Plague Pit
Bloodthirst
Ogre
Ghoul

Novels of the Supernatural

Whispering Corner
The Dark Domain

For Carole and Brian Hershman

PROLOGUE

This is the last book I shall write.

It will not be aimed at faithful readers who have an appetite for my brand of horror fiction, it will never be submitted to my agent who gave me up in understandable disgust, it is to be solely for myself – an act of catharsis.

It will be written without literary considerations, though I shall endeavour to recall – with an author's word processor memory – some passages of the novel I was engaged upon while an occupant of Whispering Corner. My aim is solely to set down the events which cast me in the role of a character in one of my own more macabre stories.

At the moment, these events and their implications are so chaotic in my mind that only by cataloguing them do I believe I shall be able to achieve a sane perspective of what led up to the ultimate tragedy. This is being attempted in another world – almost another time – from the Dorset woodland where I fulfilled a dream by buying that queer old house, where love came unexpectedly, and a unique combination of creative imagination and the paranormal laid upon me the terrible burden of belief.

Because of the daytime heat which hangs like a curse over this coast I shall type through the hours of darkness, but if there are times when illicit alcohol brings release or I cannot bear to face the still-menacing past I have the consolation that for the first time I am free from the tyranny of a deadline.

Perhaps when this self-imposed task is completed I shall be able to come to terms with both the way my career has ended and the horrific situations I once inflicted upon my characters. Perhaps as an exercise in expiation it will free me from the dreams which continue to haunt me on this far shore. Mostly, however, I believe that this narration will enable me to decide whether or not I am guilty of murder.

Jonathan Northrop

Chapter 1

Twin patterns of light flared on the rain-spattered windscreen, killing the driver's vision and panicking him as the maroon Peugeot rounded a curve in the forest lane. When the wipers momentarily cleared the glass he saw an orange Mini angled in a ditch so that its headlights not only raked him but transformed the ancient trees on either side into a monochrome tunnel.

Silhouetted against the halo was a swaying figure whose arms moved in a slow-motion attempt to flag him down.

Braking too hard, he felt the big car slide on mud which had been washed over the pot-holed tarmac. The swinging beams of its lamps transformed the silhouette into a young woman, and the driver had a fleeting vision of a face white like a clown's and framed by long fair hair. He closed his eyes, braced for the sickening thump as she vanished beneath the bonnet. But the tyres gripped and the world steadied.

He elbowed open the door and ran through the downpour to her and could not help but notice the erotic way her wet blouse clung to her breasts – a guilty reaction doused by the sight of blood mingling with raindrops on her temple.

'Please help me,' she murmured. 'It came out of the woods.'

He caught her as her legs buckled . . .

Yet again, I knew that what I had just written was a lousy intro. I closed Word, ignoring its protest that the file had not been saved by clicking, 'No', the equivalent of screwing up a typescript and throwing it into the waste-paper basket.

I prowled the flat, impatient for the Cona to reheat the coffee and wondering whether it was too early to have a proper drink to settle my panic. I am embarrassed to admit that I once described a character in one of my stories as feeling 'as though a hand of ice had fastened on his heart', yet that was how I felt that morning. It was not just the intro, I was finally admitting to myself that the storyline of my proposed book, *Ancient Dreams*, was as trite as the opening I had been agonizing over, and I feared that as a novelist I was finished.

The truth was that I was having my first bout of writer's block.

It was something I had derided in the past when I believed I would run out of time before I ran out of words. But now I was unable to get to grips with a novel that should have been half finished, a situation which had caused me to lie to my darling agent for the first time in our association. I dared not let her think I had lost the confidence gained when for several euphoric weeks my *Shadows and Mirrors* headed the top ten fiction list.

Following that halcyon period, I really believed I was capable of producing bestseller after bestseller. However, it became apparent that my next novel had not caught the public's imagination in the same way as *Shadows*. Now I needed *Ancient Dreams* to reinstate me, yet I knew it would be almost impossible to deliver the script to the Griffin Press on time. Furthermore, Griffin had just been taken over by a big publishing conglomerate and its new masters were less likely to be lenient over late delivery than my editor Reggie Burnside, who had become a personal friend.

The reheated coffee was too bitter. I poured a shot of Courvoisier and turned it into a longish drink with Perrier water. The noble spirit had its usual reviving effect and I determined to start yet again – and this time get it right.

I returned to my work table under the window, but stood for a minute, glass in hand, gazing at pale spring sky above the rooftops on the opposite side of Coram Square. Our flat was the second storey of one of those Georgian houses that once gave such grace to Bloomsbury and had somehow survived the planners and developers who had entered into an unholy alliance to turn this once romantic neighbourhood into something out of Orwell. It was the sight of the new leaves like green mist about the square's old trees which prompted the Imp to whisper that what I needed was a stroll out of doors to get myself ready to tear into my work.

I must explain the Imp.

One of the curious things I had found about writer's block was that when I had psyched myself up to the point where I was eager to hear my typewriter's reassuring rattle – woefully missing on today's electronic machines – I would find a pretext to delay getting on with it, there would be some household chore that became suddenly urgent, an errand to be undertaken then and there so it would not interrupt the creative flow once it was in spate, or a long neglected telephone call that had to be made at once. I had code-named this syndrome the Imp of the Perverse, with acknowledgements to the master of my craft, Edgar Allan Poe.

Of course I had tried to analyse it.

To have blamed the problem I shared with Pamela would have been easy, but I refused to consider such a glib explanation. I have no time for men who use their marital situations to excuse lack of effort in pursuit of their self-proclaimed creative goals. Besides, our unspoken tensions had not affected the writing of Shadows.

If I had an inkling of the real origin of the Imp, I kept it locked in the lumber room of my unconscious along with the other bric-a-brac of life which I preferred to ignore. I admit that I am a coward when it comes to facing unpleasant realities and will always avoid them if I can. Perhaps I was successful in writing escapist literature (with a very small 'l') because I am an escapist.

2

But this morning my desperation to get the wretched book started was stronger than the blandishments of the Imp.

I opened a new file and resolutely began typing. I had accomplished half a page when the telephone chirruped and I heard the lively voice of my agent, Sylvia Stone, quite rightly known as Sweet Sylvia by her authors.

'Just ringing to remind you that we have a lunch date,' she said.

'But that's on Friday.'

'Today is Friday, old chum. Authors!' She sighed theatrically. 'Come on, descend from your ivory tower and get to La Capannina as fast as you can. I only hope that your vagueness is because you've been working your unmentionables off. How many pages?'

'You know I never number my pages until the end.'

Sweet Sylvia laughed dutifully at the old joke.

'But you are up to schedule?' she persisted. 'Now that Griffin is part of Clipper Publishing the days of wine and roses are over.'

'It'll be all right on the night,' I muttered.

'Better be. Now hurry. I'd like to have a drink with you before the Mount-William arrives.'

In less than an hour I was in the streets of Soho, skirting knots of out-of-town football fans clustering round electronic porn parlours. In my long-gone journalistic days when Soho had been part of my beat, real girls had stood in the doorways, somehow that seemed less sordid than video peepshows and snuff movies. Then an AIDS poster reminded me how our sexual mores are changing and protective taboos emerging, as they did for the Victorians under threat from non-curable syphilis.

This train of thought, prompted by the fact I was in Wardour Street, reminded me of a film producer I had once worked with on a documentary film who, at a predictable stage of intoxication, would burst from the gay closet in defiance of his sober lifestyle as a husband and father. I could imagine the fear this new plague brought him, and the dilemma it created in his relationship with his wife. Perhaps celibacy had something to be said for it after all. One gets used to it.

At the corner of Greek Street and Romilly Street was La Capannina, a restaurant which had long been a favourite of mine and one which I had used as a setting in *Shadows*. Knowing my preference, it was typical of my agent to choose it for this meeting for which she knew I had little enthusiasm. Gianni greeted me warmly, and his wife Linda smiled. 'The lady is already here, Mr Northrop,' she said. I was led from the foyer into the restaurant, where Sylvia was sitting in a favoured seat by the window with a Punt e Mes before her.

'Hello, Jonathan,' she said as I joined her. 'I was hoping you would have a packet of manuscript under your arm for me.'

I reminded her that true artists never show half-finished work and

3

quickly ordered an aperitif. If Sylvia Stone had not inherited the Hermes literary agency which her father had founded for daring young writers in the thirties, she would have made an excellent headmistress. She was tall and had never rounded her shoulders to hide the fact. Her soft greying hair was swept back and her complexion, which had never known cosmetics other than a modest touch of lipstick, must have been the envy of women half her age.

Publishers liked doing business with her because she was utterly reliable and nearly always cheerful. Her grasp of literary agreements was awe-inspiring, and should any contracts department attempt to palm a tricky little clause into the small print her tone could become as chilling as a Siberian wind. Her authors she regarded as a family whose oddly assorted members she encouraged, played mother confessor to and, if necessary, bullied. On occasion she had been known to send ginseng to those who were flagging but at a publisher's party, after a little too much sparkling Piat d'Or, I heard her remark, 'old spinsters like me traditionally end up with cats or very nasty little dogs, but I have authors. Sometimes I wish it had been nasty little dogs.'

Although she greeted me with her usual bright smile, I was aware of her surreptitious glance of concern. I became conscious of the dark circles under my eyes, in fact I had been a little shocked at the haggard face which had peered back at me from my shaving mirror that morning.

'Ready for your exodus to darkest Dorset?' she asked.

'The house is almost ready. It hasn't been lived in for over a year, and it was a hell of a mess. A local handy lad named Hoddy has been doing a sterling job on it.'

'And Pam?'

'She's staying on in New York for a bit longer.'

'She must be enjoying it.'

For a moment neither of us could think of anything to add to that particular topic.

'I thought our boozy lunches with dear old Reggie would have come to an end when Clipper took over Griffin . . .' I began.

'Officially it was a merger.'

'In the same way that Jonah and the whale was a merger. Anyway, what's the scenario for today?'

'Reggie wants to introduce you to Jocasta Mount-William. Now that she's editorial director of Griffin as well as Clipper she'll be a very important lady in your professional life.'

'And Reggie?'

Sylvia shrugged.

'Although he's been given a fancy new title, Jocasta is in fact his boss. *Entre nous*, he's desperately looking around. He'd been promised a seat on the Griffin board before the merger, but now . . .'

For a few minutes we gossiped about the merger and the personalities involved, and how smaller publishing companies were being ingested by the big ones, and who was likely to end up where in the endless musical chairs of the publishing world.

Suddenly Sylvia laid her hand on mine.

'Jonathan, when you talk to Jocasta Mount-William sound what you are – a confident bestselling novelist. I hear that as far as Griffin is concerned she has the new broom syndrome, and I gather that her taste does not encompass the sort of popular novel that Griffin has specialized in – especially horror novels.'

'She's an intellectual?'

'Cambridge degree in literature, old chum. Her claim to fame is that when she was with Icarus Press she actually made Barram re-write the opening chapter of *Marl* before it went on to win the Russell-Montgomery award.'

'Oh great,' I said. 'But what's a nice high-brow girl like her doing in the bordello of popular publishing?'

'She has the reputation of being very, very efficient, has friends in high places, and I think her brief is to raise the tone of Griffin Books by a few notches. So if she asks you about your motivation as a writer don't go into your "too lazy to work, too scared to steal" routine.'

'It got a laugh on LBC.'

'Just remember that today it's Radio 3. Ah, here's Reggie.'

Reginald Burnside was a balding young man in a very well cut suit including a waistcoat and a magenta open-necked shirt, a sartorial style he had acquired while scouting for books on the west coast of America.

'Hope I'm not late for my favourite literary agent – and author,' he said. 'Sylvia, Jonathan, I'd like you to meet Jocasta. She'll be looking after you now that I've been banished to non-fiction.'

The young woman beside him reminded me of a newspaper picture I had once seen of a female freedom fighter (or terrorist), though on closer inspection I saw that her olive battle fatigues could have only come from the King's Road. Her sun-streaked hair was cropped short, her long face was over-tanned and she wore glasses that were ever-so-slightly tinted blue. Her watch was very expensive, a diver's Rolex.

'We meet at last. I've heard so much about you,' said Sylvia in her best agent's manner.

Jocasta set the tone immediately. She gave Sylvia a mouth smile and said, 'You're with the Hermes Agency.'

'I am the Hermes Agency,' Sylvia replied in her extra pleasant voice.

'Of course. It's just that there seem to be so many agencies these days.'

5

'And fewer and fewer publishers . . .'

Sylvia's voice was honeyed, the sort of honey that comes from a Venus fly trap. But I also knew that, whatever was said to ruffle her, Sylvia, for the sake of her authors, would never lose her cool.

There was a truce while the menu was discussed and I extolled the delights of the restaurant's cheese pancakes.

'So you're the author of *Shadows and Mirrors*,' Jocasta said musingly as she handed her menu to the waiter. 'Somehow I had the impression from your book that you'd be younger. Oh well – I hope you have something worthwhile coming up for us.'

'Jonathan's superstitious about talking about his work until he's typed "The End",' Sylvia explained. 'But when it's delivered I'm sure you'll have another bestseller on your hands.'

Jocasta looked doubtful. 'I hate to be a prophet of doom,' she said, not hating it at all, 'but I checked the sales figures of your last book before I left the office, and they're very disappointing.'

'Early days yet,' I said.

'I'm afraid there has been enough time for our sales people to gain an idea, and frankly . . .'

Her voice trailed off as the hors d'ouvres arrived and Reggie gave me an encouraging wink.

'The trouble is that horror is becoming *passé*,' Jocasta continued as she deftly speared a tiny dead creature with her fork. '*Shadows and Minors* came out at the right moment. Now the public wants something different. Something like Martin Winter's *Blue Hour*. We're having phenomenal success with that.'

Sylvia said, 'Martin Winter, and good luck to him, is having phenomenal success because he's basically a film writer and he turned one of his scripts into the book-of-the-film, a film which had the good luck to be a hit at Cannes. With all that publicity it follows that the book should be a blockbuster.'

'True, but Martin touched a nerve whether in film or book form,' Jocasta said. 'What I'm saying is that the public's taste is changing, and to succeed as a publisher you have to continually gauge it, find authors to match it, and be ruthless about giving up those who don't. "Deflower and devour" horror books were OK in their day, but that day is over . . .'

'Anyone who knows Jonathan's work would hardly call it "deflower and devour",' Sylvia protested. 'When he was interviewed on *Bookworm* last month he was introduced as "one of the most intelligent interpreters of horror".'

Jocasta permitted her lips to draw back in a slight smile.

'*Bookworm* is hardly the exemplar of the British literary establishment.'

I felt it was time I joined the conversation.

'Correct me if I'm wrong, Miss Mount-William, but it seems to me that you're unhappy to have inherited me with the Griffin list.'

She paused for a moment before replying, and I guessed she was considering the fact that at one time I had made a lot of money for Griffin and, although my last book had not done well, there was a possibility that I might again.

'It would be foolish to pretend that I don't see a problem, as the sales figures bear out, but of course I hope that the book you're working on will re-establish you. How is it progressing? I understand it's due for delivery in three months . . .'

'Provided there are no unavoidable circumstances.' Sylvia quoted a clause that she always insisted upon.

'I'm sure there won't be a problem,' Reggie asserted. 'I've always found Jonathan to be most professional over deadlines. Comes from his years in newspapers, I suppose.'

'The book is going fine,' I lied. 'And I'll bring it in on time.'

'And the title? In the contract it merely says "A Novel".'

'It took me a while to decide,' I said, an extraordinary idea beginning to take shape in my mind. 'So important to get the right one,' I went on, hoping for a few more seconds before I had to come out with my decision. 'Margaret Mitchell called her book *The Old South* – luckily someone changed it just before it was printed. I can't imagine *The Old South* having the same impact as *Gone With the Wind*.'

'And your title?'

I took a reckless gulp of white wine.

'Whispering Corner.'

'Like it,' said faithful Reggie.

Sylvia choked back her surprise and Jocasta merely remarked that she would have to think about it.

As soon as she finished her main course she said that she had to go.

'There's a meeting,' she added by way of apology.

'There's always a bloody meeting these days,' Reggie sighed. 'We go along to hear what the sales side will allow us to publish.'

Jocasta chose to ignore this heresy.

'It's been interesting to meet you,' she told me. 'I'm glad *Whispering Corner* is on course. It's scheduled to appear in spring. See you in a minute, Reg.'

She headed in the direction of the ladies' washroom and Reggie gave us a wry grin.

'You will have gathered that horror is not the favourite genre of my new boss.'

'This situation must be so disappointing for you,' said Sylvia, actually patting his hand.

'You can't keep a good man down,' he laughed. 'There may be an announcement in *Publishing Weekly* before long. But it's only to be expected that Jocasta will want to promote her own authors, so be sure *Whispering Corner* is a winner. I don't want to be downbeat, Jon, but what you badly need is another success. You can only coast along on a past one for so long and you know the old adage, You're only as good as your last book. *Shadows and Mirrors* was a very fine novel but your last didn't live up to it. I'm not saying it wasn't well written,' he added hastily, 'but I think you felt you were in a position to experiment. Subtlety is all very well, but you did tend to overdo it.'

'So sorry there wasn't a disembowelled corpse on every page that didn't feature a rape scene,' I said bitterly.

'Jon, just give this one everything you've got. Since I edited your first novel I've recognized your ability and I know you've got it in you to write a bestseller again . . . Ah, here's the Knightsbridge Guerrilla.'

When Reggie and Jocasta Mount-William passed into the pale sunlight of Romilly Street I signalled urgently for a couple of brandies – mine a large one.

'I think we need these,' I said.

'I certainly do,' Sylvia agreed. 'Jocasta might have been a bit much, but you . . . what's this new title you suddenly sprang on me? What the hell happened to *Ancient Dreams* that you're supposed to be half way through?'

'*Ancient Dreams* became a modern nightmare. I'm sorry, Sylvia, but I've been lying to you about its progress – couldn't admit I had writer's block, I suppose. And when I did get some of it down I'd tear it up afterwards. No one could have believed in my characters because I didn't believe in them myself

Sylvia could not prevent her surprise – no, shock – showing on her face.

'You mean that the book that the Mount-William is expecting in three months just doesn't exist?'

I nodded, and ordered another brandy,

'Do you want me to get you out of the contract?'

'No way. I'm going to write a novel called *Whispering Corner* in place of *Ancient Dreams*, it's going to be delivered on time and it'll have a brand new storyline that'll have film producers queuing at your door.'

'I wish you luck,' said Sylvia. She was not impressed by my sudden surge of self-confidence and I was very aware that she was hurt because I had not mentioned my difficulties earlier. 'How do you plan to get a whole novel written in such a short time?'

'I'm going to bury myself in the country and do nothing but write morning, noon and night. I'll live my book and my characters will come so alive they'll take over the plot just as they did in Shadows.'

'Did you really believe that, or was it a good conversation piece?'

'It was true – spooky but true. They definitely developed wills of their own, and I felt so intimate with them that when I came to the last page I was bereaved. My companions had gone.'

'At least *Whispering Corner* isn't a bad title.'

'It's the name of my new house. The atmosphere of the place should help. It's very secluded.'

Sylvia glanced at her watch.

'I must rush. I'm seeing the editor of Heritage at three thirty. Could you do a piece for him – after you've finished the book – on your house? With a name like that . . .'

'I doubt it. It's just an old place that happens to be in a wood.'

'No historic associations? No rare architecture? No ghosts?'

'None of those things.'

'But that name . . . where did that come from?'

I shrugged.

'The estate agent had an idea the name referred to a spot in the wood before the house was built, but he was rather vague. I'll certainly research it when I get down there.'

As we left the restaurant Sylvia said quietly, 'Listen, old chum, the next time we come here I want you to hand over the *Whispering Corner* script and tell me it's the best thing you've done.'

* * *

It was the sound of the telephone which saved me from the nightmare. My heart was pounding from a combination of fear and brandy and I sat bolt upright in my sweat-soaked pyjamas for several disoriented seconds before the incessant sound forced me to stumble into the small hall where the telephone stood on my wife's prized Pembroke table.

'Hello?' I croaked into the receiver.

Music and laughter crackled in my ear. Somewhere someone was having a party while I wondered if I was about to have a heart attack.

'Jon . . . what time is it over there?'

'Pam, it's very late. Maybe four in the morning. Are you ringing from New York to ask me the time?'

The tone of her laughter told me that she was several drinks ahead of the game.

'Darling, I get so confused with this time business. I forget whether it's forwards or backwards. We're having a party in Liz's studio. It's in an old warehouse, overlooking the Hudson.'

'How splendid,' I said and slumped down beside the Pembroke.

'Have you heard from Steve?'

'He's very happy with his course in Sheffield. He rang me a couple of days ago. He told me to give you his love if . . . when we next spoke.'

'Give him mine. How's the bloody old novel going?'

'Just fine.'

'Jon, we're having a celebration.'

'I guessed that.'

'It's for me.'

I began to shiver. Perhaps it was the shreds of the nightmare which clung to me, or perhaps I was cold, or perhaps it was Pam's tipsy laugh.

'Can you guess what we're celebrating?'

I said I had no idea.

'Jon, wonderful news. I've landed some work with the Feinstein Agency. How long? Can't say. At least three months. I'm working on the launch of a new perfume.'

'That's nice,' I said automatically as the shivering grew worse. 'What's it called?'

'Hello? There are voices on the wire. Are you the Wichita Lineman? Did you say, "What's it called"?'

'Yes.'

'*Fleur de Lune*. Watch out for it in the glossies in a few weeks' time. Isn't it marvellous? To be back with a campaign after all these years. It was Liz who got me the introductions. She's been fantastic. What? You sound sort of funny.'

'I just came out of a bad dream.'

'Not those bloody stairs again?'

'Well, congratulations on *Fleur de Lune* . . .'

'The perfume is supposed to come from some sort of Asian lily that only blooms in the moonlight. That gives it the name, see?'

I said that I did.

'Think of the copy I can write round that idea.'

'I could write a book round that idea.'

'Those bloody voices again, can't you hear them? Must be the CIA. Tell Steve I'll give him a ticket to come over here for a holiday at the end of term.'

'I will.'

'Look, Jon, I think the way things are at the moment is best for both of us . . . hey, that's my champagne . . . sorry. What I want to say is that . . . well, nothing dramatic has happened. I just happen to have landed a job over here, and you've got a book to finish in England and . . . and we're still friends?'

'Friends,' I said.

'Liz wants to say hi. I'll write and let you know how the work goes. OK?'

'Pam . . .'

'Hi.' Liz's voice came on the line, triggering off a mental picture,

10

out of date now, of Pamela's trendy college chum who had married an American advertising man and now, successfully divorced, followed her intense but short-lived enthusiasms. I gathered that the latest was sculpting shapes of feminist significance out of basalt.

'Pam told you the great news?'

'That she has a job.'

'Yeah. And about time too. She's had to subjugate her talent for far too long. She's her own woman again.'

She did not disguise the note of satisfaction in her voice. She had never forgiven me for getting Pamela pregnant in our young days, seeing me as the factor which had spoiled what she regarded as a glorious friendship.

'I'm very pleased for her,' I said.

'You don't mean that. You think you're the only one allowed to be creative . . .'

I guessed that like the rest of the party she'd had a goodly intake of champagne and I held the receiver away from my ear.

'. . . you were so full of shit you never realized that woman's potential,' she was saying when I brought it back into place, and I wondered why American expressions were so anal in character.

'Can I speak to Pam again?'

'No. There's a photographer here from *Village Voice* and she's being photographed with Mercedes . . .'

'Oh, good,' I said, not having a clue as to why she should be photographed with Mercedes, whoever she was. Someone to do with the new perfume, I supposed.

'By the way, Jonathan, I read your last book. To be perfectly honest, I hated it.'

'That's its best recommendation yet,' I said and hung up.

I climbed back into the bed whose sheets were damp from my nightmare, and lay in the dark feeling desolate. I knew I should be glad for Pamela's sake that she was back in her profession of advertising copy writer, but it only emphasized the fact that now we no longer had the shared responsibility for our son our marriage had run its course.

The thought made me lonely. It was not as though I was losing a lover – as our separate beds had long testified – but while Steve had been growing up we had been a family unit. Then, a few months ago, he had gone to college to study the history of art and we were suddenly face to face with the reality of our situation. Logically it was the best thing for us to go our own ways, I hoped retaining some sort of friendship, so why did I feel so distressed? Regret for the might have been, or a sense of loss of shared history? Though the marriage had been unsatisfactory for us both, we had produced a child together and Pamela had been the biggest single influence on my life. Now everything was changing, and I was apprehensive of the future.

I tried to tell myself that this was the witching hour when the human organism is at its lowest ebb, and that things would seem better in the morning light. Like Pamela I had a new life to start, and at least I had Whispering Corner to start it in. The place was fast becoming a symbol.

Chapter 2

I awoke from a sleep of exhaustion still feeling exhausted. My movements were clumsy as I went into the kitchen to heat the Cona and the place where I had lived for the last eighteen years no longer felt familiar.

I downed my coffee, dressed, put old clothes and reference books into suitcases, raided the drinks cupboard and carried everything down to my car as though London was about to fall into rebel hands. I made another trip upstairs to collect my laptop and make sure that everything electrical was switched off, and then I was on my way. I had not even bothered to shave – that I could do when I reached Whispering Corner. Automatically I pressed the Radio 3 preset button on the radio and Dian Derbyshire playing Mozart's Piano Concert Number 21 came like an omen of better things as I drove through the morning traffic towards the M3. The combination of the music and doing something positive lifted the shadow cast by the night.

After the heady success of *Shadows and Mirrors* I decided to buy a country house in Dorset. I contacted a number of estate agents with precise details of what I required, but such houses rarely came on the market, and when they did their prices made me realize that what seemed a great deal of money to an author was pretty run-of-the-mill to those in more stable professions.

'The trouble is that you want a stately home for the price of a seaside bungalow,' Pamela said.

Predictably she had not shared my enthusiasm, saying that she would miss London. I had suggested that as a compromise we should keep the flat – which was in her name as she was living there before we were married – and divide our lives between the city and the country. But nothing suitable materialized, until one day I received a letter from an estate agent saying that a house had come on to his books which he thought would fulfil my requirements, adding that as it was within my price range it was a remarkable offer.

A couple of days later Pamela – her coppery hair complemented by a jade green trouser suit – travelled with me to Lychett Matravers to meet our genial pipe-puffing agent, Mr Johnson. We climbed into his silver BMW and drove through the village to a vista of unspoiled countryside with rolling hills in the distance.

'It'll need some work on it,' Mr Johnson warned as he piloted us along a narrow road towards a low wooded plateau. 'It's been standing empty for some time.'

'Why?' Pamela asked suspiciously.

'Legal complications. When the old lady who owned it died at the beginning of last year her will – if ever she had one – was never found, and it seemed that she had no heirs in this country. Finally a relation was located overseas, after which it had to go to probate. That has just been completed, and the new owner is only interested in selling, as soon as possible. That's why it's going at such a low price. I'd say that with a bit of redecoration it would be ideal for a writing chap like you. All the solitude you want without being too far from the amenities.'

At the word 'solitude' Pamela winced but said nothing. Soon we were driving through woods which, as we turned into a narrow lane, took on the wilder aspect of a forest.

'The Brothers Grimm would have loved this,' Pamela remarked brightly as Mr Johnson pulled up opposite two lichened columns which, topped by eroded heraldic beasts, had been ornamental gate posts.

The carriageway was too overgrown for an ordinary car to follow. Mr Johnson tapped tobacco into his pipe bowl and, resigned to the effect the walk would have on his gleaming brogues, led the way on foot. Pamela and I followed, and I almost laughed at the look of disgust on her face when she noticed a splash of orange fungi on the bole of an ancient ash.

As we picked our way I savoured the woodland hush and the effect of the new leaf growth which dimmed the light to a greenish gloaming. Had I been describing the three of us making our way past the pallid plants and saplings which had taken over the shadowed path in one of my novels I would have made the most of an 'oppressive atmosphere' or perhaps a 'sense of hostility towards intruders'. All that was missing was the mutter of distant thunder.

In reality I felt none of this. My vivid and slightly sinister imagination had stood me in good stead when I began writing horror novels, but I understood my craft too well to be influenced by it any more than a conjurer believes in real magic.

The path curved and we emerged from shade into sunlight. At the far end of what once had been a large garden stood the house, and I fell in love at first sight with its eccentric architecture. Walls of mellowed stone supported a steep central gable flanked by a smaller one on either side. All three were surmounted by gargoyles which must have been the pride of the Victorian owner who had added the Elizabethan-style chimneys which twisted like barley-sugar sticks behind them. Butterflies jinked over the lawn of knee-high grass as though DDT and subsequent poisons had never been invented. On each side there was a line of extraordinary green shapes resulting from topiary being allowed to lapse. What a delight, I thought, if they could be trimmed back to the fabulous bestiary they had represented.

Pamela, having decided that humour was her best weapon against my folly, pointed to a massive tangle of briars and made reference to Brer Rabbit.

Mr Johnson was extolling the tranquillity of the surroundings when he put his foot into an ornamental pond whose slime had been camouflaged by weeds. He swore fervently before regaining control and offering Pamela an apology. This she graciously accepted, and then said to me, 'It looks like a setting for one of your ghastlier efforts. You could re-christen it Usher.'

I could understand her reaction. The neglected old house, with its blind windows and high slated roofs, did have a certain melancholic atmosphere. Still, take any old stone-built house that has been vacant for a year, surround it with a dark wood, and you'll have something like an illustration for an M. R. James story.

'How old is it?' I asked.

'Two hundred years,' said Mr Johnson, rubbing his shoe with a handful of rank grass. 'Give or take a score or two.' He straightened up. 'Of course it has been improved from time to time.'

The work of the 'improvers' was evident. Some windows had been enlarged, spoiling the original proportions, yet enough of the basic Georgian design remained for the house still to be a pleasure to the eye.

'It's certainly a house that several Jacks built,' Pamela said as we halted before stone steps leading to French windows guarded by a pair of weed-filled antique urns. 'Fancy adding brick to that stone.'

She waved at the extension into which the French windows had been set. To me it did not look so bad – the brick had weathered and was now mostly covered by ivy – but Pamela was a purist and to her the effect of the grey stonework had been marred by the addition.

After a struggle with a protesting lock, Mr Johnson opened a heavy door and we entered a huge, old-fashioned kitchen. After the small noises of the outdoors it was hushed and still, and I noticed Pamela shiver. Again, if I had been describing that moment in one of my books I could have done a good purple passage on how the house seemed to be waiting . . .

Of course it was only waiting to be redecorated.

Mr Johnson led us into the drawing-room and stood like a benign uncle with his back to the empty fireplace while we walked about raising wraiths of dust.

'I love these high ceilings,' I said. 'To have enough space is the greatest luxury today.'

'But how do you heat it?'

We went into the large hall and up a curving staircase to the first floor which comprised three bedrooms and a vast Victorian bathroom containing a cast-iron bath standing on lion's-paw feet. One of the rooms could be converted into an ideal author's study – in my imagination I saw its walls lined with books – while from the window I would have a pleasant view of the garden area, which gave a sense of enclosure due to the thick ranks of trees which bounded it.

15

Hundreds of hours of manual work would be needed to redress the neglect which had allowed blackberry to grow with jungle ferocity where once formal flowerbeds had delineated the border between husbandry and nature. The prospect of physical labour did not daunt me. Like a lot of writers I welcomed an excuse to quit my desk after several cramped hours and indulge in a completely different activity.

Leaving Mr Johnson cowering behind a screen of pipe smoke while Pamela gave him a hard time to compensate for my noted lack of sales resistance, I climbed some narrow stairs to the top floor. Here were small rooms whose sloping ceilings followed the angle of the roof, which had once housed servants and lumber. The air was hot and stale and I guessed many years had passed since the windows had been opened. I tried to open a door disfigured by peeling brown paint – as was every door in the dingy passage – but it was locked fast.

Somewhere an insect hummed. Opening the door of the next room, I was sickened by a carpet of dead birds in various stages of decomposition. The poor creatures had entered through a small hole in a filthy window-pane and once inside had been unable to find their way out again.

In need of fresh air, I went down to the hall and out through a door with panels of stained glass depicting pre-Raphaelite maidens with downcast eyes. I found myself in the front garden, a wicket gate in the tough hedge opened to a pathway leading through the wood. It must have been here that the previous occupant made her last stand against weeds and old age.

I had a sudden picture of young Edwardian ladies in long pastel dresses, escorted by youths in white flannels, blazers and boaters, coming through the wicket gate with bantering laughter. Perhaps they had arrived for a game of croquet on the velvet lawn at the back – with charades and songs round the piano in the evening – unaware that their world was about to be swept into the dustbin of history, that somewhere in the Balkans an assassin was loading his revolver and before long Rodney would die entangled in the wire of the Western Front and Bertie would be disembowelled by a Boche bayonet.

I wondered why I had imagined Edwardians. Why not Victorians – or a Regency party? The house would have been long established when Prinny was building his Arabian Nights palace. It would have been tempting to think I had been influenced by some psychic tremor lingering in the air, but I knew better.

I went back to Mr Johnson.

'What's the name of this place?' I asked.

'Whispering Corner,' he answered.

'I'll take it.'

As I cruised along the motorway at an easy eighty, I reflected on the significance of the moment when I decided to buy Whispering Corner. It must have been at that point that subconsciously Pamela and I realized we would be parting, that now Steve had left home there was only habit to keep us together and that was not strong enough.

Of course I deluded myself at the time, thinking that Whispering Corner would give both our lives a new dimension, but within a week Pamela was planning to visit her old friend Liz in New York. For the next few weeks we were both preoccupied with our projects, she with her preparations for going abroad, I with the business of getting the old house refurbished. Strangely we were more friendly towards each other than we had been for a very long time.

Then one morning I drove her to Gatwick and watched her 747 haul itself into a louring sky before returning to Bloomsbury to start on *Nightfall*. But the book did not get written and Pamela did not return after a month as she had originally planned.

Thinking about the new novel ahead of me I feared a panic attack coming on as I wondered how the hell I could meet my publisher's deadline, but I managed to quell it by telling myself that in new surroundings I would be able to concentrate on it to the exclusion of everything else for the next three months. I would ignore all other problems and immerse myself totally in my work.

Work – as a terrible slogan once stated – makes us free, and I saw my salvation in *Whispering Corner* and the house which had inspired its title. For the rest of my journey I turned plot ideas over in my mind without any significant result. This would change, I reassured myself, once I was a literary hermit in the heart of the wood.

I did not start work that day, instead I spent the time settling in and setting up my study overlooking the wilderness garden. It smelled of new paint and I was filled with a sense of anticipation when I put my Acer laptop on the new desk in front of the window and, like Simenon, sharpened pencils for the forthcoming opus. I had been lucky enough to interview him in my journalistic days and now I remembered him telling me that the actual writing of one of his novels was nothing, he often did it in less than a week. The real writing had already been done in his head over a much longer period, and the whole story was clear when he began to put the words down. And here was I with twelve weeks to get my book written but so far with only its title in mind. It was dark when I finally unpacked the last tea chest which I had sent down from London, and arranged my beloved Hiroshige prints above my bed. Weary, I went down to the kitchen to make a bacon sandwich and fix myself a drink. Like the other fittings the stove was new, the product of a wonderful shopping spree with which I had celebrated the purchase of the house. Of course I had not been able to afford to furnish it fully, half the rooms were still empty, but thanks to Hoddy, the hardworking young handyman with the intense eyes, everywhere had been decorated apart from a locked room upstairs for which I had been unable to find the key.

With a glass of brandy in my hand I opened the French windows to the night. There was a scatter of stars and the surrounding trees had become black shapes against a blue-black sky. It was unbelievably peaceful, the only sound being a night breeze whispering through the leaves. I was to find that this soft southern wind, carrying a tang of sea salt, seemed to catch this particular part of the wood so that the lighter branches of the trees were continually restless. Perhaps it was the rustling of their leaves which had been responsible for the name Whispering Corner.

I finished my drink and went up to my bedroom where I lay on my new bed beneath my new bottle green duvet, and drifted into a sleep which held no nightmares for me that night.

Next morning I was optimistic as I went to my desk. I switched on the laptop and opened a new Word file. I typed WHISPERING CORNER at the top of my first draft. Beyond the window sunlight filled the tangled garden. On the yet unscratched surface of the desk I had laid out my dictionary, Roget's Thesaurus, the Pearlcorder for verbal notes and a jar of sharp pencils and a note pad for odd jottings. Everything was poised. The moment had come to begin the novel which had to re-establish me in the best-seller list.

'Title written,' I said aloud. 'Now all that's required is a hundred and twenty thousand words of vibrant prose!'

My problem was that I still did not have a plot. When I had considered it over my coffee and burnt toast in the stone-flagged kitchen I had decided to let my main character follow in my footsteps with his arrival at a house based on Whispering Corner, and hoped that the story would develop from there. While making sure it did not become autobiographical, I might as well cash in on my experience to provide an authentic background.

Once I had established my character I would gradually introduce the supernatural element, not too fast to begin with so that my readers would be lulled into suspending their disbelief. What the supernatural element would be I did not yet know, I would cross that Vistula when I was over the Rhine.

First I must sketch my character. Let's call him . . . I looked round the study in search of inspiration. The names of characters are very important as I believe that certain sounds and combinations of syllables can suggest types of personality. A newspaper I had used for packing caught my eye, the name FALCO was emblazoned in a headline on the sports page. Let's call him that, and for a Christian name, James. I had never used James before.

I gazed down on the garden and in my imagination it suddenly became the setting for the novel's opening. I began to type fast.

> *James Falco pushed his way down the overgrown path and suddenly beheld the house known as Whispering Corner. For several minutes he stood on the edge of what had once been a graceful lawn but was now knee-deep with feral plant life. In his late twenties, he had the appearance of an outdoor man – a look accentuated by denims, a tartan shirt and fell-walking shoes. His skin was pleasantly tanned from a recent walking tour along the byways of Normandy. And it had been a walking tour – no hitching for Falco . . .*

I paused. Why no hitching for Falco? And furthermore, what gave him his independence? If he had an ordinary job he would never be able to live at Whispering Corner.

Suddenly I felt an old excitement as my character began to come into focus, to come alive. Dr Frankenstein would have known exactly what I felt like.

I continued typing.

> *A freelance artist, Falco was on call to several advertising agencies, and in between commercial assignments he concentrated on his private work. Now his sketchbook – and Falco used his sketchbook as others use cameras – was filled with scenes of forgotten France . . .*

That should fill the bill, I thought.

> *He wished he had his drawing materials with him so he could capture the old house as he saw it with his vision still fresh. His eyes caressed its ancient stonework, tall brick chimneys like pieces of Gaudi-inspired sculpture and triple gables like dark sails against the pale Dorset sky . . .*

Good. I'd got the location in.

> *Falco had inherited the house from his aunt, who had died intestate. He carried only a childhood memory of her, a frail woman who wore very old-fashioned clothes. As he grew up he had heard on the disapproving family grapevine that she had become a recluse, living alone in some 'awful' place in the middle of a Dorset wood. 'She'll probably start a witches' coven down there,' James remembered his father joking. 'Remember how she was an ardent spiritualist? And then a Swedenborgian?'*
> *For the first time James began to wonder deeply about his aunt, his father's elder sister who for some reason seemed to be better off than*

the rest of the family. He vaguely recalled something about her fiancé's being killed on a bombing raid over the Ruhr in the Second World War.

Looking at the empty house, its windows like blind eyes, so obviously unlived in, he wondered if it reflected her life – eccentric and empty.

Whispering Corner was his now, and he'd bring it – and the garden – back to something of its former glory not only for his own pleasure and comfort but as a memorial to the lonely lady who had spent much of her life there. It would be a pleasurable task because he had instantly fallen in love with Whispering Corner, and with that came the conviction that here he would do his best work.

Looking back on what I had written I decided to alter the fact that Falco's aunt had died intestate. Instead she would have willed it to him, ignoring the rest of the family. There might be a specific reason (which I could develop later) as to why she wanted him to have it.

Apart from that change, I was pleased with the start I had made because I felt that if I looked into the garden again it would be possible to see Falco standing waist deep in purple willowherb at the far end of the garden. My old fears about having written myself out were beginning to recede and I had a feeling that the storyline was about to develop.

This was a moment when in the old days I would have lit a cigarette, and I found that my hand was reaching for a packet of Pall Malls that was not there. Although I had given up smoking after a minor heart attack some years ago, there were still times when I longed to tap a king size out of its glossy red packet.

I resumed typing.

Falco began to cross the garden. Briars clutched savagely at his jeans, reminding him of an illustration he had once drawn for the Sleeping Beauty story in a high quality fairy tale book – the sort of work he hoped to be able to concentrate on.

Whispering Corner would make a splendid background for such illustrations – Beauty and the Beast, for example. Was it simply because it was empty that he sensed there was a touch of strangeness about the house? Or was the impression merely formed by the neglected garden and the vague notion that its last owner had been a bit odd?

When the place was restored it would have a benign atmosphere. He could picture his friends coming down for long, lazy weekends, eating alfresco at a white wrought-iron table shaded by a fringed garden umbrella. And croquet! He must introduce that as the fun feature of his new home. There was something pleasantly Edwardian about these ideas.

He would get himself a striped blazer to play the part.

He suddenly froze. Through the glass of the French windows he could see a man hanging.

Chapter 3

I was dismayed as I read the last sentence I had typed. It had not been intended. Even though it had been my fingers on the keyboard, it was as though I had been watching a message from a foreign land suddenly appear on the screen.

My plan had been for Falco to enter the house and explore it as I had done on my first visit, in order to set the basic scene for the book. So why had I written in a hanged man? Who the hell was he? And what effect would he have on Falco?

After peering stupidly at the words I remembered that I was still the author. I could easily cross out the sentence, or have Falco deluded by his own reflection.

To introduce horror so early, before the reader knew enough about the main character to identify with him, would be a mistake. Or would it? Raymond Chandler said that when he reached an impasse in a novel he had a man burst through a door with a gun. I wondered if I was subconsciously using a similar trick. After all, there was nothing in the opening to make the reader desperate to turn the page.

Perhaps some inbuilt story-telling mechanism had recognized this and tried to remedy it.

I decided to compromise. I'd let the incident remain in such a way that it could be worked into the story later or deleted once I knew what the plot was about. I resumed typing.

For a moment Falco stood without moving, before it occurred to him that the man might not yet be dead. The thought released him from the paralysis of shock and he ran towards the house, stumbling as long grasses lassoed his ankles.

He made for a white glazed door and, not as yet having a key, hurled himself against it. Amid the cracking of glass and rotten framing the weight of his desperation wrenched it from its hinges and he staggered into a large, cold kitchen. Next he was in a gloomy hallway where dust billowed from under his feet. There were several white-painted doors which he flung open one after another in an irrational panic that he might not be able to locate the room in which he had seen the body suspended like some levitating yogi.

The middle door revealed the drawing-room whose French windows opened on to the garden.

There was no body hanging in the stale air.

Falco ran back into the hall and flung open the remaining doors, but all that did was prove that he had already found the right room.

He returned to it and sank into a shrouded easy chair. He told himself that he must have been deceived by his own reflection, a bizarre trick of the light on the grimy glass. It could not be anything else, and yet . . . the face he had seen was older than his, the hair was dark whereas his was fair and his tongue had not been protruding from purple lips.

That gets over it, I thought. It could be a ghost that Falco sees or a psychic glimpse of a future event, either of which can be worked into the story as it develops.

I read what I had written, and although I saw that I could probably utilize Falco's unexpected experience I had a niggling feeling about the way it had appeared. In the past my characters had taken on lives of their own and my plots had taken turns which I had not intended, but this had only happened when I was well into the work, when my 'people' had had enough time to come alive. For it to happen on the second page was so curious that I could not let it pass. In trying to analyse it, I took into account the fact that I was using my own situation as my background. Could it be that when I was in the garden some light effect had implanted an image in my imagination without my being aware of it?

Even then I knew that if that was the answer I would be relieved.

To test out the theory I went downstairs, put on my new wellingtons and walked to the spot in the garden where Falco would have made his entrance. I turned so that I'd see Whispering Corner just as he would have done.

Then the absurdity of it struck me. In my eagerness to get the novel started I had placed Falco into my situation, and now I was putting myself into his. I had a sudden flashback to my childhood, when I had held pocket mirrors of the same size opposite each other to create endless corridors out of their mutual reflections.

Nevertheless, I approached the house with my eyes on the French windows through which Falco would have seen the suspended horror. All I could see was the reflection of a flock of cirrus clouds fleeing before the southerly breeze. I moved my position, hoping that by altering the angle of sight I might still find a clue to the origin of the unbidden scene, but all I got was a mirrored view of dark trees instead of light sky. I climbed up the steps between the twin urns whose moss half obscured the bas-relief of nymphs and pursuing satyrs, and still there was nothing to suggest the impression of a hanged man behind the glass. I was about to turn away in disappointment when I gave an exclamation of surprise – and fright. In one of the panes a shadowy figure had loomed. I spun round and the ominous reflection resolved itself into the un-alarming figure of a middle-aged postman.

'Morning,' he said cheerfully as he handed me a letter redirected from London. I could see it was from my bank, the usual statement I supposed, and I thrust it into my pocket.

'It's been a long time since I came here,' he said. 'You going to do something about that drive? It's full of bloody brambles.'

'It's going to be cleared,' I promised. 'Did you used to come here often?'

'Naw. The old dear used to get the usual bills and a few overseas cards at Christmas time, that's all. Must've been lonely, just her and her cat. First time I came she were throwing bread on the lawn for the birds. I thought that was nice, until I realized she were using it as bait for the cat's benefit. Funny, I think I saw it just now as I came through the trees. I suppose it could be another, but there aren't many pure white cats about,'

'I'll look out for it,' I said.

He nodded. 'Hope you settle in all right,' he said as he turned to go. 'Be a sight too lonely for me. Just wait until winter comes.'

A couple of minutes later I heard the distant sound of his van start up and then fade. Solitude returned and at that point I should have returned to my desk, but the Imp had followed me and whispered that a young man like Falco, with his inquisitive artist's eye, would explore his new surroundings. Apart from the overgrown driveway leading down from the lane I had not yet gone beyond the precincts of the house and I decided to collect local colour for half an hour.

I went to what I thought of as the front garden and through the wicket gate on to the path which led through the trees. Later I learned it was called Church Walk, being an ancient track which ran through the wood to the centuries-old church of St Mary the Virgin.

The branches of the trees met overhead so that I had the impression of walking down a tunnel, an effect which was heightened when high earthen banks rose on each side. At a point where the path curved sharply the roots of a huge tree flowed down the bank like a cascade of intertwined serpents. There was something menacing about the twisted roots, and I made a mental note to have Falco sketch them as a background to one of his fairy tale illustrations. I could imagine a child being scared that they would reach out to grab passersby and pull them into the earth.

I descended the path for several more minutes and then it emerged from the trees to continue between the edge of the wood and the barbed wire fence of a farmer's field in the centre of which a small herd of black cattle socially chewed the cud. On the other side of the shallow valley a cornfield provided a contrast to the expanse of grassland curving towards a dark horizon of forest.

I was filled with delight. This panorama of unspoilt countryside, the scents of growing things, the trilling of a bird deep in the woods on my right . . . this was what I had hoped for when I began my dream of a rural life.

With a light step I continued down the grassy path until I came to a stile set in the lichened wall of St Mary's churchyard. Among the numerous stone crosses and time-softened memorials to forgotten lives rose the square Norman tower of the church which, with its backdrop of bright windswept sky, looked like an illustration out of the pages of *Heritage* magazine. I climbed over the stile and picked my way among the ancient tombs to where a burly man in his middle thirties brooded over a pile of smouldering weeds. He was prematurely bald – a condition compensated for by a full beard – and his heavy eyebrows gave him a sombre look. He wore jeans, an old sheepskin coat and a clergyman's collar.

'Good morning,' I said.

He started, and his solemn face became unexpectedly youthful as he smiled. His eyes of darkest brown shone with a gentle light which, if it reflected his nature, suggested that he was completely suited to his calling.

'Sorry. Looking into a fire always makes me introspective, I'm afraid,' he said. He held out his hand, then, aware of the grime of his labours, started to withdraw it, but I shook it just the same.

'You must be Jonathan Northrop,' he said. 'I'm Henry Gotobed.'
I could not help smiling at the Old English surname.

'It's better than Cometobed – if you're a vicar,' he said with a grin which suggested it was an old joke. 'I understand from Hoddy that the redecorating is finished up at Whispering Corner, and that you've just moved in.'

I nodded. 'If you see Hoddy, would you be kind enough to tell him that I've found a few little things that still need attention? There's a box room door I haven't been able to open.'

'Certainly. I see him quite often as he does little jobs about the church. One of God's simples, but very willing, I had planned on visiting you today – to welcome you to our community and . . .' he smiled shyly '. . . I must confess to a vested interest.'

'Yes?' I said, thinking that a request for a donation to the organ fund was coming a little sooner than I had expected.

'I'm afraid that, in my spare moments, I'm a bit of a horror buff and . . . well . . . for some time now you've been my favourite author. I loved *Shadows and Mirrors*. The last chapter was amazing. Well, I'm endeavouring to write a book myself . . . oh, not in your field . . . and I did wonder if you could spare a few minutes to give me some advice.'

'What's your subject?' I asked, stepping back as a shift in the breeze whirled aromatic smoke about me.

'It's historical,' he replied. 'When I came here I happened by chance to read Alexander's *Phantom Britain*.

He wrote, 'this place is supposed to be haunted by Sir John Maltravers who was associated with the murder of Edward II and that might have something to do with the Whispering Corner phenomenon.

When I heard that the author of *Shadows and Mirrors* was actually taking over Whispering Corner I thought I might ask for a few words of advice. Awful cheek, I know, but I'm desperate to get started'.

That's something we have in common, I thought. Aloud I said, 'Why not come up to the house and have a chat and a dr . . . coffee.'

'I'd rather settle for the drink,' he said with his shy smile. 'I'm sure it would be such a help to me, but perhaps you're in the middle of your next novel. I'd hate to play the role of Coleridge's "person from Porlock" who caused him to lose his inspiration half way through *Kubla Khan.*'

I assured him that my work was far less inspirational and added, 'What was the Whispering Corner phenomenon you mentioned?'

'Oh, that. It's one of our quaint old bits of Dorset folklore. The story is that when you pass a certain bend in Church Walk you sometimes hear the murmur of soft disembodied voices which are never quite loud enough for the words to be distinguished. You would have passed the spot coming down here. There's a huge tree overhanging it with a lot of its roots exposed. Obviously the name got transferred to your house through being so close to the spot.'

'Have you any idea how the legend came about?'

'Well, as I said, there's a very vague tradition that Sir John Maltravers was involved in some way, but I haven't been able to find out how. I think he was probably tacked on to a much older legend – in this case going back to the time of the Black Death in the fourteenth century. In those days Lychett Matravers was huddled about this church, though it's hard to imagine now we are surrounded by empty fields and woods. The village was particularly badly hit by the plague, and when most of its inhabitants were dead the survivors decided to leave the valley for the hills above Poole harbour where the sea breezes kept the air pure. According to the legend those villagers who could still walk set off up Church Walk, which would have been the main track to the south then. It is said they rested at the spot now called Whispering Corner, and that many who were badly afflicted died there. The tradition is that the whispering which gives the place its name is an echo from that time.'

'A supernatural replay of the plague victims.'

'Precisely. The strange thing is that after the Black Death the survivors never returned to their village. Instead they built a new one where the present Lychett Matravers stands, and that's why this church is now so isolated from it.'

I looked at the serene landscape beyond the stone walls of the graveyard.

'So, apart from the church, nothing remains of the original Lychett Matravers?'

'In the fields to the right of the wood there are mounds said to be the foundations of the old village dwellings. Nothing more.'

Returning up Church Walk I felt like a veteran prospector who after many disappointing seasons in the wilderness, has struck pay dirt. The legend the vicar had just told me was pure gold as far as my novel was concerned. Something would happen after Falco's arrival at Whispering Corner to trigger off a psychic time-bomb which had been primed since the Black Death.

Of course, I'd have to rework the legend, it was too straightforward as it was. Perhaps some of the villagers had made a pact with Satan to avoid the infection, or perhaps a local robber baron had taken advantage of their distress to plunder the village and their posthumous desire for vengeance had survived down the centuries, waiting to be activated.

I laughed aloud as ideas began to pop, one leading to another as they had in my creative days.

What could set off the phenomena which would scare the hell out of Falco? Suppose . . . suppose he was a descendant of the baron who had razed the village . . . ? No, trite!

I reached the bend where the tree roots clawed at the bank and I felt the least I could do was acknowledge my debt to the legend. I stood still and strained my ears, but all I heard was the susurration of my own blood and not a single whisper.

I returned to my laptop more confident than I had been for weeks. Bless the Reverend Gotobed and his interest in old wives' tales.

For a while I worked steadily, describing Falco's exploration of his new home and his moving-in. I hoped I was making it interesting enough to hold my readers but sufficiently low-key that they would be totally unprepared for the first shock.

What concerned me now was to introduce my heroine as soon as possible. As yet I could not visualize her or her background, or her reason for turning up in the middle of a Dorset wood. This was worrying because women have never been secondary in my novels. A reviewer once said that I always fell in love with my heroines, which may not have been far from the truth.

I stopped typing and considered the problem. Could the heroine be an ex-girlfriend of Falco who wanted to rebuild their relationship? No. Let her be someone new in his life. Supposing Lorna – that was it, her name was Lorna, a name invented by R. D. Blackmore for his heroine Lorna Doone . . . supposing she is the author of a children's book which she wants Falco to illustrate . . .

As I glanced thoughtfully out of the window I had the curious sensation that something I had just written was coming to life.

A young man appeared by a huge hornbeam at the edge of what had once been the lawn, his lower half submerged in weeds. He stood stock still and although he was about fifty yards away I could see that he was an outdoor man.

In his mid-twenties, he had keen bronzed features and long, sun-bleached hair almost down to his shoulders. If his denims and tartan shirt had been transformed into a robe he would have had the appearance of an Old Testament prophet, an effect heightened by the fact that he was holding a straight branch in the manner of a staff. Then, like the fictitious Falco, he advanced across the garden.

I hurried downstairs and appeared at the French windows just as he reached the steps leading to them.

Seeing me standing there startled him, but as I opened the glass doors he said in an unmistakable accent, 'G'day. You fair made me jump. Must have been a trick of the light.'

I felt a curious little shiver, a goose walking over my grave.

'What did you see?'

'Nothing really. It was just that the windows all looked blank, as though the house was deserted, then – shazam! – there was a figure there. The magical appearing act!'

'The place won't look so deserted when I get the curtains up, but as you can see it's well and truly occupied.'

My words were a challenge but easily repelled. 'That's a relief. I hope you're Jonathan Northrop.'

'Yes,' I admitted warily.

'Great. I'm Warren Turner. I've come down from London in the hope of meeting you.'

'Really? You'd better come in,' I said, my heart sinking at the possible prospect of my second would-be author in one day.

'Thanks.' He shrugged off a light pack and followed me into the kitchen.

'You could use a cup of tea?'

'I reckon.'

While I filled the kettle he said, 'I hope you don't think I'm some sort of nut, but the fact is I just wanted to meet you. Back home in Australia a couple of years ago I saw a film on Channel Nine based on your book *The Dancing Stones*.'

'Oh yes?'

He was referring to a book about the folklore connected with Britain's megaliths I had written before I was in a position to concentrate on fiction.

'That film really got to me. I bought your book and then read everything I could about stone circles and prehistoric religious sites. I came over because I wanted to see them for myself. I suppose you could call it a sort of pilgrimage. Do you understand?'

I nodded. The book, and the documentary film based on it, had raised quite a lot of interest in Britain's ancient monuments and this young man was not the first to have sought me out.

'Anyway, I hope you won't take it amiss that I just wanted to say hello and thanks.'

I handed him a steaming mug.

'Have you seen many circles yet?'

'Those up north. I found the Castlerigg Circle fantastic, and Long Meg and Her Daughters. I'm just back from Brittany where I visited Carnac.'

'How did you know where to find me?' I asked, annoyed at the possibility that my publishers had given my address to a stranger.

In reply he opened his wallet and held out a newspaper clipping. It was a piece from a diary column revealing that Jonathan Northrop, one of Britain's leading writers, had bought a house near Lychett Matravers where he was finishing his latest novel, which his publishers hoped would be another *Shadows and Mirrors* after the disappointing reaction to his last book.

'What is the betting that the new Gothic masterpiece will be named after the scribe's new home – Whispering Corner?' the columnist concluded.

'So it was no problem to track you down,' said Warren, 'and here I am. But if you're busy I'll be on my way to the Badbury Rings.'

I felt a pang of envy. How wonderful to be in one's twenties again with nothing to weigh on one's mind other than travelling from one prehistoric site to another. Perhaps it was the freedom he enjoyed which gave him his ease of manner. Although I had only known him for a few minutes he no longer seemed to be a stranger.

'Are you hungry? I could do with a bacon sandwich,' I suggested.

'I can see you're a big fry-up man,' he said, nodding to the pile of unwashed dishes in the sink and the frying pan with its patina of bacon fat. For all the new stove and the gadgetry of my modernized kitchen, I had attempted nothing more adventurous than bacon and eggs or toast that usually ended up as a burnt offering.

'I worked in a restaurant before I came over,' he remarked. 'Food is my profession.'

His words hung meaningfully in the air.

'How are you on *chilli con carne*?' I asked.

He rolled his eyes and kissed his fingers in burlesque imitation of the archetypal French chef.

* * *

And that was how Warren Turner came to stay at Whispering Corner. I suggested that, being sick of my own pathetic cooking, he could have a bed for the night in return for making supper. The deal was struck and he went off to the village to hunt for ingredients while I returned to my study.

29

Perhaps it was not surprising that when I tried to visualize my character James Falco took on the image of the young Australian.

Late in the afternoon Warren began work in the kitchen and, never having seen a professional cook at work before, I was amazed at the speed and deftness with which he prepared the food. There was even style in the way he cracked an egg.

When thickening dusk merged the surrounding trees into oncoming night there was a tap at the door and the Reverend Gotobed stood without, holding a plastic folder.

When he realized I had company he tried to beat an immediate retreat. The very last thing he wanted to do was intrude. He'd only come to leave some of his early chapters for me to glance at if I didn't mind. He'd come again at a more convenient time.

But it was not difficult to persuade him to stay. As a bachelor it seemed that he had nothing more than television or his work to occupy his evening, and I could see that he would relish both the company and the food whose spicy smell was infiltrating the house.

I offered him an Amontillado – Warren and I had already enjoyed several aperitifs – and once he was in a comfortable chair with a glass in his hand all thought of returning to the vicarage for his boil-in-the-bag supper vanished. And while off-stage Warren intoned a dirge about bushrangers and Botany Bay, no doubt a gem from Australia's cultural past, the Reverend Gotobed – or Henry as he asked to me call him – endeavoured to start a literary conversation.

The fact is I am not literary. I am unable to recognize the underlying symbolism, social significance and psycho-philosophy which critics are so good at discovering in an author's work, often to his utter surprise.

To me the function of a novel is to entertain, and I had no intention of getting involved in an analysis of horror fiction with Henry. As soon as I could, I steered him on to the subject of the previous occupant of Whispering Corner.

'I suppose you could describe Miss Constance as an eccentric. She was certainly a recluse,' he said. 'She lived here alone after the death of her father, who I believe was something of an amateur astronomer. Apart from an annual visit to a war cemetery in France, Whispering Corner was her world. Generations of school kids used to scare each other with stories that she was a witch, and I suppose in an earlier age adults would have thought so too, because of her habit of holding conversations with her cat, a great white beast named Mrs Foch. I remember the animal had the most malignant eyes.'

'I hear that it's still around in the woods,' I said.

'I wouldn't be surprised. Miss Constance taught her to hunt, as though she wanted her to be able to fend for herself when she was no longer around to feed her. Mrs Foch ran off after Miss Constance was found dead here . . .'

He trailed off, perhaps thinking that such a remark might be disagreeable for a new owner.

'What did she look like?' I asked, my interest in Miss Constance rising.

'Nothing witchlike. She was small, with a rose and white complexion and large sad eyes. As a girl she suffered a tragedy. Her fiancé was killed in the first Battle of the Somme. She remained faithful to his memory, as the old expression went. The garden was her consolation. I'll never forget when I made my first visit here. She was wearing a white muslin dress and held a parasol in one hand and a trowel in the other for all the world like an illustration from an Edwardian ladies' magazine. But she would put on her wellies and dig like a navvy when necessary. Part of her eccentricity was her dress. She wore thirties-style clothes – probably had such a large wardrobe in her heyday that she never used it up. When she came to church on Christmas Day the younger women used to giggle at her get-up, but I thought she looked rather splendid. The only other day she came to church was on the anniversary of D-day each year. My predecessor always made sure there was a good display of flowers on the altar that day. A kindly thought.'

* * *

The supper was a great success, thanks mainly to Warren, not only for his cooking but also for his enthusiastic conversation. I have found that ninety per cent of social conversation is about other people, so unless you know what old Hugo is up to or the latest scandal about Tracy and Tim you'd better forget it and concentrate on the food and booze.

As none of us shared mutual friends we were, in fact, three strangers unexpectedly gathered together, the talk was fresh and full of interest. Warren certainly charmed Henry with his talk about the ancient Christian shrines he had visited such as Walsingham and Lindisfarne. The fact that he discussed them in the same breath as pagan sites did not disturb the vicar at all. Soon they were in a heated discussion on the merits of the Celtic Church and whether the Synod of Whitby had done the religious life of this country a disservice. This topic exhausted, they moved on to ley lines.

I smiled to myself as I heard Warren expounding his ideas. Ever since I had written *The Dancing Stones* I had received letters from people who liked to believe that there was something mystical about Britain's cromlechs and the imaginary lines which were supposed to link them into some sort of anagogic pattern. It seemed to me that with the old-established dogmas no longer shielding us from the chaos of existence, many seemed so eagerly seeking new areas of faith, ranging from belief in the power of ancient 'earth energies' to the utterances of Rolls-owning

31

messiahs.

The concept of ley lines – really the old straight track ways which criss-crossed prehistoric Britain – was rediscovered by the photographer Alfred Watkins in the early twenties when, on a peak in the Bredewardine Hills, he had a vision of an orderly relationship between standing stones, holy wells and ancient pagan sites. He examined Ordnance Survey maps with new eyes and found that many such sites were in exact alignment with each other and, as he ruled lines across his maps, perceived the reality of his hilltop notion.

After careful investigation Watkins published his book *The Old Straight Track* and, though he only saw his ley lines as paths by which prehistoric man travelled about the country, there are now those who believe they are mysterious channels for geometric power – Warren for one.

Turning to me, he said, 'Did you know your house stands on an intersection of leys?'

'I hadn't the faintest idea.'

'It makes it quite special,' he continued, 'And it explains why it is so close to the church. Early churches were often built on pagan sites which were inevitably ley centres. It was supposed to endow them with some sort of psychic force. A conjunction of leys creates conditions conducive for paranormal manifestations. Britain's best known haunted sites are nearly all situated on ley centres.'

'That might explain the whispering phenomenon here,' said Henry quite seriously, and he went on to relate the legend to Warren whose eyes lit up.

I poured more drinks and sat back while my guests grew more and more animated. In researching material for my horror novels I have been through the gamut of the occult, and while I recognized its entertainment value I had no more faith in what my friends were discussing than I did in werewolves. Yet Warren's talk about Whispering Corner's being on a ley centre could not have come at a better time. The terrors that my hero Falco was about to endure could certainly be linked to such an ancient mystery.

Chapter 4

'You look rough,' Warren said as I walked into the kitchen next morning. 'I've got coffee perking and I reckon that's just what you need.'

I nodded and sank into a chair.

'Too much booze last night,' I said, but for once that was not the reason. I had experienced something for which I could find no explanation, which had robbed me of sleep. I had no intention of telling Warren about it knowing he would put some fanciful interpretation on it.

At midnight Henry had bidden us an effusive goodnight and departed with an unsteady step up Church Walk, after which I had had a final nightcap with Warren and then gone to bed. I felt better than I had done for a long time, thanks to good food and company and the fact that at last I had begun to feel I knew where I was going with the novel. Ideas were coming together and as I closed my eyes I estimated that if I could produce two thousand words a day for the next twelve weeks I should be able to deliver *Whispering Corner* on time.

I may have been asleep for an hour when I awoke and was conscious that I was not alone. A sound of breathing came from the other side of the double bed. For a moment it was as though I was back in the days when Pamela and I used to share a bed and I would sometimes wake to hear her regular breathing.

But for several years I had been sleeping alone,

Pamela was on the other side of the Atlantic and I was no longer in the family home.

Then who?

Surely Warren was not a sleep-walker, or interested in sharing my bed. I slid my hand over the sheet, expecting to touch human flesh. Nothing. Yet the rhythmic breathing continued.

Then I thought I had the explanation. I was lying on my side and as my head had slipped down from the pillow my face was pressed against the mattress. Through some acoustic effect, probably due to the coiled springs it contained, I must be listening to my own breathing.

There was an easy way to test the theory. I held my breath.

The gentle sound continued.

I must confess that then I had a moment of fear, not of some inhabitant of the ghost world, in which I did not believe, but for Pamela. I knew there were cases when a telepathetic signal at the point of death manifests itself as a touch on the shoulder, the sensation of a hand being clasped, a murmured name. Could this breathing mean that she had been taken ill or mugged in the subway?

'Pam!' I cried aloud.

No response, no quickening intake of breath, no sigh.

For what seemed several long minutes I lay perfectly still, not knowing what to do and reluctant to investigate further.

At last I forced myself to act. I sat up and groped for the switch of the bedside lamp. The sounds became fainter.

As the light came on silence filled the room. Now that I was more awake my fears for Pamela receded. Experiments have shown that telepathy works in close proximity, but I doubted if the human brain was capable of transmitting a message for a couple of thousand miles. I automatically ruled out the possibility of the supernatural, but what could it have been? It was too lifelike to have been the aftermath of a dream.

The only conclusion left was that it was something connected with my own mental state, perhaps an oblique warning that I was in danger of a nervous breakdown. I knew that hearing imagined sounds can be one of the symptoms.

I pulled the duvet back over me and tried to escape into sleep, but it was impossible. A phantasmagoria of disturbing thoughts – anxiety over *Whispering Corner*, regret over my failure with Pamela, a sense of life having slipped away too quickly, of loneliness – paraded the corridors of my mind.

Sunlight was edging through my slatted window blind when I finally dozed off, only to be wrenched into wakefulness almost immediately, or so it seemed, by my alarm radio switching itself on.

Now I sat with my hands round a mug of coffee while Warren cheerfully prepared scrambled eggs and toast.

'I'll be getting out of your hair this morning,' he said. 'I'll hitch to Glastonbury – the Isle of Avalon.'

'Why not make your base here for a few days?' I heard myself suggest. 'I'm so under the gun with my novel I haven't time to cook and anyway I can't even boil an egg. If you looked after that department . . .'

I knew that it was not just decent meals I wanted, after my experience in the night I did not want to be alone with my neurotic fears about an impending breakdown. With someone else staying at Whispering Corner I would have to make the effort to remain normal.

'That sounds good to me,' Warren said. 'To tell the truth I'm a bit tired of youth hostels and thumbing lifts from smart young salesmen in their fast cars. I'd like to be in one spot for a bit, and what could be better than this place? Funny, I feel I almost know it.'

He looked thoughtful, then added, 'If you're sure it's OK by you, I'll earn my keep, I'll have a go at the jungle out there and see if we can make a garden of it.'

Over breakfast Warren turned the conversation to the film of my book *The Dancing Stones*.

'Did a television company buy the rights off you?' he asked.

'No. A chap called Charles Nixon, who had been involved in the film world and wanted to try his hand at producing, approached me with the idea of forming a company to make it ourselves. He said he had the right contacts and I had the copyright, so why let some big company do it and take the profit? I agreed, and we formed a hundred pound company called Pleiades Films.'

'Just like that?'

'Yes. I agreed that he should have sixty per cent of the shares because he'd be putting more time into the venture.'

'Must have cost a lot.'

'I put some cash into it, and Charles managed to arrange an overdraft with the Regent Bank. We both worked without salary. We hired a director and a camera crew and went round the country filming megaliths.'

'You make it sound easy.'

I laughed, remembering the problems that had beset us.

'No film is ever easy. I certainly enjoyed my part in it, though. Writing is a lonely business, and getting involved with a group of people dedicated to a creative project made a pleasant change. Once the team got together it was like an instant family. Great fun.'

'Is Pleiades going to make any more films?'

I shrugged. 'Unfortunately *Stones* did not live up to Charles's expectations. It never sold in America, which is essential if a film is to be profitable these days, so we never made anything out of it. What it did earn was swallowed up by the production costs. In fact I believe there's still a small overdraft, but Charles said that'll be cleared by repeat fees and odd sales to cable or satellite television.'

I finished my coffee. It had been pleasant to breakfast with company, and the anxiety caused by the odd happening in the early hours had gone. I rose, intending to go up to my study, but once more the Imp of the Perverse pounced.

'Are you any good at picking locks?' I asked Warren, and explained about the room I had not yet entered.

'Sounds interesting,' he said. 'Who knows what we might find in a sealed room?'

'A skeleton with a poniard in its ribs sprawled over a table strewn with yellowed cards,' I suggested.

We collected the few tools I possessed and I led him to the top of the house. He set to work on the old-fashioned lock, while I pondered on what I should write that morning. Having done my scene-setting, the next thing was to introduce the legend of the whispering and bring in Lorna, the girl with whom Falco would become emotionally involved who would share with him the increasing terrors of the old house, to be heralded by a mysterious murmuring. I considered various ways of introducing her, and found improbabilities in all of them. Then it occurred to me that I might be able to salvage the opening scene from the abandoned *Nightfall*.

'Got you!' I heard Warren exclaim in triumph as the lock surrendered with a metallic snap. 'You can make your entry now.

But the white gloss paint which Hoddy had used on the woodwork still held the door fast to the jamb and we had to throw the combined weight of our shoulders against it. The result was that the door suddenly gave way and we toppled into the stuffy room like a couple of Keystone Kops.

There was a patina of dust everywhere and the tightly shut window was so begrimed that daylight filtered through but dimly.

'No skeleton of a murdered gambler,' said Warren, 'but that's interesting.'

A brass telescope stood in front of the window. It was a beautiful example of Victorian craftsmanship with the legend 'Norbury and Poole, Optical Mfs., Liverpool' inscribed on its barrel. When I examined it I found that it was securely clamped on its tripod so that it pointed beyond the garden. I rubbed part of the glass pane with my handkerchief in order to see what it had been aimed at, but when I went to look through the telescope I found that the eyepiece was missing.

'Miss Constance's father must have done his stargazing from here,' I said. 'He'd get a good view of the southern sky.'

'That telescope would be worth big dollars to an antique collector,' said Warren. He threw himself into an easy chair in the corner and a faint haze of dust rose from its cretonne cover. 'The old girl must have used this as a sitting room,' he said, indicating an ornate blue, gold-rimmed cup and saucer, a brown stain in the bottom of the cup being all that remained of coffee which had never been finished. I looked at a framed photograph on the discoloured wall of a young man in uniform posed in front of a studio backdrop of a cataract, rocks and ferns, and I experienced a vague sense of guilt as though we had broken into something sacrosanct.

Beneath the photograph of the soldier stood a small cabinet. I opened it and saw that it contained several lacquered boxes, some bundles of papers tied in old-fashioned red tape and a leather bound book embossed with the words 'My Autographs'. These relics summoned up a mental picture of Miss Constance sitting up here alone with the mementos of her past. I felt it would be wrong to see what trinkets the lacquered boxes contained or read the messages from long gone friends in the autograph book. But a loose sheet of lined and yellowing paper caught my eye because it had a poem written on it in pencil. I read,

> Those swift-sped days of freedom now are gone,
> Those hours of joy are but a memory,
> The muse can come no more, she is alone,

Her work is finished with this elegy.
She is calling,
Sadly calling.
Time is come, and only I am free.

Up looms the dark, dim future, and it holds
With steel-bound fingers all my destiny.
No human eye or heart upon this earth
Will ever see inside its mystery.
It is calling,
Sadly calling,
Time is come, you arc no longer free.

And so like clouds above, all swiftly passing,
Our joy and sorrow comes alternately.
And over all I seem to hear this message,
Endure – take all that comes unwearily.
Something's calling,
Gladly calling,
Time will come when you will yet be free.

Underneath, in faded violet ink and penned in precise copperplate, were the words, 'Arthur's last poem. Written on the eve of the D-day offensive.'

'Let's go. I've got work to do,' I said as I replaced the paper in the cabinet.

'I'll clean the room if you like,' Warren volunteered. 'It wouldn't take long to emulsion it with a roller.'

'Leave it for now,' I said.

* * *

The following week passed pleasantly. Apart from a visit to the Badbury Rings close by, Warren was happy to stay at Whispering Corner and tackle the garden, clad in cut-down jeans. The long grass was scythed and the yellowish stubble mown so that it soon regained the semblance of a lawn. Then, with berserk energy he attacked the encroaching brambles.

With Warren taking care of the household chores I got up early each morning and spent the day in my study, but even in these ideal conditions I was disappointed by my progress. I would type a few paragraphs and then, thinking of what I should be writing next, I would drift into an almost trance-like state. My powers of concentration were at a low ebb and I had a tendency to doze.

It was then that I began to experience hypnagogsis, that hallucinatory state which comes occasionally as one is being overtaken by sleep, bringing an illusion of voices. It seemed as though different people were saying sentences which held no more sense than the mysterious radio messages in Cocteau's film *Orphée*, enigmatic messages one felt would have great significance if only one had the key to decipher them. Once, however, I distinctly heard a voice repeating in rapid succession 'IcannotIcannotIcannot . . .'.

At the end of a week Warren said that he wanted to visit Glastonbury for Beltane, an ancient Celtic festival celebrating the fire of Bel. Afterwards he would go on to Cornwall. On the morning he left he told me that he'd soon be back, he wanted to finish the work he had begun in the garden,

'You're welcome any time,' I said. 'The thought of going back to a diet of cornflakes and bacon sandwiches gives me the horrors.'

After he vanished through the trees I returned to my study and introduced my heroine Lorna into the story by the device I had used in *Nightfall*. She drives to Whispering Corner to persuade Falco to illustrate a book of children's stories she has written, believing that the possibilities of its success will be much greater if he is associated with it.

Following the car accident, Falco makes her stay the night at Whispering Corner, and – because I wanted to get to the emotional possibilities between them as soon as possible – the next day he takes her to see St Mary's church.

I sat at my desk and began . . .

'Have you any commitments, James?' Lorna asked as she and Falco strolled in the churchyard reading tombstone inscriptions. 'An estranged wife with a gaggle of children or a sultry mistress lurking in the background?'

He took the lightly phrased question seriously and shook his head.

'I did have someone,' he said. 'But that ended quite a while ago. What about you? I can't believe someone like you . . . I mean someone as attractive as you are . . .hasn't got a lover.'

It was her turn to shake her head so that for a moment her fair hair fell across her face.

'I've had my share of lovers,' she answered in a matter-of-fact voice. 'Too many.'

'Why too many?' he asked.

She looked at him with wise grey eyes. 'You have to kiss a lot of frogs before you find a prince.'

'And did you ever find one?'

'I thought so for a while. But it turned out he was nicer when he was a frog.'

Falco laughed.

'And you – what happened to your girlfriend?'

'She was my wife – she died,' he said simply.

I stopped typing.

Until that moment it had not occurred to me that Falco had a tragedy in his past. I had thought to explain his present lack of emotional involvement by something less dramatic, his fiancee having left him for someone else, for example. From the point of view of the storyline this was better, it gave an acceptable reason for his wishing to change his lifestyle and begin a new era at Whispering Corner.

Yet it was odd how Falco's words just seemed to appear on the screen, a reassuring portent that my character was coming to life. At that stage I could not imagine what his wife had died from, but no doubt that would emerge in later conversations.

Reviewing the novel so far I knew that after establishing Lorna I must quickly introduce the character I thought of as the villain. It was not enough for the two young people to be threatened by unearthly powers in their refuge from the world, as they would begin to regard Whispering Corner, there also needed to be an element of human conflict, an older character with a very positive personality who endeavoured to manipulate them for his own malign ends before the final betrayal. He should be someone in whom they placed their trust, because the betrayal of trust – the sudden alienation of the familiar is the basic element of horror. That was a bitter lesson I had learned early in life. 'Granny, what long teeth you have!' is probably the most chilling line in folklore.

At the moment I could not visualize the character who would take on this role, but it was not long before I was to have a model.

I typed for the rest of the afternoon, sometimes deleting a few lines as better ideas occurred, or making notes on my note pad to be incorporated in the final script. I grew increasingly intrigued by Lorna. I wanted her to be a slightly mysterious figure, the eternal enigmatic female, to provide a contrast to Falco's relatively simple character.

By sunset I had written a couple of thousand words, my best stint so far. What alarmed me was the knowledge that this would have to be my target every day if I was to meet my deadline.

My head ached and my back was stiff when I left the study and went downstairs for a brandy and Perrier. Holding the glass, I went out into the garden, which smelled of newly mown grass. The low sun gilded layers of stratocumulus and stippled the lawn with tree shadows. Blue dusk was gathering about Whispering Corner and the air would soon be filled with soft rustlings as the woodland prepared for night.

I sank into an old deckchair which Warren had unearthed somewhere to allow the peace of the moment to seep into my being. I was weary. The night before I had sat up late, listening to Warren extolling his ideas on the mystic elements of nature. Now as I lay back in the faded candy-striped canvas my eyelids drooped and I slipped into that indolent twilight state between wakefulness and sleep.

I became aware of dissociated words and phrases forming in the recesses of my mind, the hypnagogic murmurings I had experienced before. Different voices competed like those heard when seeking an elusive station on a short waveband. Among the broken sentences a harsh military voice shouted, 'Move, you buggers, move!' It was replaced by a woman reciting a line from the poem which I had read in Miss Constance's sanctum, 'The muse is gone . . .' And this was submerged by a babel of nonsense followed by a line I had heard before, 'IcannotIcannotIcannot.'

It brought me out of my dream state with a physical jerk. My heart was pounding, and despite the fact that the temperature had fallen with the dusk there was a sheen of perspiration on my forehead.

I sat up in the deckchair, breathing hard and trying to shake off the lingering sensation of despair. If I had been of a credulous nature, it would have been easy to associate my experience with the tradition of Whispering Corner. Back in the house it took another brandy and Perrier to bring me back to normal.

That night I slept so well that when I woke the sun was over the tops of the trees. After a couple of cups of strong coffee to erase the lingering effects of a sleeping pill, I went unshaven to my study and began to work on the character of Lorna. I worked steadily through the day and into the night, and was rewarded with a feeling that at last the novel was progressing.

And for the next few days this pattern continued. Each day I sat in my study in my dressing-gown, my stubble softening into a beard and my diet consisting of bacon sandwiches.

One evening I heard a tapping at the French windows and when I went to investigate I saw the Reverend Gotobed – Henry – smiling on the other side of the glass. I let him in with a feeling of embarrassment at my unkempt state and the hint of Courvoisier on my breath. Either he was tactful or I fitted his concept of an author caught in the fever of creativity, because he never raised an eyebrow and agreed to join me in 'one little drink'.

He told me that he was just back from London where he had spent a fruitful day in the Reading Room of the British Library. Handing me a large used manilla envelope, he said almost shyly, 'Here are some notes I took at the same time. They relate to this house and I thought they might be of help to you as you are setting your novel here. Oh, don't bother with them now. Look at them at your leisure.'

I thanked him and put the envelope to one side. I could imagine the sort of material it contained – a quotation from the Domesday Book, extracts from some ancient title deeds and population statistics over the last century. But it was a kind thought and I hope I responded correctly.

Next morning a letter arrived embossed with the winged-helmet emblem which told me it was from my agent.

'Why don't you get a device known as a telephone installed like most civilized people?' Sweet Sylvia wrote, and went on to say that Radio City had been in touch with her, asking if I would take part in Charity Brown's chat programme in a couple of days' time.

'I said I was sure you would be interested,' Sylvia wrote. 'I hate the idea of your losing even one day on *Whispering Corner* but one cannot ignore Charity's radio show. Such publicity would reassure your new editorial director that you're hardly a back number. Please call me from a village phone box urgently.'

Having at last established a work pattern in which all my time was devoted to the novel, I resented the prospect of having to drive up to London. But Sylvia knew best, I told myself, and after shaving off a growth of beard whose greyness came as something of a shock, I set out along Church Walk in the direction of the village. There I put a call through to the agency and told Sylvia I would be happy to do my bit on Radio City.

'Splendid. I did insist that you'd be the only author,' she said. 'There'll be three other guests, one of whom will be the obligatory pop star, I expect. But I do happen to know that you'll be rubbing shoulders with royalty.'

'What?'

'King Syed of Abu Sabbah has agreed to go on air.'

'King who of where?'

'Syed of Abu Sabbah. The person at Radio City told me that Abu Sabbah is a tiny kingdom on the Red Sea. No one seems to have heard of it. No oil, I suppose. Now, old chum, dare I ask . . .'

'It's going,' I said.

'How many words?'

'You know I never count them.'

'Same old answer to the same old question. But do get it finished on time. I think Jocasta Mount-William would love an excuse to hold your book back, I understand she's using every trick in the book to push the Clipper fiction list more what she sees as upmarket.'

'Don't worry,' I said, feeding more coins into the phone slot. 'I eat, sleep and drink bloody *Whispering Corner* . . .'

'Good. But go easy on the drinking bit, especially on the show. No remarks like that pearl about critics being like eunuchs in bordellos.'

'*In vino veritas*,' I said.

'Well, no *vino* tomorrow night.'

'I promise. I'll stay cool, give the popular answers and plug my forthcoming book.'

'Take a serious line, that'll go down well with Clipper. The artistic aspect of the horror genre . . . drop a few names like Henry James and de Maupassant and any other literary worthies you can think of.'

We chatted for another minute and then I trekked back past Jenny's Lane to Church Walk. Before plunging into the shadowed woods I surveyed the gentle countryside whose fields and distant hills were so freshly green and I felt good. *Whispering Corner* was taking shape, I was still rated highly enough to be invited on to one of Britain's most popular radio shows and I was in love with my new home. I felt that I was regaining control of my destiny.

Chapter 5

The steel band theme music faded. The 'on-air' light glowed. Charity Brown began the introduction to her show.

'You may not know it, but today is Beltane, a very special festival for the ancient Celts and still a time when witches celebrate,' she told the microphone.

A beautiful black girl, Charity looked like a model in a dress whose patterning of burnt umber and gold had a medieval look. Unlike her colleagues, she shunned the almost regulation jeans and Radio City T-shirts. Her un-trendy elegance had become her trademark and caused her to be nicknamed the Princess by other members of the staff, a nickname which I believe she relished.

'So being an old pagan feast day, I thought it'd be fun to invite guests who have something to say about folklore – and perhaps the supernatural,' she continued. 'First, I am honoured to have with me His Royal Highness King Syed of Abu Sabbah, who is especially interested in the folklore of his own country.'

The dark man seated next to Charity at the baize-topped table inclined his head. In his beautifully tailored suit there was a hint of the film star about King Syed, a junior Omar Sharif, a gossip columnist later dubbed him.

'And we also have with us Mandy Devine,' said Charity. 'Her hit single is still at number one, and I understand she has a really spooky story to tell us. Sitting next to Mandy is the Reverend Dr Andrew McAndrew, a Church of England clergyman who is regarded as the foremost exorcist in the country, and whether you believe that evil can be cast out of people or not, I know you'll be fascinated by what he has to say on the subject. Last but far from least, we have Jonathan Northrop, the author of *Shadows and Mirrors*.'

With the seemingly effortless skill that had made her a top broadcaster, Charity set the scene and got the chat under way. She knew to the second how long to let anyone speak and how to get someone else started. She launched Mandy Devine into a story about how she and her group saw ghosts when appearing in the old Opera House at Firbridge-on-Sea.

'Right in the middle of our act I realized that we weren't alone on the stage,' said Mandy in her professional cockney. 'It weren't half eerie to have them shadowy figures round us. At first I thought I was seeing things like, because of the strobes. But they were there sure enough because the rest of the group saw 'em.'

'How extraordinary,' said Charity. 'What were they doing?'

'Rockin'. They had guitars like, but they were rockin' to a

43

different beat to us, if you know what I mean. Afterwards I found out we weren't the first to see 'em. They were supposed to be the ghosts of a pop group that got killed in an accident.'

A good story, dreamed up by her PR people, I thought.

'You must have experienced the paranormal, Dr McAndrew,' said Charity, neatly switching to the elderly priest. 'I understand that the reason you have been so successful as an exorcist is because you have a psychic streak inherited from your mother – the "sight" as they call it in Scotland.'

I watched him with professional interest as he launched into an amusing childhood story about a spectre in the Orkneys where he grew up. I believed the casting out of demons was rubbish – real popular press stuff – but I gained the impression that the old chap sincerely believed in what he termed 'the ministry of exorcism'. One Sunday newspaper had labelled him the Devil Hunter, but it was hard to equate such a cognomen with the small, silver-haired man sitting beside me.

Everything about him seemed mild, even his face gave no hint of his outré calling. His cheeks were rosy and his expression was the essence of mildness, apart from his eyes. Despite his age, and I believe he was close to his three score and ten, they were as clear as crystal and disturbingly blue.

After he had finished his tale Charity turned to King Syed.

'Obviously Abu Sabbah is Islamic,' she said, 'but do you have the same sort of folklore creatures as us? Ghosts, for example?'

'Oh yes, we are highly haunted,' he responded with his charming laugh. 'And as I am sure Dr McAndrew will agree, our exorcists are kept busy getting rid of them, especially in the desert hinterland where the tribesfolk have not yet been encompassed by the twentieth century. And not only ghosts. You have vampires and we have ghouls.'

'There's a distinction?'

'An unpleasant one. Your vampires gain sustenance from the blood of the living, our ghouls devour the flesh of the dead ...' And then he went on to talk about jinn, who had developed into our pantomime genie.

When it came to my turn Charity asked me the usual question, what made me write horror novels? Remembering Sweet Sylvia's strict injunction I did my serious bit, solemnly explaining that there was a social need for such literature and it was this aspect which fascinated me.

'The world is going through a period of disillusionment,' I said pontifically. 'After Darwin scotched people's belief in fundamental Christianity, science became the new religion. At the beginning of the century it appeared that the god Science would bring about a worldwide Utopia. Now we know that as well as benefits it has brought pollution and weapons of spectacular horror – and I don't just mean nuclear bombs. On a less dramatic scale the god Science has handed us the tools of terrorism, napalm, car bombs, chemical weapons in the Gulf War. Remember when Beirut was bombarded with phosphorus shells? In the hospitals the bodies of children who had been hit had to be kept under water to stop them burning. That is real horror.'

'And your sort of horror?' Charity asked.

'Pure escapism. We turn from reality to fantasy. There is catharsis in being scared by something we know will never actually harm us. We are aware that vampires don't exist, yet there's a curious satisfaction about allowing ourselves to be scared stiff by Dracula ...'

'How can you be so sure that vampires do not exist?' asked the Reverend McAndrew in his soft voice.

I was not going to let the old boy upstage me so I said pleasantly, 'I agree that there might be a few deluded individuals who believe they are vampires, just as some women in the sixteenth and seventeenth centuries really did believe they had the power of witchcraft. A few came forward and confessed to it even though they were not under suspicion. The human mind is capable of endless self-deception.'

I then went into the bit about horror being a basic ingredient of fairy tales. 'They used to terrify me rigid,' chimed in Mandy Devine, and the talk became general until Charity steered it to the king.

'I agree with Mr Northrop,' he said in his carefully modulated voice. 'Our Arabian Nights stories, which have proved so popular in the West, are founded on horror. Poor Scheherazade had to be able to tell a tale a night to a sadistic caliph for a thousand and one nights in order to save herself from execution. Imagine, Mr Northrop, how you would feel writing under such conditions, knowing that you would be literally killed if your fictional output let you down for a single day.'

'Your Majesty enjoys horror stories?' Charity asked.

'Rather. I became a horror buff when I was at Harrow. I discovered such writers as Ambrose Bierce, Algernon Blackwood, M. R. James, William Hope Hodgson, H. P. Lovecraft ... what pleasure they all gave me. Now I believe their worthy successor is Jonathan Northrop.'

A royal endorsement! I thought. If only Jocasta Mount-William was listening!

During the break for commercials Charity encouraged us with her dazzling smile and assurances that it was going fine, but she would like more anecdotes.

'You must have had some odd experiences in your time,' she said to me.

'I feel rather a fraud, but I really don't believe in psychic phenomena,' I answered.

'Perhaps it is that you will not allow yourself to believe,' said Dr McAndrew gently.

'Stand by,' came the voice of the engineer from a loudspeaker. The Doggo commercial came to an end and Charity swung into action by asking the priest how he performed an exorcism.

Twenty minutes later the programme was over, and I hoped that Sylvia would be pleased. I had managed to mention the forthcoming *Whispering Corner* twice.

As Charity escorted us to the foyer King Syed turned to Dr McAndrew and me and invited us to have supper with him at the Hilton. The little priest thanked the king with grave courtesy and explained that he had to catch his train. But I was intrigued enough to accept. Collecting 'characters' is part of a writer's trade.

A Radio City Rover – followed discreetly by a Special Branch car – took us to Park Lane while the king made conversation, asking me how many hours I worked a day, how many words I averaged and so on. After a few minutes I realized he was genuinely interested, and instead of giving stock answers I found I was enjoying discussing the writing process with him.

'Jo, my American wife, was a press photographer when we married, so I have some comprehension,' he said. 'She will be pleased to meet a fellow professional. Although she makes an excellent queen, I fear that at times she misses her old days on the *Voyageur* magazine.'

At the Hilton we went immediately to the Rooftop Restaurant. The king had a table reserved on the raised floor by the vast windows which provided a panorama of the glittering city below, and a slender young woman with bronze hair down to her shoulders was already seated. The Arabian sun had given her skin an olive tone, and her expression of gravity was heightened by deep hazel eyes with glints of emerald.

'Your Majesty,' I said as the king introduced me to his wife.

'Jo, please,' she said. 'We are trying hard to be incognito. And please call my husband Syed. He's still not used to his titles.'

'Which include the Sword of the Desert, the Leopard of the Righteousness and the Commander of the Faithful,' said the king.

'Surely "Commander of the Faithful" was one of the titles used by Haroun Al-Rashid?'

'You are right. The royal line of Abu Sabbah is descended from the Abbaside dynasty. Haroun Al-Rashid was the fifth caliph, from 786 to 809.'

'To go to Abu Sabbah is like walking back into the Arabian Nights,' said Jo.

'My country is very Third World,' the king resumed after a waiter had taken our orders. 'We have no oil and the income from camel hides and dates is limited. Yet my people are content with a way of life they understand. They do not have television, but neither do they know poverty. They still fear Allah and look to me for justice, but I cannot say how long this state of affairs will last. I must follow my brother's example of leading them gently into what is left of the twentieth century, but it must be done so that the best of the old way of life is retained while the best of the new is gained. It is with this thought in mind that I am building a college as a memorial to my brother, King Hamid.'

'You'll remember that he was assassinated a year ago,' Jo said.

'Of course,' I answered gravely, though in truth I had never heard of King Hamid.

'It happened when he was leaving the mosque of El Saad,' the king continued, an expression of sadness on his face. 'A youth ran up the great steps towards him holding a petition. The royal bodyguard would have kept him back but Hamid – in the tradition of our house – waved him forward. The murderer knelt before him with a rolled up scroll, and then suddenly struck him in the chest with it. It contained a stiletto blade which pierced my brother's heart. He died instantly, and the crowd tore the assassin to pieces.'

His words were simple but they conjured up a vivid picture in my imagination, the white mosque against a raw blue sky, the intent faces of the faithful watching their king bend over the kneeling fanatic, the sudden wail of desolation as he reeled back . . .

'The Hamid IV College will be the key to my plans for modernization,' the king continued. 'English will be spoken, and our most promising young people will attend free – yes, even our young women.'

Jo gave me a sly grin. 'Nothing chauvinistic about Syed,' she murmured.

'There, in air-conditioned classrooms, they will be awakened to the very best that the outside world has to offer. Not just self-defeating technology, but arts and philosophy and of course literature.'

As the supper passed I warmed to the king and his witty and attractive wife. If Abu Sabbah did survive modernization it would owe a debt of gratitude to this ex-American photo-journalist who I guessed was the practical power behind her husband's throne.

At eleven o'clock I said that I must go. It would take me nearly three hours to drive home and I ought to start work reasonably early in the morning if I was to catch up with my schedule.

'Before you leave, Mr Northrop, I will tell you what is in my mind,' said the king. 'I want you to come to Abu Sabbah.'

My face must have shown my surprise.

'He would like you to be the writer-in-residence at the new college,' Jo explained.

The king nodded. 'I understand such a post is quite usual in America,' he said.

I replied that I was honoured but as I could not speak Arabic.

The king dismissed this with a regal wave.

'The students will speak English,' he declared. 'Also I have it in mind that my writer-in-residence will make a collection of folk tales which have been handed down the generations in my country. My *rawi* – my personal story-teller – has them in his head, but it requires the skill of someone like yourself to put them into a form which will give them a niche in the world's literature. I want them preserved. Otherwise, when television does come to Abu Sabbah – when there are portable television sets in the tents of the desert tribes – the impact of reality shows will obliterate our folklore.

'Of course you would be paid for your work, and I think you would find the time spent in my kingdom a unique experience. You might even base one of your novels on our folklore – the legend of the ghoul might inspire you, for instance. And then there would be the satisfaction of bringing enlightenment to enthusiastic young people.'

I protested that I was hardly suitable. What was needed was someone with a first-class degree and lecturing experience.

'Lecturers I can have!' exclaimed the king. 'I want a working writer so the students share in practical communication. I want the author of *Shadows and Mirrors*.'

A gust of wind whirled raindrops against the glass walls of the restaurant so that the ribbon of car lights along Park Lane was refracted into a thousand crystal shards.

'Syed does not expect an answer now,' Jo said. 'But do consider it. Abu Sabbah is a different world, and one I think you would enjoy.'

'I'd miss that,' I said jokingly, pointing to a champagne bottle up-ended in an ice bucket.

'For a giaour there could be a dispensation,' said the king with a smile. 'Why not come out for a holiday and see how you like it? Then you could make up your mind. There's no terrific hurry, the college won't open for a few months yet. Meanwhile, I shall have a letter sent to you confirming what I have said.'

I thanked him and bade the royal couple goodnight.

A few minutes later I was walking along the seemingly endless concrete corridor to the car park beneath Hyde Park, and it occurred to me that if I failed to make a success of *Whispering Corner* a few months' retreat on the Red Sea coast might be a good idea.

But definitely no books about ghouls.

As I drove past the glare of Heathrow towards the M25 the gusts of rain had increased to a steady downpour, and by the time I had swung on to the M3 my windscreen wipers were switched to 'fast'. I pressed a cassette into the player and the car was suddenly filled with great growling chords from Weather Report. I was cocooned in warmth and sound, and I did not mind that I had to drive at reduced speed as the rain danced over the road surface in my headlights.

I was glad that I had gone up to London. I felt I had said the right things – the things that Sweet Sylvia would approve of – on the Charity Brown show, and I had enjoyed supper with the first royal couple I had met. But most of all, as a professional character hunter, I was delighted to have met the little Anglican priest who specialized in exorcism. To most people his calling must seem like a relic from medieval times. Mild, almost timid, he might appear, but I guessed that his mind was as sharp as his piercing blue eyes.

Oh yes, Dr McAndrew, you are certainly a find, I thought. Do not be surprised if a character based on you should appear in the pages of *Whispering Corner*, sir.

The Peugeot 604 has a unique windscreen wiper system. The two blades are mounted close together so that the driver's side of the glass gets an extra sweep, but even with this refinement I found visibility difficult when I was close to Lychett Matravers. The rain had become an unrelenting downpour and as I turned into the lane which led through the woods I was relieved that I would be home in a couple of minutes.

Suddenly twin patterns of light reflected on my windscreen. When the wipers momentarily cleared the glass I saw that an orange Mini had skidded and come to rest in the ditch. Its headlamps were aimed straight at me, illuminating the ancient trees on either side so that their tossing foliage appeared to form a tunnel.

Silhouetted against the faceted halo was a stumbling figure. I braked hard and my heart lost its rhythm as the car continued to slide on the mud which the rain had washed on to the road. My own headlights transformed the silhouette into a young woman with a blanched face and short black hair. Fearful that I would see her vanish under the bonnet of my skidding car I yelled a useless warning and instinctively eased the brakes long enough to enable the tyres to grip before braking again. She was still several yards away when I pulled up.

I pushed open the door and ran to her through the curtain of rain, and I could not help noticing the erotic effect created by the wet transparency of her clinging shirt. But my reaction was dispelled by the sight of blood mingling with the rivulets of rain on the side of her face.

'Please help me,' she murmured and I caught her as her knees buckled. For a moment I stood stupidly in the middle of the woodland tunnel. My first thought was to lay her on the wide back seat and drive her to hospital, until I realized I had no idea where the nearest hospital was. I had lost my mobile phone a few days before and had not yet replaced it, so calling for help was out of the question. I could be an hour or more in this rainstorm trying to find the way. The best thing would be to take her to my house and get an ambulance to come for her.

I carried her to the car and sat her in the front seat, as it would be easier to lift her out by myself from that position, and then drove carefully to the entrance of my drive, which Warren had cleared of the briars and saplings which had blocked it. It was only when I reached the garden that I realized it would be impossible to call an ambulance. Having been so telephone-oriented in London, I had momentarily forgotten that as yet I had not got one installed in Whispering Corner.

There were two alternatives – to back the car up to the lane and drive in search of a hospital, or to take her into the house and do what I could myself.

I decided on the latter course as I believed she needed to lie down and get warm. I reasoned that she could have no dangerous spinal injury since she had been able to get herself out of the car.

I crossed the lawn to unlock the house and switch on the lights, then returned and carried her towards the French windows. The movement roused her, and she muttered something in the slurred tone of one in shock.

'You'll soon be safe and warm inside, and then I'll get help,' I reassured her. Suddenly, I remembered that I needed to get the house a new telephone line and myself a new mobile to replace the one I had lost.

She put her arm round my neck as though afraid I might drop her. I moved awkwardly over the waterlogged grass, finding her dead weight difficult to manage. I was panting by the time I laid her on the sofa, placed a rug over her and directed the warm breeze of a fan heater on to her.

'First things first,' I said as she shivered under the covering. 'I just want to see where you're hurt.'

As gently as possible I ran my fingertips over her head, which I guessed had struck the windscreen when her car went off the road. To my relief her skull felt firm to the touch beneath her springy hair, nor did she give any exclamation of pain which would have indicated that I had located a fracture. But I did feel the gash from which warm blood flowed with the alarming profusion of head wounds.

'I'll get some antiseptic and fix this temporarily,' I said.

'Don't cut my hair,' she whispered, vanity triumphant over adversity.

In the kitchen I switched on the electric kettle, then returned to swab the deep cut and bind a pad of gauze against it.

'You look like a tennis player with a headband,' I said as I tied the bandage. Talking for the sake of talking.

'Feel cold,' she said.

'Hot tea coming. You must be shocked and no wonder. But do you hurt anywhere else?'

'My leg, a little, but it's my head. Everything seems to be revolving rather slowly. I think I was knocked out for a while.' She made a valiant effort to sit up, but fell back with a grimace of pain.

'Take it easy. You may have slight concussion. The good news is that nothing seems to be broken.'

From the kitchen I brought out two mugs of tea, hers sickeningly sweet with the sugar I had put into it as an antidote to shock.

'Better,' she said between sips. 'It's stopped my teeth chattering.' She swivelled her eyes round the room. 'Where . . . ?'

'You're in my house which is right by where you crashed. It's called Whispering Corner.'

'Ah. What about the car?'

'I'll take care of that. Top priority is to get you dry and warm.'

I fetched a heavy bath towel and a nightshirt which my son had given me as a trendy present last Christmas.

'Help me get these things off,' she said. 'I'll manage my bra and pants.'

'By the way, I'm Jonathan Northrop,' I said as I eased her soaking sweater over her head.'

'Hi,' she said with the palest ghost of a grin. 'I'm Ash. Ashley Matheson.'

Her lightly tanned skin was goose-pimpled with her drenching and I gently towelled her. The rain had made her underwear semi-transparent, revealing the large aureoles of her breasts and a generous pubic shadow. Had the circumstances been different the Old Adam might have been breathing heavily in my ear, and as she began to unfasten her bra clip she murmured with a brave attempt at humour, 'If the bells of hell weren't going ding-a-ling in my brain this could be fun.'

'I'll get more tea,' I said, and retired tactfully. When I returned her clothing was a soggy mound on the polished floorboards and she was wearing my nightshirt with the rug wrapped round her.

'I should have thanked you for your help,' she muttered. 'Sorry. I'm not quite myself. There's a buzzing in my ears, it's like being at a party where everyone's talking at once.'

I shrugged her apology away. 'You must rest now. In the morning we'll get medical advice, to be on the safe side.'

I picked her up, carried her upstairs to the spare bedroom I had furnished in the hope that my son would visit me in his vacation, and laid a duvet over her. Her eyes closed in sleep and she began breathing heavily.

Hoping I had done the right thing, I turned off the main light and left her. By now I was shivering with cold myself, but before I could get out of my wet clothing I had to take a torch and trudge up the drive to where the headlights of Ashley Matheson's car still shone. I lifted a small suitcase from the back seat, turned off the lights and locked the door with the key I took from the ignition.

As I walked back I heard a creaking above the hiss of the rain and the rush of the wind harrying the wood. It changed into a sharp splintering and ahead of me an old beech crashed across the drive. Sick at the thought of what would have happened if I had been a few steps ahead, I inspected the tangled branches and realized immediately that it would be impossible to drive the Peugeot out.

I was marooned with Ashley.

* * *

Next morning I awoke knowing that I had been dreaming ill-omened dreams. The details had dissolved, but the lingering sense of menace was strong. Then I remembered my guest and, putting on my dressing-gown, hurried to her room, half afraid that she might have lapsed into a coma. Her face was still unnaturally pale, and rather than turn her head she swivelled her eyes towards me. 'How do you feel?'

'Still got a crook headache, but I slept, thanks to your kindness,', she answered. 'You married?'

'Yes. Separated by the Atlantic Ocean, though.' I heard myself add, 'And not only that.'

'I thought you might be on your own. There's not a single feminine touch in this room. Sorry. I only asked because I didn't want to . . .'

'I understand. But believe me, you're no trouble. The guest is god and all that.'

'I'll get out of your hair as soon as I can.'

I smiled at her, not wanting her to go yet. The coincidence of her arrival and the fictional meeting of Falco and Lorna was too remarkable to ignore. And so far I knew nothing about her. She had no accent to indicate her origin, though one word she had used did give a suggestion. However, my curiosity could wait. Now I was worried in case she had concussion, remembering alarming stories of people suddenly collapsing after unattended damage to their skulls. I gave her a couple of Paracetamols for her headache and told her that I was going out for a few minutes. Putting on a waterproof jacket, I set out along Church Walk in the direction of the vicarage. The rain had eased to a bleak drizzle, the only sound being that of heavier drops, which had coalesced on the leafage above, striking the waterlogged loam. With the warmth of the morning coils of vapour drifted among the mossy trunks and exposed roots like the aerosol mist favoured by pop groups and directors of horror films.

When I left the shelter of the trees I saw that the sky, normally such a delight to me, was a sickly white, and there was something in the clammy atmosphere which brought back the feeling I had awakened with. I was glad to reach the vicarage, where I recognized the grotesque door-knocker as an old sanctuary knocker, once you had grasped its ring on the church door you were safe from the posse. And when I .entered the cosy house with its well worn furniture I felt f had indeed gained sanctuary from the opaque alien world outside.

'Heard you on the radio last night,' Henry Gotobed greeted me. 'Must have been fun to be on the same show as a king. And what did you make of McAndrew? He's got quite a reputation in ecclesiastical circles.'

I responded briefly and then explained about last night's incident. 'I think a doctor should have a look at the girl before she gets up,' I finished. 'But not having a phone, or knowing a doctor down here ...'

Henry nodded. 'I'll ring Dr Valentine for you,' he said. 'I'm sure he'll come when I explain. He's one of our churchwardens.'

I thanked him. While I drank a cup of tea prepared by Mrs Turvey, who came in each day to 'do' for the vicar, he telephoned the doctor and gave me a thumbs-up sign.

'He'll be over as soon as he can,' he said a moment later. 'Now, shall I ring the garage to collect the young lady's car?'

As I was preparing to leave, Henry asked, diffidently, 'By the way, have you had time to read the BL material I gave you?'

'I haven't had a chance, what with having to go up to London, but I hope to start on it as soon as I get Miss Matheson sorted out.'

'It might just give you an idea or two.' He sounded almost apologetic. 'I was quite excited when I came across it. I started off by looking to see what the BL had under Lychett and it was quite surprising what I unearthed.'

'Thanks again,' I said, anxious to get back to Whispering Corner to make sure that Ashley was still all right. As I walked back through the weeping woodland I wondered if my anxiety over her was heightened because I found her presence so intriguing. We had exchanged no more than a few dozen words and I had no idea what she was like under normal circumstances. And yet, and yet.

I went through the white wicket gate and was struck by the sombre appearance of the house I had fallen in love with. Now its gables were no longer picturesque, against the sky bled of colour there was a harsh defiance about them like the turrets of a medieval castle constantly under siege by the erosion of time. A remark of Pamela's returned to the effect that Whispering Corner must have two personalities, a romantic one to reflect the summer and something like a backdrop for Macbeth in winter.

Inside I hurried up to the spare bedroom, where I found the duvet in a tangle on the bed. Ashley had disappeared.

Chapter 6

For a moment I stood staring stupidly at the rumpled bed. Then the obvious explanation came to me – she had gone to the bathroom.

'Ashley, you OK?' I called.

There was no reply and I felt a ripple of panic. Throwing propriety to the winds I pushed open the bathroom door, half afraid of seeing her lying on the blue floor in a faint. But the room was empty and a minute later I had ascertained that the rest of the house was too.

I ran into the drizzle, again half expecting to see a sprawled shape on the wet lawn. Instead I saw a figure in my red and white striped nightshirt standing beneath the hornbeam at the far corner of the garden.

'Ashley!' I shouted as I ran towards her. 'What the hell are you doing? You'll get your death of cold!'

She slowly turned her head towards me.

'I was afraid. I had to get out,' she said between chattering teeth.

'There's nothing to be scared of. You must come in now.'

She turned her bandaged head from side to side with the solemnity of a disobedient child. I came to the conclusion that it must be pressure on her brain that was causing her to act irrationally, and I cursed myself for not having taken her in search of a hospital last night before the tree fell.

I took her clammy hand. 'You can't stay out here in the wet,' I said gently. 'Everything will be all right now. I'll see that you're safe.'

'It was the voices . . .'

'Voices?'

'Yes. Several voices running through my head.'

'That's called hypnagogsis,' I said. 'People get it just as they're going to sleep. I've had it since I've been down here.'

The last sentence made me pause. A question hovered in my mind, but I shelved it. The essential thing was to coax Ashley back into the warmth.

'It seemed as though they – the voices – were yelling at me, telling me to go.'

'Hypnagogic voices never make sense,' I said lightly. 'You just listen to my voice telling you to come inside.'

The remote expression left her face. She smiled wanly and I led her by the hand back to the house.

'Get yourself dry and back into bed until Dr Valentine comes,' I said. 'I'll make a cup of tea to warm you up.'

Having given her a fresh bath towel I went down to the kitchen, but as I took a couple of teabags out of their green glass jar my fingers were trembling. What had I expected to find in the garden? A dead body?

I was dramatizing. Yet when I looked back on the feeling I had when I found the house empty it was like a premonition of disaster.

I carried two cups of tea upstairs and found Ashley asleep in bed, her cheek on her arm. I sat in a chair by the bed and drank from one of the cups. The girl's breathing was shallow and when I laid my fingers on her forehead her skin felt unnaturally dry and hot. I'd be relieved when the doctor arrived.

Ashley opened her eyes half an hour later.

'I drifted off – no voices this time. You should have woken me. The tea must be cold.'

'I'll make some more.'

Through the kitchen window I saw Valentine arrive, a broad ruddy-faced old man with tight curls of silver hair.

'I hope you didn't have too much trouble finding the place,' I said as he shrugged off his dripping trench coat.

'None at all,' he replied in a pleasant Dorset accent, 'I used to visit Miss Constance, God rest her. Let's have a look at the patient. According to the vicar she had a road accident last night and you played the Good Samaritan. What do you think is wrong with her?'

As I led him upstairs I explained my worry about concussion. I left him sitting on the edge of the bed, his red sausage fingers lifting Ashley's eyelid with surprising deftness.

When he came downstairs he said that to be on the safe side he would have her X-rayed.

'Will she need an ambulance?'

'No, I'll take her to the cottage hospital myself. I'm due there anyway.'

He brushed away my thanks and explained the location of the cottage hospital so that I could visit Ashley. A few minutes later I held an umbrella over her as she walked unsteadily up the drive and past the fallen tree to where the doctor's Volvo estate car was parked.

'I'll visit you this afternoon and bring the traditional grapes,' I told her as I helped her inside.

'Please bring one of your books,' she replied. 'I'd like to read *Shadows and Mirrors* again. Now that I've met you it'll be fun to try and pick out the autobiographical bits.'

Dr Valentine backed carefully out into the lane and I was left alone.

After the events of the last twelve hours I did not feel like starting to write immediately. To appease my conscience I took up the folder which Henry had given me. Inside were a number of pages in neat handwriting and photostats of several octavo pages of old-fashioned text in two columns, a running head proclaimed *The Gentleman's Companion*. I sprawled on the sofa and read the printed heading on the first page,

Notes on the Experiences of the Lawson Family in the House of Colonel Elphick in the Wood on the Edge of Lychett Village.

Beneath this he had written, 'According to *The Gentleman's Companion* the house in question was built around 1750 by Sir Richard Elphick who subsequently lived there with his wife Arabella and his sister-in-law Evelyn. In 1758 Arabella died and her sister remained to run the household for Sir Richard. What was described as an 'attachment' developed between them, which set the district seething with gossip. In those days marriage between a widower and his sister-in-law were forbidden and if they had an intimate relationship they would have been technically guilty of incest. Sir Richard and Evelyn ignored the gossip, if indeed they were then aware of it, and continued as leading members of the Dorset social set, frequently giving lavish entertainments at the secluded house. When these entertainments ceased in 1762 and Sir Richard and Evelyn no longer followed the local hunt, rumours circulated that Evelyn was pregnant. As time passed and no evidence of a birth was forthcoming there were malicious whispers that Sir Richard, who placed great value on his outward respectability, had had the newborn child secretly done away with.

'It seems that this gossip was taken seriously, because when Sir Richard wished to start entertaining again hardly any of his old acquaintances accepted his invitations. Indeed, the couple appear to have been ostracised by the leading county families. Sir Richard's response was to drop any further attempts at reviving social intercourse with his neighbours and, having sacked most of their domestic staff, he and Evelyn lived in melancholy seclusion. She died in 1770 and he followed her by taking his own life a few months later.

'The house passed on to his nephew Colonel Wardley Elphick and, as the colonel was on duty overseas, it remained empty for some time. In 1775 Enoch Lawson, a well-to-do merchant with business connections in the West Indies, leased the house and settled his wife and young family there before setting out on a long business visit to Kingston. After he departed Mary Lawson began to experience the phenomena which were to drive her and her children out of the house within a year. A highly educated and intelligent woman, she was more intrigued than frightened at first, and she kept a diary of events which she later turned into her 'Narration'. This remained a curiosity in the Lawson family until 1872 when it was published in the September issue of *The Gentleman's Companion*, causing considerable interest as psychic matters were in vogue at that time.

'To give you a flavour of the "Narration", I have included several photostated pages of the magazine. Having briefly described the house and her situation there, Mary Lawson wrote that soon after moving in a young nursemaid came to her complaining of hearing disembodied voices during the night. At first Mrs Lawson, who had a no-nonsense attitude towards servants' fancies, dismissed the story as the imaginings of a girl who was probably emotionally upset 'having had to forsake the weekly tryst with her beau in Kensington for the solitude of a house in a remote rural setting'. It was only when the girl threatened to give up her position that her mistress began to take the matter seriously, doubtless encouraged by the fact that her two oldest daughters, aged five and seven, told her that they were frightened by a voice they heard during the night. Mrs Lawson did not consider that there was any supernatural cause behind their distress – she believed that they had probably overheard the servants discussing the nursemaid's fears. Having questioned the girl again and been impressed by her sincerity, Mrs Lawson decided that she had been deluded by some natural cause such as the sound of wind-tossed branches close to her top floor bedroom. Born and bred a Londoner, the girl was 'unacquainted with the diverse sounds and rustlings of nature'.

'Mrs Lawson therefore placed the nursemaid in a downstairs room insulated from the 'diverse sounds' and allowed her two daughters to sleep in her. bedroom. The change had no effect and Mrs Lawson wrote that she was becoming exasperated with their "wilful fancies" – until she heard the whispering herself.'

This was followed by a photostat of part of Mary Lawson's 'Narration' as it appeared in *The Gentleman's Companion*, which read,

'I betook myself to bed close to midnight, having composed a long epistle to my absent husband giving him a full account of our quiet domestic life in this charming part of the country and having ensured that all was secure in the house. I recall that I was fatigued and as soon as my head rested upon the pillow I began to doze. In that vague borderland between wakefulness and slumber, I became aware of a sibilant whispering. Although I could not distinguish the words, I comprehended that it was an exchange between two people, one, a female voice, seemed to be protesting against something that was said vehemently by a deeper male voice.

'This experience, which I first took to be a random dream generated in my semi-conscious state, had the effect of banishing my drowsiness, but instead of the acrimonious dialogue fading with it, to my puzzlement and, it must be admitted, apprehension, the incomprehensible argument continued. Meanwhile Louisa and Annie awoke, crying out that there were people quarrelling in the room. I hastily took them down to the parlour. Despite the rare comfort of hot chocolate, however, they continued to weep and my efforts to calm them met with no success until the sounds subsided.'

Mary Lawson now accepted that there was something strange happening in the house. However, she was a very determined lady, and she refused to be put out by the experience even though a couple of servants – one was the nursemaid – packed their bags. She wrote, 'I decided that as we were all God-fearing, church-going people who could count on the benevolent protection of Him who orders our lives, we would outbrave the disembodied voices. I recalled that many houses have traditions of unaccountable manifestations and that their owners have come to no harm but accept them as household curiosities. With these thoughts in mind I endeavoured to quell the fears of my girls, trying to explain in simple terms that what we heard were probably echoes from a bygone time which for some reason, not yet explained by Science, has not entirely died away, and I concluded that no harm could befall them provided they remembered their prayers.'

For a while there were no more unaccountable sounds and Mary Lawson congratulated herself that in some way her practical attitude to the phenomenon had put an end to it. But this was not to last. The "Narration" continued, 'At the beginning of the year 1776, when the vocal manifestation had been replaced in our minds by seasonal festivities, I became conscious of a hollow murmuring which seemed to fill the whole house. It was like no other sound that I have heard and could not have been caused by the wind as it occurred on the calmest nights.

'At times it was interspersed with the return of the original voices, although now the female voice was no longer protesting so strongly but more sorrowfully at something the male voice was urging upon her. As before, it was impossible to distinguish the actual words.'

From the "Narration" it was possible to see how the scale of the phenomenon steadily increased and new forms of haunting began. 'Some time after the voices returned I, then sleeping in the bedroom over the kitchen, frequently heard the noise of someone walking within in the room. Although we often made instant search, we never could discover any appearance of human or brute being. I once or twice heard sounds of music and one night in particular three distinct and violent knocks as though someone was beating with a club or other heavy weapon against the door downstairs. These were followed by a stifled cry, as though of a woman in anguish, after which there was a silence almost as alarming as the unaccountable noises. There seemed to be no regular pattern to these occurrences. Sometimes we would go for a week without hearing anything unusual, sometimes the peace of the house would be disturbed for several nights on end.'

The "Narration" continued for several more pages, giving a graphic description of the mounting tension in the household. The voices would now end abruptly with a scream that slowly died away.

With her husband still abroad, Mary Lawson turned to her brother Captain Myles Stafford for help. In response to her letter he came down from London and soon experienced the disturbances, as did a neighbouring friend, the Reverend Dominic Bracey, who had agreed to help Captain

Stafford investigate the house. After a thorough search of the premises the two men sat up for an all-night vigil in the hall. Soon after midnight the Reverend Bracey heard the footsteps of someone walking across the floor of the main reception room. He threw open the door and shouted, 'Who goes there?'

The "Narration" continued, 'Something flitted past him and he cried, 'Look, against the door!' My brother was awake and heard the Reverend Bracey's challenge. To their astonishment they continued to hear various noises but, although they examined everything everywhere, they could see nothing and found the staircase door fast secured as I had left it. We inquired of the Reverend Bracey what he had seen at the door and he replied that it was something like a moving shadow with nothing to cast it.

'My brother sat up every night during the week he spent at our house. In the middle of one of them I was alarmed by the sound of a gun or pistol, discharged quite close to me, and immediately followed by groans as of a person in agony or on the point of death. My brother now earnestly begged me to leave the house.'

Mary Lawson took his advice, leaving with her family in August, 1776, to settle in a house in Curzon Street, London.

The photostats were followed by a further note in Henry's handwriting, 'Unfortunately the material I found at the BM made no mention of what happened to the house after the Lawson's left it, and I did not have time to pursue the matter further. I shall do my best to find out more when I next go up to London. 'Meanwhile I do hope that these notes will be of some use and that the suggestion that your house was once haunted will not disturb you. In fact, with a legend like that in its background, it makes an ideal setting for an author of horror novels!

'P.S. I forgot to mention earlier that in *Hilliard's Traditions and Anecdotes of Notable Wessex Families* (published in 1864) there was the suggestion that some contemporary "slanderous scandal mongering" in connection with Sir Richard Elphick, who resided in Dorset, hinted that he had hastened the end of his wife in order to take advantage of her sister. Good stuff!'

For a long time I lay back holding the papers and blessing Henry. Here was a whole *raison d'etre* for the supernatural activity which my characters were about to face. Now there was no need to go back to the fourteenth century for the vague Black Death tradition, here was a splendid ready-made story that could be built up from the whisperings, as described by Mary Lawson, to truly horrific manifestations – manifestations which would threaten the sanity of Falco and Lorna. And the idea of the 'Narration' could be introduced in exactly the same way as it had come to me. Falco would strike up an acquaintance with a parson who had come across it in his researches into parish history.

I wondered if Mary Lawson knew of the previous history of the house. The phenomena she claimed to have experienced fitted in so perfectly with the story of Sir Richard and his sister-in-law that it would have been a remarkable coincidence if she had been unaware of it. I decided that if one could ever get to the truth behind what happened in the house 213 years ago it would probably have had a psychological origin. Perhaps Mary Lawson had unconsciously created a situation based on her servants' fears to focus attention on herself. With her husband abroad for a long period and her household in the middle of a country wood, she may have seen the so-called haunting as a lever to escape her social solitude. If so, she had been successful, it had got her to Curzon Street,

But whatever the cause, it was the effect that interested me, and my fingers flexed with eagerness to get on with my story. In the study, where raindrops on the windowpanes gave me a highly impressionistic view of the garden and the surrounding trees, I decided to work on the chapter where Falco, who has not yet received the explanatory 'Narration', hears the whispering, after Lorna's arrival. And as I switched on my laptop, I could not help reflecting on the similarity between that fictional scene and the real-life arrival of Ashley at Whispering Corner.

Then, thinking about Ashley and Lorna, I found that the features of the real girl began to blur those of my heroine. It was hard to imagine Lorna's long fair hair when I thought of Ashley's short dark curls, Lorna's blue eyes darkened and took on the tiny golden flecks which I had noticed in Ashley's eyes. That was when I knew that I would be using Ashley as the model for Lorna. And why not? It seemed as though whatever joker it is who watches over drunks and authors, having put me through the horrors of writer's block, had relented at last and was now providing me with all the material I needed to get *Whispering Corner* finished on time.

I began . . .

Falco suddenly sat up in bed. Beside him Lorna lay asleep, her back turned to him, her head resting on her arm and her dark hair . . .

I had moved ahead in the story to write this scene while the inspiration from the 'Narration' was fresh upon me, but even so I was surprised that they had become lovers so soon. My next job would be to go back and write the big romantic scene in which they came together. Meanwhile I decided that I did not like the idea of Falco suddenly being wide awake. At this point the whispering would not be loud enough to jerk him out of his sleep. It must be insidious.

I deleted the lines and began again.

Falco slowly opened his eyes. For a moment he had no idea of

what had woken him. In the moonlight streaming through the window he saw that Lorna, after their wild love-making which had ended in contented oblivion, had turned from him so that all he could see was her short dark hair on the pillow. She breathed softly, with the regular rhythm of someone safely in the lower levels of sleep.

He rubbed the back of his hand across his face in a characteristic gesture. If she were asleep then who was whispering? His instinct told him they were alone in the house. The whispering was not the monosyllables of burglars, yet what could explain the voice – no, two voices – murmuring words that he could not quite make out? It was like hearing a hushed conversation through a wall, reminding him of nights spent in cheap hotel rooms in his wandering days.

Suddenly one of the whisperers spoke more loudly. In a tone hardened by some deep emotion a woman cried, 'Never! Never! Never!'

Then there was silence except for the hiss of the blood in his straining ears.

Puzzled, he got out of bed and went to the window to look out into the garden, now a place of silver and shadow (Note, Put in a description of the garden with the dark woods pressing upon it for weird effect. Strange shadows?)

Lorna turned in the bed to see him silhouetted against the glass.

'Hold me tight,' she murmured as she stretched her arms out to him. 'I've had a beastly nightmare. A couple were whispering . . .'

I had typed about a thousand words when, glancing at the clock, I realized that it was time to get busy if I was to visit Ashley that afternoon. I would have to clear the fallen tree from the drive before I could set out in the Peugeot for the cottage hospital.

First I went down to the cellar in search of an axe. I had hardly ventured into the place apart from a perfunctory look to make sure that it was dry when I moved in. Deciding to leave it until I had a couple of days free to clear out generations of accumulated junk and whitewash the walls, I envisaged turning it into a games room for the entertainment of Steve and his college friends if they came to stay. I was anxious that even though his mother and I no longer shared the flat in London, there should still be a place which he could regard as a home base.

The feeble yellow light emitted by an un-shaded and grime-encrusted bulb was just strong enough to throw shadows over piles of long abandoned household objects. The whitewash on the walls, which might have been fresh when Queen Victoria celebrated her diamond jubilee, was peeling like some ghastly skin disease. Although the flagged floor still I appeared to be dry, there was an odour of decay in the air that I concluded came from the small cellar beyond, which had probably been designed as a wine cellar.

It brought to mind Edgar Allan Poe's story *The Cask of Amontillado,* which as a journeyman horror writer I regarded as one of the finest examples of our genre – horror without relying on the supernatural element. Poe would have loved my cellar. And obviously it would figure in the terrors of my unfortunate characters.

I remembered having seen an ancient carpenter's bench against one cobwebbed wall – what on earth could spiders trap in this vault? – and now when I wrenched its drawer open I found assorted tools. I removed a rust-red saw and hurried up the steps to light and fresh air. Thankfully I shut the heavy door behind me – a door whose polished outer surface gave no hint of what lay below – and fastened the ornate iron bolt which must have been cast at least a century ago.

Outside the drizzle had stopped and streaks of blue were appearing in the sky as a fresh wind dispersed the vapour which had been brooding over the landscape since the storm. I drew the saw across the smooth grey bark of the trunk – it was too heavy to move intact -and fancifully wondered if the trees were hostile to this oasis in their midst, a semi-cultivated garden, a house -or to me.

The saw was as blunt as it was rusty and frequently I had to pause to get my breath back. On one occasion when I straightened up I saw that I was being observed by a pair of green eyes from a bank of ferns.

'Mrs Foch? Puss, puss,' I whispered soothingly, hoping that the bedraggled white cat regarding me was Miss Constance's pet. Because I loved Whispering Corner I had developed a sentimental affection for the previous owner to whom it had been so important, and if I could take care of her only companion it would be the least I could do for her memory.

'Mrs Foch? Mrs Foch?'

The animal responded to the sound of the name as though it recalled a dim memory of happier times. She moved out of the shadow of the fronds and I could see that once she must have been a prize animal. Now, though, her long white fur was matted and there was a wound on her head.

'Come home, puss,' I coaxed as I carefully extended my hand towards her. A rumbling purr began, but the next moment I was aware of something flashing past my shoulder and part of a dead branch struck the cat in the chest. With a hiss Mrs Foch vanished into the dripping undergrowth.

'What the hell?' I shouted, jumping to my feet.

Hoddy the handyman stood further up the drive, a sullen expression on his usually open features, a lock of hair hanging over one eye. He held a long-handled axe.

'Why did you do that?' I demanded.

''Cause I don't like cats and I hates that one,' he retorted. 'Damn' witch's cat. If you'd let it get closer it'd have clawed your face.'

His antagonistic tone matched mine. I got control of my anger. As Henry Gotobed once remarked, Hoddy marched to the beat of a different drum and I knew it would be wrong to upset him. There was something about the way he swung his axe at a sapling which endorsed the view.

'Vicar told me to come and help you clear away this old tree,' he said in his old cheerful tone. He cast an amused look at the pitiful cuts I had made. 'Reckon it'd be harvest home by the time that saw got through it.'

Later we dragged the severed trunk to the side of the drive and I took some money from my pocket.

'You don't need to pay me for a bit of a job like that, Mr Northrop,' he said. 'You paid generous for the work I did on the house.' But he did not protest as I put a couple of pound coins in his hand.

'Now, tell me, what have you got against that cat?'

He combed his hair with his fingers.

''Tweren't just the cat. It were the old woman. She used to overlook folk, and when she did the cat was always with her. In them days it were something else, if you get my meaning.'

'How do you know about Miss Constance overlooking people?'

'When I went to school. All us kids knew. The older ones would warn the younger ones when they came to the infants. I tell you, Mr Northrop, we kept well clear of this part of the woods in them days, what with her and them ghosts from the plague times whispering to each other on Church Walk and . . .'

'And . . . what?'

He suddenly turned his innocent smile upon me.

'You're just asking me these things to put in them scary books you write.'

I had to laugh at his perception.

The noise of an engine came from the lane. The breakdown truck had arrived to tow away Ashley's car. When I returned from talking to the mechanic I found that Hoddy had vanished. I tried to call the cat back but in vain, and I thought that if Miss Constance had lived in the seventeenth or eighteenth century she would have probably been hanged as a witch.

At the Cottage Hospital I found Ashley lying comfortably in a four-bed ward.

'How kind of you to come when I've already been such a nuisance,' she said in her accentless voice.

'Before we worry about that, tell me what's been happening to you.'

'I was X-rayed when I arrived and I had a jab. I think it was penicillin, or something like that, as insurance after I got so soaked and cold. The doctor said that they take bumps on the head very seriously and after seeing the X-ray he wants an EEC done. I don't like the sound of that.'

'Just routine, I expect,' I said with the cheerful optimism that visitors assume as soon as they enter a hospital ward.

She asked about the car.

'It must have hit a tree when it left the road,' I told her. 'The mechanic said the engine had been knocked back several inches with the impact. No wonder you got such a bang. Don't worry, though. The garage will get in touch with the company you hired it from. It'll be covered by insurance. Anyway, a car is the last thing you'll be needing for a bit. Dr Valentine said you should rest up for a few days when you're discharged from here.'

'Perhaps I can find a guesthouse, then,' she said.

I remained silent, sensing that it was not yet the time to say what I had in mind, and busied myself instead with fighting to get a box of chocolates out of its wrapping of sealed plastic. 'How did the accident happen?'

'I suppose I must have skidded on the wet road. I can't remember clearly. I've still got such a bloody awful headache.'

'Is there anyone you'd like me to contact?'

'I haven't got anyone in England. Anyway you've done enough already.'

I shrugged.

For a while we said nothing, and I came to the conclusion that Ashley was not the sort to volunteer information about herself. If I wanted to know anything about her I would have to ask the questions.

'You're from Australia?'

'What makes you think that? I don't talk like an Aussie, do I?'

'No, but you used the same word that an Australian friend who stayed with me used – crook.'

'I'm a New Zealander.'

'Oh, sorry. You on a tour – is that why you were on the road so late at night?'

'Actually I'd been to your house.'

'Whispering Corner?'

'Right. All my life I've wanted to see it.'

My face must have shown surprise.

'My aunt was a family legend.'

'You were related to Miss Constance?'

'She was my great-aunt. Her brother emigrated to Godzone and set up as a dairy farmer in Taranaki. His son – my father – never came to England, never knew his aunt. All I can remember were the stories my grandfather used to tell about her, how she became eccentric after her fiancé was killed in action. When she died Dad inherited the house, but all he could think of was selling it and raising some cash. Things haven't been too good for farmers out there since Britain joined the Common Market. Of course, I was sorry that I'd never seen the place, having heard Grandpa's stories about it. You know how things get magnified in family anecdotes, when I was a kid Whispering Corner had become a cross between Shangri-la and Wuthering Heights. So when I arrived in England the first thing I wanted to do was visit it, even though it had passed out of our hands. That's how I came to be there.'

'So late at night?'

'I'd only just arrived from Auckland – the longest air journey in the world. I was full of jet-lag. And instead of resting up in an hotel as I should have done, I decided to come straight down to Dorset, see Whispering Corner and find somewhere to stay in the neighbourhood while I got my plans sorted out. To begin with I felt all right. It must have been false energy, because I hired a car and drove down no trouble. Then, after a lot of difficulty – the locals aren't exactly brilliant at giving directions – I found it in the late afternoon. I parked the Mini at the end of the drive and there it was. The house of my dreams. Only there was no one at home.'

'I was in London, doing a radio,' I said apologetically.

'Anyway, I had a wander round the garden – you could make something of it if you really wanted to – and I must admit I pressed my nose against your windows.'

'How disappointing for you, having come all that way.'

'It's funny the effect seeing the place had on me. As I said, it had become part of a family legend, and I honestly didn't expect it to live up to what I had imagined. Yet when I saw it I was not at all disappointed. It seemed sort of . . . Oh, it sounds ridiculous . . . well, it seemed to be waiting for me. I loved it at first sight.'

'I know what you mean,' I said. 'I felt something like that when I first saw it. You must be sorry that your father didn't hold on to it long enough for you to have stayed in it for a while.'

'At least I can say I've been inside it, and I am glad that it's you who bought it. Anyway, after I'd had a poke round, the old jet-lag caught up with me and I decided to have a doze in the car. I thought I'd wake up in a few minutes, or when the householder came home. When I did wake up there was rain drumming on the roof and it was close to midnight. I'd been asleep for hours, and I was still dozy when I started the motor. My idea was to drive off and find a hotel. I didn't want to stay in that dark wood with the wind doing its best to uproot the trees.'

I could imagine the scene, the lonely little car with rain sluicing over it and the roar of the wind filling the woodland.

'I started up the drive,' Ashley continued. 'It was steep and slippery and I gave it the gun, with the result that I shot forward – and after that everything's hazy. I have a picture of tree trunks appearing in the headlights.'

'Were you dazzled by lights?'

She looked puzzled.

'Why?'

'Just a thought.'

'The lights I do remember after I had come round and climbed out of the Mini were yours.'

'I'm afraid I'll have to interrupt your tête-à-tête,' said a nursing orderly pushing a trolley. 'Time for your EEC.'

'I won't have to have my head shaved?' Ashley cried in sudden alarm.

'You can keep your lovely curls, my dear,' said the nurse. 'They just put little microphone things against your head with a dab of special grease to give a good contact. Nothing worse than that.'

'Goodbye. See you tomorrow,' I said.

I drove back to Whispering Corner. It was only as I began to type that I reflected that not only was I being served with the material for my book and provided with a perfect model for my heroine, but I had not thought about Pamela for twenty-four hours.

Chapter 7

There was the sound of surf in my ears. As I opened my eyes the bedroom swam into focus and I realized that it was not rollers creaming up some dream beach but the wind soughing over the treetops. For a while I lay 'baking', as they say in the north. Early morning sun streamed through the window, which was still waiting for the curtains I had bought down from London. Such unfinished touches underlined the newness of my tenancy, keeping me aware of the house, its details were not yet blurred by familiarity, which was important if I was to give a vivid picture of it in my novel. The fact that I was borrowing from reality did not bother me, the point was that I was still the storyteller.

There were several pages of careful writing ahead of me, and it was with a sense of anticipation that I sat at my desk a little later. I reread the last few pages I had written, having reached the point in the story where frightening phenomena, based on those in the 'Narration', were soon to occur. To add to their impact on my two characters, I wanted to set them in contrast to the happiness Falco and Lorna feel after they recognize their mutual attraction and become lovers.

I set the scene by describing how Lorna, who remains at Whispering Corner to get over her accident and persuade Falco to take an interest in her book of stories, decides that after a diet that seemed to comprise only boiled eggs and oranges it was time he had a decent meal. She goes to Poole to buy ingredients for a dinner of avocado soup, coq-au-vin, syllabub and applewood-smoked cheese to accompany coffee and brandy. To complete it she buys a bottle of champagne.

When Falco comes weary-eyed from his studio early that evening he finds that the table in the dining-room has been laid as though for a dinner party for two. Two tall candles are already burning, and Lorna appears in a long grey and silver dress he had not seen before. To enter into the spirit of the evening he changes his usual denim for a dinner jacket. Then, with a Jacques Loussier CD on in the background, the champagne is ceremoniously opened and a leisurely supper begins.

Through brief snatches of conversation over the dinner table I endeavoured to give more insight into my characters. My own criticism of what I had already written was that Falco and Lorna lacked depth, and when the frightening aspects of the story began I wanted the reader to be able to empathise with them. Falco mentions his childhood, saying that he has no difficulty in working alone because he was an only child, brought up by an aunt in a lonely Cumbrian village. Lorna is more reticent about her background, but she gives the impression that she has been deeply hurt by an ill-starred relationship. Then, a Sinatra CD providing a fitting background, she asks Falco to dance.

'It's not my forte,' Falco replied. 'So forgive me in advance if I tread on your foot.'

'It's quite easy. You just need to hold me and shuffle. We're not in a "Come Dancing" competition.'

I described the dining-room of Whispering Corner as I imagined it would look in candlelight, the lone couple dancing on the carpet, their shadows merging on the walls.

'This beats disco dancing,' Falco said. 'Don't they call it "touch dancing"?'

'It seems to me our ancestors knew a thing or two after all,' Lorna laughed. 'I remember a record, an old 78 that my grandparents used to play, called "Dancing in the Dark". I loved it as a little girl.'

As they moved close to the table Falco pinched out the candles, and the smell of the extinguished wicks brought back a fleeting remembrance of when he was an altar boy snuffing out the candles after mass.

'Now you're really dancing in the dark,' he said.

Sinatra sang about strangers in the night and Lorna murmured, 'That's appropriate,' as they danced from the darkened dining-room into the living-room. Here moonlight flooded through the French windows, whose curtains never needed to be drawn in this remote spot. Outside, the garden and the trees surrounding it were etched in silver and black as definite as an Aubrey Beardsley drawing.

As they paused to look out Falco was surprised at the effect holding Lorna had upon him. He was acutely aware of the touch of her slim hand on his shoulder, the exciting osmosis of some rare energy between their bodies.

It had been a long time since he had experienced anything like this. Since the death of his wife the prospect of finding love again was something he had not considered. And though champagne and brandy had played their part in forming this unfamiliar mood, he was far from drunk – on alcohol, at least. No, this feeling of intoxication had a different and more fundamental cause.

'Chemistry,' he said. 'It must be chemistry.'

'That's an odd remark to make at a moment like this. Unless you mean . . .'

'That's the only expression for what we're feeling – what I hope we're both feeling . . . that the chemistry in each of us is just right. Perhaps I'm presuming too much because of how it affects me.'

She smiled at him as they stopped dancing and stood hand in hand, looking out at the trees. 'Alchemy. I'd rather call it alchemy than *chemistry.'*

'Why?'

'It has a touch of magic about it.'

'Then it's not just me.'

By way of reply she tightened her grip upon his fingers. *'Out there . . . it's rather like one of your illustrations,'* she said. *'Like the night wood in The Cat o' Nine Tales,'*

'You've a good memory.'

'Let's go out. It'll be like walking into your drawing. We might even meet the Magic Cat.'

He smiled at the recollection of the story he had illustrated.

'You know what would happen if we did meet him?' he said.

'We'd be granted a wish. Let's go out and try. If the Magic Cat doesn't appear, there might be a shooting star.'

I paused to reread what I had been writing. I wondered whether I was making it too romantic, yet that is how it was. What I mean is that instead of the sun-dappled garden beyond my window it appeared – to my inner eye – to be drenched in moonlight. And there was a sense of enchantment enveloping my characters on this particular night. I felt that I was merely a reporter in the wings of their stage and I must continue to describe their story as it unfolded.

Telling myself that I could alter the text later if necessary, my fingers sprinted over the keyboard as I described how they walked into the garden, an elegant couple who as a joke had put on evening wear now in perfect keeping with the theatrical scene.

Hands clasped, they moved across to the hornbeam, the summer airs warm about them, until they paused beneath the ancient tree. From one of its branches a swing dangled on rusted chains. Lorna sat upon the bleached wood seat and Falco stood behind her, his hands on the chains, ready to launch her into flight. She shivered when the cry of a hunting owl came from the woods and Falco let go of the swing and put his arms round her, holding her breasts. She raised her hands and laid them over his, not to move them but just to hold them. He held his face close to her dark curly hair, his nostrils filled with her perfume.

'Look,' she cried suddenly. *'There's the Magic Cat.'*

Unable to point without letting go of his hands, she nodded to where a white cat was emerging from the shadow of the trees. Tail erect, it regarded them with smouldering eyes.

'It must be the cat that belonged to the previous owner,' said Falco. *'The local kids used to say that she was a witch and it was her familiar.'*

'So it is a magic cat. There's a hint of witchcraft in the air tonight.'

'It took to the woods after she died. I'd like to look after it – I

feel I owe the old dear something.'

'I'll get a saucer of milk, for a start,' Lorna said. But before she could move from the swing the cat stepped back into shadow and vanished.

'It's magicked itself away,' she murmured, turning to look into Falco's face. 'But I did wish. Sony I can't tell you what I wished, but perhaps you can guess.' She paused and then said seriously, 'James, you told me that there is no one in your life.'

'That's true. Not since the death of Irene.'

'Your wife?'

'Yes. For a long time after she went I seemed incapable of any sort of feeling. One of T. S. Eliot's hollow men. You see, I felt that I had contributed to what happened. I know it's very common for people to feel guilt when someone close to them dies, but this was different.'

'Was it some sort of accident?'

'You could put it like that. She jumped from an apartment window in Manhattan.'

After a silence Lorna said, 'You were there?'

'No. She was out there, working.'

As I saw what I had written my fingers froze. Where had those last few sentences come from? I had never intended Falco to have had such a tragedy in his past. Certainly he was a widower, but that was a device to explain his present status and liking for solitude. Something in my subconscious must have wanted to make the story more dramatic, but it filled me with repugnance. Angrily, I deleted the last few lines and resumed at the point where Lorna tells Falco that she had made a wish.

Chemistry! Thought Falco. They knew so little about each other, yet at this moment he felt he had always been aware that she would come – the pre-destined lover-friend.

He also felt that all would take its correct course without worry or tension. It was the first time he had accepted the possibility of falling in love since Irene died, and now all he needed to do was marvel and enjoy.

He leant forward and they exchanged their first kiss. Almost chaste at first, it changed as the chemistry worked within them. Falco's fingers tightened cruelly as he pulled Lorna closer, and each was aware of the hardness of the other's teeth behind the pliancy of their lips.

When they drew back they looked into each other's eyes, enigmatic in the moonlight, and then their mouths came together again. This time Lorna did not allow him to crush her, moving her head so that her mouth remained soft against his, then he was aware of the tip of her tongue drawn teasingly across his lips.

They walked back to the looming bulk of the house without need to speak. They both knew that what was about to follow would be inevitable and right, and they cherished this knowledge as though it was some precious wisdom granted only to them.

Again I wondered if I was overdoing the romanticism. I tried to tell myself that as an artist Falco dealt in ideas and feelings, that a century earlier he would have belonged to the pre-Raphaelite movement. And again I decided that it was not for me to judge at this point, but to get it down 'the way it was'.

I continued typing.

Back in the living-room they stood for a moment like a pair of silhouettes against the French windows before Falco turned and poured brandy into two glasses.

He handed one to Lorna and raised the other.

'A toast,' he said.

'To us,' she answered, and there was the clink of glasses touching.

Falco drained his so quickly that his throat burned. He began to unbutton the row of tiny buttons down the back of her silver and grey dress, then jumbled with the hook of her bra.

'You're out of practice,' she said, amused.

'True. I'll need co-operation tonight.'

'You shall have it.'

Reaching behind her, she unfastened the hook for him and then shook herself free of both bra and dress while he drew in his breath at the sight of her, like carved ivory in the moonlight.

'I please you?'

'Very much.'

He ran his fingertips gently over the swell of her breasts and felt the firming of her dark nipples. Her fingers were busy with the buttons of his shirt, and then she tugged it open and they felt the heat generating from their skins.

'Now, at this moment, I want you to know I'm in love with you,' Falco said in a low voice.

'Of course. It wouldn't be happening otherwise.'

He slid to his knees before her, his mouth moving down her skin as he did so.

'Darling,' she murmured, her eyes closed as a surge of pure physical pleasure spread through her.

'Upstairs,' he said, leaning back on his heels.

'No, here, in the light of the enchanted garden.'

She sat on the carpet, rolling down a stocking. He sat beside her, his arm over her shoulders, both of them looking out at the silvered trees.

'I shall remember this scene for ever,' she said, abandoning the attempt to remove her other stocking. Then, the one stocking giving a

curious suggestion of a harlequinade, she lay back on the thick carpet, and the sight of her open for him brought Falco upon her.

The gravity they had displayed towards each other was swept away. All that mattered in the world to Falco was to feel himself become part of her, all that mattered to her was to receive her new lover.

Her arms tightened round him as he lay upon her, his mouth hard against hers as he writhed desperately to enter her, earlier gentleness replaced by a force over which it seemed he had no control. Lorna murmured with the pain of his onslaught and released her arm, and he cried out with relief as her hand eased him into the dark warmth that had become the centre of his universe.

Entwined together, hearts racing, they rode their waves of mutual pleasure. Falco closed his eyes and buried his face in the shampoo-scented curls, aware only that the heat which had begun in his loins was spreading like a fever through his body until his nerves and muscles could stand the tension no longer. Behind his eyelids everything seemed to explode in a nova of lights, and Lorna, with a shuddering cry, went limp beneath him in the little death.

When Falco opened his eyes the garden outside was a place of deep shadow. Lorna lay with her head on his arm, her hair soft against his chest. The sweat which sheened them was cold and he felt her shiver. He climbed to his feet, helped her to hers and then, without switching on any lights, led her up to the bedroom. There was no need to say anything as they pulled the duvet over themselves and just before sleep overtook him Falco knew that all he wanted now lay within his arms.

I pushed the laptop away with a sense of relief. Now the story would roll on more easily. It had needed this happy intimacy as a contrast to what was about to happen.

Having finished the scene, which had developed more easily than I had expected, I went down to the kitchen to make myself a cup of coffee. Waiting for the water to boil, I put my hand in my dressing-gown pocket and felt a crumpled envelope. When I took it out I saw that it was the letter from the Regent Bank which I had thrust away unopened several days ago. I tore it open and saw at once that it was not the usual statement sheet but a letter from the Marchmont Street branch where I had my account. I knew the manager well enough for him to begin any correspondence with 'Dear Jonathan', and it was with uneasy surprise that I saw 'Dear Mr Northrop'. I carefully poured out my coffee and read, 'I am very disappointed that neither you nor your partner Mr Charles Nixon has replied to my earlier letters regarding the account of Pleiades Films. The amount at which the company overdraft now stands is £48,510.15p, which is unacceptable. Therefore, as a joint and several guarantor, you are required to pay this sum into the company account within seven days in order to prevent the matter being passed to our legal department for immediate action.'

I reread the letter and could only conclude that the bank's computer had gone mad. Several years ago, in order to pay the film laboratory for the final work on *The Dancing Stones,* Charles Nixon and I had signed joint and several guarantees to secure an overdraft of five thousands pounds. After that the film had been finished and sold and the company, Pleiades Films, had not been involved in any further productions. Now I realized that I had not actually seen a bank statement since then, though I presumed that they had been sent to Charles as managing director of the company. As a shareholder and director I should have been informed of any problem by the bank.

To demand such a ridiculous sum from me within a week could only be an error on the part of the bank. Even if Charles had gone mad with the company cheque book – and although he was an odd character I had never had reason to suspect him of dishonesty – the Regent Bank would surely never have allowed the overdraft to soar to such a figure.

There must be a simple explanation, but nevertheless the letter was worrying enough to put me off returning to work until I had got the matter sorted out. I dressed and then, after collecting all the ten-pence pieces I could find – I had not yet replaced my lost mobile – and set out up Church Walk to the phone box in Lychett Matravers.

After the rain of the previous day the track was muddy underfoot, but the varying shades of green making up the wood were more lush than ever, and when I left the trees and gazed out over the gentle landscape towards Beacon Hill and heard the insect hum of a distant tractor the peace of the scene did something to quell the disquiet caused by the bank's letter.

* * *

When I reached the public telephone, I dialled the number of Charles Nixon's maisonette in Richmond. After a wait I heard the Welsh lilt of his wife.

'Hello, Olwen,' I said. 'It's been a long time. How's things?'

'Oh, Mr Northrop . . .'

She did not tell me how things were, and I had a mental picture of a pale, severe-looking woman perpetually wearied by the force of her husband's exuberance.

'Is Charles about?'

There was a long pause – a pause which, when I thought about it later, was just a little too long.

'Charlie isn't here at the moment.'

'When will he be in?'

Another pause. 'I've no idea. Cedric, his young actor friend is with him. They are location hunting. That can take ages.' She sighed.

'I'll ring later.'

'I have to go to Ystrad – my mother's poorly. So if you don't get an answer you'll know Charlie is still away.'

'I'll keep trying.'

I was still more uneasy when I hung up. If something had gone wrong with the Pleiades account I dared not contemplate the consequences. The next step was to find out the truth of the matter directly from the bank. Not wishing to carry on such a conversation punctuate by the clash of coins being fed into the pay phone, rang Marchmont Street to make an appointment. Mr.. Barnet, the assistant manager, would be able to spare me a few minutes the following afternoon.

* * *

Usually I enjoyed driving through the Dorset countryside before getting on to the M3, but the next morning I could not relax. My thoughts were focused on Pleiades Films. When the company had been formed I had agreed that Charles, who had the day-to-day problem to contend with, could sign the company cheques. This meant that, not having received any bank statements, I had no knowledge of Pleiades' financial situation apart from the fact that the really profitable deals with America and Japan that Charles had so confidently predicted had never materialized. However, I did know that some months earlier the film had been sold to one of the new satellite television companies and, thinking about now, I was sure that the money from the sale should have cleared the original overdraft I had guaranteed.

The last time I had seen Charles was almost a year ago. I had run into him in a restaurant in Wardour Street, where he was lunching an eager young actor who, he declared, would be ideal for the leading role in a television series based on *Shadows* for which he claimed he was about to get financial backing. As usual I congratulated him, though I had heard such announcements a dozen times before and each time the deal had mysteriously faded away. Nonetheless, it impressed the young actor immensely and I hid my amusement. Now I wished I had taken more interest in Charles.

In London I plunged into the tunnel leading to the car park beneath Hyde Park and then walked to where my agent had her office high in a building of faded elegance.

'I'm glad to be in touch again,' said Sylvia as she poured a pre-lunch gin and tonic. 'Without a phone you might as well be in Outer Mongolia. You must get yourself a new mobile, I'm desperate to know how the novel is going.'

'It's going,' I said. 'I've been lucky in some ways.' And I went on to tell her about Mary Lawson's "Narration".

'You certainly sound more confident,' Sylvia said. 'Do bring it on time, for goodness' sake. Ever since Clipper took over I've been having problems. You know how Marian Avent is always behind schedule? The old company understood and scheduled accordingly, but when I had to tell Jocasta Mount-William that Marian would be a month late delivering *The City of Glitter* she wanted to break the contract. Thank goodness for my little clause about "unavoidable delay". Still, I can't swing that one too often.'

Lunch with Sylvia pushed the anxiety over the bank's letter temporarily to the back of my mind. She brought me up to date on publishing gossip and the doings, always told with affection, of fellow authors whom she represented.

It was therefore with a more confident air that I arrived in Marchmont Street and entered the Regent Bank where, after a ten-minute wait, I was ushered into the assistant manager's office.

'Coffee?' asked Mr Barnet as we shook hands and smiled at each other as though everything was all right in the world.

When two cups of anonymous liquid from a beverage dispenser had been brought in by a junior, he looked at me with an alert expression.

'It's about the Pleiades account,' I began.

'To be sure. We've been sending out letters to the managing director about it for some time now, but neither you nor Mr Nixon has seen fit to reply.'

'You should have written to me direct. I've only just learned about it – that's the reason I came straight up from Dorset. There must be some mistake.'

'Legally we are only obliged to write to the managing director. If you choose to remain out of touch with the workings of a company of which you are a director – and a joint and several guarantor – that is your business. The bank has behaved perfectly properly.'

'Mr Nixon never passed anything on to me.' I said, 'We haven't been in touch for some time. After the film was made the company virtually ceased to trade, and anyway I've been too busy with my books to be involved with it.'

'But I'm afraid you are involved,' said Barnet gently, holding up the agreement I had signed.

'That was merely for an overdraft of ten thousand pounds to get *The Dancing Stones* completed. If that overdraft wasn't cleared, as it should have been, by the film's earnings, then Nixon owes you five thousand and I owe you the same amount – not nearly fifty thousand pounds!'

Barnet permitted himself a little chuckle at my naivety.

'It was an open-ended agreement,' he said. 'There was no

specified limit. On the assurance of Mr Nixon that Pleiades was about to sign up with a television company to produce one of your books we allowed the facility to be increased, but although he gave us continual assurances that the deal was about to go through nothing happened. It seems to me that Mr Nixon lives in a fantasy world. The overdraft, on the other hand, is a reality and it has to be cleared.'

'If you thought Nixon lived in a fantasy world why the hell did you allow him to go on using the account?' I knew my voice was rising but I was too angry to control it. 'You should have bloody well warned me it was creeping up.'

'I repeat, the company was kept informed, but our letters were ignored. There is no legal requirement to inform someone in your position separately. You could have arranged to have company statements sent to you at regular intervals, but you chose not to do so.'

'It isn't that I didn't choose – I just never thought of it,' I said more quietly. 'At the time the most important thing was to get the film completed. The signing of the guarantee seemed such a routine matter.'

'It isn't a routine matter now, I'm afraid. We have had instructions from Head Office . . .' He let the words 'Head Office' hang in the air with the same reverence as a parish priest announcing that he had just had a call from the Vatican. 'Unless the overdraft is cleared, legal action will be taken. I suggest that to save yourself trouble you make funds available in the next couple of days and clear the whole matter up.'

'And what about Nixon?' I demanded. 'Why aren't you asking him? He was the man with the chequebook.'

'If we have to go to law, and I most sincerely hope it won't come to that, our legal department would go for a summary judgement against him as well. But realistically he is not worth chasing. I understand he only rents his maisonette, whereas as well as a flat in London you own a substantial property in Dorset. Under law we can proceed against the guarantor who is most likely to settle. You can, of course, take legal action later to recover what you can from your co-guarantor.' He glanced none too surreptitiously at his watch.

I felt I was in the middle of a nightmare. All I could think of asking was where the money had gone.

'That is something you might learn from the company accountants – if the accounts are up to date.'

As Barnet showed me to the door he said, 'I'll get the latest figures sent to you. As you know, interest increases every day.' Then an amusing thought struck him. 'One thing, Mr Northrop. 'You might be able to make use of such a situation in one of your novels.'

* * *

'You ought to be locked up for your own protection,' exploded Paul

76

Lincoln, my accountant, to whose Kingsway office I had hurried after my visit to the Regent Bank. 'You mean to say that you signed this joint and several without checking with me first?'

'You must have been away at the time. It seemed such a minor thing. We needed money to get the show prints finished and it was so easy – a good lunch with the manager, sign a form and away we went.'

'No joint and several is a minor thing,' said Paul, his glasses flashing as a shaft of westering sunlight illuminated his office with its mini-jungle of plants and club furniture. 'How much do they want from you?'

Feeling like a schoolboy in the head's office, I handed over the crumpled letter from the bank.

'Jonathan, how could you let it go as high as this?'

I went through the same routine as I had with Barnet, Paul's silence making me feel more and more stupid.

'We'll worry where the money has gone later,' he said. 'I'll get the bank to send me a copy of the agreement you signed, but I'm sure they'll be certain of their ground. Can you pay if off?'

'You know I can't. I put everything I had into buying Whispering Corner and renovating it. I've only got a few hundred quid in my current account. So what do I do?'

'How much is the Bloomsbury flat worth?'

'That's out. It's always been in Pamela's name.'

'So that only leaves Whispering Corner. It's likely that it'll have to go.'

'But it's my home,' I protested.

'When the bank gets judgement they can force you to sell it,' said Paul with gloomy relish. 'As far as the court is concerned it would be regarded as a second home, a luxury. Of course we'll get a good solicitor and delay as much as possible. When the time comes he might be able to get you a Tomlin.'

'A Tomlin?'

'When the bank gets judgement against you they'll have the right to seize your property at any time without further application to the court, but they might allow you a Tomlin, which means you pay off a set sum monthly. Of course, if you can't pay on the dot they move in. You might be lucky and get away with paying around fifteen hundred a month.'

'You know that would be impossible,' I said. 'I only get my royalties every six months.'

'How about that book you're working on? The payment for delivery would be something to throw into the pot as a goodwill gesture, and then we might be able to do a deal, assign future

77

royalties and so on.'

'So everything depends on getting *Whispering Corner* finished,' I said.

Paul nodded. 'You look like you could use a drink, old man.'

Chapter 8

It was a serene evening as I drove back to Dorset. The sunset was particularly good, a wall of castellated clouds which, as the sun departed in a golden nimbus, took on the most delicate shades of pink to contrast with a backdrop of mauve sky.

But the celestial artistry was lost on me. As I sped into the darkling world no music sounded from the car's speakers, there was no sense of pleasurable expectation at returning home – I had a pain in my stomach and I was so angry that at times my knuckles were bloodless as I gripped the steering wheel.

'Fool!' I kept reviling myself. 'To get into this bloody situation because you were careless about signing a piece of paper.'

I knew Paul Lincoln had not been bluffing when he talked about having to sell Whispering Corner unless I got the novel finished and made enough on translation and paperback rights to fend the bank off for a while. But that was rather like throwing a baby out of a sleigh to halt a pursuing wolf pack, it would soon be in full cry again. Even if I were granted the Tomlin thing, there would be several miserable years ahead when everything I earned went straight into the Pleiades account. It was not just the debt, Paul told me that the accumulating interest must be roaring up the chimney at the rate of several hundred pounds a month.

At a stroke I had lost the fruit of the lean years when I was attempting to get established as a novelist, of the books that only just covered their advances before vanishing without trace, of the nights driving a minicab when my credit ran out, of the feelings of guilt when Pamela saw those red unpaid bills on my desk.

Even when success came with *Shadows and Mirrors* much of the money it earned went to pay off old debts. The rest redecorated our flat, bought me a new car and established a decent bank account until Whispering Corner came along. If I sold the house and cleared the Pleiades debt there would be some money left over, but a dream would be gone.

When I thought about Charles Nixon I literally felt the bile rise in my throat. But it was myself I blamed. Dozens of incidents should have rung warning bells, but had been dismissed as funny or eccentric. I had a sudden vision of one of the last times I had been with him, lunching some American who, he assured me, was going to sell *Shadows and Mirrors* to one of the big networks for us. His long, normally pale features were flushed and the lenses of his granny glasses flashed as he held the floor while the American paused at regular intervals to look up from his steak au poivre to say, 'Is that right?'

Charles, a great flirt with waiters, suddenly complained of the heat, and when one of the handsome Italian boys opened a window for him he pressed a five pound note into his hand.

Why did that cameo return now? Something to do with extravagance, I suppose. It had been an omen which I failed to recognize, even though I knew in my heart that we were all playing make-believe, the big producer, the Hollywood salesman and − God forgive me − the distinguished author.

In my anger at myself, Nixon, Pleiades Films and the Regent Bank I had pressed the accelerator pedal down until the speedo needle was wavering at the 100 mph mark. The last thing I wanted was to be stopped by a police cruiser, so I slowed to a sober sixty. The dusk was turning to darkness as I turned south from Salisbury and realized with a fresh sense of resentment against a hostile world that I would be too late to visit Ashley. I needed a drink when I finally parked the Peugeot in the drive and approached the dark house. The gables looked like sinister black triangles against the starshine, yet it seemed unusually welcoming when I got inside. Here was home − but for how long?

In the living-room I only switched on a heavily shaded table lamp, preferring to sit in the shadows with the brandy and a bottle of Perrier on the marble coffee table beside me.

The first drink helped.

It steadied me enough to play a Dian Derbyshire CD. Mozart's music, played with her amazingly sensitive touch, began to calm me enough to try and think more constructively. Somehow I had to find a way to keep Whispering Corner − I had accepted the fact that I would have to pay the bank − and I tried to think of alternatives. For a moment I believed that the answer might lie in raising a second mortgage, but the sum owed by Pleiades was too large. The prospect of a mortgage company's financing someone like myself, self-employed with no regular income and owing such a massive debt to a bank, was remote.

Several brandies later I came to the conclusion that my only chance lay in writing myself out of trouble. I had to write as I had never written before in the hope that *Whispering Corner* would live up to *Shadows and Mirrors* and get paperback and overseas sales in time to enable me to offer a sum large enough to prevent a forced sale. It would be a race between my finishing the novel and the bank's getting judgement against me.

I was reminded of Sir Walter Scott. He toiled at his novels to clear debts incurred by a business partner for which he was no more responsible for than I was now, and in doing so brought about his own death through overwork. The thought of Sir Walter slaving through the lonely nights while he suffered increasingly ill health made me raise my glass in his memory, and I found when I came to fill it that the bottle was empty. I swayed slightly when I got up to get another bottle from the kitchen and my fingers were clumsy with the stylus when I put on another CD.

The truth was that I was drunk. But there are times when one needs to get drunk, and after such a day I felt that this was one of them. I lay back on the sofa balancing a glass of Courvoisier and Perrier while notes of piano music filled the room like showers of sparkling raindrops shaken from fantastical flowers . . .

It was the sound of a baby crying which woke me. There was a wet patch on my chest where my drink had spilled when my fingers relaxed on the glass, and beneath that my heart was thumping unpleasantly – always the penalty with brandy.

The sobbing continued as I tried to sit up. When I swung my legs over the edge of the sofa the room rocked gently like a moored boat caught by the wash of a passing vessel. I was already in the grip of a hangover, and I sat with my head in my hands until the room steadied. But at least I was awake now and could tackle the problem of the crying. I got to my feet and walked very carefully to the door, where the sound was louder. Apart from the crying the house seemed very still. I switched on the light in the kitchen expecting to see something – a bundle of cloth, I supposed.

Nothing.

I went into the old scullery, pulling open the doors of the big cupboards, but all was in order. The sound was more urgent now, nearer screaming than crying, and I began to panic. It was as though something terrible was happening, something that I could stop if only I could find out where it was going on. It was the stuff of nightmares, but I knew by my pounding heart and the sweat beading my face that I was uncomfortably awake.

Then I saw that the cellar door was still ajar after my search for a saw, and it was from the cellar that the pitiful cries were emerging.

'Take it easy, I'm coming,' I called as I pulled back the door and stood at the top of the steps gazing into sheer blackness. The coldness of the air came as a physical shock, I was shivering as I ran my hand along the wall until I located the old-fashioned electric switch. Enough light filtered through the grime on the bulb for me to make out the shadowed heaps of junk round the walls, trunks piled on top of each other, a wooden-rollered mangle like a medieval torture instrument, a broken-legged chaise longue . . . but nothing living, nothing that cried.

It could only be in the second cellar, through the arch. As I descended the steps with exaggerated care the brandy sweat on my face turned to drops of ice water. I was reminded of a dream which had recurred during the latter years of my childhood, in which some irresistible power was forcing me to descend a staircase into darkness.

With only a couple of stumbles I reached the dirty stone flags of the cellar and crossed to the entrance of the second cellar, my eyes straining to see by the amber light which elongated my shadow. Apart from some empty crates at the far end the place seemed empty. I stepped through the doorway, hands outstretched to feel along the stone shelves where long ago bottles of blue-blooded port had stood in cobwebbed dignity.

And the crying stopped.

It did not fade away as it does with an exhausted child, but ended as sharply as a radio switched off. There was no baby in the wine cellar, only ancient dust and darkness and now a silence so complete that I could hear the pulse in my ears. I backed into the main cellar.

Now that I was convinced there was no living child to rescue my only thought was for myself. I wanted to get out of the cellar. The puzzle about the crying could wait until later.

I knocked against the mangle in my hurry, cursing the inanimate object childishly, and I was halfway across the floor when my body stopped. It was as though my energy drained away like water when a bath plug is pulled. I just stood there, feeling ill and wondering whether I was about to collapse. I told myself that it was the result of too much brandy, that I was stupidly pissed. A minute may have passed while I stood in the silence, taking deep breaths and trying to break the paralysis which had overwhelmed me. I decided to count to ten, and on the word ten I would move. It did not succeed the first time, and when I started counting again I became aware of the shadows. In certain corners they seemed to be forming into menacing shapes. It was just another symptom of my disorientation through stress and alcohol, but I must admit that at the time I was as afraid of those shadows as any unfortunate character I had terrorized in my fiction.

I counted to ten again and this time I had enough willpower to put one foot after the other. The pathetic cellar light appeared to dim. Out of the corner of my eye I kept a wary watch on the shadow-shapes which seemed to be becoming more mobile in the gathering gloom. I hauled myself up the steps. The temptation to rest for a moment, to slump against the handrail, was almost irresistible, but fear kept me going. Fear of exactly what I did not know, any more than I knew what awaited me at the bottom of the staircase in my childhood dream.

And then I was back in the house, back in its accustomed warmth with its tang of new paint, and when I had shot the cellar door bolt on my fears I fell full-length on the sofa. And it seemed to my morbid imagination that somewhere in the house something was again faintly crying.

* * *

It was the sound of intermittent tapping that dragged me back to consciousness. I sat up painfully, grateful that my heart was no longer fluttering inside my ribcage like a trapped bird. As my eyes focused I saw a figure pressed against the French window. I shambled over and admitted the Reverend Gotobed.

'My dear soul,' he said, his voice full of concern. 'I was so anxious when I saw you sprawled on the sofa. Are you all right? You look as though you've seen a ghost.'

'I had rather a bad night,' I said vaguely.

'I can see that.' He could not help glancing at the empty brandy bottle on the coffee table, then became embarrassed in case I thought he was making a moral judgement.

'Let me make you some coffee,' he added, and as a surge of dizziness made me sink down on to the sofa I made no objection. While he was in the kitchen I took my pulse. It was too fast but steady, it's when it misses the beat that I worry. The smell of fresh coffee in the percolator made me feel a little better.

'I just thought I'd pop over and see if you'd had time to read the "Narration",' Henry said as he put a steaming cup down beside me.

'I have indeed — it was fascinating. It's given me some marvellous ideas for the current novel. I'm very grateful.'

'So glad. I couldn't believe my luck when I came across it. What a coincidence that you should come to a haunted house, in the light of what you write.'

'I don't believe in hauntings really. I'm sure there's a logical explanation for the "Narration". We only have the word of Mary Lawson, no corroborative evidence . . .' My words disappointed Henry, I could see, so I added, 'But still, it makes a great story. It certainly affected me last night.'

He was so obviously interested that I felt it would be churlish not to discuss it with him, despite my aching head.

'The story was vivid enough to have a curious effect on me,' I explained. 'Yesterday was a bastard, if you'll excuse me putting it that way . . . an unexpected financial problem which will take a bit of solving. The result was that I drank far too much brandy. I didn't intend to, one glass must have followed another without me realizing it until I passed out. Then I had a sort of hallucination, because when I came round it seemed that I heard a baby crying. It was so realistic that I actually went searching for it down in the cellar. Of course there was nothing there, and now I see how the story of Sir

Richard Elphick must have triggered off the illusion or whatever it was – the unwanted child would most likely have been done away with in the cellar, or at least the body would have been buried down there. Anyway, the hallucination affected me enough to scare me half to death when I was down there. Now that I'm sober it's obvious that the whole thing was in my imagination.'

'You don't think it was possible that in some way you tuned in, as it were, to an echo of the past?' Henry asked tentatively.

I shook my head and then wished I hadn't. 'Echoes from the past, psychical reverberations – they're just modern euphemisms for the age-old ghost thing.'

'Why are you so sceptical of paranormal phenomena when, if you'll forgive me, they've been your bread and butter?'

'It's illogical,' I said. 'Just supposing a human being does have a spirit, why should it return after death in the likeness of its old body which it obviously no longer inhabits, to go through some trivial act? The ghost tradition began when one of our prehistoric ancestors was asleep in his cave and dreamed of some dead member of the tribe. Not understanding the mechanism of dreaming, he concluded that they had made a brief return from the dead. It's just superstition, like . . .'

'Like religion?' said Henry gently.

'That's what I was going to say,' I admitted. 'No offence intended.'

'And none taken. I can sympathize with your point of view. Neither religion nor the paranormal is logical, yet there may be more things in heaven and earth, Horatio, than are dreamt of in your philosophy. Is it necessary that the only things that can be accepted are those we can explain? Imagine trying to explain colour television to an early Victorian. At this stage of scientific knowledge the idea would have been mad, yet we accept it as part of everyday life. Religion has been dismissed as superstition, yet the further man goes into physics the more likely the metaphysical seems. Victorian theologians made an error in ridiculing the advances in scientific thought, they should have seen the hand of God in evolution. Alas, they were too indoctrinated by Hebrew folktales.'

I drank my coffee while he paused reflectively.

'Jonathan, what happened to make you lose your faith so completely? You told me that you used to be an altar boy, so there must have been a foundation there.'

It was the very last question I wished to discuss at that – or any other – time, so I merely said, 'As I grew up I began to think for myself.'

'Sorry,' said Henry, abashed at the brusqueness of my tone. 'Not my business, of course.'

'It's me that should be sorry. I'm not behaving very well,' I said. 'I must confess that I have a thumping head. Serves me right.'

Henry brought me a second cup of coffee with Christian conciliation, and said, 'I do hope something will turn up to solve your financial difficulty – I shall pray that it will. You should be free to concentrate on your novel. Now I'll leave you to rest. Have a hot bath and get some more sleep and I'm sure you'll wake up feeling better.'

I took his advice.

* * *

After I woke up in the early afternoon my headache had gone, though I still had that post-drunk sensation that my skin was not a good fit. The first thing was to try and contact Charles Nixon, so I set off up Church Walk in the direction of the village phone box. Today there was no wind, and the wood was remarkably still and soothing to the spirit. The air, redolent of leaf mould, was a pleasure to breathe and I would have enjoyed my walk had it not been for the nature of my errand. If I managed to get hold of my partner I doubted whether it would achieve anything, I had a bet with myself that I would get a one-way spiel on how he was selling *Shadows* ('They're mad for it, Jonno, mad for it!') to Universal or MGM or perhaps Channel 4 ('Big co-production deal!') and the money would be through before the bank ('How dare they speak to you like that!') could do anything.

As it turned out my call was unanswered. His wife must have gone to Wales and Charles, who worked from home, was either on one of his 'location-seeking' jaunts or just not answering the phone.

Returning down the path I managed to push Charles and the Regent Bank out of my thoughts and concentrate on what I was about to write. The brandy-inspired delusions I had suffered the night before suggested the next scene in my novel. Now that Falco and Lorna had become lovers the time had come to introduce the sense of menace which is about to overshadow their lives. Paranormal forces inspired by a story similar to that told in Mary Lawson's 'Narration' are about to be unleashed upon the couple, their new-found happiness in contrast to the ancient evil which seeps – from where?

The cellar, of course.

That is where an unspeakable deed had been done, the murder of an innocent by a man obsessed by his need to keep a respectable face in the local squirarchy. Or did he use the strength of his personality to force the mother of the unwanted child to do away with it? And was that his first crime? If he was capable of killing a baby, murder obviously did not present a problem to him. Had he murdered before? Had he killed his ailing wife so that the attraction between him and his sister-in-law could burgeon within the walls of Whispering Corner? Or had the incestuous affair started while she was still alive and he had silenced her when she found out?

As I went through the old wicket gate into my garden I tried to recapture something of what I had felt last night when I found myself in the cellar almost legless from drink. Much had faded as dreams fade before the onset of daily life, but some impressions remained, such as the chilling effect of the crying even though it had been illusionary, and the sensation of stark fear when it seemed that shadows were moving about me in that damned cellar. Then I went straight to my study, eager to get the words down while the mood was upon me.

I described how Falco had been at work in his studio all day roughing out the illustrations for Lorna's book. As evening draws on she prepares supper for them both. Having found each other, they are in the mood for a quiet celebration. Falco insists on candlelight again and an appropriate musical background. During the meal he asks Lorna about herself but her answers are vague, at this stage I wanted her to remain an enigmatic character. She talks about her ambitions as an author of children's stories rather than about her personal life, and then deftly turns the conversation back to him.

As I wrote I hoped that I was building an atmosphere of pleasant intimacy, of romantic cosiness which my readers male and female (and not least myself) could imagine enjoying. Then I wrote,

Lorna interrupted Falco in mid-sentence.

'What's that? It sounds like – like a baby crying. Turn the music off.'

He obeyed with the air of someone indulging a lover's whim, then looked puzzled.

'I do hear something. Wait a minute – I know what it is. A cat. It must be the Magic Cat that you saw in the garden. It's come back to its old home and now it's shut in somewhere.'

'That's no cat . . .' Lorna began but, amused by the idea, Falco went to the door and began calling, 'Puss, puss. It sounds as though it's in the cellar. Get some milk, darling, it'll probably be famished.'

He opened the door to the stairway which led down to the cellar and shivered as the cold hit him.

'Poor little moggie if she's been shut in down here,' he said as he groped for the light switch. An ancient electric bulb cast yellow light but failed to illuminate any movement below. 'Probably scared to death,' he muttered as he went carefully down the steps. The mewling sound became faint, as though having led the man to this spot it was now receding.

'Puss, puss,' Falco called with less conviction. He stood in the centre of the stone-flagged cellar, thinking he would pay the handyman to clear the whole place out. It was as eerie as hell the way it was.

'Puss, puss.'

Somewhere in the house above Lorna screamed. Falco bounded back

up the steps, tripping and barking his skin agonizingly on the brickwork.

'Lorna!'

There was no response. He ran into the living-room. The French windows were open and he could see Lorna huddled on the steps between the two ornamental urns . . .

My alarm clock trilled and I came back to reality. It was time to go and visit Ashley.

The next couple of days were the lull after the storm in my affairs. The knowledge that I was likely to lose Whispering Corner filled me with a dull anger in place of panic, and the previous sense of urgency about my novel was redoubled now that it seemed to hold the only hope I had of being able to come to an understanding with the bank. I began work early and broke off only when hunger forced me down to the kitchen for a snack. I was amused when I imagined what Warren, who I presumed was still visiting megaliths in the west, would have said about my bacon sandwiches.

The highlight of my day was an evening drive to the cottage hospital to visit Ashley. The doctor had diagnosed delayed concussion, and there was something about her EEG which suggested that more tests should be made before she was discharged. She suffered from severe headaches, for which she was given analgesics, and always seemed to me to be sleepy despite the valiant effort she made to appear bright and cheerful during the visiting hour.

On my first visit after my ill-starred trip to London she expressed concern over my haggard appearance, which I explained as a combination of too much work and a manic session with a bottle of brandy.

'Only myself to blame,' I said lightly.

And bloody Pleiades films! I thought bitterly.

Although I looked forward to making these visits I learned very little about Ashley from them. She seemed to like to talk about books most – afterwards it struck me that this was a safe neutral topic – and when I took her a couple of Judy Gardiner novels she declared that she was one of her favourite authors. When I mentioned that I knew Judy I rose in her estimation. But after a few minutes' chat her eyelids had a tendency to flutter and it seemed to be an effort for her to keep a conversation going. At this point I would make a remark about 'companionable silences', and a few minutes later leave the little ward and walk down the over-lit corridor with a sense of vexation.

There was something about Ashley that intrigued me. Although I knew why she had visited Whispering Corner, there was still an air of mystery about her. When I sat in the chair by her bed, especially when she was dozing. I could not help imagining her as Lorna in my novel. Now I wonder if that was why, at that point, she held such interest for me.

When I knew that she could not see me I found myself scrutinizing her for copy, the slight unevenness of her teeth, a mole high on her right cheek, her unusually long fingers, the habit of holding the back of her hand against her forehead while sleeping as though protecting herself against a glare – everything was grist to my literary mill. I was embarrassed when a nurse came in and saw me in rapt contemplation of the patient, and from then on I had to endure her suspicious looks whenever she saw me.

My only other human contact at this time was Henry Gotobed, who made a habit of looking in once a day, ostensibly to lend me a book on local history or ask for some advice regarding his literary opus. I think I had become a cause he rather enjoyed, and I was touched by his surreptitious glances towards the table on which I kept my drinks to check on my brandy consumption.

I found no difficulty in proceeding with *Whispering Corner* from the point where Falco finds Lorna unconscious on the steps outside the French windows. When she comes to she explains that after he had gone in search of the cat it seemed that an invisible hand took hold of the candelabrum, raised it slowly in front of her and then hurled it across the room. Falco sees the candelabrum lying on the floor and the wallpaper on the far wall spattered with wax.

'*You mean it just happened by itself – it rose up in the air and then hit the wall?*' Falco asked, an uneasy thought in his mind.

From the sofa Lorna nodded her head.

'*I never guessed anything like that could be so terrifying,*' she whispered. '*All I remember is that I had to get out, and when I reached the steps everything went black, as they say. I know it must sound crazy to you but, James, it did happen. It just rose up as though the Invisible Man was lifting it.*' She shuddered and ran her fingers distractedly through her short hair while Falco handed her a glass of brandy.

He crossed the room and looked at the dribbles of wax which had solidified on the wallpaper, and the candelabrum, one of whose arms was badly bent with the impact of striking the wall.

'*I've never believed in that stuff,*' he said. '*It's not been scientifically proved.*'

Lorna looked at him wide-eyed. '*But I'm telling you I saw it happen,*' she said in a quiet, determined voice. '*Do you think I threw it across the room? Are you suggesting that I made the story up?*'

'*Of course not. Most likely you felt faint, grabbed the candelabrum and it shot out of your hand . . .*'

'*So, as I was going into a swoon, the candelabrum left my hand with enough force to bend it.*'

'*OK, that's a stupid theory,*' Falco conceded. '*It's just that I*

can't take that psychic . . .' His voice stopped in mid-sentence.
Somewhere in the house a baby was crying.
I decided that was a good point to end the chapter.

Chapter 9

Looking back on the days following Ashley's dramatic entry into my life, I find it quite extraordinary how swiftly my mood could change. Often during the witching hours of the night I would wake up with a panic attack and lie in the darkness with mad sums going through my head, sums in which I tried to work out how I could pay the Regent Bank and still keep Whispering Corner. Sums that of course never worked out.

Sometimes my mood was a calm, almost melancholic, depression about the novel I was writing. Reviewing what I had written I would come to the conclusion that the whole thing was ridiculous. I was merely putting down words in a Pavlovian reflex. Then I would tell myself that I ought to return to reality and do something positive such as take up King Syed's offer and go and teach English Literature in Abu Sabbah.

Reflecting these moods were dreams – or did my moods reflect my dreams? – which would have delighted a psychoanalyst for their textbook quality. I remember one in particular in which I was seated at a *bal masque*. Costumed dancers whirled in wild rhythm, then the music changed and they began a formal minuet. Something about their automaton-like movements gave me a sense of foreboding. They stopped and in the following silence a couple approached where I was seated in shadow. They were dressed as Harlequin and Columbine and when they removed their masks I saw the faces of Jocasta Mount-William and Charles Nixon. At that moment a spotlight focused upon me and laughter rolled from the assembled company. Then, to my horror, I realized that I was seated on a lavatory.

I found the best antidote to the negative phases was to have a brandy and get to work. As my anxiety subsided and I gained control of my thoughts, a calmer frame of mind took over and I became immersed in the relationship between Falco and Lorna, and the growing atmosphere of menace which hung over them. It seemed to me that since these two characters became lovers they had come to life, their feelings for each other animating them in a way I had not known even with the best of my previous characters.

A curious aspect of the developing story was that while I was deeply involved in their discovery of each other and enjoyed writing their conversations, the gathering storm of paranormal activity seemed to develop automatically. I began to share the sense of claustrophobia that was enfolding them.

A couple of days after my return from London I telephoned my accountant in the forlorn hope that he might have found a way out of the mess.

'I've got a copy of the form you signed from the bank,' Paul Lincoln told me. 'There's no doubt about it, they've got you over a barrel. There was no limit on how high the overdraft could go. The way people cheerfully sign away their birthrights never ceases to amaze me.'

'But I should have been warned,' I said, warming to the old theme.

'Barnet was right when he told you there was no legal obligation on the bank to do so, but, having said that, they should have protected your interests, especially when they must have had an inkling of the sort of character your partner is. My private opinion is that someone boobed in allowing him to have such a facility when no money was coming in, and now they're trying to rectify it by clobbering you before head office clobbers them. But that doesn't help you.'

'I just don't know what to do,' I said dispiritedly.

'You just get your book finished and hope that your agent can get some quick sales. Meanwhile there's nothing that can be done at the moment. When the bank gets a writ issued against you we'll need a red hot solicitor.'

He talked on for a while, explaining the legal steps that must be followed before the bailiff actually knocked on my door.

The depression engendered by this conversation lifted as I returned to Whispering Corner and saw its steep-angled gables appear through the symphony of greens which made up the woodland. The early summer light gave it a comforting quality, its patches of ivy dark green against ancient brick, its windows no longer blank but shining in welcome. I felt that since my arrival the house had become subtly reanimated, and whatever happened in the future nothing could take away the pleasure I had found in it. That, like the love one feels for a dead friend, would remain for ever.

An airmail letter was waiting for me. As I picked it up I realized that over the past few days my thoughts had revolved so closely round the bank and round my novel, and the part Ashley was playing in it as Lorna, that everything else had become remote. I had rarely thought about Pamela until I slit the envelope she had addressed.

In the letter she wrote enthusiastically about her work on the perfume launch and the breathless – her word – time she was having in New York. She closed affectionately, as though to an old friend, and left me with a vague feeling of dissatisfaction.

At the end of the day I drove to the cottage hospital for my usual visit to Ashley. Each time I saw her she had improved, her speech growing more confident and the tendency for her eyes to close lessening. When she had been in hospital for a week she announced,

'I'm having another lot of tests tomorrow and then, if they're OK, I can go home.'

'And where is home?' I asked, prepared for this development.

She answered that she would go to London and find accommodation. On the notice board at New Zealand House there would be advertisements from girls looking for flatmates. No problem. But I saw that despite her confident tone she was not looking forward to the effort it would involve.

'You won't feel like traipsing round bedsit land yet,' I said. 'You really need to have a quiet period after concussion. I can just imagine what it'd be like if you moved in with a bunch of lively kiwi girls – the ghetto-blaster blasting, telly on until close-down, all-night parties . . .'

Ashley gave an amused shudder.

'And their boyfriends! Big muscle-bound brutes named Bruce and Kevin singing rugby songs and cracking tubes . . .'

'Not Bruce and Kevin!' She was laughing now.

'Definitely Bruce and Kevin. But you do have another option.'

'I have?'

'You could stay at Whispering Corner until you're fit enough to brave the big city.'

'That's kind,' she said, giving me a level look with her cool dark eyes. 'But you have your novel to finish and I'd only be in the way.'

I shook my head. 'There's more than enough room for two in the house. We could go for ages without bumping into each other. And no strings,' I added.

'No strings?'

'I promise.'

She gave a little smile and I thought I must have sounded pompous.

'I'm having a raving affair with my heroine at the moment,' I said to lighten my words. 'I couldn't be unfaithful to her.'

'If it's not my eager young body you lust after, why?'

'I suppose you could call it friendship,' I replied. 'And it seems to me that as you had such bad luck when you came to see your great-aunt's old home it might be nice for you to live in it for a little while.'

'Yes, I'd love that. Maybe I'd pick up her vibes. But are you sure that's the real reason? You haven't got a complex about helping lame dogs . . . ?'

What was the real reason? I looked at Ashley with her black curls on the pristine hospital pillow while the blood-red hospital blanket decorously outlined her breasts – so full for someone as slender as she – and I had to admit that I found her a highly attractive young woman. Yet this was not the reason I wanted her to be my guest.

Probably the least endearing aspect of a writer is his detachment. No matter how involved he may become in human situations, no matter how much he may enjoy himself or suffer, there is part of him standing to one side, a neutral observer taking notes for future reference. This alter ego will even seek copy in his own tragedy, he will store the dialogue when a lover announces the end of an affair, analyse emotions by the open grave. Once I believed I was dying and as I was rushed into hospital I was aware of the other me – the recorder – observing my reactions and quite aloof from the pain as I was wheeled to what I expected to be my doom.

There was no doubt that the idea of having Ashley about the house was pleasant, but at that moment it was as Lorna that I really wanted her.

So it was agreed that she would recuperate at Whispering Corner. I drove home in the twilight with a rare sense of elation, savouring the sky darkening to indigo, the curving fields blurring into dusk, the black aerobatics of the bats and the woods losing their innocence with nightfall.

All I needed now was a villain for my puppet theatre.

The next day I brought Ashley home. Perhaps it is odd to use that expression, as she had never lived at Whispering Corner, but it indicates how my mind was working at the time. Although Ashley fiercely denied it, she was still weak from the effects of concussion and a week in a hospital bed. After a boil-in-the-bag supper she was relieved to go up to the bedroom I had prepared for her.

'Thanks for everything,' she said at the door as I bade her goodnight. 'I can't tell you how thrilled I am to be staying in my great-aunt's house. It must sound crazy, but it's like a childhood dream come true. I feel there is something very special about this place. Or is that just my imagination?'

'I felt that from the moment I first saw Whispering Corner,' I answered. 'Perhaps there is something in Lawrence Durrell's idea of Spirit of Place. Sleep well, and tomorrow you can explore the ancestral pile to your heart's content.'

I went to my study and started to work against the background of the Dian Derbyshire CD. It was well after midnight when I sat back with the dazed feeling that comes after an intensive stint at the laptop, and when I went to bed soon afterwards I had a recurrence of the hypnagogic voices which had repeated meaningless sentences in my head after my arrival at Whispering Corner. Again there were the disjointed phrases, and a sibilant voice repeating over and over, 'The time will come . . . the time will come.'

This did not worry me. I had looked up hypnagogsis in one of my reference books and was reassured to read that it is not an uncommon occurrence, especially when one is fatigued or anxious.

Next morning I awoke to a glorious day. From my bedroom window I saw the tops of the trees moving in a gentle sea swell, while the cloudless sky appeared to have transposed its colour from the Mediterranean. The vividness of the scene communicated an excitement to me, the sort of excitement I had felt as a young man waking up in a strange city when anything seemed possible. Even my usual morning depression – with its desperate financial reckonings, imaginary letters to the Regent Bank and imaginary conversations with Charles Nixon – was absent. And I remembered that I had a guest.

I shaved, dressed and went down to the kitchen to make breakfast. Though the bacon was a little too crisp – some epicures might have said charred – in places, the second batch of toast was passable. I was opening the window to allow the fumes of the first lot to escape when Ashley appeared at the door in a cream towelling robe.

'Something smells good,' she lied. 'Am I invited?'

'This breakfast feast is in your honour.'

'Then I am honoured . . . I think those eggs are done.'

While I snatched the frying pan from the glowing ring of the stove she seated herself at the table and exclaimed, 'What a bright, peaceful morning. It makes me feel as though Whispering Corner likes me being here. It is kind of you to let me stay.'

'How do you feel?'

'The headache's gone. The funny thing is I can't remember much of what happened before I was taken to hospital. Did I really run out into the garden or was that a nightmare?'

'You ran out all right and scared the hell out of me,' I told her. 'Have you any idea what made you do it?'

'I think something upset me.'

'At the time you said that voices frightened you and you had to get out.'

'That's interesting. I don't remember hearing anything now, but it might have been caused by the concussion.' Then she laughed. 'It couldn't have been the whispering of the plague victims, could it?'

'You know about the legend?'

'Oh, yes. My grandfather told us about the ghostly voices with great relish. It was all part of the mythology of Whispering Corner. It was that old story which gave the house its name, wasn't it?'

'So I believe.'

'Do you think I heard ghosts, then?' She looked amused at the idea and I could imagine her writing it as an anecdote in a letter to the folks back in Taranaki.

'No,' I said. 'Even if there was such a thing as the whispering you wouldn't hear it here. I'll show you the spot. It's a bend in Church Walk where, according to the vicar, the plague refugees were supposed to have rested. It would be easy to think you could hear something like soft voices there – the wind makes the trees rustle quite loudly in that part of the wood. If you're superstitious you can imagine all sorts of weird things. Since I've been down here I've heard voices just as I'm going to sleep. If I believed in old wives' tales I could imagine I was having a supernatural experience, in fact it's quite a common symptom caused by fatigue or tension.'

'You suffer from tension?'

'I was a bit worried about my novel being behind schedule,' I said lightly.

'I guessed you were under some sort of stress when you visited me,' she said. 'I'm afraid that I'll be in the way and make matters worse.'

'Nonsense.'

'I'll do the cooking. That'll give you a bit more time.'

'That's a deal,' I said. 'A young chap stayed a few nights here a couple of weeks ago. He took over the catering and it made a great difference.'

'Now I know why you really wanted me here,' Ashley laughed.

'When I bought the house I had to have it redecorated,' I said, 'But there's one room which escaped the handyman's attention because the door was locked. I had to break in, finally. Later on I'll show it to you. Miss Constance used it as her sanctum and there are still a few mementos of her there.' And I went on to tell her about the poem that had been written in wartime.

'I'd love to make a copy of it,' she said. 'It's sort of sad that a few lines on a piece of paper are all that remains of her great love affair.'

'That's exactly what I thought when I found it.' After breakfast I took myself off to my study and resumed the story. Falco is unable to accept the idea of the supernatural, and fears that the girl he has fallen in love with has a split personality. The only explanation he can think of for the so-called poltergeist incident is that she threw the candelabra at the wall herself and immediately afterwards was unaware of what she had done.

Falco watches her actions and reactions surreptitiously but not surreptitiously enough and Lorna has a shrewd notion of what he suspects. Afraid of bringing their thoughts out into the open, both endeavour to behave normally, and the growing tension that results is only relieved by frantic – almost despairing – love-making.

I knew that soon two things would have to happen in the story. Firstly a petty quarrel will cause Falco to lose his self-control and voice his suspicions, and Lorna will leave Whispering Corner in anger. Then Falco will come face to face with the supernatural himself. This time it will be something more dramatic than a candelabrum flying across a room.

Secondly, my instinct as a story-teller warned me that the element of human iniquity must soon be added to that of the paranormal. The trouble was that at that stage I had no idea of the character of my villain or his – or her – motivation in bringing harm to the couple.

I had just reached the point where Falco and Lorna are about to turn on each other when there was a tap at the door and Ashley entered wearing boutique jeans and a dark red shirt which complemented her olive complexion.

'I don't want to disturb the muse,' she began. 'But you said . . .'

'I'd show you round,' I finished. 'Don't worry, Melpomene is ready for her coffee break. Just give me a few minutes.'

'Melpomene? I should have thought Calliope would have been your goddess.'

While I typed she looked about the room with curiosity, especially at my reference books.

'You into black magic?' she asked.

'Of course not,' I answered emphatically. 'But I've made a study of the occult to get authentic backgrounds for some of my novels.'

'Your readers would be disappointed if they knew what an unbeliever you are,' she said. 'But there are things that can't be explained. When I was a little girl I believed in the local taniwha. The Maoris believed it was a sort of supernatural water monster. In the creek near our farm there was supposed to be a taniwha who claimed a life every year, and sure enough I can't remember a year going by without someone being drowned in it.'

'There were probably dangerous currents,' I said.

'You would say that.'

'But I like the idea. Someday I might use your taniwha in a novel.'

As I led her to the small room I had told her about, she said, 'You take some idea – like the taniwha legend, for example – and develop it into a whole novel?'

'Yes. I suppose you could say that the book I'm working on now owes a lot to legends connected with this place. Once a theme is established, though, the story goes its own way.'

'If Whispering Corner comes into it I'd love to read what you've written.'

'When it's finished,' I said. 'I have a complex about anyone reading half-finished work. I don't even show it to my agent or the publisher.'

'Are you afraid they might make suggestions?'

'I suppose I'm afraid they'd say it was no damned good. And to start altering the plot could ruin the overall effect I have in mind. Once it's finished it can go out into the world and stand on its own, but until then it's vulnerable. Here's the room.'

'And to think that less than a couple of years ago my great-aunt was sitting in here,' Ashley said excitedly. 'Why didn't I come over when she was still alive? I'd love to have talked to her. Was she very lonely, do you suppose?'

'I gather so – apart from Mrs Foch, her cat,' I said. 'Here's the poem I told you about.'

From the drawer of the small desk I took the ruled paper with its pencilled words and handed it to her. As she read it a tear slid slowly down her cheek.

'Sorry,' she said as she knuckled it away. 'It's just that something like that bridges the years. I can just imagine Great-aunt Constance getting this poem in a letter from her fiance's commanding officer, telling her how gallantly he had died for King and Country and enclosing these verses which had been found in his pay book. I can see her now, standing at the gate, the postman tramping away while she unfolds the poem. Sometimes I feel as sorry for people who are dead as those who are still alive. It's to do with time, I think. Just because all those years have gone by it doesn't mean that things hurt any the less when they happened. The agony was real then, and perhaps somewhere it still is.'

'What do you mean by that?' I asked, intrigued by what she was trying to say.

'It's hard to put into words. I suppose I mean that the present we're living in now is just the point where the future is becoming the past. I think we're like . . . like the playback head of a tape recorder. On one reel is the future, on the other the past and we only experience the moment when the tape passes the head. But that doesn't mean the past isn't there, it's just that it's stored away. Somewhere on the tape of the past a young girl called Constance is reading this poem by the wicket gate. Perhaps I feel so strongly about Constance because at last I'm in her house' – I mean, what was her house . . .'

I went to the window, making a mental note yet again to try and obtain an eyepiece for the telescope which stood in front of it. It was a beautifully constructed instrument and deserved to be brought back into use.

'I'll make a copy of the poem and you can have the original,' I said, but later when I looked for it I could not remember where we had put it. 'Hey, look. If I'm not mistaken there's Miss Constance's cat.'

Ashley hurried to the window and I pointed to the end of the garden where a large white cat was edging out of the undergrowth.

'I think she's gone feral,' I said. 'I'd hoped to look after her – it was something I could have done for the old lady.'

'That's a nice idea. Let me have a go. I'll try and give her some milk.'

I remained at the window while Ashley went downstairs, and then I saw her emerge on to the grass carrying a soup bowl full of milk. The cat froze, crouched belly flat, and watched the girl with baleful eyes. Ashley's soothing words floated up to me. 'Mrs Foch, Mrs Foch, puss, puss.'

She managed to get within arm's length of the cat, set down the bowl and backed away. Mrs Foch smelled the milk, a smell which must have reminded her of the good old well fed days. She inched forward until her nose touched the rim of the bowl and then began to lap ecstatically. Ashley turned and gave me a triumphant wave, and it was this sudden movement that sent Mrs Foch racing into the woods as though all the demons in cat hell were after her. Ashley shrugged ruefully at her mistake and walked back to the house.

It's strange what remains fixed in the memory for no apparent reason. When I try to visualize Ashley now I always see her standing on the grass giving that rueful little shrug.

Chapter 10

I stopped typing, eased my stiff back and looked out over the treetops towards the western sky which had become a palette of flame and purple. I was surprised to see the sunset. Time had raced, indicating how engrossed I had been in the chapter I had just finished. In it Falco finally admits to himself – and to Lorna – that the house he has inherited is haunted, its manifestations based on the story told in Mary Lawson's 'Narration'. Now I worked out the number of words still to be written and divided them by the number of days to the deadline and found that at my present output I was only a week behind schedule. If I could manage an extra couple of pages a day it would be possible to catch up and my agent would be able to deliver the typescript to Jocasta Mount-William exactly on time.

Ashley – always nervous of disturbing a genius at work – tapped her light tap at the door.

'Come,' I called in a jokey executive voice. With that chapter behind me I felt unusually light-hearted. The concentration it required had shielded me from thoughts of the looming financial crisis.

Ashley entered and I drew in my breath at her appearance. Since her arrival at Whispering Corner she had worn her designer jeans and a succession of shirts of varying shades of red. Now, for the first time, I saw her formally attired – and she looked marvellous. Her dress was a long, clinging, silken affair of black and gold – golden diamond shapes against a jet background which suggested an Aubrey Beardsley illustration or the garb of a medieval *jongleur*.

'Ash, you look like a fashion plate come to life,' I told her.

''Specially for you,' she answered. 'As is the supper I've been preparing. I felt we ought to celebrate tonight.'

'Anything in particular?'

'No. Just a no-reason celebration. I've been so happy here in my great-aunt's house that I felt I wanted to make an occasion before I go.'

As she stood there with that soft dress emphasizing the supple lines of her slender body, I felt a pang of dismay that she was thinking of leaving, that soon she might be enjoying a richer life while I remained with only my imaginary characters for company. But I was determined not to let this feeling show. If I had been Falco's age things might have been different, but I was not Falco and I had no wish for Ashley to remember me as a middle-aged amorist. So I kept it light.

'I've got a bottle of champagne hidden away,' I said. 'It was in case of emergency, like finishing a novel or selling rights to Hollywood. But why wait? Like the song says, the best of times is now.'

'Great. Now I must dash back to the kitchen.'

'You're not cooking in a dress like that?'

'Only finishing off. And I have a plastic pinny I bought in Poole along with the other goodies for tonight. The worst is over now but I don't want any last-minute disasters. I just came to ask you to come down in half an hour.'

'I'll be there,' I said. 'Leave the booze and music to me.'

As Ashley had obviously gone to a great deal of trouble I decided to show my appreciation by entering into the spirit of her evening. After I had showered and shaved away the day's stubble I put on a formal smoking jacket. Then I went downstairs, got out the Moet and put on a Jacques Loussier CD. In the dining room I found the table beautifully laid for two, with an arrangement of woodland flowers and ferns in the centre and two tall candles already burning.

'Perfect,' I called.

'Glad you like it,' she called back from the kitchen. 'Open the champers and we'll have a drink before I start serving.'

I poured the hissing wine into a pair of flutes and when Ashley came flushed from the hot stove we raised our glasses in a mutual toast.

'I'll bet Great-aunt Constance used to dress for dinner long ago,' Ashley said. 'Maybe she and Arthur had a meal together like this before he went off to France. I'd like to think their ghosts are approving of us tonight. I wonder if people – after they've died – can revisit places that meant a lot to them.'

'Doubt it,' I said. 'But if it were so I think it would be something more sinister than Miss Constance which would return to Whispering Corner.' And I told her briefly about the 'Narration'.

'I'll have some tales to tell if I go back to Godzone,.' she said. 'Hey, look how much we've drunk already, and I bought wine for the meal. If I don't stop now I'll be incapable of serving. Be seated and I'll bring in the first course. Chilled vichyssoise OK?'

'Very OK.'

The meal was pleasurably long. During the course of it I put on several CDs to keep the background music going, and we got through both the champagne and the white Macon which Ashley had bought because I once remarked that I loved the Macon country.

The wine and the intimate atmosphere, and most of all Ashley's face mysterious in the candle light, loosened my tongue. There was a temptation to tell her of the pressures upon me, to shed the load temporarily by dumping it on someone else, but I had enough self-control to steer away from that dangerous track.

At first the talk was about my days in journalism and the people I had met, and then the making of *The Dancing Stones*. Anything to do with film seemed to fascinate Ashley, but I tried to switch the conversation to her.

'Tell me something about you,' I said.

'Why?'

'Because it's boring if I keep on about myself.'

'But, Jonathan, you haven't told me anything about yourself. You've told me a series of amusing anecdotes and precisely nothing about you as a person.'

I laughed. 'Then that's two of us. So let's trade. One deep penetrating question each. OK?'

'OK. You go first.'

'All I really know about you is that you were brought up on a farm in a place called Taranaki and like a lot of young New Zealanders you've come to Europe for the obligatory visit. And your great-aunt was the previous owner of Whispering Corner. Apart from that you're an enigma. You're like someone in a beautiful mask, I have no idea what's behind it. I don't even know what you do for a living.'

'The mask analogy is pretty good. I've played so many roles that I sometimes wonder what's behind the mask myself.'

'You're an actress?'

She nodded.

'So that's why you haven't got a typical kiwi accent. I should have guessed. You trained in New Zealand?' She explained that on leaving high school she went to the Wellington Teachers Training College and during her course became involved in children's drama.

'I went from school to school with a special group putting on things like *Dr Dolittle's Circus* so we could get the kids to join in as animals and performers. From then on I was hooked. There were not a lot of opportunities – very little live theatre - but I was determined, and after my elocution classes I did get some parts on TV after appearing in a few commercials. Then I went over to Sydney because the film industry there is really taking off. But...' Her voice trailed off. 'Things didn't work out as I hoped. So, as England is the centre of the theatre world, I decided to try my luck here. I'd love to get a stage part. I want a live audience rather than cameras. Back home I was a little fish in a pond. Here I know I'll be a tadpole in an ocean, but I'm game for a try.'

I asked her which role she had enjoyed most.

'Antigone,' she answered without hesitation. 'Now it's my turn. Tell me about your marriage. When I was in Poole I went to the library and looked you up in *Contemporary Authors* and it said you married Pamela somebody and have a son.'

'That's right.'

'And from what you said the morning after my accident Pamela

101

does not share your house.'

'She's working in New York,' I said. 'We went our different ways after our son left home. He had been the keystone of the marriage. With him gone it became apparent that we were two individuals who shared the same roof but little else.'

'That's sad. Were you in love when you got married?'

'I honestly don't know. At the time we were greatly attracted to each other. She was on the rebound from an advertising executive who had ditched her and I had just come to London and was very lonely. But the question was really taken out of our hands. Pam became pregnant and in those days abortion wasn't the automatic answer to the problem. And when I see my son today I'm bloody glad it wasn't. We did what we thought was the right thing at the time and got married, but looking back on it I see that it was the worst reason for a marriage. There's a thought at the back of both parties' minds that it was not done through choice or love but merely to satisfy convention. Of course it's different now, abortion, one-parent families, life together without the blessing of holy matrimony – they're all quite accepted. I guess Pamela and I never had a chance to find out whether we were in love. Anyway, it's past history now.'

'What a waste.'

'It wasn't so bad. We did remain friends most of the time, and it's not too late for her to pick up her career again. She's very happy in New York, and I expect before long I'll hear she's met someone there she can really love.'

'And you?'

I shrugged. 'I'll carry on writing, I suppose. I'd like to travel.'

'To Abu Sabbah?'

'Perhaps.'

'And get married again?'

'I don't think so. I think I'd be scared I might find someone I could really love but wouldn't be able to make her happy. I suppose I feel guilty that it didn't work with Pam. If I'd had more understanding we might have made a better go of it.'

Ashley looked at me through the candles, which had burned down to half their length.

'Looking over your shoulder is bad, Jonathan,' she said. 'You know the poem about the Moving Finger having writ . . . '

'Moves on, nor all thy Piety nor Wit shall lure it back to cancel half a line, nor all thy Tears wash out a word of it,' I quoted.

'. . . and it is impossible to alter the past. You should look to the future. Your wife and son sound as though they are making out. It's time you gave yourself a new start.'

'In what way?'

'Enjoy life, to begin with. I guess it's the champagne and the Macon that's making me talk more than I ought to, but I've hated to see you under such tension.'

I was genuinely surprised. I had believed that I had managed to hide my worries very creditably. 'What tension?' I asked unconvincingly.

'Come on, Jonathan! There are times when stress positively radiates from you even though you try to hide it – and all those empty brandy bottles under the sink! I can't believe it's working on your novel that makes you like that. Something's bugging you . . . but of course it isn't my business.' She paused. 'You're not having a doomed love affair or anything like that? It isn't a woman, is it?'

I couldn't help laughing. 'There are other things besides love affairs that screw up peoples' lives. With me it's a case of fading talent and a joint and several guarantee, and that's all I'm going to say about it tonight. I'm really enjoying our evening and we're not going to spoil it with boring problems. Right?'

'Right!' She raised her glass, which I had refilled.

For a moment we sat looking at each other over the rims of our glasses and then I said, 'You've asked if I have a romantic – for want of a better word – life. Now it's my turn to ask you.'

'I have been in love. Once!' she answered simply. 'It didn't work out. Even so, I'm grateful. At least I know what it's about. But like you I'm enjoying myself tonight and the hell with past regrets.'

The evening seemed to accelerate as we talked and laughed together, and when I got up to go the bathroom I found I was a tiny bit unsteady, though my mind was clear. Excited but clear.

'Put on another CD while I'm away,' I said. 'Try the Stan Getz.'

When I returned Ashley was dancing to 'The Girl from Ipanema'. The candlelight glowed and rippled on the moving gold of her dress.

'Dance,' she said, holding out her arms. We danced easily to bossa nova music, and if the wine we had drunk made us sway a little amorously to the rhythm it also made me feel more confident than I usually did when dancing.

'What an archaic couple we must look, you in your smoking jacket and me in my long dress, dancing in the dark like a clip from a thirties film,' said Ashley with a soft laugh.

'*Evergreen*, perhaps.'

We danced into the living-room, and through the French windows we could see the midnight moon shining above the jagged treetops. As we paused to gaze at it I felt Ashley tighten her arms about me and the softness of her lips against mine.

'Sorry. I just wanted to do that,' she said.

'You beat me to it by a fraction.'

The music continued but the dancing was over. We stood hand in hand looking at each other, both smiling.

'Do you know why I wanted to do that?' Ashley asked.

'Because it's a romantic moment.'

'Yes. And?'

I shook my head.

'Because I've fallen in love with you.'

Her words took me by such surprise that I could think of nothing to say.

'Are you thinking, how boring?' Ashley asked. 'Being sort of famous as a writer you must meet lots of literary groupies who fling themselves at you.'

'Of course,' I said lightly. 'I live in the middle of a wood to escape them.'

'You haven't escaped me.' Her hand tightened on mine almost painfully. 'I wasn't going to say anything, and here I am giving myself away at the first opportunity.' She suddenly sounded angry. 'Mind if we go outside? I feel hemmed in.'

I opened the windows and we stepped into the garden, walking across the lawn to where a swing was suspended from a branch of the hornbeam. The kiss Ashley had given me, and her words, had released long suppressed sensations which bubbled through me like the bubbles in champagne.

Ashley sat on the swing seat. I stood in front of her and taking hold of the rusted chains pushed her away from me so that she swung back into my arms. I kissed her hair, her scented hair, and she said, 'If I'm making a fool of myself, don't do that. I'll go quietly. You don't have to be polite.'

'Ash, the truth is that I've been wanting to do that.'

'Then why the hell didn't you?'

'Because I was afraid you'd think I was an ageing Romeo who'd invited you here under false pretences.'

'Fool,' she murmured.

'Old fool,' I said.

'Hush. That's the very last word you must ever use. I'm in love with you and that's all that matters to me. I must say I was relieved when you told me about Pamela.'

She stood up from the swing so that we could embrace properly. The feel of her body pressed close against mine brought a surge of excitement, and the inevitable result made her look up into my face with a mocking smile.

'Say it. Just once.'

'I love you, Ashley, I . . . '

'That's enough. We can talk tomorrow if you wish. Words might break the spell now.'

One of my favourite words is 'glamour', not in the Hollywood sense but in its original meaning, and it really did seem as if a glamour had fallen upon us.

Ashley shivered.

With my arm round her shoulders we walked back across the lawn, pausing once to kiss. This time I was briefly aware of the touch of her tongue and I definitely knew that talking was for the next day.

With a sense of *deja vu* I stepped into the living-room and poured the last of the wine into two fresh glasses. I sank down on the sofa with mine, and there was a silken rustle as Ashley slid down beside me. The moonlight flooding through the oblong panes of the French windows illuminated her face so that it looked like a black and white portrait taken by a master photographer. And to me at that moment Ashley was truly beautiful.

'I have a confession to make,' she said as I slipped my arm round her. 'I used to smoke. And right now I need a bloody cigarette like never before.'

'Sorry. I haven't a packet in the house.'

'I have. I was evil and bought a packet in Poole. Maybe subconsciously I knew I might need one for a moment like this. You don't mind if I have one?'

She got up gracefully and went to the kitchen. I lounged back, glass in hand, looking out at the silvered garden. We were almost strangers, but nature ignored that. The chemistry was there and that was all that mattered. It made me feel as though I had known her always.

She returned and sat beside me. I took the matches from her and lit her cigarette. She inhaled with relief.

'That's better,' she said. 'Everything seems funny inside. I'm not used to telling men that I love them.'

For some minutes we sat in silence. I had my arm round her, my hand cupping her warm firm breast. Both of us were calm – the calm before the storm which I knew would whirl away all restraint. Sometimes she turned her head and in the glow of her cigarette I could see that she was smiling at me, but most of the time she looked out into the garden.

'Tomorrow it'll be just another garden with trees round it,' she mused, 'but tonight it's like a stage set. I feel almost as though I'm taking part in a production, that tonight nothing's quite real.'

'What I feel is real enough,' I said.

'What I meant . . . you and I are real but the surroundings are not. Perhaps there's something magical about Whispering Corner.' She stubbed out her cigarette. 'Oh, Jon, I do love you tonight.'

Ashley kissed me, and strangely I found that the smoky taste of the cigarette on her breath added to the excitement. We lay back on the sofa side by side, my arm about her, and I began to unfasten the tiny, infuriating buttons down the back of her harlequin dress. When I had finished she sat up and gave a little shrug, and the soft material slid down to her waist. Now there was more than her face for me to admire in the moonlight. Her breasts were like full exquisite fruits. She stood up and allowed the dress to rustle about her feet, standing above me like a proud statue carved from old ivory as the moonlight drained her natural colouring.

'You take over now,' she whispered.

I hooked my thumbs in the elastic of her briefs, and felt my breath catch as I slid them down and beheld her as naked as a sculptured Aphrodite. I laid my cheek against the satin of her belly, my arms enfolding her while she looked down upon me and twined her fingers in my hair.

'You taste of the ocean.'

'Then I must be a sea witch,' she said.

'More like Venus rising from the foam.'

'I like that better, but this isn't fair.'

Parting my hold, she sat beside me and began to undo my shirt.

A woman can unclothe herself gracefully – as Ashley had done – but with a man it is impossible since the advent of trousers. I tore off the bow tie I had worn to give the smoking jacket a more formal look and went through the absurd ritual of struggling out of my pants, kicking off my shoes and pulling off my underwear while Ashley watched with a slightly mocking expression.

As I fumbled to get free I feared that this pantomime, this comic entr'acte, would kill the mood which had built up between us, but as I pulled her to me and felt the delicious heat of her breasts against my skin it returned. Ashley was all I wanted. As I embraced her it was as though I was holding the world, and she knew and responded.

'Bed – please,' she murmured.

I laid her down on the carpet. The sight of her lying there, surrounded by our tangled garments and so defenceless in the silver radiance streaming through the windows, caught me by the throat. She looked up wide-eyed as I knelt above her.

'I'll never forget this moment,' she murmured. 'Whatever you want, my darling.'

I should have been more gentle but I was swept along by the mysterious force which has ensured the continuity of life on this planet since time immemorial. I was only aware of the heat of her skin and my all-consuming need, and then her brief, bitten-back cry as she guided me home.

We woke like two people coming out of a trance to find ourselves cold and uncomfortable. The room was black, the moon having vanished beyond the trees and only starshine illumining the glass panes of the French windows.

'What did you say?' Ashley murmured.

'Nothing.'

'But I heard you talking. I don't know what about but it woke me up.' She yawned. 'Let's go to bed properly. I'm exhausted.'

I felt the same way, exhausted in the true sense of the word by our intense love-making. She was shivering as I helped her to her feet and her nakedness had no effect on me. Desire had burnt itself out for the moment, the mood was now one of sleepy companionship.

'Don't put on the light,' she said. 'My eyes couldn't take it, and I don't want to know what time it is.'

Holding hands we went slowly up the dark stairs to my room. There was just enough starlight coming through the window to enable me to draw back the duvet for her.

'Thank God for bed,' she said. 'I think the champagne and the Macon was just a bit too much.'

'The champagne had nothing to do with it,' I said as I slid in beside her.

'You plied me with liquor and took advantage of me! That's my story and I'll always stick to it.'

After the hard floor the bed was bliss. Ashley lay with her back to me, my arms encircling her – like millions of couples that night, no doubt – but as I felt her soft shampoo-scented hair against my face I was filled with a sense of wonder that this girl who had come so unexpectedly into my life should reciprocate my feelings. At the back of my mind I knew that there would be problems – there always are where the human heart is concerned - and I thought the fact that at least fifteen years separated us could be one of the foremost. But tonight was our night and as we plunged back into sleep, our bodies fitting against each other so naturally, I refused to harbour negative thoughts.

When the false dawn was diluting the night we woke – or half woke – and made love again, but this time it was a gentle reflex in contrast to the urgency which had overwhelmed us earlier on. I can only say it was sweet and loving, symptomatic of the instant intimacy which had sprung up between us.

After she had felt the spasm of my climax Ashley lay still in my arms, and so we lay and so we slept.

The sun was high and the room filled with warm summer light when I next opened my eyes. Ashley slept on, the back of her hand against her forehead, and despite a lustful stirring in my loins I resisted the temptation to waken her. Instead I put on my dressing gown and went downstairs to make coffee and perhaps a simple breakfast to carry up to her.

The dining table which had been so carefully laid last night was now a confusion of dirty plates, the tall candles were burnt-out stumps, and on the living-room carpet our garments lay like a reproach for our uninhibited night. I quickly gathered them up, filled with a ridiculous apprehension that the Reverend Gotobed might appear and be shocked by the evidence of our lovemaking.

The events of the night were blurred, but Ashley's soft dress mingled with my clothing over my arm was proof that my world had tilted, that nothing would ever be quite the same.

A few minutes later I took coffee, toast and a boiled egg up to the bedroom where I sat on the bed while Ashley ate voraciously.

'Jonathan, there's no need to talk now, is there?' she asked as she put a dab of butter into the over-boiled egg. 'What I want more than anything now is a shower and then a walk in the woods by myself to calm my soul. To realize that you're suddenly and deeply in love can be a bit mind-blowing at first. You don't mind, do you?' she added anxiously.

Soon afterwards I watched her walk into the trees in her familiar jeans and a lumberjack shirt, and then I went to my study. On opening the door I experienced that sickening sensation one gets with the realization that one has been burgled.

Books were scattered across the floor as though hurled from their shelves by a violent hand. Certainly they were too far from the bookcase to have fallen out, or even to have been dropped by some intruder searching for small valuables or money hidden behind them.

I looked round the room. Nothing else seemed to have been disturbed. In the top right drawer of my desk was my wallet intact despite the fact that it held a number of five pound notes and credit cards. My expensive shortwave radio had not been touched, nor had a valuable French carriage clock which had been in my family for several generations. I checked the window and found it bolted, then hurried round the house. Nothing appeared to have been disturbed and there were no signs of anyone having forced an entry.

It was obvious that Whispering Corner had not been burgled, and I returned to the study to try and work out what had happened. I stooped to start gathering up the books and then decided to leave them to show Ashley on her return. I was so puzzled that childishly I wanted someone to share my bewilderment. In truth it was something more than bewilderment. Perhaps because books are so much a part of my life there was a touch of obscenity about it. I was uneasily reminded of the sensation I had felt when I ventured down into the cellar, something that was deeply worrying because I could not explain it.

This feeling became so strong that I found I could not sit at my desk and work. Instead I carried the laptop down to the kitchen and put it on the table there. I tried to get back to Falco and Lorna, and sought inspiration from the way my own feelings for Ashley had overtaken those of my characters, but I was making coffee when Ashley hurried in.

'Milk, quick!' she said.

I took a bottle out of the refrigerator and she poured it into a bowl.

'You've seen the cat again?'

'I've made contact with Mrs Foch,' she said as she hurried out into the garden.

I followed and saw Ashley slowly approaching the cat, which stood warily in the centre of the lawn.

'Mrs Foch, Mrs Foch,' she said coaxingly. The cat watched suspiciously while Ashley put the dish down about a yard from her and then knelt to await developments. After a moment the animal could no longer resist the temptation. With a strange little cry she stalked forward and began lapping the lovely liquid.

And she only flinched momentarily when Ashley gently stroked her back just long enough for her to be reminded of human contact without being scared by it.

Ashley backed away and looked at me with a smile of triumph.

'I saw her in the woods and kept calling her name. She must have recognized it because she followed me back here. I think that's a good omen.'

Chapter 11

'It must have been a polter-whatsit,' exclaimed Ashley when I took her up to my study and showed her the books scattered over the floor.

'Poltergeist – means "noisy ghost" in German,' I said. 'Psychic researchers think it's a mischievous elemental force, usually triggered off by young children or teenagers with sexual problems.'

'Well, there are no young children here and we're certainly not teenagers with sexual problems. Are you sure no one broke in? I hate the idea of that more than a noisy ghost.'

'It wasn't an intruder.' I showed her how the window had been fastened.

'A ghost then? I'm sure Great-aunt Constance wouldn't have done anything as stupid as this.'

'Let's forget about ghosts,' I said more irritably than I intended.

She regarded me with a quizzical smile. 'Why? Aren't they your bread and butter?'

'Sure, but let's keep them to the pages of my manuscript. In my story *Whispering Corner*, the *fictional* Whispering Corner is haunted. But in real life that's impossible. There's a logical explanation for everything.'

I knelt beside her and helped to replace the books. When they were back in place Ashley straightened up and said, 'So what did cause the books to fly into the middle of the room?'

'I must admit I don't know, but that doesn't mean there's not a logical explanation.'

'You don't think I did it as – as a sort of practical joke?'

I looked at her and burst out laughing. 'That's the very last thing I'd think. What on earth made you say that?'

'I don't know. It just popped into my mind.'

'That's the craziest thing that ever popped into anyone's mind. Listen, let's make today a holiday. We'll do whatever you like.'

'Great. After last night it would have been a terrible anticlimax for this to be just another day. Let's have a picnic.'

While she went to prepare the food I took a piece of ham from the refrigerator and laid it on the step of the open French window as an offering to Mrs Foch, who was now sitting by the empty milk dish. Before long she tested it with her delicate pink nose and then set to work to devour it. When it had gone I placed another piece on the floor a few feet inside the room. Still hungry, Mrs Foch came inside. When she had eaten the ham she began to move about very slowly, sniffing the new carpet and furniture as though trying to reconcile the new scents with

110

her old surroundings.

'I think we can get her to settle in her old home,' said Ashley, coming into the room. Mrs Foch bolted through the open French windows, but only as far as the bottom step.

She was still sitting there, legs tucked beneath her, when we set off in the Peugeot for the huge Stone Age hill-fort known as Badbury Rings a short distance to the north of Lychett Matravers. When we reached the vast mound rising above the flat countryside I parked the car and we began to climb up the slope. It was easy to see how effective the great defensive trenches that encircled the fort must have been in the days when log palisades were set above them. Ashley, bewailing the lack of a camera, was fascinated by the place and told me that in New Zealand Maori hill-forts, known as *pas,* were built on identical lines.

When we reached the top I threw down the car rug on a stretch of grass and lay back while she unpacked our lunch. By turning my head I could see an expanse of Dorset landscape laid out like a green map, lush pastures, coppices of darker green, the occasional vivid square of rape and here and there roofs and spires of distant hamlets.

Turning my head again I watched Ashley filling bread rolls with egg curry while the fingers of the warm breeze tugged at her curls. At that moment I could not remember when I had been so content. Anxieties over my novel and the Regent Bank had receded with last night's revelation.

During the picnic we chatted easily, laughing at each other's jokes with the familiarity born out of our new intimacy. Then Ashley suddenly seized my wrist and said, 'Jon, tell me it's all right. It's not likely your wife will want to come back, is it?'

I shook my head, sincere in my belief. 'No. The sad truth is that neither of us have anything to come back to now. Of course I hope we will always be friends simply because of shared history, but Pam has found herself a new life, and I'm about to do the same.'

We stayed on our vantage point where long, long ago perhaps a Celtic lookout strained his eyes for the caterpillar column of a Roman legion, until the distant dots of humanity moving along the great ditches and over the sheep-cropped slopes headed home to tea and telly, and we were alone in the evening world.

With the departure of the Lilliputian visitors the character of the Rings underwent a subtle change. Birds fleeing the oncoming dusk, swooped low with forlorn cries, there were rustlings in the bushes as night creatures stirred, and the character of the wind changed, no longer a playful daytime breeze like a jolly character in a children's story who makes the washing on the line dance but something cooler and almost visible – a moving tide of shadow. It made us both shiver and I stood up to go.

'Please, not yet,' Ashley said. 'Let's wait, at least for the evening star.'

I picked up the end of the rug on which she was sitting and draped it over her shoulders. For a while we remained silent, both rapt in our view of the darkening world where suddenly a distant speck of light glimmered. Now, as I write in another world, the courses of our lives have undergone such a sea-change that in fancy I sometimes wish I could barter the future to be back in that moment of the past.

Ashley laughed softly, and said 'Back home when I was a kid I used to go up on a hill like this and watch the sun set on Mount Egmont, which is our look-alike of Mount Fuji, and as the light went I imagined I was the only person left in the world. '

'What had happened to the others?'

'I never thought that out,' she said with a reminiscent smile. 'They just weren't there – not nuked or anything nasty. Anyway, I felt like that again just now, only this time I was the only *other* person left – until that light went on. I'm so happy being up here alone with you that nothing else seems to matter. Tomorrow, though, we must talk. I want you to explain what the problem is that seems to be hanging over you.'

'As I said, it's just trying to get this wretched book finished on time,' I said lightly.

'Are you stuck with the story?'

'No, it seems to be developing well at the moment. The atmosphere is building up nicely – it's time I'm short of. Look, there's your evening star. She's a planet really.'

I pointed to where Venus hung like a glow-worm against a blue-black curtain. I tightened my arm about Ashley and she turned her face to me.

'Jon, I want you . . . here and now.'

And despite the constraints of our clothing we made love while the dark wind flowed over us.

* * *

There is no need to detail the next few days except as they confirmed that I had fallen deeply in love with Ashley and she appeared to return the feeling. As yet we had not felt the need to discuss the future. I was in agreement with Ashley, who said, 'Let's just set our sails together and see where the winds blow us.' But of course there was no more talk of her leaving Whispering Corner.

Only one odd incident is worth mentioning. After supper one evening I went upstairs to my study to bring down a copy of *Shadows and Minors,* which she had dutifully declared she wanted to read, and when I entered the room I found that once again my books had been dumped in the centre of the floor. This time it had happened with such violence that one had its cover partly torn off.

My first – and very stupid – reaction was that it was a joke played by Ashley because of my conviction that every action, no matter how bizarre, had a logical explanation. My respect for books is such that it makes me over-sensitive to what I regard as misuse. A coffee cup placed on the cheapest paperback sets my teeth on edge.

'You didn't need to chuck them down quite so hard,' I shouted down the stairs in a peeved tone.

'What are you on about, darling?'

'Your trick with the books.'

'Sorry, I don't know what you mean. I'm coming up.'

She came up the stairs carrying Mrs Foch who, while still suspicious of me, had been gradually enticed back into her old home and now allowed Ashley to comb out her matted fur and treat a wound that had gone septic after some desperate encounter in the woods. But when Ashley reached the study Mrs Foch, perhaps startled at seeing me, emitted a yowl, clawed herself free from her benefactor's hands and vanished from sight.

Ashley ruefully ran her scratches against her lips and asked, 'Now, darling, what's all this about a trick?'

'It's happened again,' I said and pointed to the books.

'Weird!' Ashley exclaimed, then a puzzled expression crossed her face. 'You said something about a trick. You don't honestly believe that I . . . ? Oh, how could you even think such a lousy thing?' She flushed beneath her light tan and her cool dark eyes looked straight into my face. 'If you think I'm the sort of person to do that you've got a bloody odd idea of me,' she said in a deceptively low tone. 'I may not be one of your genteel poms but even in the backblocks where I come from we do have some respect for the printed word. Look at that book – it's almost lost its cover. Do you really think I'd have done that?'

'For goodness sake, Ash, you know I could think nothing bad about you. It just flashed through my mind that you might have been having a bit of fun at my expense.'

She did not reply but knelt by the books, handing them up to me to replace.

When this was done she said in an altered voice, 'Jon, does anyone else have a key to this house?'

'Not that I know of, except perhaps Hoddy. He must have had one when he was working here.'

'You told me he thought my great-aunt was a witch. Perhaps he's got a fixation about black magic or something. Those books that were thrown down were your occult reference books. He probably saw them when he helped you to move in and he may think they're

113

Satan's handbooks or something.'

'You could be right,' I said. 'You see, there's a logical explanation after all . . .'

'You're really afraid that there might not be one, aren't you? Why?'

'I'll have a very discreet word with Hoddy tomorrow,' I said, ignoring her question. 'If he was responsible it means that the first time he must have come in while we were asleep.'

'Or when we were making love. He might even have watched us.' Her nose wrinkled with distaste.

'I didn't hear anything,' I said.

'Darling, a Boeing could have landed in the garden and we wouldn't have heard it.'

* * *

Next morning I had something more than Hoddy to worry about. The postman brought a recorded delivery letter which I signed for in my dressing-gown. With a sense of foreboding I took it into the kitchen where I had been making tea to share with Ashley. As I tore open the buff envelope the sense of insulation from the outside world which she had given me melted. Reality returned as I read that the Regent Bank's solicitors had been instructed to bring legal proceedings against me for the full sum owed by Pleiades Films. Unless I immediately cleared the amount they would apply for a possession order on my house situated at Church Walk, Lychett Matravers.

Paul Lincoln had warned me that I would be receiving such a letter, but when I stood with it in my hand all the old anxieties returned and I was filled with anger that the idyll of the last few days should be spoiled.

'Something wrong?' Ashley said as I took the tea in to her.

'Just a business problem,' I said, trying to sound casual. 'Authors should be allowed to live in ivory towers and not be bothered by mundane money matters.'

'Poor darling, you look as though it's something more than you're trying to make out. Want to talk about it?'

'Not at the moment.'

I felt reluctant to explain the Pleiades overdraft to Ashley for the simple reason that I had no wish to appear a fool in her eyes. I could imagine her exclaiming, 'But surely you must have seen the bank statements? You don't mean to say you never checked on the company of which you were a director?'

I still remembered my feeling of shame when I had to admit my carelessness to Paul Lincoln.

'It's no big secret,' I added. 'But I'd better put a quick call through to my accountant.'

I dressed quickly and set off on my well worn path to the phone box.

'No need to panic,' said Paul when I got through to him and read out the letter. 'It's just another station on the line. Now's the time to get a solicitor, I suggest you use Swan, Floyd and Company. I've found them pretty reliable on this sort of thing. I'll speak to them on your behalf if you wish. I don't suppose you've been able to contact your partner?'

'I've rung his number each day but no luck. I'll try again as soon as we're through.'

'How's the novel coming? Keep the midnight oil burning on that.'

'It's fine,' I said, feeling guilt that I had fallen behind schedule these last few days.

I dialled Charles Nixon's number next and for the first time I got a reply.

'Yes?' came a young Thespian voice. I guessed that with his family away in Wales Charles was making the most of his freedom to entertain young actors who were initially impressed by his promises of film parts.

'I'd like to speak to Mr Nixon,' I said.

'Who calls?'

I told him. I could almost see the hand being put over the mouthpiece, but it was done inefficiently and I heard a faint, sibilant 'It's Northrop'. There was a pause and then the voice said, 'Sorry, he's away on business. Location hunting.'

'Oh yes?' I said. 'Who are you?'

'I can't see that it's any business of yours, but if you must know I'm a colleague.'

'Great. You'll know when Charles will be available, won't you?'

Another pause, and this time the only sound was static on the line. Again I could picture Charles miming a message not to tell me anything.

'When Charlie gets in touch with me, I'll tell him you rang. Don't pester him! The poor dear is so worried. Goodbye.'

'Tell him now,' I said. 'I know he's with you.'

There was a hiss of indrawn breath and the line went dead.

As I walked back along Church Walk to where the great tree spread its octopus roots over the bank and the plague victims were said to whisper their venerable secrets, I seethed with anger. Charles Nixon had cast a blight on my life at a time when I should be enjoying it to the full. It now seemed obvious that he had cynically run up the overdraft in the knowledge that the bank would look to me for its repayment because I was an easy target. I sat on a tangle of roots to give myself time to calm down. I did not want this miserable business to infect my relationship with Ashley.

She must have been watching for my return because as soon as I went through the white wicket gate she came out to greet me.

'Not too tough?'

'Not the end of the world,' I said and even managed a smile.

'I feel a bit guilty,' she said, slipping her hand in mine. 'I've been taking up so much of your time, and I know you're worried about the deadline for your novel. I'll spend today writing to the folks back home so you can lock yourself away and get a huge number of pages done. OK?'

'OK,' I said. 'I think poor old Falco is in for a tough time.'

When I went up to my study I decided that before I began work on *Whispering Corner*, I would draft a letter to Charles. I quoted the bank's letter to me and asked him to answer several points which included why I had not been informed of the overdraft, where the money had gone and what the hell he intended to do about honouring his guarantee. Before I printed the letter I deleted 'what the hell', and considering the mood I was in, it was remarkably restrained. Very firm, but restrained.

* * *

When I came down from my study, back aching after a day at the laptop, head aching from trying to create the fear which gripped my characters when they were confronted by the materialization of a past event, I found a stiff drink prepared for me in the dining-room and the table beautifully laid with a vase of wild summer flowers flanked by two candles. I was deeply touched by the work Ashley had put into cheering me up. It would be churlish not to respond, and I did my utmost to shrug off my gloom and enter into the spirit of the evening.

'Something smells very good,' I said, entering the kitchen.

'Casseroled steak cooked in Guinness,' she said.

Mrs Foch, who had responded to Ashley's overtures by gradually reverting to the role of a pet in her old home, rubbed enthusiastically against her ankles and purred rhythmically.

'You'll get your share,' Ashley promised.

It was a heart-warming domestic scene and I had to fight off the bitterness which rose like bile when I remembered that soon such an evening in Whispering Corner would be impossible.

A day at a time, I told myself. Just live for today. And I made such an effort not to think of the future that when we sat down to eat I actually had Ashley laughing at jokes dredged up from my old newspaper days. Thanks to a few drinks and Ashley's company I did not have to work at being cheerful for long. I really did throw off the depression which had been louring over me all day.

When we were finished the smoked cheese and port which Ashley had bought in Poole, she suddenly said, 'I've no right to ask about your problems, but what I do want to know is whether they have anything to do with you and me.'

For a minute I hesitated, but then I decided to tell her about Pleiades Films and the Regent Bank in order to dispel any idea that there was anything wrong between us.

'So you really might lose Whispering Corner?' she said when I had finished. She was really troubled, and not just on my behalf. Now that she was living in her great-aunt's old home it had come to mean a lot to her. In a sense she would be losing Whispering Corner as well. 'No wonder you've been on edge. But there must be some way round it.' She made several suggestions, most of which I had already considered and rejected, and in the end she began to accept the fact that I was legally responsible for the debt. Now it was her turn to look depressed, and I said, 'It hasn't happened yet. Something will turn up. If the thought of it spoils the time we have together then my problem will be doubled.'

We sat in silence for a while. I wondered if Ashley regarded me as a fool for having allowed myself to get into this stupid situation, and I expected some remark to this effect when she looked up and said, 'Jonathan, is it because of this Pleiades business that you drink so much?'

I was honestly surprised. 'I didn't think that I drank a lot,' I said defensively. 'I must confess that I have had the odd brandy when I've been a bit depressed. And it does help to keep me going when I'm tired, but I'm hardly a toper.'

'No? It's just that when you're not working you do seem to have a brandy in your hand quite often.'

'Well diluted with Perrier,' I said. 'I have a thing about having a glass in my hand. Don't worry, Ash. I'm a world away from seeing purple snakes.' But as I said those words I had a memory of that strange and frightening night I descended into the cellar. Brandy had been responsible for that.

'I was silly to mention it,' said Ashley. 'It's just that I love you so much and, you see, my father had a drink problem.' She shrugged. 'He's not so bad now, but when we were kids he would have a bout every so often and then things were grim for the family. The rest of the time he was a kind and loving man, but when he came home with rum on his breath we knew all hell was about to break lose. Funny how things in childhood remain with you.'

'You're damn right,' I said and was surprised at the bitterness in my voice. 'That's what real haunting is, not phantoms, but what

Poe called "sheeted shadows from the past", shadows of things we can sometimes hardly remember which follow us through life.'

'Sorry, Jon, but I must go to bed,' Ashley said. 'I'm exhausted. It's just hit me – I don't know why.'

'Because only a few days ago you came out of hospital, and you were warned it'd be a while before you were a hundred per cent. Now it's up the wooden hill to Bedfordshire.'

She smiled at the old-fashioned nursery expression, and hand in hand we went upstairs to her room. As yet she had not moved into my bedroom. 'Don't take this amiss,' she had said, 'but things have happened so quickly between us that I don't want to get into a marriage routine and lose the courtship.'

'You'll come and say goodnight?' she said as we reached her door.

I put on my pyjamas, then went along the landing to Ashley's room. She was asleep. I lay down beside her, pulled the duvet over me and savoured her warmth, my fingers resting gently on the swell of her breast. As I became drowsy the old hypnagogic voices began their quarrel until I crossed the borderland into sleep.

It was Mrs Foch – the new domesticated Mrs Foch – landing heavily on the bed that roused me. For a few moments I lay still in the darkened room. Beside me Ashley slept on. Then I caught a noise, a noise I sensed rather than heard, that suggested someone moving about. I felt no fear, rather indignation. It occurred to me it might be Hoddy sneaking into the house to vent his anger on my reference books.

I eased myself cautiously out of bed so as not to disturb Ashley. The bedroom door was ajar, and once through it I made sure that it was closed properly. Then, in the fading moonlight, I began to descend the stairs in an increasing state of bewilderment.

The first odd thing I noticed was a dark oil painting, I think of a pastoral scene with a ruined tower in the background and framed in ornate gilt, hanging on the wall halfway down. All my pictures were in plain silvered frames. Where the hell had this picture come from? Had Ashley bought it for me and hung it there as a surprise gift? If so it was strange that I had not noticed it earlier.

But Ashley could not have hung striped wallpaper on the walls which I'd had painted Lilywhite. It was as though I was descending into a stranger's house.

A repetition of the sound which had aroused me dispelled the bewilderment. The intruder was my priority and I continued down to the hall, where a candle in a brass candleholder burned on a great polished chest I had never seen before. The air was filled with the aromatic smell of a log fire.

This transformation – this slipping through a tear in the veil of time – had been so rapid and *mundane* that I could not immediately comprehend it.

The sound of someone talking softly led me across the hall to the half-open door of the room I used as a dining-room, my naked feet feeling the texture of alien rugs. And it was at this point, gazing at a scene of two centuries ago, that my disorientation was transmuted to fear.

It is a trite thing to say that one is paralysed by fear – too often I had used that expression in my novels – but that is what happened to me. I stood motionless and speechless at the door, and yet I was still capable of taking everything in. My recording mechanism was still functioning.

Inside the room a log blazed in a large fireplace and by its dancing light, coupled with that of several oil lamps, I saw a four-poster bed with hangings of rose brocade. Lying beneath a patchwork counterpane, her head propped against several lace-edged pillows, was a woman whose white, wasted face still held a hint of its former beauty. Beneath the cover her chest rose and fell rapidly as she fought to speak, and there was a familiarity of timbre which evoked my hypnagogic experiences.

It was not illness but outrage which caused her speech difficulty, outrage directed at the man standing close to the fire. His broad, bulging back was turned towards me and he appeared to be dressed as a gentleman of the eighteenth century. Neither of the occupants of the room were aware of me standing in the doorway.

When exhaustion halted the invalid's words and she lay panting, the man addressed her in a cold and deliberate voice. Although I was unable to distinguish his actual words any more than I had been able to distinguish hers, the tones of both echoed their enmity.

The woman on the bed gulped back her breath, made an extraordinary effort to half raise herself upon the pillows, and then answered the man with such vehemence that her parchment features twisted into anguish like a mask in a Greek tragedy.

The man stepped up to the bed. He laid his hand on her chest and pushed her down, then tugged a pillow free and pressed it over her face. He leaned over her, both arms rigid as he used all his weight and strength to smother her.

On each side of the pillow stick-like arms flailed, and the counterpane writhed as she kept drawing up her knees and kicking with a strength unimaginable from the poor emaciated frame.

The only sounds were the soft grunting – the sound that accompanies great physical exertion – of the man and the cheerful crackle of the log in the grate. Now he was kneeling on the bed to apply more weight to the pillow, and once he glanced over his shoulder as though in fear of being discovered. I had a glimpse of a broad florid face which in middle age still retained something of the handsome arrogance that must have turned many a girl's head and heart when he was a youth.

If I had been in the real world, of course, I would have dashed forward to save the woman, but this was not my world and I remained as paralysed as Lot's wife.

The threshing of the bedclothes diminished. The waving arms with their opening and closing hands fell back, and the man slowly raised the pillow and held it ready to ram it back into position.

The woman's mouth gaped, the eyes were wide open and already glassy in death.

Roughly he seized her jaw, shaking her head from side to side as though to satisfy himself that no ember of life remained, then he replaced the pillow with its dainty lace beneath her head, straightened her fair-grey hair over it and rearranged the bedclothes. After glancing round the room as though to satisfy himself that nothing would proclaim his guilt, he walked past me at the doorway so close that I noticed the dandruff on his velvet collar.

An elderly servant woman scurried from the direction of the kitchen in answer to his call. She threw up her apron to cover her distress when she saw the still form. She was followed by a young woman in a wrap of blue Chinese silk whose face was similar enough to that of the dead woman to indicate they were sisters. Pressing her hand across her mouth she threw herself on to her knees by the bed and seized the hand of the corpse.

The murderer followed them into the room slowly, mopping his face with a handkerchief to remove sweat rather than tears.

And then nothing.

Nothing!

* * *

I stood looking into my darkened dining-room. There was no fire, no four-poster, no figures.

The paralysis which had held me during that brief, horrifying drama released me and I walked across the hall and sank down on the stairs, once again covered by carpet bought at John Lewis's. I was shuddering and deathly cold, and crying like a child whose sobs rack its whole body. After a while the hysteria passed and in snuffling shame I wiped my wet face on the sleeve of my pyjamas.

I climbed awkwardly to my feet, my movements slow and my fingers and lips trembling like someone in shock. What I needed more than anything was brandy. I made it to the drinks cabinet and took a mouthful straight from the bottle. My throat was scorched but the sudden influx of alcohol did halt the jumping of my nerves. Now all I wanted was to go upstairs and literally and figuratively pull the covers over my head.

It occurred to me then that perhaps the scene in which Sir Richard Elphick had murdered his ailing wife Arabella was the climax of some cyclic replay and from now on there would be no more phenomena. I recalled that many people who claimed to have seen ghosts – especially landlords of haunted pubs – declared that the manifestations happened on their arrival in new premises and that once the point had been made, as it were, there was peace.

This theory was dashed when I was halfway up the stairs. A babble of voices seemed to explode in my head. Not the low bickering of the old hypnagogic voices but mad, angry, screaming voices. It was like a gust of sound from an air shaft of hell, and its impact on me was so great that I had to clutch the banister.

Perhaps they were like the voices which echo through the minds of the criminally insane. While the actual words were impossible to distinguish, there was no doubt as to their terrible meaning.

'Ashley!' I heard myself cry and I forced myself to run up the stairs to her bedroom.

At the door I saw a white figure kneeling on her bed in horrific repetition of what I had witnessed below, a white figure bending over Ashley who, with a slight smile on her face, lay unaware of the arms, those lint-white arms, reaching for her.

Chapter 12

With fear only for Ashley, I lunged across the room and flung myself on to the attacker. He – it, whatever the thing was – simply collapsed under the impact and I was left grasping a tangle of white bedding. Only that, a hideous linen origami which had been animated by the same spirit of evil whose action replay I had just witnessed downstairs.

Under my weight – I was lying half across her – Ashley's eyes snapped open.

'What . . . ?' she began. 'Jon, what's wrong with you?'

My expression alarmed her as much as the abruptness of her awakening. She sat up, drawing as far away from me as she could without actually falling out of bed.

'What the hell have you been doing with the bedclothes?' she continued. 'Ugh! You've wet the bed. You're smashed – you stink of brandy . . . '

She ran out of words and gazed at me in the dim light from the window with an expression of fright on her usually calm features. There is nothing worse than feeling suddenly threatened by someone familiar, but for a moment I could say nothing to reassure her. My lungs were pumping too painfully for me to be able to speak coherently.

Ashley switched on the bedside lamp.

'What a mess,' she murmured. I did not know whether she was referring to my appearance or the tangle of bedclothes. Then she added wearily, 'Stay here. I'll get some coffee. Maybe that'll sober you up a bit.'

I shook my head. 'Don't go down,' I managed to say. 'Not drunk.'

'You could have fooled me,' she said.

'Listen, Ash,' I said between gasps. 'This is going to sound crazy, but please believe me . . .'

'There's certainly something crazy round here. You landed on me like an All Black making a tackle.'

'All right. I know how it must seem to you, but please just listen.'

I moved off the bed – Ashley was right, the tumbled candlewick counterpane was damp – and sat in the white rocking chair in the corner of the room. Shattered by my experience in the dining-room and now faced with Ashley's hostility, I had never felt a greater need for a drink.

'Just let me tell it from the beginning,' I said, 'but remember I can only say what happened – I can't say why.'

Ashley nodded. 'OK, but make it good.' Her words triggered

something off in me. The events of the past few minutes had stretched a thread within me almost to breaking point, and her implied judgement before I had a chance to make my defence snapped it.

'Correct me if I'm wrong,' I said in the cold, reasonable voice which comes only on those very rare occasions when I am filled with anger, 'but – until the bank chucks me out – this is my house. In my own house I should be allowed to have hallucinations, get blind drunk if I wish and even – as you accuse me – piss on the bed. Because it's my house, my booze, my bed – and my bloody ghosts.'

'So sorry I mistook your hospitality,' she replied. 'I didn't realize there was a price tag on it . , .'

'Price tag?'

'Yes, the price of my accommodation is to accept whatever the Great Author may say as Holy Writ and obey the Eleventh Commandment, "Thou shalt not criticise, no matter what the provocation".'

'One thing I do know for sure and it's interesting that such a cheap jibe should come into your mind – is that I've never played the Great Author. And another thing I know for sure is that there was never ever a price tag on your staying here.'

'Not even my bed?'

Her anger forced words out before she could bite them back. Their effect was devastating, all the magic that had been generated between us was turning to dross.

'That's it,' she said finally in a voice so low and dull that it was difficult to hear. 'I know I've blown it. I just don't know what's got into us tonight . . .'

'I do,' I said in sudden sick comprehension. 'It's what *they* want.'

'They? Who are *they?* I just don't understand you. I don't understand anything this bloody night. I'll go in the morning.'

'Don't talk rubbish. Just listen to me for five minutes. A few minutes ago I saw a murder take place. And – no! – it was not the DTs but something that happened a couple of centuries ago . . . ' And I went on to describe in detail the scene I had witnessed, and then how on reaching the bedroom I had seen a figure created out of bedclothes bending over her in the same way that Sir Richard Elphick had bent over his wife Arabella.

'The sheets were animated by a psychic force,' I said. 'It needed something by which to manifest itself.'

'I can't believe that you're telling me this,' said Ashley in a hushed voice. 'You've always been such a cynic over supernatural matters.'

'That's true, but there can be no other explanation for the

123

drama I saw. I went down those stairs into another world. I could even smell the smoke from the fire . . ,'

'But did it seem real? I mean, did the figures look as real as I do sitting here?'

'Real, all right,' I answered, remembering the dandruff on Sir Richard's collar when he went past me to announce his wife's death. 'And yet there was something about them – the phantoms, for want of a better word – that's hard to define. Although they were real enough to cast shadows there was a lack of substance. Have you seen a hologram?'

Ashley nodded.

'Like that. A hologram image looks perfectly real, yet you can pass your hand through it.'

'And all this really happened? I mean, you weren't sleep-walking and it wasn't a nightmare?'

'It would be a comforting explanation, but no – it was real.'

'Jon, I've wondered about ghosts in the past. I mean, people seeing phantoms and so on. Does something actually appear or is an image projected in the mind of the beholder? Were there ghosts actually moving about down there or did something lingering from the past create the images in your brain?'

'I only know that what I saw there was a re-enactment. A re-run of your tape of time, if you like. What concerns me is that thing – the bedclothes man – I saw bending over you. That was something different. Up here a power was at work – perhaps a blind elemental power – using the bedclothes to take on a shape and mimic the old murder.'

'But even seeing that might have been in your mind,' said Ashley reasonably. The hostility had gone from her voice but she was still mistrustful. I could not blame her for that. If our roles had been reversed and she had been telling me about the haunting I would have put it down to the concussion she had recently suffered.

'It wasn't a hallucination,' – I told her wearily. 'Those sheets didn't get twisted up by themselves. Besides, they're wet. According to a book on the occult in my study pools of water are frequently found where poltergeists have been active. That dampness is not a figment of my imagination, and I certainly wasn't responsible for it. No, Ash, there is something malign here, and I think its power is growing. It began with those hypnagogic voices I was hearing, the sense of fear that made you run into the garden after your accident, the feeling of terror I experienced in the cellar, and now full-blown manifestations. I am convinced that it was its influence that made us bitter with each other just now. We were being forced to act like Sir Richard and Arabella'

'Jon, I don't actually disbelieve you, but I can't believe it

124

either.'

'You'd believe it if you'd just watched a woman being smothered.'

'I'm sure I would, but I didn't see it.'

'I understand,' I said wearily. 'How can I expect you to believe it, when I've been such a materialist myself? It's funny – it only takes one experience like that to prove to me that there is something beyond the bricks and mortar of our world.'

Suddenly I felt close to tears again, and perhaps something in my voice warned Ashley of this.

'All right, darling, what shall we do?'

'I think we should get out of the house for tonight, at least, and then we'll think of something. Please bear with me. We'll take the car and drive to the coast and watch the sun come up.'

'Of course, darling.'

I did not care that her tone was placating so long as she agreed to come with me. I was shaking again and suddenly I began to appreciate the truth in the old saying about 'going to pieces'. I had an absurd feeling that I was physically about to break up and parts of me would fly off in different directions. I afterwards discovered that this is one of the classic portents of a nervous collapse.

I went to my room for slacks and a sweater while Ashley put on a black tracksuit emblazoned with the New Zealand emblem of a silver fern. My ears strained for the slightest noise and as I returned to Ashley's room my eyes sought any movement in the shadows, but the house was still.

'Ready?' I asked.

'Yes. Have you seen Mrs Foch?'

'We'll let her out as we leave.'

I led the way down the stairs. Together we went into the living-room – still thank goodness as I had furnished it – and while I tried to coax Mrs Foch from under a chair Ashley went to the French windows.

'Shit!' she cried, that word of despair which is usually the sudden and final exclamation of a pilot on the flight recorder of a crashed aircraft.

I hurried over to Ashley, whose face was blanched by more than the moonlight.

'Ash . . . ?'

Then, I looked out of the window at an altered landscape.

The trees which normally crowded the garden of Whispering Corner were now much further from the house and held at bay by tall dense hedges, and down each side of the lawn stood a row of statues, doubtless plundered from Greece.

Even the moon was in a different quarter.

It was sunlight streaming through the bedroom window that awakened me. As my eyes focused I found myself looking into Ashley's calm face, sleep having erased the tension of the night. My arm was round her protectively and as I moved to ease the cramp she opened her eyes.

For a minute she lay in silence as memory returned.

'Was it true, Jon, what happened?' she asked finally. 'Had everything changed outside the house?'

'It seemed to us that it had,' I said cautiously. 'It was interesting that we both experienced the phenomenon.'

'Interesting? It was bloody horrendous!'

'At least it proved something to you – that what I had told you was not just a product of the DTs.'

'Sorry about that,' she said. 'But what was I to think? You did smell of booze and you seemed to be on the edge of hysteria. But that's understandable,' she added quickly. 'I wasn't exactly calm when I saw how the garden had altered.'

For a while I lay without speaking, turning over in my mind the events of the night, events which twelve hours earlier I would have thought incredible. Perhaps, in the light of morning, I might have been tempted to explain away my experience in the dining-room and the figure on Ashley's bed as hallucinatory symptoms of an approaching breakdown, but Ashley had seen the transformed garden – so transformed that we dared not venture into it.

'What are we going to do?' she asked at length.

'Get up, shower away the terrors of the night and have a good breakfast. Then we'll decide,' I said in a positive voice.

'Everything seems so normal again in the daylight,' she said. 'It's hard to imagine now that we're in a haunted house. It's odd. I always felt the atmosphere here was friendly.'

'Oh, I'm sure there's nothing sinister about Whispering Corner itself,' I said with conviction. 'After all, your great-aunt lived here all her life without any ill effect. It's just that for some reason we don't understand something tragic and evil has been reactivated from the past. The house can't be blamed for that.'

'For as long as I live I shall never forget looking out and seeing everything altered,' said Ashley. 'It was like being in another country . . .'

'Didn't someone say the past is another country?' I said.

'What do you think would have happened if we had gone out into it?'

'I really don't know. I suppose it would have been rather like things in the dining-room. Everything appearing real but somehow superimposed upon us. The trouble is that there seems to be no rhyme or reason to it. The garden was as it must have been a couple of centuries ago, yet inside the house everything was normal by then. And nothing more happened when we came up here.'

'We were not *aware* of anything happening, but goodness knows what may be going on around us. I mean, there are radio waves about us the whole time but we're not aware of them. They mean nothing until we turn the set on.'

'I wonder what turned this set on?' I mused.

'I'm going to take your advice,' said Ashley, getting up. 'Scalding water and coffee, that's what I need.'

For once the sight of her pale olive body caught in the warm sunlight failed to give the usual erotic tug at my feelings, nor did she unconsciously hint at the coquette with a swing of the hip or breast as she usually did.

'At least you should get some inspiration for your novel out of all this,' she said with some irony as, slipping on her robe, she went to the bathroom.

For a few minutes I continued to lie in bed. Ashley's words had given me food for thought. What had happened would not help the novel because in it Falco and Lorna had already been menaced by the supernatural. It was reviewing what I had intended to put in the story next that would be significant.

After I had showered away some of the weariness from my body I went down to the kitchen. Ashley was preparing breakfast and the wholesome smells of bacon frying, bread toasting and coffee percolating did for my spirits what the hot water had done for my body.

When we were sitting opposite each other at the table Ashley said, 'Jon, I want you to know that whatever you decide is fine by me. I'll hang around. OK, cobber?'

'Very OK, cobber,' I said, picking up my knife and fork.

'It may be that last night was a one-off,' I suggested, once the bacon and eggs had been demolished and we were spreading lime marmalade on our toast. 'Nothing out of the ordinary may ever happen again. On the other hand . . .' I shrugged.

'Could it – the haunting, I mean – actually do us any harm, do you think?'

'I don't know. But perhaps there's a way to find out.'

I had not known the role my villain was to play in my novel, or how he was to be introduced. The memory of an interview I had once done for my paper returned now to give me what I needed. Falco would turn for help to a spiritualist, and he would take advantage of the situation for his own ends. As yet I could not visualize him but I was confident that his character would develop once I had introduced him. And I would follow Falco's example, and I knew just the medium to approach.

'I met Angela Thurlby in my Fleet Street days,' I said. 'Of course I didn't believe in the paranormal then and I took rather a cynical view of her.'

'I can believe that,' Ashley said.

'Yes, but it didn't stop me giving her a fair write-up.'

'What was the story?'

'She claimed that someone "came through" to give her the whereabouts of a child that had gone missing.'

'Was she right?'

'Yes. At the time I thought it was clever deduction or sheer good luck. But I must say that she quite impressed me – especially as she never tried to make any money out of her so-called gift.'

'Do you think she'll come here?'

'It's possible. I should imagine that what happened here isn't exactly run-of-the-mill in the world of parapsychology, and she might be intrigued by it. In a minute I'll see if I can find my old contacts book, then I'll go to the village and phone her.'

'I'll come with you,' Ashley said quickly.

* * *

Angela Thurlby arrived at Whispering Corner as dusk was gathering in the woodland, driven down in a Volvo estate by one of the helpers she had said she would need for her séance.

She had remembered me when I telephoned her Kensington flat.

'Of course I know who you are – you did the best write-up I've ever had, and since then I've read your books. Not exactly accurate, but entertaining. Now what can I do for you? Do you want some technical advice?'

'Not exactly,' I said, and went on to tell her of the night's events as precisely as I could.

When I had concluded she said promptly, 'It sounds fascinating, my dear. I shall come down immediately if I can prevail upon Mr Peter to drive us.'

'Us?'

'My little team. There'll be five of us. They've worked with me for years and are absolutely indispensable for something like this. They boost my receptive powers.'

Now the little group crossed the lawn and I went out to greet them. It was quite a few years since I had interviewed Angela, though I had seen her several times on television when some producer had decided to do a beat-up on spiritualism, and I saw the years had been kind to her. Although well into her fifties she was still slim, unlined and very well groomed. She came from an old Anglo-Indian family and she had the vivacity and charm so characteristic of that section of Indian society.

Angela had left Lucknow as a young girl and it was in London that she discovered her psychic abilities, after a chance visit with a couple of giggly companions to the spiritualistic headquarters in Belgrave Square. Now she introduced her acolytes, Mr Peter, a middle-European with sad eyes who had a fashionable ikon gallery in Church Street, Nigel Chambers, a fresh-faced young man in beautifully tailored slacks and blazer who I gathered was an apprentice medium, Estelle Baker, an anorexic-looking girl with a spiky haircut whose accent was pure docklands before it became yuppie-belt ('a fantastic sensitive, my dear'), and Mrs Kelly, a kindly widow whose powers as a scryer, I was assured, were not infrequently though unofficially put at the disposal of the police.

Inside the house this oddly assorted team – the *crème* of her circle, Angela Thurlby assured me – fell upon the cakes and tea provided by Ashley with silent ferocity. Their leader merely required 'pure, pure water'. I gave her Perrier.

'Now tell us exactly what happened,' said Angela as the jaw movements of her colleagues began to slow. I complied, giving a straightforward account of the events which had led up to the climax when Ashley and I had looked out upon an unfamiliar landscape, but I withheld any mention of Mary Lawson's 'Narration' or the story of Sir Richard Elphick. I was still enough of a sceptic to want to see if the spirits could provide the medium with background information.

'My dears, it seems that dormant forces have been released,' Angela said. 'We must discover what has triggered it. You haven't been dabbling, have you?'

'Dabbling?'

'Black magic. Psychic experiments.'

'Of course not.'

'Not even working out some sort of ritual for one of your creepy books?'

'No.'

'Until last night Jon was an unbeliever,' Ashley said.

Angela Thurlby nodded. 'I guessed that from the time he interviewed me. But why should people believe until something happens to prove the existence of the psychic world to them?'

The group muttered agreement.

'I take it that neither of you has experienced anything like this before?'

'Never,' Ashley and I said together.

'What I find utterly fascinating is that you had a simultaneous experience at the French windows. I do wonder what it is that could cause such a powerful manifestation. You don't know if this house was built on an earlier site – say of a church or tumulus?'

'To my knowledge it was built on virgin land,' I said. 'Although I had a friend staying here who was into ley lines and he believed that there was a convergence of them at this spot.'

'And what was that supposed to do?'

'He linked it to a local legend about a part of the wood where the whispering of plague victims is supposed to be heard.'

'Interesting,' said Angela. 'There are areas where conditions are such that the paranormal is intensified. In one of his stories Algernon Blackwood described a place as "a point where the veil between" – meaning between this world and some other dimension – "had worn a little thin". Perhaps it is so here. Before we form our circle it would be interesting to visit the spot where the whispering has been heard.'

We trooped out through the wicket gate and along Church Walk. The air was hushed and darkening about us though the sky that appeared between the leafy canopies of the trees retained a pale luminosity. Nigel looked down regretfully at his glossy shoes as we followed the earthen track, but the rest of the group appeared to enjoy this essay into the countryside.

'You are so lucky to live in such a charming location,' Angela remarked.

'It wasn't so charming last night,' said Ashley.

'I am sure it is some troubled spirit which will leave you in peace once it has been placated.'

'How do you placate a trouble spirit?' I asked as doubts about my plan to bring in a medium grew, especially when she replied, 'Often it is done by prayer.'

'Here we are,' I said as we reached the bend in the path overshadowed by the huge tree whose roots held the mossy bank like the fingers of an emaciated giant. 'This is where the legend says some of the fleeing plague victims rested and died. The wind seems to catch this part of the wood, and I'm sure it was the rustle of leaves which fuelled the legend.'

'Estelle,' said Angela.

The girl stepped ahead of us and squatted in the middle of the path, the palms of her hands pressed over her eyes in concentration.

'Hush, please,' said Angela. 'My forte is in spirit communication, but Miss Baker has a remarkable aptitude for sensing atmosphere.'

We stood respectfully hushed, Mr Peter looking more mournful than ever and Nigel and Mrs Kelly ineffectually waving at the gnats dancing out of the gloom.

'Tell us what you are feeling?' Angela coaxed softly.

'Nuffink,' replied the sensitive.

'Concentrate, my dear.'

Silence, and then a slight rustle as an exhausted current of air died among the trees.

'There's something sad-like,' said Estelle. 'Unhappy voices. I dunno what they're saying. Yeah. Could be prayin', but it don't sound like the way we talk . . .'

My doubts increased. Considering I had just told the legend of the whispering voices Estelle's remarks hardly came as a revelation.

'It's chilly,' said Mrs Kelly, shivering.

'Yes, it's getting dark,' said Nigel.

'Cold, that's what I'm getting,' Estelle said. 'It's like there was a lot of people cold, whisperin' away to each other in the dark, all afraid . . .'

I dared not catch Ashley's eye.

We returned to Whispering Corner in the dusk and at Angela's request went into the dining-room where the table was 'ideal' for her purpose.

'We need to find out everything we can,' she said, opening a briefcase. 'Sometimes I do go into a trance and the spirits speak through me. No need to be afraid if that happens, though you may find it a bit strange at first. But we'll try the Ouija to start with. So much faster than having to count the raps the way the old-timers used to do it.'

From the briefcase she took out a small tape recorder and a number of plastic squares each with a bold letter or numeral which she began to space out round the edge of the circular dining table. On opposite sides of the table she placed two squares bearing the words YES and NO.

'Oh, I know this,' said Ashley. 'We used to do it as kids. It was amazing what the glass spelled out. A great party game.'

Angela pursed her lips but made no comment until the letters were set out to her satisfaction.

'If anyone wants the loo now is the time to go,' she said. 'Once we start we mustn't break the circle.'

A few minutes later we were ready to begin the séance. A table lamp on a bookcase provided enough light for us to read the letters clearly and we seated ourselves round the table with the sexes alternating as though we were at a dinner party. Angela placed a crystal glass bottom upwards in the centre of the table.

'I am sure you know all about this – especially you, my dear,' she said with a thin smile at Ashley. 'When the time comes each will lay the tip of the middle finger on the glass. Whatever you do you must not exert pressure on it.'

Inwardly I groaned. Estelle the Sensitive had hardly left me speechless with awe, and now it seemed we were in for what Ashley rightly called a party game. I wondered which one of the team had the job of steering the glass to the correct letters. As I knew that Angela never took money for such a performance I wondered why she did it, and could only conclude that she must get some satisfaction out of being the centre of the charade. What had possessed me to turn to her for help? If I'd had any sense I would have been on the couch of a first class psychiatrist at this moment . . , except for the fact that Ashley had experienced some of the phenomena too, and we both couldn't be mad in exactly the same way,

'Ready, my dears,' said Angela. 'Jonathan, I know you are new to this, but just take your cue from us. Whatever happens – and this is terribly important – don't break the circle. Together we generate harmonic vibrations to shield us from . . . well, whatever it is that disturbed you both.'

Harmonic vibrations!

I thought with irony how different the supernatural scenes I had portrayed in my novels were from this cosy little gathering round the Ouija board.

'Now, Jonathan and Ashley, just follow us,' Angela continued. 'Place your hands on the table, one hand on that of a neighbour, and for a few minutes let us sit in silence and prepare ourselves by quiet meditation.'

I obeyed – having invited them down I had to go along with them – and placed my right hand on the table. I felt the hot moist palm of Estelle on the back of it, and in turn I laid my left fingertips on Ashley's hand which she turned to give them a surreptitious squeeze. Then, like the others, I lowered my chin to my chest and endeavoured to clear my mind. The only sound was the measured tick of an old case clock Pamela and I had bought in Portobello Road soon after Steve was born, and for which I had the sort of affection that grows round inanimate household objects as the years pass by.

Now conscious of the beat of its brass heart, I began to think of Pamela by association. I wondered if she had found someone, as I had, or whether she had been too caught up in the rush of her perfume campaign to have much of a social life.

I remembered that I was supposed to be clearing my mind, and I really tried. But the cool skin of Ashley's hand beneath my fingertips brought new thoughts into my mind. One thing I had decided was that if this attempt failed to throw light upon the situation at Whispering Corner I must take her away from here. Throughout the day I had not been able to rid my mind of the menace epitomized by that scarecrow figure of tangled linen. That was something for my novel, and I thought how curious it was that Ashley and I had experienced a haunting precisely when I was writing about Falco and Lorna's being threatened by the supernatural. Was I writing a book, or was the book writing me?

Of course I had to admit that just as their background – indeed the very name of their story – was based on Whispering Corner, so the plot owed a lot to the real-life 'Narration' of Mary Lawson. The similarity between fact and fiction, therefore, was not as remarkable as it might seem at first sight.

A sigh brought my attention back to the fact that I was supposed to be part of a séance. Angela had raised her head and said quietly, 'Now we are in a state to receive our unseen guests.'

Unseen guests! The strangler shape I had seen poised above Ashley was hardly an unseen guest, but I did not know how much Angela believed of what I had told her. People who claim to have had so-called psychic experiences tend to exaggerate them, and I had to admit to myself that my account of the night's events must have sounded far-fetched. Angela asked us to place our index fingers on the glass in the centre of the polished table top, and in low tones asked any spirit present to communicate. For a minute the only sound was the regular breathing of my companions, then again Angela asked, 'Is there anyone there?'

When there was no response she said reassuringly, 'Sometimes it takes ages for the conditions to become attuned. I sense there are difficult vibrations here, some elemental force trying to create a barrier.'

'Bleeding lot of force around tonight,' agreed the Sensitive.

'I must say I'm not picking up anything at all, not a single thing,' Nigel complained. 'And not even a hint of Big Bull.'

I felt Ashley's fingers grip my knee at the mention of the young man's spirit guide, and I knew she was making a brave effort to keep a straight face.

'Maybe you was mistake,' said Mr Peter in resigned tones. 'Often people are mistake about psychic things. Something go bang in the night and – pouf! – they think it spirits.' He looked at me with sad reproach.

'Patience, my dears,' Angela said.

At that moment the glass jerked into life.

Chapter 13

As anyone knows who has tried the Ouija, the glass slides as though by its own volition and I found this startling at first. It made a series of circles within the border of letters, moving so fast that in turn we had to stretch out our arms so that our fingers would not slide off.

'You take over, Nigel,' Angela said to her apprentice, removing her fingers from the glass and sitting back.

'Do you wish to tell us something?' he inquired of the empty air.

The glass moved even faster, making circles across the table top towards the piece of plastic with the word YES on it, then it suddenly died.

For half a minute we looked at each other enquiringly in the subdued light, then Nigel repeated his question.

Slowly the glass began to move in a straight line until it reached YES.

'Contact!' murmured Mrs Kelly. 'See, Mr Peter, it was no mistake.'

'Maybe yes, maybe no . . ,' Mr Peter was interrupted by a sudden movement of the glass.

'Who are you and what do you want to tell us?' Nigel demanded.

The glass began to slide in such a frenzy that we had to half rise out of our seats to keep up with it. First it darted to the letter A, then R, then A again - and it came as no surprise to me that the rest of the word it spelled out in this way was BELLA. Then it paused.

At that point it occurred to me that someone like Angela who had devoted herself to psychic matters might easily have come across Mary Lawson's "Narration".

'Arabella, did you pass to your new life a long time ago?'

The glass wavered, moved backwards and forwards touching letters that had no meaning, and then as though making an effort spelled out T I M E C H A N G E S.

'When did you pass over?' asked Nigel.

The glass danced to the numerals and indicated 1758.

'What caused your passing?' he continued. By now I was aware of the tension that gripped the circle, the group gazed at the glass as though it held some ultimate revelation. For a moment it was still again, then it began to make its now familiar clockwise circular motion, going faster and faster so that Ashley's hand fell away but still it increased its speed, the glass rim screeching against the polished surface of the table. Then it struck a letter so hard that the plastic square on which it was printed spun away to the floor.

'M,' everyone muttered.

A few seconds later the word MURDER had been indicated.

A sigh of satisfaction went up from the sitters. Here was a real-death drama, and I wondered who was manipulating the glass. Obviously someone who knew the story of the 'Narration', and I decided it was probably Nigel Chambers. I believed the other members of Angela's group were as sincere as Angela appeared to be. But I guessed Nigel was the ambitious sort, I suspected he wanted to become a name in the psychic world with an eye on the television and lectures that would follow. I decided to keep an unobtrusive eye on Nigel.

'Who murdered you?' he asked, perspiration beginning to glisten on his forehead.

The glass made a few reluctant circles, then slowly nudged the letters DICK one after the other.

'Why did Dick harm you?'

The glass slid to NO and stopped. It was as though the force which had animated it – and which I had no doubt was Nigel's right arm – had gone out of it. But despite my feeling of frustration I had to admit he was playing it well. After the real manifestations of last night, I had hoped for something better than this glorified parlour game. And yet – even here – the subconscious observer was at work, notes on how the sitters looked and reacted were being stored for future reference.

'Are you still there?' Nigel asked after a minute.

No response from the glass.

The sitters shifted in their chairs, their muscles becoming uncomfortable as they kept their arms extended over the table.

'Gone,' said Angela. 'Arabella has gone. Something blocked her, something to do with the tragedy. I sensed that she was still full of grief. To her it might seem that it had only just happened, the time scale is different on the other side. When we can explain time we will understand the paranormal.'

Her last words struck me as containing a pearl of truth, but before I could ponder it the glass came to life again. After what I now regarded as the obligatory screech round the table to get up speed, rather like a skater circling an ice rink, it lunged at the word NO and kept hitting it.

'Another is with us,' said Angela.

'Peace,' said Nigel. There is no harm here. We ask who you are.'

NO NO NO NO, continued the glass.

'Your name?'

The glass backed away from NO, made a series of wild tangents in which nonsense words were spelled out like a young child playing with computer keyboard. Then it paused like someone calming themselves after a hysterical outburst and deliberately spelled E V E L Y N .

The sister, I thought. Someone certainly had been doing his homework!

'Evelyn, you lived here?' Nigel asked.

The glass touched YES.

'And you passed over here?'

Again the affirmative.

'What caused your passing?'

A G U E

'You were happy here?'

Y E S S S S N O

'You mean there was a time when you were happy, and a time when you were sad?'

Y E S

H A P P Y T H E N M A D

'Do you mean sad or mad?'

S A D M A D S A D M A D

'What went wrong in your life?'

B A B Y Y Y Y

'A baby? Did you lose it?'

The glass zig-zagged in a frenzy. I found it extremely difficult to keep my finger in place. Top marks for drama, Nigel old fraud! I thought.

'You must tell us what happened,' he said in a very positive voice.

The glass paused as it had before after a bout of desperation, then deliberately touched five letters.

S M O T H

Nigel was about to say something but Angela gave a frightening groan and slumped back into her chair.

The sound was so unexpected that we drew our hands back from the glass, which remained with its facets gleaming by the letter H.

'Something's happening,' cried Estelle.

'She trances,' Mr Peter declared.

Angela's eyes rolled up so that only the bluish whites were visible. She groaned a second time and then, horribly, a deep male voice issued from her gaping mouth.

'Madam, you shall do as I say or by hell, madam . . .'

The angry tones were cut by a woman's voice.

'You cannot mean it, Richard . . . '

For a moment I looked for the speaker and then realized that the second voice was also issuing from Angela – a dreadful dialogue from the same mouth.

'Madam, do you dare to think that I am going to allow this weakly *thing* to ruin you and me? You know the church rule, madam, on a bastard born between such as you and me – you knew the peril when you crawled between my sheets with your quim afire, by hell – and there are enough viper tongues in this county, among those that used to fawn at my table, to destroy us. How they'd laugh to see us topple, those bastards and bitches with their Sunday faces and envious hearts.'

'But you're talking about . . .'

'Yes, madam?'

There was a long pause.

'Murder.'

'Murder, is it? Would it have been murder if the midwife's trick had worked? You play with words, madam. Murder! 'Tis no murder to cull the runt from the litter.'

'How can you talk like that when I am so weak? No matter what you say, I cannot do as you ask.'

'Then I shall, madam. A minute in the pail, and . . .'

'Is this all love means?'

'You would see us disgraced and yet you prate about love. If it were not for what I thought was love, madam, I would not be in this midden. You throw the word murder at me, but it was for you.'

'What was for me, sir?'

'Stop playing the innocent. She might have lived for years.'

A scream issued from Angela. 'Arabella! Arabella, and now . . . you want me to . . . dear God! No, I shall get help. I shall run to our neighbours . . . you shall hang before I . . .'

Angela's head jerked as though she had received an unseen blow across the face. A sobbing. 'I shall tell. I shall tell.'

'You are lunatic! I'll settle all now . . .'

'Don't take her . . . please . . .'

'The hell with you, madam. You think I like such work!'

A cry seemingly endless issued from Angela's froth-flecked mouth. Then there was another noise. The glass began to spin about the table under its own volition, scattering the letters on to our laps. Then, with a report like a rifle shot, it exploded.

When Angela played back the tape in her recorder the explosion of the glass was followed by shouts of alarm and fear we were not conscious of having made.

I remember we threw ourselves back from the table, Mr Peter and Estelle went over backwards in their chairs and the next thing I was aware of was Ashley looking at me and screaming. When I saw myself in the wall mirror I saw why, my face was a mask of blood. A fragment of glass had buried itself in my forehead, a part of the body which tends to bleed very profusely when cut.

'I'm all right,' I kept telling her while I pulled out the splinter and pressed my handkerchief against the spot.

Gradually our voices subsided. I was not the only one to have

137

been cut, another glass fragment had drawn blood on Mrs Kelly's hand and a red blot had appeared over the heart on Ashley's cream blouse. Like me she picked out a piece of triangular glass that had sliced the material and half embedded itself in her flesh, repeating 'I'm all right!' just as I had to her. Once the glass was out she pressed her fingertips against the wound to slow the bleeding.

It was Angela who gave us the most concern. She sprawled back in her chair, a frightening rasping sound coming from her throat and her eyes still rolled up. It seemed likely to me that she had had some sort of stroke.

'I must get a doctor,' I said, making for the door. 'I'll phone from the vicarage.'

'Wait a minute,' said Nigel. 'I think she's coming round. She'd hate an outsider to be involved.'

I paused and saw her eyes return to normal, and although her breast rose and fell as though she had been running for her life her breathing lost its alarming death rattle sound. Like the rest of us, her first words were to announce that she was all right. Then, while Ashley went to the bathroom for sticking plaster, cotton wool and the old-fashioned iodine which I preferred to modern antiseptics, I poured everyone a generous measure of brandy.

'Please do something about your face,' said Nigel as I handed him a glass. 'You make me feel faint.'

'Of course.' I retired to the kitchen to wipe away the gore with a dishcloth.

'Here, darling, you can't do that,' said Ashley, coming through the doorway. 'Let me.'

She dabbed away the blood with cotton wool and then applied iodine, causing a spasm of pain which I would never have got with a modern bland antiseptic.

'What on earth happened in there?' she asked as she pressed a plaster against my skin.

'I really don't know,' I admitted. 'Perhaps Angela can explain. Obviously we had a re-run of the "Narration".'

'At first I couldn't help wondering if it was being faked, I mean, most likely someone into the ghost business would have read about Mary Lawson's experiences here.'

'I thought so myself when the messages started to be spelled out, but why go to all that trouble? Money doesn't come into it.'

'You're a well known author,' Ashley said. 'If you were to draw attention to it – even write a book about it – it would be fantastic publicity for someone wanting to become famous as a medium.'

'But that exploding glass was no fake,' I said. 'Remember Mary Lawson wrote about a loud report at the height of the manifestations. Perhaps this was some sort of repetition.'

On returning to the dining-room we found that now the initial shock was over an air of excitement pervaded our guests. Only Angela, who looked exhausted but otherwise normal, remained silent and thoughtful as though working out in her mind what to tell me.

'Sit beside me, my dears,' she said as she caught sight of us. 'I must thank you for introducing us to such remarkable phenomena. Such violence is rare. For such a physical effect the psychic force was of tremendous intensity.'

'Was?' said Ashley.

'Oh yes, it's over now.'

'How do you know?' Ashley asked.

'When you are a medium with years of experience you just "know" these things. It is part of the gift.'

'So what really happened just now?'

'The force – a force bred out of a long-ago mix of extreme despair and what we term evil – for some reason became re-activated, feeding upon itself until its very intensity burned it out. It was like an electrical overload burning out a circuit. The destruction of the glass was the final surge.'

'Like a fuse going,' suggested Ashley.

'Exactly.'

It sounded rather glib to me – I have always been wary of easy comparisons – but I suppose it was what I wanted to hear.

'What do you think it was that re-activated the force? I don't think the previous occupant, who had lived here since the war, ever found the place to be haunted.'

From a silver mesh handbag Angela took out a packet of Sobranie Lights and I noticed that her be-ringed fingers were still trembling as she lit up and inhaled gratefully.

'Who can say what reawakens a dormant psychic force?' she said. 'In science everything is logical. Recognized causes and effects can be expressed in mathematical formulae. But when it comes to the paranormal we are like explorers who have just landed on the beach of an unknown continent. I experience the paranormal almost every day, I see its effects, but I can only guess at its causes. That is why my group is independent. We could not belong to any organization with dogmatic views or religious convictions. All I can suggest is that it was something to do with you or Ashley which triggered all this off. Perhaps there is some hidden psychic quality of which you are not aware.'

'It couldn't have been Ashley,' I said hastily. 'I was hearing those voices before she arrived here. And there's nothing psychic about me.'

'Certainly you do not have that sort of aura,' said Angela. 'Being a writer, though, you do have *imagination.*'

'But what happened tonight was hardly imaginary,' protested Ashley, her fingers touching the bloodstain on her blouse.

'I didn't mean that.' Angela smiled enigmatically. Then she said, 'Could I have a very hot cup of tea with loads of sugar, please? I know I'll be all right after that. A séance always drains me, and tonight ...' Her fingers fluttered like a pair of fans.

'Of course.' Ashley went to the kitchen.

'I think it would be a good idea if you took Ashley for a little holiday,' said Angela, to whom our personal relationship was obvious. 'Give things a little time to settle down.'

'But you said that everything was over.'

'It is, but there still might be a lingering disturbance in the ether, the ripples after the stone has vanished into the pool. You understand?'

'A very sound idea,' I said.

Twenty minutes later Ashley and I watched the tail lights of the Volvo vanish in the shadowed lane as Mr Peter headed back to London with Angela's little group.

We turned and walked down the dark drive to the house which, when we reached the garden, made a dramatic shape against the starshine, its three gables and illuminated windows giving it the hint of a Halloween mask.

'If you feel nervous I'm sure Henry would be happy to put us up for the night,' I said, 'though it might be difficult explaining why we need his hospitality.'

'Me – nervous?' cried Ashley in mock surprise, then seriously, 'I think Angela was right. The atmosphere seemed to change somehow after the glass blew. Now all I want is to get to bed, and for you to kiss my wound better, and then sleep, blessed sleep. I feel as if I've just run a marathon.'

Together we walked over the grass towards the house.

'By the way, is your passport in order?' I asked.

'Seeing I've only just arrived in the Mother Country it ought to be,' she answered. 'Are you going to take me for a naughty weekend in Paris?'

'Something like that,' I answered.

* * *

Ashley dozed beside me as the aged Boeing 707, with the Flying Leopard insignia of the Royal Abu Sabbah Airline emblazoned on its fuselage, followed the electronic trail which led to the Mediterranean and thence to the Red Sea and our hope of a reprise from the tension which had gripped us at Whispering Corner.

140

That morning we had gone to the village and I had put a telephone call through to the royal palace of Abu Sabbah. For several coin crashing minutes I spoke to officials of ascending importance – 'the royal eunuchs', Ashley called them, refusing to be impressed by the fact that I was phoning a real live king. Then the voice of Syed came on the line, saying how delighted he was that I was responding to his letter.

I told him that because of some unexpected free time. I should like to take up his invitation to visit his country with a 'dear companion', as he had phrased it.

'You will be most welcome,' he said. 'Are you immediately free? I ask because we have a flight leaving Gatwick this evening, and there will not be another for a week. Could you make it do you think?'

Delighted, I replied that it might be possible.

'Excellent. I shall have first class reservations ready for collection to Gatwick.'

After expressing my thanks to the king and saying how much I was looking forward to seeing how his college was progressing, I rang Paul Lincoln to explain that I would be away for a while and would he please keep an eye on the Regent Bank situation for me.

'I hope you're taking your work with you – you know how important it is to raise money from that bloody book.' he said.

'I am and I do.'

Next I broke the news to my agent, who impressed upon me the need to return with the completed manuscript, 'I'll be more productive with a change of scene,' I reassured her.

On the way back to Whispering Corner we met Henry Gotobed, When I explained that I was taking a holiday he promised he would keep an eye on the house and open cans of Whiskas for Mrs Foch.

'I'm hoping to spend my fortnight's holiday on another research spree up in London soon,' he said. 'While I'm at the British Library I'll try and find more information about Mrs Lawson's "Narration" and Whispering Corner.'

At the house we packed our bags and Ashley bemoaned the fact that she had hardly any clothes smart enough for palace wear.

'You look marvellous in the silver and grey,' I said. '1 doubt if we'll spend much time at the palace, anyway. Syed said he would provide a guest bungalow for us in a secluded spot on the seashore so that I could have tranquillity in case I wanted to do any writing – which I certainly do.'

I went into the dining-room to tidy up after the séance. It had been instilled into me since childhood that one always left one's home immaculate when going away, and now that it was fixed that we were leaving that very day I felt an irrational pang of guilt. When I looked round the room I saw that all I needed to do was rearrange the chairs and collect the fragments of glass scattered over the carpet. It was remarkable that there had been no serious injuries considering that we had been grouped round the table when the tumbler had gone off like a glass grenade. I found a heart-shaped piece of glass actually embedded in the wall and I left it there. Evidence, but for whom?

In the late afternoon we drove along the light-dappled lane and out into the warm landscape of hayfields, the still tender green of corn and here and there the sulphur squares of rape. After the security ritual at Gatwick Airport, we were shepherded to the 707 with the courtesy one received before the boom in cheap air travel made it impractical. And once we were airborne we realized why. A stewardess in a long-skirted beige uniform and filmy headscarf hurried to us with a decorative bottle of Perrier-Jouet in an ice bucket.

'We had an email from a very important person in Abu Sabbah saying that you are his guests and must be treated as such,' she explained as she poured the champagne into a pair of flute glasses.

'I'll travel on this airline again,' Ashley said.

'I'm afraid you'll have to,' the Arab girl answered. 'The only other way out of Abu Sabbah is by camel. Will you have a European supper or our special kebab dish?'

We settled for the kebabs, and by the time the meat arrived on its bed of spiced rice we were slightly euphoric with the wine.

'It's so good to be getting away for a while,' Ashley said. 'Although I love Whispering Corner, the stress there has been too much over the last few days. I was afraid you were on the way to a breakdown.'

'I wasn't that bad,' I said defensively.

'You didn't hear yourself muttering in your sleep. But it was nothing to be ashamed of – what with the difficulties over the book, and the bank, and finally the spook invasion. It was a lot to carry alone.'

'I never felt alone.'

'Nor were you, my darling. But one thing I now realize about the haunting – it must have been much harder for you to accept the manifestations than someone with an open mind. Like a life-long atheist being suddenly confronted by a vision of Our Lady of Sorrows.'

'Quite,' I said, and let it go at that.

When the kebab trays had been removed and Ashley had drifted off on a tide of champagne bubbles, the stewardess returned with a sheaf of glossy magazines.

'This is a very nice one,' she said, proffering a copy of *Voyageur*. 'It just reached us from New York. Our queen used to work on it as a photographer,' she added with a touch of shy pride.

'I know,' I said. The magazine still smelled of ink and art paper. The girl gave me a smile as bright as her silver leopard badge and moved on to the next row of seats. I started to turn the pages and there it was – a full-colour, double-page advertisement for the new perfume which had enabled Pamela to return to her career as a copy writer.

Reading it I felt proud of Pamela, and at the same time an ache of regret. She had so easily found a new lifestyle without me. And the pain I felt was a sadness from the past, for something that never quite was.

I turned to the book reviews.

Chapter 14

After the aircraft touched down and had followed the path of coloured lights to the small floodlit terminal building, the cabin door opened and over-heated air was sucked into the air-conditioned cabin like breath from an oven. And as we straggled across the spongy tarmac, sweat breaking out on our faces, the hot soft darkness was full of the indefinable redolence of Arabia.

When we reached the impassive immigration official and placed our passports on the table his face became almost friendly for a second as he said, 'Mis'r North, you go through with lady.'

We went through a door to where a khaki-uniformed policeman with a low-slung pistol was waiting.

'Mis'r North? This way, *min fadhlek.*'

He led us out into the sultry night where a Rolls-Royce, marred by a coat of military khaki, was waiting. The policeman opened the door for us and I saw that there was already an occupant – King Syed.

'Welcome to my small kingdom, Jonathan and . . .'

I hastily introduced Ashley to His Majesty.

'You both must be exhausted. Such a beastly flight. I propose to take you straight to the house where you will be staying so you can catch up on your sleep. Everything is prepared for you and there is a maid and a reliable watchman. Tomorrow night my wife and I shall be delighted to entertain you to a quiet dinner at the palace.'

As I settled on the seat opposite him I felt my foot touch a hard object.

'Sorry, that is my machine-gun,' Syed said. 'Alas, we live in difficult times. It used to be Marxists, now Fundamentalists. But do not worry, this car is armoured.'

He gave an order in quiet Arabic and the Rolls seemed to float forward.

'Our luggage,' Ashley exclaimed. 'Er . . . Your Royalty.'

'It has already been placed in the boot.'

Now that the doors of the car were closed the air-conditioning took over so effectively that we suddenly felt chilled in our perspiration-soaked clothing.

Syed turned to Ashley.

'Jo, my wife, is eagerly looking forward to meeting you,' he said. 'Considering her American background, she has fitted in remarkably well to this medieval state, and any reservations my subjects had about a foreigner becoming their queen evaporated when she embraced Islam. But it is natural that she should like to spend time with people from her own world. There are very few Western women

144

in Abu Sabbah, and those who are here with their diplomatic husbands are not exactly in tune with Jo who made her own career before she married me. Do you ride?'

'I used to ride to school when I was a kid,' Ashley replied. 'I'd love to be on horseback again.'

'Excellent. Since she came here Jo has developed a passion for riding. I am sure she would be delighted if you would accompany her.'

I was pleased to see how easily Ashley and the king got on together and I was happy to let them chat while I gazed out of the windows of the big car. It would be trite to say that I felt I was back in the days of Haroun-al-Rashid, but let's be trite. The car glided like a low-flying magic carpet, its headlights catching the date palms that lined the highway, and the occasional group of white shrouded figures squatting round tiny camel dung fires on the roadside. Once we overtook a string of camels, led by men wearing the shawls known as *kaffiyeh* on their heads, carrying produce for the morning's market. Sometimes we slowed to pass through villages of square white buildings huddled round a mosque, and one caught glimpses of men drinking coffee from tiny brass cups through the open doors of dimly lit cafes.

Once the strip of cultivation which flanked the road gave way to desert sand, and in the harsh moonlight I saw a small domed building rising from the sand.

'That is the shrine of a saint,' Syed explained casually. 'He was martyred several centuries ago by the Turks, but the locals speak about him as though it was yesterday. Time has a different dimension here.'

A few minutes later the car turned off the road and lurched along a track until it reached a group of carob trees and a single-storey Moorish-style house. Beyond, a stretch of sea gleamed like burnished pewter.

'Your residence,' said Syed. 'May you be content here.'

'It's wonderful,' Ashley said enthusiastically.

The old watchman, carrying a Lee Enfield .303 which must have originated from the North African campaigns of the Second World War, and a young maid in a black *chawdor* bowed and smiled.

'She has enough English to serve you,' Syed said. 'I hope everything has been prepared satisfactorily. Take it easy tomorrow, and the car will call for you at sunset.'

We thanked him and followed the servants into the house. There we were offered sweet tea and our luggage was placed in a spacious bedroom with goat skins scattered on the polished wood floor. Ashley hurried to the large window and angled the Venetian blinds so that she could look over the white beach to the sighing sea, then she took me by the hand and led me out on to a terrace fragrant with flowering vines planted in ancient amphorae.

'I can't believe this,' she murmured. 'Last night all hell was breaking loose in Whispering Corner, and now we're looking out on the Red Sea. And it feels so safe and peaceful.' She laughed. 'I'll bet that old saint will watch over us.'

'I must say Syed has done us proud.'

'He must be keen for you to take up that post at his new college.'

'It might not be a bad idea if I go broke . . .'

'Darling, while we are here try and put all negative thoughts out of your mind.'

'You're absolutely right,' I said, ashamed of sounding low-key on such a night. Although we were both weary from the long flight, the sight of the sea reflecting the Arabian moon and the caress of the warm breeze had the effect of easing our fatigue.

'On a night like this Antony must have given up the world for Cleopatra,' murmured Ashley in a half-humorous way.

'And Abla gave her heart to Antar,' I agreed.

'Ant – who?'

'Antar was the Middle Eastern equivalent of Robin Hood,' I told her. 'He started life as a black slave and became a desert leader. Abla was his Maid Marian.'

'With you I learn something every day,' said Ashley, mocking my tendency, endemic among authors, to repeat an anecdote at the drop of a hat. She ran her fingers down the side of my cheek to show that she did not really object and said, 'I'm going in for a swim to wash away the journey.'

With quick movements of her fingers she unbuttoned the light cotton dress she had worn for the flight and it slid to her ankles. Her white underclothes followed it to the tiles, and she stepped out of the tangle and turned to me with a slightly mocking smile.

'Coming?'

I must confess that the sight of that smile and her lithe body – even though I had come to know it so intimately – sent a breath-catching ripple of excitement through me. In this hot shadow world she stood poised for a second like an alabaster figure carved by a master sculptor, then with a shake of her dark curls she turned and ran down the steps and across the beach to the sea.

As soon as she was far enough in she dived into a small wave creaming towards the shore. A moment later she was standing up again, thigh-deep in foam, and she *glowed.* Her skin was luminous with phosphorescence. Her raised arm beckoned me and then she turned and swam away from the beach.

Wishing that I was a stone lighter and that my waist tended

146

more to the concave than the convex, I undressed and sprinted over the still warm sand. I have always been a good swimmer and soon I began to overhaul Ashley's dark head, which rose and fell with the slight swell. She turned and saw me, and changed from breast stroke to a stylish crawl. The race was on but after a few minutes I was almost level with her, she half rose out of the water to fill her lungs, then dived out of sight. I followed the wake seething behind her until she turned and held her arms wide to me before soaring up to the surface. I saw her legs move lazily above me to keep her floating comfortably.

I followed and broke the surface beside her, my own arms now glowing with pale fire.

'You look magical,' she cried. 'You're alight. What is it?'

I told her that she looked the same, thanks to a microscopic organism that thrived in these warm shallow waters.

'A microscopic orgasm!' she cried with a peal of laughter.

I made a jokey retort about casting aspersions and we floated side by side, our legs moving gently to keep us in position. To the south a halo against the black velvet sky indicated the position of the old city.

Our hands touched and locked and we turned towards each other. I put my free hand behind the nape of her neck and drew her laughing face towards me until our lips touched. Then under we went, into the black sea, our arms round each other and strings of bubbles trailing us.

At last we had to break our embrace and kick up to the surface to gulp air like drowning sailors. When we had regained our breath we floated on our backs again, our linked fingers preventing us from drifting apart.

'I do love you,' she said impulsively.

'And you,' I said, which was our ritual of endearment.

'You know what I want?'

'And me.'

'Here. In the sea.'

'We'd drown.'

'But what a way to go,' she laughed.

I caught her desire, and I was no longer a middle-aged man but had the illusion of youth upon me. In the caressing sea, under the moon which in this Tropic of Cancer acquired a golden voluptuousness, it seemed anything was possible.

Ashley turned towards me.

'Mermaids and tritons must manage,' she said, still joking but with a throaty undertone that I had come to recognize during our nights together in Whispering Corner. 'Come, darling.'

Treading water we came together, our arms round each other,

and while we kissed our salty kisses I felt her legs encircle my thighs. My response was automatic and a second later I felt myself enter the warmth of her body. In the shine of the phosphorescence I saw her eyes widen and her mouth smile at me with a mixture of affection and eroticism.

There are difficulties in making love in such circumstances. Any movement of our bodies resulted in our faces dipping below the surface, and so we had to be content to float together while we rose and fell to the immemorial cadence of the sea. And in this yielding liquid world the anemone-like response of my lover was rapidly bringing me to the point of climax. I tried to hold back, tried to dissociate my mind from the surges of pure physical pleasure which beat from my loins . . .

'I can't bear this any more,' Ashley muttered. 'Let's make it to the beach.'

She wrenched herself away from me and briefly vanished under the glimmering surface, while the shock of exposure to seawater postponed my looming climax.

Ashley surfaced a few yards away and began to swim towards the shore. We had drifted further out than we had realized and both of us, already breathless, were panting by the time we felt the coral sand beneath our feet. We were actually swaying as we waded ashore and lost the support of the sea.

I took Ashley's hand to lead her up to the bungalow, but she shook her head and pulled me down beside her so that wavelets hissed and died about our ankles. In the moonlight I saw a dazed look in her eyes and her slack mouth seemed incapable of speech. She was possessed by the demon of unfulfilment. That expression of uninhibited need aroused me more than any of the carnal triggers I had ever known and a hot tide of lust – sheer unapologetic lust – flowed through my system in a physical reaction so powerful I winced with the unexpected pain of it.

Before I could roll over to take her, Ashley straddled me, her fingers digging into my shoulders, her body moving as she sought to give me entrance. Then once more there was the electrifying spasm of entry and Ashley rode me, her head thrown back, her eyes shut and her breasts showering me with drops of seawater which the moon transformed to pearls. If Death had tapped me on the shoulder during those frenzied minutes she would have had to wait.

At last Ashley gave a soft cry of triumph and as she reached the end of her race I felt myself fountain within her. Then we lay side by side, barely conscious, while the wavelets splashed our feet and creamed along our legs.

* * *

Sunlight slanting through the slats of Venetian blinds cast slim stippled bands of shadow on the naked body of Ashley lying beside me. During the hot night we had sleepily cast aside the cotton sheet and now the heat was increasing with morning so that already her skin was beaded with perspiration. Summer was not the ideal season to visit Abu Sabbah, but I was not going to begin finding fault. I recognized that King Syed's invitation had probably saved me from something nasty. I was several thousand miles away from my problems and here with luck I would get back on to schedule with my novel.

Eager to begin work I rose gently, slipped on a light robe and went in search of the coffee whose aroma permeated the bungalow. In the kitchen the maid looked up from the brazier on which an ornate coffee pot was balanced.

'Salaam aleikum,' I said, having tried to memorize a few words from a phrase book on the flight.

'Good morning, she managed. 'You sleep good?'

'Very good.'

I took the coffee to the bedroom where Ashley was waking up.

'I love this heat,' she said as I gave her a cup. 'It's me for the beach until we go to the palace. You'll be working on your novel?'

'Of course.'

'I wish you'd let me read what you've written. I feel shut out, somehow. If I read it I could tune in to your difficulties with it.'

'Sorry.'

There was an urgent knock at the door.

'Please, you get up,' cried the maid. 'Queen come.'

I went to the window and between the slates I saw Syed's wife riding a black horse and leading another along the dazzling beach.

'A royal visit,' exclaimed Ashley. 'What the hell shall I wear?'

'As she's bringing a spare horse I expect you'll be invited to go riding, so I suggest you put on your cotton jeans.'

A couple of minutes later I saw the watchman bow low and take Jo's bridle. On the terrace I introduced her to Ashley, who with some instant magic looked like a model for casual outfits. Perhaps because she came from a warm climate she wore her jeans and tailored shirt with the same sort of flair as Jo. Seeing them together I guessed they would have much in common.

The maid brought out a brass tray with coffee and sherbet and extremely sticky little cakes, and we lounged in worn deckchairs and squinted at fishing boats creeping along the coast, dark elegant craft riding a sea of sparkles. Jo told me how pleased her husband was that I had accepted his invitation, especially as his enthusiasm for his new college increased in ratio with its construction.

'And I'm so glad you brought Ashley,' she continued. 'I came to see if you'd care to come for a ride? We could go along the coast towards El Saad. There's a lovely little oasis where we could have a picnic lunch,' I could see Ashley was longing to go, but she glanced at me before she replied.

'Do go,' I said. 'I'll be sitting over a hot laptop all day and I'd feel guilty at neglecting you if you stayed here.'

'In that case . . .'

'That's settled, then,' said Jo, standing up and dipping her fingers into a bowl of water and floating petals proffered by the maid. 'Jonathan, have a good day. I'll look forward to seeing you at the palace tonight. Meanwhile, I hope the words come well.' She turned to the maid and said, *'Fi amàn Illah.'*

I watched the two girls walk to the horses and felt a sense of approval as Ashley swung into the saddle as easily as Jo, then they cantered off, their laughter borne back to me by the salty breeze.

The hot empty day stretched ahead of me like a colonnade in an abandoned city, and to counteract the sense of loneliness created by the sight of the dwindling riders I hurried to begin work. A few minutes later my body may have been sweltering on the littoral of the Red Sea but my mind was back at Whispering Corner.

I found what I hoped would be the coolest place in the bungalow, a small room with a large window which looked out over the sea and should catch the cool breeze which came off it to replace the heated airs rising above the land. On a table in front of the window I placed my laptop. At least I'd got some first-hand material to use in *Whispering Corner* now.

I glanced over the last few pages I had written and deleted the beginning of a manifestation episode. Lorna and Falco would experience exactly what Ashley and I had experienced, and all I had to do was write it the way it was.

I began to type quickly and enjoyed one of those rare moments of exhilaration when the words seem to tumble over each other in their hurry to be put down. There was no question of writer's block or any of the doubts about my work which had beset me, now I was in command, and I *was* Falco as he went down the stairs . . .

And even as I described the re-run of the murder my mind was racing ahead to what would be the climax of the chapter – the terrible figure composed of bed clothes crouched over Lorna. That would be one of my best scenes.

I never wrote as fluently or as fast as I did that day by the Red Sea, even though the breeze took on the breath of a furnace at noon when the palms stood in puddles of shadow cast by the merciless sun blazing directly overhead.

Of course I did much more than merely recreate my experience,

I sought to describe it in words that would arrest the reader's attention, make him or her feel that like Falco they were on the brink of something unspeakable. And I knew that I was succeeding. That was the joy of it as the shadows lengthened again and the breeze lost its heat, and when the red disc of the sun finally balanced on the rim of the sea I keyed in the last word, saved the file and slumped back in my chair.

If anyone deserved a drink it was me, and I was just about to go in search of the duty-free when I saw Ashley cantering along the shore. I went out on the terrace to welcome her and when she saw me she finished her ride with a spectacular gallop.

'Jo has lent Houri to me for the duration,' she said breathlessly as she slid from the saddle and handed the reins to the watchman. 'We've had a super day. I'm sure I'm going to get my tan back. We must hurry now and get ready. The royal Rolls will be calling for us at sundown. What sort of a day have you had?'

'Productive and hot,' I said as we went inside.

'Isn't the heat wonderful! I'm starting to feel my old self again after the accident. How many pages?'

'Twelve.'

'Aren't you good? You see, you needed the change of scene. Now let's get dressed for the banquet. If we hurry we might have time for a drink to steady our nerves.

Chapter 15

I never thought I'd write the words, 'It was a scene from the Arabian Nights', but in this case the cliché is a perfect description of the entertainment provided for us by King Syed. After the Rolls had glided into the palace courtyard an official ushered us through a maze of passages and halls to the banqueting chamber. Here one wall was composed of arched casements, some screened by delicate fretwork of carved marble, which were open to allow the breeze to enter from the dark sea. The other walls were covered with azure leather embossed with geometric designs in silver leaf.

A small fountain splashed musically into a sunken basin in which swam golden carp, and antique lamps of chased silver burning scented oil cast a soft rose light over the low tables on which delicacies were already piled. The rugs scattered so profusely over the floor would have been worth a fortune in a London oriental carpet dealer's emporium.

Syed, having abandoned the casual military uniform he often wore for a white silken robe worked with gold thread, came forward to greet us, Jo following the regulation step behind. Like her husband, she was in traditional dress and wore a transparent veil over the lower part of her face. Behind the couple loomed a tall Arab with a drawn sword, the traditional defender of the kings of Abu Sabbah, and besides the symbolic scimitar he had an Uzi machine-gun hanging from a shoulder strap.

The king welcomed us with his usual warmth and charm and began a round of introductions, mostly to Abu Sabbah dignitaries but also to a couple of laconic American geologists engaged on a vain hunt for oil, and a worried-looking Danish architect who was responsible for designing Syed's college. Apart from Ashley and the queen there were no other women present.

As we were the guests of honour we took our place on the cushions at the king's right hand.

'Do not be afraid that you will find a sheep's eyeball staring at you from the couscous,' Syed told us. 'My late brother took his chef from the Tour d'Argent and he remained to cook for me. And I trust you will agree that this Chateau Mouton Rothschild has survived its journey.'

'I thought you weren't supposed to drink alcohol,' said Ashley.

'Most of the men here will drink only tea or sherbet,' said Syed. 'Some of the younger ones will put a tiny amount of salt in their wine.' Ashley looked puzzled. 'Technically it turns the wine into vinegar.'

'But you can't fool God with a pinch of salt,' Ashley protested.

'Exactly,' said the king and he smiled enigmatically. After the excellent meal – a mixture of French and Arabic cuisine, Syed said, 'And now we shall be entertained by my *rawi*. A *rawi* is a traditional court storyteller, and it is a tradition that I like to keep going. My *rawi* Zahir Khaled could be described as my poet laureate. He is an expert on Islamic literature, which he will teach in my college.'

An elderly man with a white beard, wearing a robe of Damascus silk and a blue turban, entered. After bowing to Syed and Jo, and then the assembled company, he began to recite a story. In perfect English – I was told later that he had a Cambridge degree – he related how the high-born wife of a merchant drugged her husband every night in order to visit the necropolis outside Bagdad where she made love with a fearsome ghoul which dwelt among the tombs . . .

'I thought this would be your cup of tea,' Syed whispered. 'When Zahir has concluded I would be honoured if you would regale us with one of your tales. This is not a royal command but a request from one of your fans – you know how much I have enjoyed your horror stories.'

'It is me who will be honoured,' I replied. Listening to the delightful rising and falling cadences of Zahir's voice I had little doubt as to how I would compare with him. The guests hung on his words as he invoked the horrors of the ghoul's lair in a ruined mausoleum, the colourful life in old Bagdad and the splendours of the Caliph's palace. I became fascinated by the man. Here was true story-telling, in the tradition of the Greek poets who recited over their lyres and the *skalds* of Iceland who wove their word pictures in smoky Viking halls. Finally he resolved the story with the ghoul held for eternity by the Seal of Solomon in an underground vault, the wicked wife forced to live as a beggar in the refuse mounds without the city and the young merchant being restored to health and fortune.

After Zahir had modestly acknowledged the compliments of the guests, Syed turned to me with a smile.

'We have heard an old Arabian horror story,' he said. 'Tonight we have with us the master of the modern variety. Please,' he added to me with a gesture to indicate the floor was mine.

I decided to risk entertaining the company by extemporizing in its traditional genre. I felt nervous, but I was buoyed by a new-found enthusiasm for story-telling. Stepping into the centre of the floor, I bowed to the king and the guests and then, holding up my right hand in the traditional gesture for attention, I began, 'In the name of Allah, the merciful and compassionate.'

The guests looked at me with curiosity and old Zahir smiled in acknowledgement. Dropping my hand, I continued, 'Know, O King, that it was the custom of your illustrious ancestor Haroun Al-Raschid, the Caliph of Bagdad, to put aside his princely raiment in favour of the garb of a private citizen and – with his faithful *wazir* Jaafer – to wander in the streets of his city to observe the welfare of his subjects and to enjoy what adventures might befall him . . .'

* * *

It was my own cry that wrenched me from my nightmare. My heart was beating alarmingly fast and the sheet which covered me was soaking with my sweat. Still in the grip of terror I gazed about me in incomprehension at the room decorated by parallel strips of moonlight admitted by the Venetian blinds, and for several long seconds I wondered where the hell I was.

'Darling!' Ashley sat bolt upright beside me, her breasts and stomach caught in the bands of light.

'Bad dream,' I muttered, still half in its grip, still descending those hellish steps. 'It's something that's recurred from time to time. Sometimes I've gone for several years without experiencing it.'

'Well tell me – what happens?'

'In the dream I'm going down a flight of steps . . . knowing there's *something* at the bottom.' Childlike, I felt a great desire to bury my face in the pillow and cry and cry until all the badness was gone.

She put her arms round me and rocked me. 'Tell me. Get it out of your system.'

'There was something that happened when I was a boy,' I said. 'It was to do with the death of my mother. I was eight or nine at the time. It made a big impression.'

Ashley said nothing, just sat like a tiger-striped statue beside me in the bed. Her silence encouraged me to continue, to speak the unspeakable, to confess what I had confessed only once before, to my wife in the early days of our marriage.

'I was an only child, and my mother was quite a few years younger than my father. They were in great contrast to each other,' I said. 'I never felt as close to my father as I did to my mother. Her I could love without restraint. She was as extroverted as he was introverted. Perhaps it was because she was a staunch Roman Catholic. She did not need to question her universe. She took me to mass, and I became an altar boy. How I loved it. I believed *everything*. I believed I had a guardian angel – in fact I used to talk to him. Life was wonderful at that point. I adored my mother in return for her unstinted love. I loved the attention my father gave me and I felt secure in the arms of Jesus. Then it all went wrong.'

'Your mother died?'

'Yes. One night she fell from the top storey window on to the stone steps in front of French windows. Rather like those at Whispering Corner, actually. There was even a stone urn on each side of them. Anyway, something woke me up. I can't remember what it was, a cry perhaps, or the thud of her body. Something told me I had to go downstairs, and down I went in the dark . . . and that's all I can remember. I gather the child psychologist who saw me later said that seeing my mother's broken body on the steps was so traumatic that I refused to acknowledge those few minutes of my life. I understand that I was found trying to put her shoe back on her foot. That's the obvious background to the nightmare . . . going downstairs knowing that the ultimate horror awaits me there but not aware, in the dream, of its nature.'

'You mean, you don't expect to find your mother lying there?'

'No. You see, I have no conscious memory of that. Everything around that time remains pretty vague, in fact, though the funeral does stand out in my memory. It was so hard to believe that my mother – my pretty, singing mother – was in that box in the church where I had been an altar boy. That day the incense made me feel sick and the faces of the saints seemed to mock . . .

'The conscious effect of the . . . tragedy . . . was that I realized the futility of my faith. Where was my guardian angel on that night? Where was my mother's? How could gentle Jesus allow this dreadful, dreadful thing to happen? I *knew* the whole religious thing was a con. From then on I have had no metaphysical belief. Life is a product of patterns of electrons. I believe that we are nothing more than a dance of atoms with the ability to recognize our existence, and fool ourselves that there is something more to it than that.'

'Jon, is that why you were so adamant there was nothing in the paranormal?'

'Of course. Superstition is the other side of the religious coin. It is belief in forces that cannot be explained. To me the supernatural, both religious and occult, was a compact between the conning and the conned.'

'Now I understand what upset you so much over the haunting. It wasn't the manifestations so much as what they meant.'

'Yes,' I said wearily. 'The séance was my Road to Damascus. Of course I'd been deluding myself almost from my first days at Whispering Corner. I should have recognized that there was something odd going on when I began hearing those voices in my head, but they were too easy to dismiss at the time as natural hypnagogsis. But there were other things. I heard breathing beside me one morning though there was no one there. And I had a frightening experience in the cellar.'

'And the books,' said Ashley. 'Remember how they were strewn on the floor? And we thought it was Hoddy.'

'I'm still not sure about Hoddy,' I said.

'So when did you admit to yourself that there were ghosts in the house?'

'When I went downstairs and found the house had changed – that I was in the Whispering Corner of Sir Richard Elphick's time.'

Ashley said nothing for a minute, then asked, 'How did your mother come to fall that night?'

'I was told that she was leaning out of the window, trying to rescue Mia, our cat, who had got herself in difficulties on the ledge, and that she must have leaned too far and lost her balance.'

'What a horribly stupid accident.'

'It wasn't an accident,' I said. 'At that moment, for some reason I have never been able to discover, she had no wish to live.'

Chapter 16

I must admit that I had probably been more disturbed by the events at Whispering Corner – and even more by the fact that such events were possible – than I cared to acknowledge. But I pushed on with my novel, and though I felt a certain repugnance I capitalized on my own recent experiences.

In contrast to the glare outside the house my workplace was full of shade, and the scene of shore and shimmering sea through the window was like a bright television picture in an unlit room. When I started work in the morning such a brilliant view made it difficult to focus my inward eye on vistas of gentle Dorset landscape, but once I began typing I ignored the harsh light and almost forgot the heat. Falco and Lorna returned from the wings of my imagination and with them came the menace that threatened Whispering Corner. The séance scene was a natural one to bring into my story, but although an exploding glass is dramatic enough in real life I felt that the printed page needed something more powerful to cause a sense of shock. And I believed I had the answer to that.

When I described Falco going down the stairs and finding the house changed it was like a re-run of my own experience, and then with a sort of sick excitement I wrote how he saw the figure on the bed attacking Lorna.

The girl lay asleep, unaware of the lint-white figure bending over her, of the thin bandage arms reaching for her.

Without a thought as to what it was, Falco lunged across the room and flung himself on the intruder. For a moment he -or whatever it was – turned his head and Falco heard his own cry of terror as he saw that the shadowed face was his. It was like looking in a mirror and seeing his reflection with every trace of colour bled off, or seeing his own effigy fashioned from linen.

Under Falco's onslaught the figure collapsed. He was left grasping a tangle of white bedding no longer animated by the mimicking spirit of evil.

Any revulsion I felt in recalling the incident was changed to enthusiasm by this extra twist. An elemental force that took on the shapes of those it was persecuting. 'Nice!' I thought. It opened up storyline possibilities as well as introducing an extra dimension of horror.

I decided that what I had just written deserved more thoughtful writing, and I set to work on it.

By the middle of the afternoon I had typed over a couple of thousand words, and suddenly I was exhausted. I went through into the bedroom, darkened it as much as possible by tilting the slats of the blind, and threw myself on the bed like every other sensible inhabitant of Abu Sabbah.

* * *

'Sorry, darling. I tried not to disturb you.'

I opened my eyes at the sound of Ashley's voice. Wearing only white briefs, which emphasised the new tan she was acquiring from her sunbathing sessions with Jo, she lay beside me.

'Have a good ride?' I asked.

'Mmmm. Even I found it a bit too hot.'

Our fingers locked as we lay inert as a pair of effigies on a crusader's tomb, greater contact than that would have been unthinkable in the stifling gloom of the room.

'I love you, Jon,' she said a little later.

'And I you,' I responded.

'That's all that really matters, isn't it?'

I agreed drowsily.

For a moment I thought she had drifted into sleep but then she said, 'Last night, when you were talking about what happened when you were a boy . . . you didn't tell me why you thought your mother's death was not an accident. I thought maybe you felt you'd said enough, and then I found you'd drifted off to sleep.'

She was right. I had not wanted to talk about it any further then and had feigned sleep, which soon became real enough. Now I felt able to go on. 'What my father did not realize when he told me what had happened was that at the time Mia was asleep on the foot of my bed.'

'But why should she want to do away with herself? You told me how cheerful and religious she was.'

'I don't know, Ash, and I don't suppose I ever shall.'

'What happened to you and your father?'

'I was sent to be looked after by my Aunt Elizabeth in London. My father used to make efforts to visit me at first – take me to Madame Tussaud's and so on – but Mother's death had come between us like a sheet of plate glass. We were so bloody nice to each other. Later he went to live in Canada. He married again and I believe his new wife got him off the booze – he'd become a very dignified drunk. He writes to me twice a year, Christmas and birthday, but they're letters from a stranger. Sometimes I feel I should make an effort and go over and see him – take Steve with me to meet his grandfather – but there's always been a valid reason to put it off until next year.'

'You don't really want to see him, do you?'

'No. He's part of the past – like being an altar boy.'

'Do you blame him in some way for your mother's death?'

'I don't know. It was all long ago.' Her fingers tightened on

158

mine. 'I just want you to know, Jon, how much you have done for me,' she said.

I felt genuine surprise. I had fallen in love with her and hoped it was a mutual reaction, but I was not conscious of having done anything for her.

'I guess you may not have realized it, but I was pretty emotionally mauled when I came to Whispering Corner. You made everything right for me. You gave me my confidence back, you made me heart-whole, to use an old-fashioned word, and you gave me the gift of love. Thanks to you I'm living again, and I doubt if a younger man could have done that.'

Ashley's words brought me a sense of deep satisfaction as we drifted towards sleep, so it was odd that by the time I heard her give a gentle snore my thoughts had turned to Pamela. I told myself that I must find out if it was possible to send a cable of congratulation on the advertisement I had seen in *Voyageur*.

'Are you going riding today?' I asked Ashley when I carried coffee into our bedroom the next morning.

'Not today, thank goodness,' she said. I've still got a headache from yesterday. The sun was so fierce when we were riding along the beach. Mad dogs and Kiwis – I suppose. I'm going to stay in the shade all day. Wish you'd let me read what you've written.'

'When it's finished and corrected,' I said. A few minutes later I looked out to see a column of dust approaching, then a Land Rover appeared through the carob trees with Syed at the wheel and his bodyguard sitting in the back seat.

'Good morning, Jonathan,' he called as he skidded to a halt. 'Can I lure you away from your laptop? I have a free day and I would like to take you and Ashley sightseeing. Remember that crusader castle I told you about the other night? How about a trip out there?'

'I'd be delighted,' I said. 'But I doubt if Ashley would feel like the journey. Although she's used to the sun down under it's been a bit too much for her here.'

Syed was immediately concerned for her welfare, offering the services of his personal doctor, until Ashley appeared and reassured him that she was suffering from nothing worse than a throbbing head.

A few minutes later, I was seated beside him in the Land Rover, lurching along the track towards the Abdulla Highway – named after Syed's redoubtable father, the last king of Abu Sabbah to keep a harem.

'Apologies for the autoroute,' said the king as he deftly piloted us round a flock of goats. 'Aid for motorway construction evaporated when it was realized we had no oil potential.'

Here and there the monotony of the landscape was broken by

whitewashed houses set amid patches of cultivation irrigated by waterwheels powered by yoked donkeys plodding in never-ending circles. Youths in grimy *jellabas* shepherding goats waved at us when they recognized the royal leopard insignia on the Land Rover and were rewarded for their loyalty by being enveloped in a dun cloud of dust. Once I saw a string of camels swaying over sand dunes like an Old Testament illustration come to life, and I wished that I had a camera.

We followed the road westward into desert country. Ahead a range of lion-hued mountains crouched like a pride of the beasts and Syed expertly steered the Land Rover along the track which had begun to switchback over dunes, the beginning of the great sand sea which rolled westward into Africa. Soon we were vibrating in low gear along the wadi which led us into the magnificent Valley of the Jinn. In parts the walls were close together, towering almost vertically for hundreds of feet. Elsewhere they widened so that there were broad drifts of white sand glittering between them. Syed was continually telling me the local legends and pointing out places where the winds had carved surreal sculptures from the living rock. Some formations rose like chimneys against the brassy sky, others were stone 'waterfalls' eternally flowing down the cliffs in petrified cascades, and others again took on the forms of mythical beasts or fairy-tale palaces. The rock had the added attraction of being multi-hued, the predominating tone being a warm honey colour shot with pink and white strata.

If I found the valley impressive it was nothing to the impact I felt when our vehicle finally crawled round a bend and I beheld, crouched high on a gigantic rock buttress, a fortress whose curtain wall and towering keep menaced the narrow pass below. Its walls of pale yellow stone were crenellated and pierced for arrow fire, and it was obvious that whoever had held it would have controlled the caravan route. A dizzy path, hewn in the valley wall, led up to an empty gateway set between twin towers.

'Now we must walk,' said Syed, switching off the engine and putting to rest the echoes which had reverberated along the valley.

The climb to the castle was exhausting in the heat, and I wondered how crusaders wearing armour had managed to stand up to such conditions.

For the next hour we explored the castle and made a picnic lunch of dates, bread and kebabs which the bodyguard cooked over a charcoal brazier. The food was wholesome – what Syed called peasant fare – but 'to make amends for its simplicity' a bottle of Chateau Mouton Rothschild was produced. The king talked enthusiastically about his college, now half-constructed, where he would take me tomorrow. He repeated his hope that I would agree to head the English department for the first year, and casually mentioned a tax-free salary which startled me. If all else failed a year's work out here could give me a chance to do a deal with the Regent Bank and thus keep Whispering Corner.

From our vantage point we had a fine view of the desert hinterland and the green coastal strip with the sapphire sea beyond, and while Syed pointed out various aspects of his tiny kingdom the wine and the atmosphere of this unique place, coupled with the thought of Ashley waiting for me at the bungalow, gave me a wonderful sense of well-being. Those whom the gods destroy they first make glad.

Chapter 17

As we approached the airport on our return journey the shadow of evening descended upon the land. Behind us the lion mountains were briefly transmuted to gold as they caught the final rays of the sun. Riding the thunder of its Pratt and Whitney engines the 707 of the Royal Abu Sabbah Airline hauled itself into a sky of mauve and flame and made a lazy circle before heading towards Cairo.

When we reached the palace the king discussed arrangements for tomorrow's visit to the college site and then detailed a driver to take me on to the bungalow. I still had my sense of well-being and I was eagerly looking forward to regaling Ashley with the stories Syed had told me about the Valley of the Jinn and the Crusader castle.

'Fi aman Illah,' said the driver when he drew up in front of the house. I responded and went inside, at first surprised that the place was in darkness until I remembered that Ashley liked to sit in the tropical gloaming.

'Ash,' I called, expecting an answer from the terrace where she was no doubt looking out over the dark water with a drink in her hand.

When there was no response I looked out on the terrace and saw that it was empty, I went into our bedroom but no figure lay on the bed, and the other rooms were equally deserted. A burst of Arabic music led me to the kitchen and when I switched on the light I saw the maid hunched at the table in front of a transistor radio.

'Ashley?' I demanded.

'She gone,' the girl said.

'What the hell d'you mean – she gone?'

She shrugged.

'Take bag – gone.'

'To the palace?'

Another shrug.

'How did she go – on a horse?'

'On Houri. She *angry.*'

I ran back to the bedroom and snapped on the light which wavered in time to the capriciousness of the generator. Both Ashley's shoulder bag and her suitcase were missing, and when I flung open the louvred door of the wardrobe I saw that apart from a damp swimsuit bundled on the floor, all her clothes had gone.

A new apprehension gripped me and I hastily looked round the room for a note pinned up where I would see it. Nothing. I went into to the kitchen where a sheet of paper lay on the table. A few seconds later my fear was confirmed, Ashley had left me.

'Dear Jonathan Northrop,' I read. 'It seems I have a lot in common with Bluebeard's last wife . . .'

The writing was that of someone in a great hurry or under stress, words ran together and there was much crossing out which only added to the impact that it had upon me.

'I still can hardly believe what I read when I disobeyed you about reading what you had written – something I did because I felt I loved you so much and was hungry to know everything about you and what you were writing, so that I could understand you better and share your problems.

'How bloody naïve I am!

'It must have been fate which made me open the file at page 137 where your Falco has it off with dear old Lorna who just happens to be his guest at Whispering Corner . . . only it was Jonathan having it off with dear old Ashley who also happened to be your unexpected guest at Whispering Corner.

'At first I was horrified that you should describe in detail that night, which meant so much to me, in a book for everyone to read. And then the penny dropped. I realize I have been nothing more than a provider of "copy" for you. And how well you kidded me along, and how you must have laughed to yourself as you watched me through a magnifying glass and arranged scenes which you could type up the next day. I suppose you call it research! At least it was interesting to read how I screw from the Great Author's standpoint!

'But how could you be so hypocritical? To pretend all you did to get responses from me because your imagination has dried up – or have you always used unsuspecting people to provide you with characters?

'At least like Bluebeard's wife I now know where I stand. I may have been too eager to fall in love with you, but at least I have enough self-respect to stop being a model for your bloody Lorna. I am leaving on today's flight and we will not meet again. No doubt this parting will provide you with a good scene for your story.'

* * *

I re-read the page and then found the text which Ashley had read, and sure enough it described the night when Falco and Lorna made love for the first time.

'You silly bitch!' I cried in anger. 'Why the hell didn't you wait for me to explain?'

To explain that the scene which had so shocked her had been written while she was in the cottage hospital, days before it was agreed that she should stay at Whispering Corner. Then it never occurred to me that such intimacy as my characters enjoyed would ever take place between us, and that in this case life had followed art, not art mirrored life.

I should have locked the damned laptop away. But that would have looked as though I mistrusted her, an unthinkable thing to do.

For a moment the hope struck me that she might not have left Abu Sabbah but have gone to seek solace with Jo at the palace. I dashed to the bedroom and wrenched open the drawer into which we had tossed our passports and air tickets on arrival. But Ashley's passport and ticket were gone and I knew that my hope had been born of desperation. Ashley would never play games, there could be no doubt that she was aboard the aircraft which I had watched shrink into the sunset sky.

I sat on the bed and for a couple of minutes my eyes were dangerously close to spilling. My indignation that Ashley had read the manuscript against my wishes and drawn the wrong conclusion was replaced by an overwhelming sense of loss. Since I had fallen in love with her she had become part of my life. I had seen us going into the future together. I had believed that some generous destiny was about to make up for what I had missed during the long years of my marriage – and now, nothing!

As I sat in that hot room with a swarm of insects swirling about the light bulb and cicadas chirping from the carobs I was engulfed by a wave of utter loneliness. Then my eyes did spill over.

* * *

'Please. You wake. The king. Please.'

The maid's words dragged me back from blessed oblivion just as it seemed I had entered it.

'Please. Very little time.'

I opened one eye and was amazed at the intensity of the midday light streaming through the window.

'Driver in hurry,' she continued as I hastily closed it again. 'You have to meet King Syed.'

I remembered that today Syed wanted to take me to his college site, but it would be impossible. Last night's brandy had proved too much for even my seasoned frame.

I shook my head, then regretted it.

'Please. Driver must hurry or he get trouble. You get up. OK?'

A thought began to form. If I was to accept Syed's offer and the release from financial pressure that went with it, I should co-operate when he was eager to show me the project that was so dear to his heart. To turn down his invitation on account of a hangover would be not only churlish but stupid.

Luckily the maid must have had experience of others in the guest house who had looked upon the wine when it was red. She proffered a glass of water in which ice cubes tinkled thunderously.

First I would deal with dehydration and then search for the painkillers which Ashley had been using since her accident. The maid brought another glass, and I carefully put my legs over the side of the bed and thrust myself into a sitting position. For a moment I had the sensation one experiences when a yacht heels into the wind, and then when everything had steadied again I said, 'Tell the driver I'll be ready in ten minutes. OK?'

'OK. Coffee OK?'

'OK.'

Feeling very un-OK I dragged myself to the bathroom where I showered and shaved in tepid water and then pulled on fresh clothing with quivering hands. Strong Arabian coffee helped to steady them and I managed to make it to where the Rolls waited in the sparse shade of the carob trees.

As soon as I was inside and savouring the air-conditioning the driver accelerated away in the direction of the Abdulla Highway, and while he swung the great car round flocks and caravans, fragments of the previous night returned ... the half bottle of Courvoisier I had drunk to dull the pain, Ashley's letter full of indignant exclamation marks.

My morbid introspection was halted as the car pulled up within the crenellated courtyard of the palace. I climbed out, very slowly, as a line of olive-uniformed guards presented their old bolt-action rifles. Then the slapping of hands on stocks heralded the appearance of Syed, who looked rather Rumanian in a military uniform. Jo followed him down the stairs from the royal apartments, and greeted me coldly.

'Off we go,' the king said. 'I'm dying for you to see the progress we've made. We're going to have the dedication ceremony today, which is why I'm so pleased that you're here. Sorry Ashley won't be with us. Jo told me . . . but you two will get together again *insh'allah.*

Jo's expression told me that she did not share the king's optimism. Ash had obviously confided in her before she left.

With an outrider on a Triumph motorcycle – a collector's item in Britain – leading the way, and a jeep with a mounted machine-gun shadowing us, the Rolls left the palace and threaded its way through narrow streets and bustling squares to the port, where sea-going dhows and fishing vessels clustered at the quay or lazily chafed at their moorings. Here we turned and followed a coast road to a low headland where a collection of half-finished buildings reared against the sky.

'You see, I have placed my college on the most pleasant vantage point in the kingdom,' said Syed. 'What views my lecturers and students will enjoy. Broad vistas encourage mental expansion.'

The car climbed a winding road to the top of the headland and drew up on a bulldozed area which would ultimately be the campus. A crowd of men in both Arab and European dress were waiting to greet the king, while behind a line of soldiers building workers waved and cheered and a few even dared to whistle when Jo climbed out from the car. Syed turned to me with a beaming smile.

'It should be ready by the end of the year,' he said.

When we reached a graceful archway, the central feature of the complex, there was consternation. A line of Arabic graffiti had been daubed on it so recently that dribbles of red paint were still trickling down the snowy marble.

An officer sent soldiers off in search of the perpetrators, the anger of the official party rose to a climax and only the king retained his usual demeanour.

'Rather like the writing on the wall at Nebuchadnezzar's feast,' he said to me. 'Only this reads "Death to the Great Satan". One of the workmen with fundamentalist connections must have painted it. Very clever of him. I am assured that it was not there ten minutes ago. However, the dogs bark but the caravan moves on.'

He repeated this in Arabic and there was a round of applause and cheering from the construction workers.

With Jo walking aloofly beside me I went painfully with the others through the arch and into a courtyard where a shrouded block of black marble was suspended in a crane sling a couple of feet above the ground.

An *imam* intoned a prayer and Syed gave a short speech in Arabic, after which the crane rattled into life. Amidst more applause the king centred the block over its base and guided it into position as it was gently lowered. Then, with a dramatic gesture, he snatched away the plain cotton covering and we pressed forward to read the inscriptions. The top one had been incised in beautiful Arabic calligraphy, the lines below were an English translation which read,

This college,
for the benefit of the people of Abu Sabbah, is dedicated to
the glorious memory of
KING HAMID III who died a martyr's death as was the
will of the Almighty.
'Drink at the fountain of knowledge and honour his
memory'

'Is the wording all right?' Syed asked as the Danish architect led us off on a tour of inspection.

'Splendid,' I answered, 'I like the "fountain of knowledge". It was an ancient belief that truth was to be found in a sacred fountain or well.'

'So Jo told me,' he said with a smile, and went ahead to walk with the architect.

'And not only at the bottom of wells,' remarked Jo as we turned into a long passage between two walls of brick. 'It sometimes turns up in very odd places – like on a computer screen.'

I did not answer. Hangover sweat beaded my face and I feared that at any moment the world would tilt and I would go reeling. And then the world did tilt.

An explosion cracked in our ears. I looked up and saw a pall of dirty smoke dimming the sky between the two walls, and then the wall on our right took on the graceful curve of a wave about to break and for a mad instant I was reminded of Gaudi's architecture.

I turned to Jo and flung her through one of the door-less doorways in the left hand wall. There was a series of concussions as a rattle of hysterical shooting cut through the tinnitus of screaming. Then the wave broke. I tried to follow Jo as thousands of bricks cascaded into the passage.

* * *

'Allahu akbar! Allahu akbar! La illaha ill' Allah! La illaha Hi'Allah!'

The plangent prayer drew me from my dream state and I opened my eyes to look out of a lattice casement whose sill was level with my bed. It was like a frame for an illustration from one of those suede-bound copies of Omar Khayyam. Silhouetted against a sky of layered lavender and rose was a minaret from whose circular balcony a *muezzin* called the faithful to the sunset prayers.

I found that, like the *muezzin,* I seemed to be wearing a turban. Remembering that the mosque stood beside the royal palace I deduced that I must be a guest of the king, though why this should be I was too enervated to comprehend.

Somewhere a woman spoke softly in Arabic. There was a rustle of draperies and when I opened my eyes again I saw Jo between me and the window, her face in shadow. .

'The nurse just told me you've come round,' she said. 'Don't panic. You're not badly hurt. Some bricks caught you and the doctor gave you an injection so you wouldn't feel too shitty when you woke up. You'll have a headache and a sore back and legs for two or three days, but nothing permanent.'

'Syed?'

'He's all right – at least physically. He and the architect had left the passage when the wall collapsed. He'll be along to see you as soon as he gets back. At the moment there's a state of emergency.'

'Who planted the bombs?'

'We think that some members of a fundamentalist group infiltrated the workforce. The charges had been placed with great care, nearly all the college is rubble now. It's a terrible blow to Syed.'

'You mean there were bombs all over the site?' I said when I had digested this.

'They went off one after another. I guess their timing was a bit out. Even so at least half a dozen people were killed and quite a few hurt. And that brings me to the gratitude bit. If you hadn't shoved me through that door I'd still be under a ton of bricks. I've got to thank you for my life. And I guess I was being rather rough on you before it happened.'

'Seeing it from Ash's point of view I can understand how you felt about me. But I could say that if Ash had really loved me she would have given me the chance to explain. Perhaps she felt that things were not working out and subconsciously welcomed the opportunity for the break. After all, the age difference . . .'

'That's crap,' said Jo.

I could have gone on to explain that perhaps my role had been to exorcise the ghost of a dead love, but I did not want to talk any more.

'I'll leave you to rest,' said Jo, sensing my ebb of energy. 'Thanks again for the rest of my life.'

She left and for a long time I gazed at the graceful minaret against the darkening sky, savouring the realization that I was lucky to be alive. In comparison with this wonderful fact my present problems were petty.

The king visited me an hour later. He looked strained and his uniform was still stained with brick dust, and he began by thanking me for saving Jo, although in truth that had not been heroic but merely a reflex action.

'Praise Allah that you were right behind her when the wall collapsed,' he said. 'The archway shielded you from the worst of it. They're still using a JCB to search for bodies under the rubble. Unhappily Zahir Khaled is among the dead. And my college is razed.'

'You are going to build again?'

'Of course. I owe it to the memory of my brother. I owe it to the next generation of my people. But next time there will be more security. Our friends from the Gulf will not be able to engineer this a second time.'

'You know who was responsible, then?'

'Oh yes. We caught several suspects and a couple have already confessed.' He smiled thinly. 'I am sorry that I can no longer offer you a post in the college until it is rebuilt. Perhaps, though, you will consider coming out again when it has risen like the phoenix from its ashes?'

'Perhaps,' I said.

'For as long as I – or the heir I am to have – retains the throne of this country you will be honoured here. Not only did you save the woman I love but you saved the succession.'

168

In the faint light I could see that Syed's eyes were moist.

'Congratulations,' I said.

'Oh, what a propitious day it was when our paths crossed at Radio City. Wonderful are the ways of God. If it had not been for that meeting the JCB might be digging out the corpse of my wife at this moment. It is traditional that the Abbasides reward those who have served their House. Jonathan, what can I do that will enrich your life?'

Forty thousand quid would sort things out very nicely, an irreverent voice chimed in my head, but aloud I assured Syed that the fact that Jo and her newly conceived child were safe was reward enough in itself.

'But you must have the grace to receive . . . please take this. It is a trifle, but it carries my gratitude and can be redeemed for a royal favour at any time in the future.'

From his finger he screwed off a heavy ring representing the head of a leopard, the emblem of Abu Sabbah, with ruby eyes. He pressed it into my hand.

Four days later I was ready to return to England by the next flight from Abu Sabbah.

Chapter 18

I arrived at Gatwick Airport in the late afternoon, and was thankful when the courtesy bus deposited me at the long-term car park and I could sink into the well upholstered seat of my car. My legs were aching badly where the bricks caught me, and as well as the blow to the head which had rendered me unconscious, several bricks had struck my back leaving livid patches of bruising, the pain of which I kept at bay with analgesic tablets provided by the royal doctor.

Because of the stiffness in my legs, coupled with the fatigue of the ten-hour flight, I was grateful that the car was an automatic as I left the airport and headed on to the motorway system which would take me most of the way to Lychett Matravers and Whispering Corner. After the heat and the harsh light of the tiny Red Sea kingdom I would have been in a mood to savour the variegated greens of the English summer landscape in normal circumstances but I was in no mood to appreciate nature. My feelings about returning to Whispering Corner were very mixed.

On one hand I knew that arriving there would place me back in the thick of financial problems, and that every part of the house would be a painful reminder of my brief days with Ashley. On the other hand I had loved that eccentric old house from the first, and it had come to represent home despite the haunting and the effect that had had upon me.

By the time I was passing the Rufus Stone in the New Forest the sky in the west was changing dramatically.

Although large patches of the landscape were still brightly lit by late afternoon sunlight, others darkened as sombre banks of nimbostratus materialized ahead of me. I was insulated from the world by steel and safety glass, but I could well imagine the hush portending the storm. A flicker of lightning – too distant for me to hear its thunder – danced along the edge of the cloud and I guessed that by the time I reached my destination the sluices of heaven would have opened. And I had a vivid memory of how it was in such a storm that Ashley had come into my life.

I was right. As I turned into the lane leading to Whispering Corner I was driving through a curtain of rain, and lightning flashes were appearing like brief galaxies through the heavy foliage of the wood. When I pulled up at the bottom of the drive Whispering Corner looked wildly dramatic, its windows mirroring cold blue flames, its steep roofs gleaming with rainwater and its gargoyles animated by the interplay of light and shadow. What puzzled and alarmed me was that the door leading into the kitchen area appeared to be swinging open.

'Oh no!' I exclaimed. That was all I needed – to find I had been burgled on top of everything else! I think I was actually swearing aloud as I limped past the overgrown mythical beasts. My clothing was wet through by the time I entered the kitchen and reached for the light switch to learn the worst.

Probably as a result of the storm the house was without electricity, so I had to rely on an old torch and the almost continuous lightning illuminating the rooms like disco lights. Everything seemed to be in order in the kitchen, and in the dining-room where I had several watercolours which had been in my family since Victorian times.

In the living-room there was no sign of an intruder, nor in my bedroom, and I began to hope that the Reverend Gotobed had inadvertently left the back door ajar after paying one of his promised visits to feed Mrs Foch. I began to relax, until I entered my study.

Once again I saw that my occult reference books had been scattered over the floor and this time many of the covers, including a valuable edition of the *Daemonologie,* had been wrenched from their spines. Then I noticed that on my desk the shape of a cross had been crudely scored.

Being a book-lover since childhood my first concern was for the books, and I knelt painfully to see if some of my particularly prized volumes had escaped. Whoever had attacked them had done so in a frenzy, many not only had their covers torn off but pages ripped out and then torn again. Depressed and angry I hauled myself to my feet, holding the remains of a once leather-bound volume of *The Golden Bough.*

After the manifestations I had witnessed in the house, culminating in the exploding glass at the séance, I was prepared to accept that in the past my books had been strewn by a poltergeist. But somehow I found it hard to imagine an elemental force pulling out pages and tearing them into scraps of paper, this destruction had the hallmark of human hands.

Hoddy!

My earlier suspicion of him returned. With his childhood belief that Miss Constance was the witch in the wood, this simple-minded fellow, who had had ample opportunity to see my books when he was doing odd jobs about the place, might have decided to perform some sort of exorcism on my 'devil's library', as I had heard him describe my shelves of reference books.

I looked again at the symbol cut on my desk and I was more than ever convinced that a human agency was responsible for the destruction. And I wondered if the intruder had roamed through my house looking for other objects to vent his righteous anger upon. Then another thought occurred, that he might still be somewhere in the house.

Forgetting in my anger that Hoddy – if indeed it was he – was half my age and considerably stronger, I left my study and began to search the house. Each time I passed a light switch I turned it on in the hope that the electricity had been restored, but the house remained an eerie mixture of darkness and flashgun illumination. I entered the room which I always thought of as Miss Constance's parlour and found that her father's telescope had been knocked over. As I swept the beam of my torch over it I saw something white and fluffy lying in the worn carpet, something that reminded me of a prize at carnival sideshows, a furry caterpillar to make the girls shriek. When I picked it up I saw that it was part of a cat's tail.

Mrs Foch's tail.

As I stood there holding it in front of my torch the lights suddenly went on. Looking down at the spot from where I had picked up the tail I saw a deep gash in the carpet which I guessed had been made by the axe blow that severed it. From here a trail of blood spots led me downstairs to the cellar entrance. The door was partly open and I guessed Mrs Foch had fled down the steps to hide. I went through the doorway and rubbed my hand over the roughly plastered wall until it encountered the old-fashioned brass switch, and when I pressed it the old bulb threw its yellow rays into the gloom. I cursed that I had not thought to replace it with a modern high-powered light, but I suppose the truth was that I had not particularly wanted to return, especially since I had an uncomfortable idea of what might have been buried there.

Now, however, the adrenalin of the indignant householder was surging through my system, and I was anxious about Mrs Foch.

There was no sign of the cat. Dark spots on the dusty steps showed that she had sought sanctuary in the cellar, but there were dozens of places where she could have gone to earth. I went down the stairs a foot at a time, each downward step reminding me painfully of the blows my legs had received.

At the bottom I saw that the blood trail led across the filthy floor to the smaller wine cellar. I did not know to what extent a cat's tail bleeds when severed, but the spots which had brought me this far were so plentiful that I wondered if the unfortunate animal had received any other injury.

On reaching the second cellar I pushed its heavy door as far as I could to one side and swept the tunnel-like recess with my torch. There were some old crates and a broken basket – an Edwardian picnic case – stacked at the far end, and it seemed the only place where the cat could have taken refuge was behind them.

'Hey cat,' I called softly.

I was answered by a faint mewing. Because Ashley had worked so hard at rehabilitating her, Mrs Foch had come to trust us. I hoped it would not be too difficult to coax her out and drive her to a veterinary surgeon.

It was very cold and quiet in the old wine cellar, almost too quiet after the thunderclaps which had shaken the house after each lightning flash. I suddenly felt uneasy, I could not stop myself wondering if the fragile bones of an unwanted infant lay beneath the hard clay floor. 'Come on, Mrs Foch,' I called, anxious to leave this place. The hidden creature responded with more pitiful mewing and I was about to step forward to pull the boxes away when there was a crash that echoed through both cellars. It was not thunder but the slamming of the door at the top of the cellar steps. I turned and looked past the wine cellar entrance, and saw Hoddy descending.

In one hand the young man held a brass cross which I recognized as having once stood on the altar of St Mary's Church, in the other he carried a small hatchet. His face was expressionless.

'Hoddy, what the hell do you mean ... ' I shouted. He turned his gaze on me and at that moment I wished I had remained quiet. The anger that had sustained me drained away. There is nothing like the sight of a man following one into a gloomy cellar with a hatchet in his hand to change a feeling of outrage into one of apprehension. Yet when he spoke there was nothing to suggest menace in his pleasant Dorset accent.'

'Mr Northrop. I didn't know you'd be home today.'

'Then why are you here?' I asked, remaining in the doorway of the wine cellar.

'There was something I had to do, Mr Northrop,' he replied.

'Like try and kill my cat!'

'Weren't your cat, Mr Northrop,' he said. 'Damn witch's cat, that. And if you look in the Bible it says suffer not a witch to live.'

'Look, Hoddy,' I said, 'if you've got it in your head that poor old Miss Constance was a witch, forget it. She's been dead for over a year.' He paused on the bottom step.

'Her cat ain't dead . . . yet. And things – bad things – are still around, Mr Northrop. I learned that working here. Maybe you can't understand, coming from the city an' all. And maybe you made things worse by bringing them books into the house and writing them things you do. Paid for one of your paperback books in the village – second hand – and it were right wicked.'

'This isn't the time to talk about books,' I said, trying to sound reasonable. 'You've been upset by the storm. Why not go home and . . . and have a cup of tea?' I added lamely.

'It's not like that, Mr Northrop. I got things to do here. The vicar don't believe me so I got to do it myself. There's evil here. Like you burying that baby ... '

I suddenly felt sick as I had an inkling of what was happening.

'And there's more to it than that, ain't it so?' he continued. 'What about that poor wife of yours? You saw her off on her sickbed ... '

'Tell me, Hoddy, how do you know all this?' I asked as coolly as I could. 'Are you sure you haven't made a mistake?'

'It come into my mind like,' he said almost conversationally. 'See, I'm different to other folks, and things come into my mind and I know they're true. Sometimes they're all jumbled, like voices whispering things I can't quite hear, and sometimes I'm told things clear as a church bell.'

'Hoddy!'

'Since I been here I been told things about you. I didn't know at first – thought you was a nice gentleman when you gave me work here – but now I know there's bad inside you. You must have got it from your mother. She were bad – that's why she did herself in. Know why she did it? I do.'

My legs went weak and I clung to the door to stop myself sliding to the floor.

Hoddy chuckled.

'Your ma weren't faithful to your dad, were she? It were all right for a while but when her boyfriend wouldn't have anything more to do with her, when she was in the club like, well ... '

'Bloody lies!' I shouted. 'But you're right about something evil being here – and it's affecting you – Get out! Get out before something dreadful happens!'

'Can't stand talking all day,' said Hoddy conversationally. It seemed he had not heard my outburst. 'Got things to do.' He began to walk across the cellar. 'Got to finish off that damn cat, and then I'll see about you, Sir Richard ... '

I slammed the door of the wine cellar shut and summoned up all my strength to push the rusted bolt into place. Fortunately the door had been made from solid oak planks and the iron bolt was massive. For the moment I was safe from the madman.

There was a knock at the door, not heavy, just the sort of knock you'd make at the door of a house where you'd been invited to supper. Whatever else had happened to Hoddy, he had not lost his natural politeness.

I leaned against the door feeling weak from my bruises, the long journey and the realization of what was happening at Whispering Corner. The medium had been utterly wrong when she said that the phenomena at the séance signalled the end of the hauntings. They had merely been the end of the first phase. Now the power behind the manifestations was ready for something more positive than parlour tricks. It was anxious to make its word flesh, and Hoddy who, as the vicar had said, walked to the beat of a different drum – was its first choice as host.

'Mr Northrop.'

Hoddy's voice was muffled through the oak. He knocked again and I ignored him.

Looking back on the manifestations which had occurred at Whispering Corner it seemed to me that the force, for want of a better word, was rather like a battery. It used its energy in a quick burst and then there was a lull while it recharged. The difference was that each time it recharged it was more powerful, and I remembered Warren Turner and his talk about ley lines, Could it be that Whispering Corner was at the centre of a mysterious conflux which provided energy for the malign phenomena?

Such thoughts flashed through my mind before I had recovered enough to consider my situation. I was in a dark cellar with a deranged man wielding a hatchet on the other side of the door, apart from the two of us the house was deserted – by human beings at least – so there was no one to whom I could look for help.

'I don't know what to do!' I heard myself mutter.

To my surprise there was a response to my words, a low mew. Then something brushed against my legs. I reached down, touched the soft fur of Mrs Foch and picked her up. As I automatically stroked her I felt the stickiness which had bled from her severed tail. There appeared to be no other wound and she seemed glad to be picked up, probably recognizing my familiar scent, and managed an attempt at purring.

'Good cat,' I whispered and realized that, ridiculous as it may seem writing it now, I felt better for her company.

Then, as though the attention I paid to Mrs Foch sparked a telepathic link with Hoddy, he called through the door, 'Mr Northrop, you ain't got nothing to be afraid about. Just let me in to deal with that damn witch cat and that'll be the end of the problem.'

'But you just told me I buried a baby down here,' I replied, to find out what his reaction would be.

'That be daft, Mr Northrop,' he said with a chuckle. 'What a daft notion. I never said no such thing.'

There was a long silence. I continued to stroke Mrs Foch and racked my brains for some plan of escape, but all I came up with was the thought that nothing lasts for ever and sooner or later the circumstances would change – I just hoped that I would still be around when they did. What worried me was that even if it appeared that Hoddy had gone away I dare not open the door in case he was waiting in the shadows with his hatchet.

Time passed. It was probably only a few minutes but in the dark it seemed to stretch like elastic and I had an absurd flash vision of Salvador Dali's melting watches.

'You there, Mr Northrop?'

The muffled voice was still . . . respectful is the word I can best use to describe it. It was just like the old Hoddy asking what colour I wanted a particular room painted.

'Of course,' I answered.

'What are we doing, Mr Northrop? I don't like it down here. Never did like this old cellar. Don't know why I'm down here.'

I realized it was the old Hoddy speaking, and I wondered if the 'battery' of the entity which had possessed him was running down. This thought suggested an avenue of escape.

'I can't come out because the bolt is jammed,' I told him. 'You go and fetch the vicar. He'll know what to do. Tell him to bring someone with him,' I added as I realized that I might be putting Henry in jeopardy. 'It'll take several men to break down this door.'

'That's right,' Hoddy agreed. 'Be a strong old door.'

'Be quick then,' I said. It's not very nice in here. And seeing that it's evening we'll say that you're on overtime.'

Overtime had always been a magical word in Hoddy's vocabulary and he answered that he'd be off right away and I wasn't to worry.

I slid down to the floor. My legs had been trembling and it was a relief to sit.

'Bye, Mr Northrop.'

Hoddy's voice was fainter, as though he was already ascending the cellar steps.

Now it was just a matter of waiting, or I hoped it was. I would face up to the cause of the situation when I was free.

On my knee Mrs Foch began to lick her bloodied fur. Weariness filled me, my eyes felt more comfortable closed, my head drooped and drooped again.

It was the crash of the hatchet striking the door of the wine cellar that jolted me back to cold reality. There was another blow, followed by a splintering sound.

'You come out of there, Sir Richard bloody Elphick,' Hoddy shouted on the other side. 'Don't you think I don't know what you're a-burying in there! And if you won't come out I'll soon have this door down and then you'll pay , . .'

His words were drowned by a tattoo of blows. The force dragging him into past horrors had recharged.

At the first sound of Hoddy's axe striking the door Mrs Foch leapt away, spitting, to hide among the old crates at the far end of the cellar. I climbed to my feet and began to fumble in the darkness in search of a weapon. As I groped along the filthy shelves I wondered how long I had before the door gave way. Hoddy was a very muscular young man and I guessed he would be aiming his blows at some vulnerable spot. I had perhaps twenty minutes before we came face to face.

To begin with I had heard him damning Sir Richard Elphick, but as his onslaught continued his muffled words changed to grunts of effort. I was almost relieved when I failed to lay my hand on an old bottle or a forgotten hammer. It would take a very hard blow to stop Hoddy, provided I was lucky enough to get it in, and the thought of the injury such a blow could cause, the possibility that I might end up with a corpse in my cellar, made me literally shiver.

I could not remember feeling so weary, and I once more slid to a sitting position to watch for a chink of light in the door to warn me that I would soon be confronting – a newspaper headline popped into my mind – the mad axeman.

It occurred to me, not for the first time, that it was like being a character in one of my own novels. I felt an inane sympathy for my poor creations – how I had put them through it! Did God feel like that after the Battle of the Somme? My mind was flitting from absurdity to absurdity while all the time the beat of Hoddy's hatchet vibrated through the confined space. And then I suddenly knew what I had to do.

Once more I got to my feet, consoling myself with the thought that whatever was to happen in the next minute at least I was taking the initiative. I would not be like some poor hunted animal gone to earth while the huntsmen bring up the terriers.

I groped my way to the end of the cellar, picked up a crate and positioned it at a short distance from the door, then placed another on top of it. Next I flattened myself against the wall and concentrated on the rhythm of Hoddy's blows. Once I got the timing I planned to act on the count of three.

One! A blow delivered.

Two! In my mind's eye I saw Hoddy's massive arms take the hatchet back above his shoulder for the next stroke.

Three! I pulled back the bolt.

The door swung wide.

As I stood to one side. I saw, in the dim cellar light, the hatchet flash into view, followed by the dark shape of Hoddy. Having swung a great stroke through the empty air he reeled forward off-balance and tripped over the crates.

With adrenalin giving me a burst of new life, I swung round the door and pulled it shut with the idea of fastening it after me. But as Hoddy had made short work of the outside catch there was nothing for it except to run. Half way across the cellar I collided with a stool and went down on all fours.

Behind me I heard the wine cellar door crash open.

Up again, I reached the steps.

Hoddy's shadow seemed to overtake mine on the once whitewashed wall. I tensed for the impact of the hatchet. Then, like some marvellous piece of legerdemain, the door ahead of me opened, and bright light streamed down. Someone shouted to me, pulled me through, slammed the door and turned the key in the lock.

'What the hell's going on?' demanded Warren Turner.

'Hell's going on,' I muttered. 'First things first. Let's get a brandy.'

'How about that drongo I saw chasing you with an axe?'

'He'll keep while I have a drink.'

'You look dreadful. Your face . . ,'

'That was from last week.'

'I know. Saw it in a newspaper . . . British Author Saves Arabian Queen. That's good for a few laughs.'

While we were talking, almost incoherently, Warren took my arm and led me to the living-room. I slumped on the sofa while he poured me a generous Courvoisier, and on second thoughts decided to join me. The sound of the hatchet striking wood echoed through the house.

'Your mate sounds lively. Shouldn't we do something?'

'Yes,' I said. 'He's had a sort of brainstorm. Could you go to the vicarage and get Henry to phone Dr Valentine and ask him to come urgently. He probably knows Hoddy anyway.'

'Leave it to me,' he said. 'How about you?'

'I'm starting to feel better.' It was true, the brandy was working its old magic.

'Supposing he chops his way out?'

'It'll take him a while,' I said. 'The doors in this house are pretty solid.'

'See you, then.'

Beneath his healthy tan I could see that the young Australian was flushed with excitement.

As soon as he was gone I had another brandy, then lay back on the sofa and closed my eyes. There would be plenty of time for explanations. At this moment I was savouring the fact that I was still alive, that I wasn't lying on the dirty cellar floor with my skull split open. Soon there would be a lot of things to be done, but this was the eye of the cyclone and even the sound of the hatchet did not disturb my moment of peace while alcohol pushed back my aches and pains.

Half an hour later the lights of a car swept across the garden and Dr Valentine arrived in his cherished old Rover.

'Evening, Henry,' he greeted the vicar. He nodded to Warren and turned to me. 'You look as though you've been in the wars. Those bruises are too mature for Hoddy's handiwork.'

'They're a week old,' I explained.

'It was in the papers , . . "Horror Writer Braves Blast To Rescue Queen",' said Henry.

'First things first,' said Dr Valentine. 'Is Hoddy still in your cellar?'

'Yes,' I said. 'He's been quiet for the last twenty minutes.'

'Henry said he took an axe to you.'

I nodded.

'Poor fellow.' For a moment I thought he was being sympathetic to me, then realized he was referring to Hoddy. Which, it occurred to me, was quite right.

The doctor opened his case, took out a hypodermic syringe and fitted a phial of colourless liquid into the barrel.

'From what Henry told me I judged it necessary to call an ambulance,' he said with a sigh. 'But I won't wait for it. I don't like the fact that you haven't heard anything. The unfortunate lad may have done something . . .' His voice trailed off as I led the way to the cellar door.

'I blame myself for this,' said Henry. 'I should have realized he was heading for a breakdown. He's been saying some rather strange things lately – wanted me to conduct a service of exorcism at Whispering Corner, of all things. He seemed obsessed by that white cat of Miss Constance's.'

Exorcism! I thought. *In that respect he had been right.*

At the cellar door I stood not quite sure of what to do next. When I opened it a hatchet-waving Hoddy might burst upon us.

'Come on, man,' said Dr Valentine brusquely.

I turned the key in the lock and stepped aside. Dr Valentine, with a confidence gained through years of dealing with the unexpected as a country GP, walked down the steps. At one glance I saw that the 'battery' of the entity which had taken control of Hoddy was exhausted again. The young handyman was standing stock still in the middle of the cellar. He had not bothered to brush back the lank lock of hair which obscured his right eye and I saw the glisten of tears on his blanched cheeks.

He made no movement when Dr Valentine touched him on the shoulder or a moment later when he smoothly injected tranquillizer into his upper arm.

'Hoddy, it's not very nice down here,' said the doctor kindly. 'Come upstairs with me, there's a good chap.'

He took his arm and without a word or change in his blank expression Hoddy allowed himself to be led upstairs. The rain-streaked French windows reflected eerie blue flashes from the ambulance which had just edged down the drive. Dr Valentine spoke briefly with the driver and his mate and Hoddy, wrapped in one of my blankets, was taken away.

'I'll have to follow to see about getting him admitted,' Dr Valentine told us. 'He's certainly in some sort of deep trauma – I just hope he pulls round. Be a lousy life for him in some institution. I suppose I should see his old mum . . .'

'Leave that to me,' said Henry. 'I'll go and tell her that he's a bit unwell and has had to go to hospital.'

'Good. I'll go and see her in the morning when I know something more definite.' He turned to me. 'You'd better come to the surgery tomorrow so I can check you out. Understandably, you look a bit rough.'

'Only bruises,' I said.

'Nevertheless.' And he went out to his car to follow the diminishing blue flashes.

Chapter 19

That night I had to talk to somebody, and I talked to Warren.

After the ambulance had left he made strong black coffee and toast and we sat together in the living-room listening to the soughing of the wind-harried trees and the hiss of raindrops whirled against the glass panes.

'You certainly turned up like the US cavalry,' I said. 'I think Hoddy would have caught me on the steps if you hadn't opened the door and pulled me through. What good fortune led you here?'

'I came back a couple of days ago after my tour round Cornwall,' he said. 'I saw some of the sites that were in your film *The Dancing Stones* – the Merry Maidens and the Hurlers and the Men-an-Tol – isn't that weird'? Anyway, I was going to take up your offer of having another week or two at Whispering Corner, only to find the place shut up. I went and saw the Rev. and he told me that you'd taken off for the Middle East, and that I was welcome to stay at the vicarage for a few days. A very hospitable bloke, Henry.'

'Very kind,' I agreed, thinking of the trouble he had taken to bring me Mary Lawson's 'Narration'.

'Tonight I was coming up Church Walk – I'd been doing a spot of decorating in the church vestry as a thank you to Henry – when I saw that your lights were on. I came round and got a bit worried when I found the door swinging in the wind – and when I came in to take a look round I heard a sort of knocking sound coming from the cellar. I thought maybe you'd got accidentally locked in – until I opened the door and saw the axeman after you. Now it's your turn. I'm dying to hear about your adventures in Abu-wherever-it-was . . .'

'Warren,' I said. 'Is there really anything in that stuff you were telling me about ley lines?'

'I think so.'

'Do you think that places reputed to be haunted are most likely to be at sites where a number of these lines intersect?'

'That's the theory,' he said. 'Maybe people experience a time slip at such places – you know, a moment from the past overlaying the present. Perhaps that's the explanation for ghosts.'

'And Whispering Corner? You said once you had an idea that lines joined up here.'

'Right. I checked it out on an Ordnance Survey map and it's an amazing example. There must be half a dozen leys joining up here. There's a very powerful one that comes up from Lychett Minster . . . I can show you on the map.'

'I'll take your word for it. So this place would be more likely to have psychic phenomena than other places?'

'Right. Remember once we were talking about how ghostly voices were supposed to give this place its name, and I mentioned then that maybe ley lines had something to do with it? Why all the interest? I think you're the biggest sceptic I've ever met, which is funny . . . '

'. . . considering the sort of novels I write,' I concluded for him. 'The thing is, Warren, I've had to readjust my ideas.'

And so I told him the story of the increasingly odd happenings that had occurred since I had taken up residence in the house, the jumbled voices in the beginning, the instance of someone breathing beside me, the sound of a crying baby that led me into the cellar and the vision of murder in the library. I was still too emotionally off-balance over Ashley to talk about her so I omitted to describe the sheet figure. Again without mentioning her I told Warren about the dramatic séance and finally how Hoddy had been possessed so that he saw me as an eighteenth century murderer.

'This takes some believing,' Warren said as I finished. 'You know I'm into ley lines and the occult, but . . . not that I don't think you're telling the truth,' he added hastily. 'It's just so extraordinary. And there seems to be no rhyme or reason behind it.'

'Ah, but there is,' I said, and I went on to tell him about the 'Narration'. 'Mary Lawson experienced the same sort of thing two hundred years ago. I'll get her account for you to read tonight,' I said, and went to fetch it from my study.

'Here we are,' I said on my return. *'Notes on the Experiences of the Lawson Family in the House of Colonel Elphick in the Wood on the Edge of Lychett Village.'*

Warren took it eagerly. 'This is like being a character in one of your novels,' he said.

'The thought has crossed my mind,' I said.

I poured us a brandy each while Warren glanced at the first page.

'Of course it doesn't explain everything, but I suppose the supernatural never has been explained and that's what fascinates people about it,' I said. 'The same with religion. It's the mystery which makes it work. Once a computer comes up with the equation for God, the Pope can hang up his triple crown and all the wonder will go out of the world.'

'I'd got the impression that you were anti-religion.'

'I tried very hard to be, although I never lose my respect for what religion has inspired – art, music and learning. It's just that I wanted it to work the way I wanted it to work, and it can't be like that.'

'I wonder if the lady who had Whispering Corner before you

was troubled by ghosts?'

'Probably not,' I said. 'She spent all her life here, her ghosts were of a different kind, the ghosts of the lost generation. It seems to me that if you're right about the ley line business it acts as a sort of catalyst that from time to time creates a climate for psychical phenomena which under normal conditions would have faded with time. Thus the whispered voices of the plague refugees have been heard occasionally, and the evil generated by Sir Richard Elphick has not dispersed. There must have been anguish and evil practically everywhere at one time or another – who thinks of Tyburn Tree when they come out of the Underground at Marble Arch? but in certain spots the malady lingers on, or at least recurs from time to time. The effect is like watching a replay of something that happened long ago, and sometimes – as we've seen with Hoddy – it is actively evil.'

'At least you're getting good material out of this,' Warren said. 'But what can you do about it?'

'Bring in an exorcist,' I answered.

The next morning I awoke feeling dreadful. My body ached from its bruising in Abu Sabbah and my mind was disturbed and gloomy following nightmares inspired by the incident with Hoddy. A near scalding shower helped a little, as did the breakfast provided by Warren. While I ate, I sifted through the letters which had accumulated while I had been away. Among letters from magazines and mail order houses suggesting that I had practically won a Ferrari or a Caribbean cruise for two I recognized an envelope from Paul Lincoln and another bearing the Hermes symbol of my literary agency. But the letter I had hoped for, a note from Ashley perhaps giving me her address, was not there. I opened the agency envelope and found a card on which Sylvia Stone had scrawled 'Ring as soon as you get back!'

The letter from Paul Lincoln added not a little to my feeling of despondency.

'Sorry to send you bad tidings, but the bank absolutely refuses to consider my suggestion of regular repayments over a specified period. I don't know why they are being so harsh over this, but they are certainly out for your blood. Perhaps your partner made them so many false promises that they are taking it out on you. The fact remains that unless they are paid off immediately and in full they will take you to court as soon as they possibly can. I am afraid there is no doubt that they will get judgement against you. The time has come to brief your solicitor, as you must be represented. Meanwhile, is there any hope that the novel will be finished soon . . . '

I did not read any further. I had more urgent matters to attend to this morning.

'I'm going to the village to phone Dr McAndrew,' I told Warren.

'I must make the effort to drive to Poole and get a new mobile. Perhaps you can have another look for Mrs Foch.' Despite our efforts to find the cat the night before she had remained hidden away.

It was a relief to get out of the house and feel turf beneath my feet. The storm had worn itself out during the night, and the sky I saw through the dripping canopy of leaves was a brilliant blue. The smell of moist earth came, pleasantly to my nostrils. Small rivulets still trickled down the path and frequently a small shower of left-over raindrops caught me as the breeze shook a bough above my head.

As I left the trees I was aware of subtle changes in the landscape. Here and there hayfields had been mown. A field of wheat had changed from green to gold, while the trees on Stony Down seemed darker with the progress of summer. The scene was a delight after the aridity of Abu Sabbah.

In the phone box I dialled the Nomansland number for the modest little clergyman I had met at Radio City on the Charity Brown Show.

'McAndrew speaking.' His voice still retained a touch of an Orcadian accent from his distant boyhood.

'I'm Jonathan Northrop. You may not remember me, but . . .'

'. . . My dear boy, of course I remember you. Can I be of any help? Do you need some technical advice for one of your books? Exorcism has been rather overdone in fiction lately, I fear.'

'I certainly need help, but I'm afraid it's over something more serious than a novel.'

I explained about Whispering Corner as succinctly as I could, pausing every so often to feed more ten pence pieces into the slot.

'I'll come,' he said simply when I had finished.

There was something so matter-of-fact about those two words that I felt that lifting of spirits we get when we pass a responsibility on to someone else.

'I don't live at too great a distance from you – just across the Hampshire border,' he continued. 'If you care to drive over and pick me up we could do what has to be done today.'

'Are you sure? Such short notice . . .' In a world in which little can happen before diaries and timetables and pocket computers are consulted, I was surprised by such an immediate response.

'Since I have retired from parochial duties I have more time for my real work,' he assured me. 'And from what you tell me no time should be lost.' He then gave me directions for driving to his village and finding his cottage when I got there.

Next I dialled the Hermes Agency and was switched to Sylvia Stone.

'So you're back in one piece,' she greeted me. 'What have you been doing in Abu Simbel, or whatever the place is called? I saw a headline "Queen Jo Owes Life to Brit Horror King".'

'We got blown through a doorway together by a fundamentalist bomb,' I said.

'You should get a medal.'

'Between ourselves, I did. The Order of the Silver Leopard of Abu Sabbah First Class.'

'Do I have to call you "Sir"?'

'No, the correct form of address would be Highly Exalted – Most Exalted is reserved for those with royal blood.'

Sylvia laughed heartily and I let her go on thinking I had invented it.

'Now tell me, how has the Highly Exalted got on with his exalted novel?'

'I didn't get much done in the last week,' I admitted.

'I expect you got blown up or whatever to get yourself an excuse for late delivery, but it won't wash. I'm having more difficulties with Jocasta Mount-William. Yesterday her secretary rang to see if *Whispering Corner* is on schedule, so please tell me when I can see the script.'

'Soon.'

'That's all you ever say.' I heard her sigh over the telephone.

'It'll be all right on the night,' I said as my money ran out.

I arrived at Dr McAndrew's house just as he was returning from walking his plump Labrador, a picture of a retired country vicar with silver hair and rosy cheeks. He wore an ancient panama, an open-necked sports shirt and a creased linen jacket.

'I'll just take Boots indoors, make you some tea and we can be on our way,' he said. 'I've got my case packed.'

Inside I examined his collection of fans, his life-long hobby, and turned to his bookcase. Among his theological books I was surprised to see a copy of *Shadows and Mirrors*.

'I must get you to autograph that before you leave,' he said as he carried in two cups. 'Bought it after I met you at Radio City. I found it very interesting.'

'In what way?'

'Your characters,' he replied in his soft voice while his sea-blue eyes watched me shrewdly. 'They appear so real.'

I gave the automatic smile I use when someone compliments me on one of my novels, usually following their praise up with the remark that, books being so expensive these days, 'I always get yours from the library.'

'It was as though they had lives of their own – as though once you had breathed life into them they became independent and took over the storyline.'

185

'That's very perceptive,' I said. 'It was certainly true of Shadows. The characters did seem to follow their own destinies, and it gave me a strange feeling when they worked out an ending for themselves which was different from what I had originally envisaged.'

'I wonder what happens to characters once a book is finished?' he mused. 'Somewhere Cinderella may have found marriage to Prince Charming boring, somewhere James Bond may have retired and be writing his memoirs. Eternity must be filled with authors' creations who were not allowed to die decently in their books.'

I smiled at his notion but he appeared to be quite serious.

'Perhaps we are all characters in a novel written by an omnipotent author,' I said lightly.

'And the Word was made flesh,' he quoted. 'St John, chapter one, verse fourteen.' Then he laughed. 'Sometimes I get quite odd fancies for a clergyman,' he said.

In the car he began to question me closely on the happenings at Whispering Corner.

'Contrary to popular belief an exorcist like myself does not go around laying ghosts,' he said when I came to the end of the recital. 'That in itself would be a full-time job . . . Oh, yes,' he added when he saw my quizzical look, 'ghosts are all about us, though they're not necessarily spirits of the dead – more psychic reflections from the past.' He went on to say that he would exorcise a spectre if it was a suffering earth-bound spirit or if its manifestation had become a focus for the powers of evil.

'Another fallacy about my work is that it consists of the ceremonial casting out of demons who have taken possession of human beings,' he continued. 'In fact only a third of the exorcisms I carry out relate to people, and even then it's only after I've got a medical opinion. Some forms of possession have the same symptoms as certain mental disorders and I always want to be sure that I'm only involved in cases that medicine doesn't provide the answer for. I might add that nearly all my cases are referred to me by doctors.'

'So what's the other two-thirds of your work?'

'Black spots. That's my term for them – sites where the power of evil has built up enough to influence those who live in the area. Such zones can be very large, like the Bermuda Triangle, or merely a few hundred square feet like roads with "black spot" reputations. There are stretches of perfectly ordinary highway with no physically hazardous aspects which nevertheless are notorious for unaccountable accidents resulting in injury and death – places where survivors of crashes tell the police that the car seemed to suddenly swerve into the path of an oncoming vehicle.'

'And does exorcism work in these spots?'

He smiled and nodded. 'If it didn't I wouldn't keep being asked to perform the ministry of exorcism in such places.'

'Tell me,' I said. 'When you perform an exorcism, do you believe that you cast out an actual demon?'

'I do not believe in thousands and thousands of little imps each eager to possess someone,' he said. 'What I do believe in is the spirit of evil. Just as I believe there is a spirit of good, there is a source of evil. And I do think a tremendous harm was done when the Church ceased to preach about the Devil, because therein lies his strength – when nobody believes in the Devil he has won.'

'So what you exorcise are not ghosts or demons but what might be called the essence of evil. But why should it manifest itself, what is its motive?'

'I think it's simply power. Evil – or its personification, the Devil – has a terrible lust for power over others.'

'So you think that my house – Whispering Corner – may have become one of these places where some sort of evil power has become concentrated?'

'From what you've told me it has all the hallmarks.'

'But ghosts are involved there. I saw them.'

'They're probably just manifestations of the evil, and they suggest to me how it's increasing its power. Evil draws evil unto itself like droplets of oil coming together to make an oil slick. This could be a classic example, first the voices, then frightening phantoms, and now a simple-minded lad temporarily possessed. I would say that the next step would be for someone living in the house to become much more dangerously possessed. But I'll be able to tell you more when we get there. Now you tell me – what are you working on at the moment?'

'A novel called *Whispering Corner.*'

'Oh, dear,' he said. 'I wonder if that's wise.'

When I asked him what he meant he merely smiled and said. 'Perhaps there would be a little too much mingling of fact and fiction for my taste.' And he changed the subject.

When we arrived at the house Warren made tea for our guest, who appeared to be a tannin addict. Dr McAndrew looked about him with interest but, other than to remark that the house was architecturally unusual, he said very little.

Warren kept looking at him unobtrusively. With his interest in the mystical and arcane he was both fascinated and disappointed, here was a real live exorcist, a priest with an international reputation for dealing with the forces of evil, but he hardly looked the part. As he raised his cup he looked more likely to be about to address the Mothers' Union than wrestle with Satan. In fact I began to have slight doubts myself. Saying a prayer over a stretch of dangerous road was one thing, but

187

cleansing my home of the power that was endeavouring to possess it might be a very different matter.

But even if my hope of expert help was to be disappointed, the exercise would not be a complete loss as far as I was concerned. Already I was picturing an exorcism scene in my novel based on first-hand experience. I even decided to get my pocket tape recorder so that I would be able to get the invocation of exorcism word perfect. Dr McAndrew could be transformed into an excellent character.

For a while we sat without speaking, Warren and I feeling more and more awkward while Dr McAndrew had a second cup of tea.

'Is there an official ritual laid down for exorcism?' Warren asked to break the silence which had fallen upon us.

'I have evolved prayers that seem to suit me best, based on the ancient Mozarabic rite.' Turning to me, he added, 'It's very strange, Mr Northrop, but while I sense something malefic here, I don't get any suggestion of supernatural characters. I do sense what you might term a psychical presence – a sort of reflection from the past – but there's nothing at all malevolent about her. Indeed I get an impression of basic goodness coupled with sadness . . . perhaps the victim of some tragedy.' He paused for a minute, his eyes unfocused, giving the impression of listening for something it would be impossible for us to hear.

'Strange,' he said finally. 'Very strange. There's something here that I haven't encountered before and I must confess it puzzles me. I have absolutely no perception of Sir Richard Elphick and those unfortunate ladies associated with him. Please don't think I am doubting your word, dear boy. Each case I deal with is different – that's what makes my work so interesting, and in this one I have a blind spot. Perhaps I shall find out why in a few minutes.'

'You'll still carry out an exorcism?' I asked.

'Of course. I told you there is something malefic here. Oh, yes, no doubt about that, and unless it is stopped it will continue to grow.'

'Why?' I asked.

He shrugged. 'God moves in mysterious ways, and so does the force of evil. I think we should get on with the work now. First I'll change and then we can begin.'

'Where do you want to do it?'

'The cellar, without doubt.'

Dr McAndrew took a battered, but once-expensive, leather suitcase into the bathroom and I seized the opportunity to slip up to the study for my Pearlcorder. When I came downstairs again I saw that he had put on white vestments and a vibrant purple stole. He took two bowls from his suitcase and asked me to put some salt in one and water in the other. When I had done so he asked, 'There's no one else in the house, is there? No children or pets?'

'Certainly no children. What about Mrs Foch?' I added, turning to Warren.

'I had a good hunt for her but I couldn't find a whisker.'

'The reason I asked is that the spirit of evil waits for the opportunity to enter someone who is unsuspecting or not even aware of the nature of evil,' Dr McAndrew explained. 'When I order it to "leave this place or person" it may find refuge in anyone spiritually weak, or children and sceptics who have no defence against something they don't think exists. I've even known animals to be infected in this way. Now, lead on to the cellar.'

I opened the cellar door and switched on the light, and could not repress a shiver as the scene of my ordeal with Hoddy was illuminated by the yellow light.

Dr McAndrew led the way down the steps. In the middle of the main cellar he opened his suitcase and took out a small folding table. He laid a white cloth over it and placed a silver crucifix in the centre with a candlestick on either side. Having lit the candles he took the two bowls from me.

'Now we come to the preliminary exorcism of salt and water in order to obtain holy water for our ceremony,' he said. Making a sign of the cross over the salt he began his ancient orison, 'I exorcise thee, O creature of salt, by the living God, by the true God, by the holy God, by that God who by the Prophet Eliseus commanded thee to be cast into the water to cure its barrenness . . .'

The intonation of his voice took me back down the years to when I was an altar boy shivering at early mass.

A few moments later he turned to the other bowl.

'I exorcise thee, O creature of water, in the name of God the Father Almighty, and in the name of Jesus Christ His Son our Lord, and in the virtue of the Holy Ghost, that thou mayest by this exorcism have power to chase away all the strength of the enemy, that thou mayest be enabled to cast him out, and put him to flight with all his apostate angels . . .'

While he continued with his prayer I noticed that he was changing. His voice, usually so soft that it was frequently little more than a whisper, was strengthening by the moment until there was a ringing note of authority in it. And in the dim light his white-shrouded body stood out from the shadows in a way that suggested a hitherto unsuspected strength. Again the word authority sprang to mind.

He now took the salt and poured it on to the surface of the water in the shape of the cross,

'The symbolism is Christian because I am a Christian,' he said matter-of-factly as he approached Warren and myself. 'But I have known and co-operated with Islamic exorcists. It is a very strong vocation with them. Now for your protection.'

I felt his thumb, wet with holy water, make the traditional mark of blessing on my forehead. He did the same with Warren and then returned to his table.

After that I do not know what I had expected ... a flash of hellfire and a whiff of brimstone? There were no dramatics, no trembling victim suddenly released from a demon, no green slime vomit or other manifestations devised by an enthusiastic special effects department. And yet there was something very impressive about Dr McAndrew as he intoned a series of prayers. Warren, who was more attuned to the mystical than me, said afterwards that he could feel spiritual power emanating from the little clergyman. Perhaps.

It was certainly like a scene from a horror film, the white figure raising his arms in the dim light, the radiance from the twin candles glimmering on the silver cross, the vague menacing shapes of accumulated junk in the background, Warren and I standing like statues in the shadows, the distant mutter of thunder as another summer storm approached. I thought the latter was particularly appropriate, and made sure that my miniature tape recorder was running. Then I concentrated on memorizing the scene for future reference.

'O God, come in Thy mercy to cleanse this place, stretch forth Thy healing hand, destroy all polluting influences and cleanse the spirits of Thy children who frequent this sullied building . . .' the exorcist recited. 'Strike terror, O Lord, into the wild beast rooting up Thy vine.'

Now there was a hint of strain in the timbre of his voice, and I noticed that his hands were trembling as he picked up the bowl of holy water. Obviously something was draining him of energy, something more than the conducting of this short service. Outside, in the real world, thunder growled louder. I guessed the climax of the ritual was at hand. Dr McAndrew appeared to brace himself, and then in a powerful voice he uttered the last words of the exorcism, at the same time sprinkling drops of holy water about him.

'Begone, thou hideous demon, unto thine appointed place and return no more to plague the servants of Almighty God!'

At that moment there was the wild cry of a cat in pain and from the dark entrance to the wine cellar Mrs Foch shot out like a white fluffy cannonball. She leapt straight on to the portable altar, scattering candles and cross, and prepared herself to spring at Dr McAndrew. Her eyes blazed emerald and her red mouth was wide as she continued to screech.

I moved forward to try and prevent her from furrowing his face with her unsheathed claws. Warren was even faster and managed to grab the frantic animal from behind. At the same time Dr McAndrew flung the remainder of the holy water over her. The effect was remarkable. Mrs Foch gave vent to a scream that hurt our ears, then crumpled up as though dead in Warren's hands.

'Help me, please,' I heard Dr McAndrew mutter. I took him by the arm as he swayed alarmingly on his feet.

'I'll get you upstairs where you can lie down,' I said, and led him to the steps. When we reached the well-lit hall I was alarmed at the grey pallor of his face, and I half carried him to the sofa in the living-room.

'Tea. Plenty of sugar,' he croaked.

I hurried to the kitchen and switched on the electric kettle. Warren came in holding the limp Mrs Foch in his arms. In the daylight she was a pathetic sight. Her long white fur was filthy from hiding away in some hole in the wine cellar, blood from her dismembered tail stained her rear legs and her head hung at an unnatural angle. Her eyes appeared to have taken on the glaze that every pet-owner fears.

'She's had it,' Warren said, still stroking the dirty fur. 'Poor bloody animal. It got her just as he warned us.'

'Something certainly sent her berserk,' I agreed, the sight of the lifeless animal bringing a lump to my throat.

Remembering the other casualty, I threw a teabag into a mug and heard Warren utter an exclamation. Mrs Foch was defecating over his tartan shirt.

'She's still alive,' he cried delightedly.

'Perhaps it's just a reflex action.'

'If you'll trust me with your car I'll take her to the vet in Poole. He might pull her round with a jab or something.'

'Hold on,' I said. 'I might need it to rush Dr McAndrew to the doctor.'

I spooned an indecent amount of sugar into the mug and hurried back to the living-room.

'Don't be anxious,' Dr McAndrew said. 'An exorcism always takes it out of me – more so as the years go by. In a few minutes I'll be back to normal.'

'You sure?'

He nodded and took the mug gratefully.

I hurried back to the kitchen where Warren had laid the cat in a washing basket and tossed him the car keys.

'Say she had an accident in the woods or something,' I said. 'Don't mention exorcism to anybody.'

'Course not. I don't want people to think I'm round the twist.'

He hurried out into the garden. Fat raindrops were falling, and the lightning born of hot summer air flashed over Morden Heath and made our old windows vibrate with its thunderclaps.

'Appropriate sound effects,' commented Dr McAndrew with touch of his old wryness when I returned to him.

That evening Warren, having returned from Poole with a drugged Mrs Foch who had been given a fifty per cent chance of survival, drove Dr McAndrew home in the Peugeot. Fatigue and pain had caught up with me again and as soon as I was alone I poured a glass of Courvoisier and Perrier. The house was very quiet. The summer storm had passed quickly. I put on a Dian Derbyshire CD and her playing of Aubcr's *Etudes* continued the work of the brandy in relaxing me.

Mulling over the events of the afternoon I did not know what to think. At best the house had been cleared of an evil influence which had unaccountably returned from the past, at worst I had obtained some colourful copy which could be incorporated in *Whispering Corner*. But I had to admit to myself that there had been something unsatisfactory about the exorcism. I certainly had no doubt about the sincerity of Dr McAndrew. I knew that during his long career he had never taken a penny for his services. He worked at his singular calling because he humbly believed he had received his ability as a gift from God.

But he, too, had been puzzled. During the simple meal that Warren had prepared for us he had repeated that it was strange that apart from a sense of evil he received not a single impression of the manifestations I had described to him.

'But it couldn't have just been in my mind. Someone else experienced them with me.'

This interested him and he asked where this person was. I had no wish to mention Ashley, so I side-stepped the issue by referring vaguely to the séance. It certainly diverted his attention, the mild clergyman grew grim and muttered about fools meddling with dangers of which they had no concept.

Now, alone in the house for the first time since Ashley had moved in a lifetime ago, I tried to review my situation. As far as she was concerned I still held to the belief that something as important to us both could not be sundered so easily, I still secretly hoped for a letter from her expressing regret that she had acted so hastily ('If only there hadn't been a plane leaving that day!') and suggesting a meeting to talk things over.

Meanwhile the fate of my house seemed to depend on when the Regent Bank could get a hearing before the Queen's Bench. If their solicitors could arrange it soon – as Paul Lincoln feared – the place would have to be sold.

Now, more than ever, I would have to work on the book to the exclusion of all else. I must forget Jonathan and Ashley in favour of Falco and Lorna, I must ignore the real Whispering Corner in favour of the fictitious. Every line I typed would bring me that tiny bit closer to solving the mess that Charles Nixon had led me into.

With this thought in mind I went up to my study, and tried to focus my mind on my characters. Perhaps influenced by what had happened in Abu Sabbah, I decided that the time had come for their honeymoon period to end. Perhaps Lorna might even walk out on Falco for a while.

Why the hell should I be the only one to suffer!

Chapter 20

'I don't know why we're quarrelling like this,' Falco said in what he hoped was a reasonable tone.

'Well, if you don't know, I certainly do,' Lorna retorted.

The sun streamed through the kitchen window, the cloth on the breakfast table was pleasantly floral, the breakfast that Lorna had cooked, still un-tasted, was good enough to be photographed for a cookery magazine, so Falco had said. So how had their bitter quarrel begun? he wondered. He could not recall what had been said, what thoughtless sentence had caused it to flare up like dry brushwood ignited by a carelessly thrown match.

'I think it's perfectly reasonable to stay here,' he continued. *'It's my home. I can't just abandon it because some weird things have happened here.'*

Lorna paused in her pacing and stood looking at Falco, who sat with his elbows on the table.

'"Weird things" is putting it mildly!' she exclaimed. *'After what happened at the séance it's dangerous to stay here. Anyone would see that except you. You're besotted by this bloody place. I'm just saddened that you think more of it than of me, after what you claimed you felt for me. I don't think you care about me at all. It's true what people say about you you're a natural recluse, and as long as you're stuck away in the middle of a wood and you've got your drawings to do you're happy and sod everyone else.'*

'But we have to stay and fight this thing.'

'James, try and grow up. This place is haunted and dangerous and a leading medium has told us we should leave.'

'If we leave it'll make a better story for his memoirs, soon to be serialized in the Weekend Herald . . . '

'After all he's done to try and help us, how can you say that about XXXXX?'

I stopped typing. The XXXXX referred to the medium, the self-seeking villain of the piece who was trying to manipulate the situation at Falco's house in order to build up his reputation as a psychic. As yet I could not visualize him – in fact I hadn't even decided on a name which I felt would suit him, hence the Xs.

In Abu Sabbah I had given him a lot of thought before the explosion, but so far he remained out of focus. This did not particularly worry me, having come so far with the book I was confident that soon he would make his entrance in my imagination. At the moment my concern was with the temporary estrangement between my hero and heroine.

Falco said nothing.

'Oh, hell. I know I sound like a fishwife – whatever a fishwife sounds like,' said Lorna, sitting, down opposite him. I hate myself when I go on like that. It's symptomatic of what's happening to us. There's something here – something that has come down from the first owner, who strangled his wife – which is affecting us, killing our feelings for each other.'

'But my feelings haven't changed a bit,' Falco protested.

'In that case please humour me *... Let's get away for a bit.'*

'OK. You go away until I've got this place sorted out and then I'll join you.'

'How can you sort it out? There's only one person who can do that . . .'

'XXXXX only wants to turn Whispering Corner into another Borley Rectory – you know, the place that used to be billed as "the most haunted house in Britain". I'm going to call in an exorcist.'

'James, you've been seeing too many movies. My nerves are like violin strings, and all I want is that we go away together for a while. Surely that's not too much to ask . . .'

Falco shook his head stubbornly, 'I can't abandon Whispering Corner.'

'In that case you'll have to abandon me, because I can't stay here another night.'

'So be it.'

I stopped again. From my window I could see the postman approaching across the lawn. And suddenly I found myself running down the stairs.

'Mornin', Mr Northrop,' he greeted me as I met him on the steps leading to the French windows. 'Funny weather we're having. More thunderstorms than most folk can remember. If you ask me there's still a lot of fallout from that Russian nuclear accident floating about and buggering up our weather.'

'Very likely,' I said, taking a padded packet and a number of letters. But when I hurriedly sifted through the envelopes, most of which were Amazing Free Offers, I felt sickened by a sense of anti-climax. I had convinced myself there would be a letter from Ashley in the pile. Surely she must have seen something in a newspaper about the bomb blast in Abu Sabbah and felt some concern over me.

My disappointment was followed by almost childish anger. At the moment the only thing that mattered was to continue with *Whispering Corner,* now at least sixty pages behind schedule, probably more if I was honest with myself, and here I was squandering concentration like a love-sick youth over a girl whose early protests of devotion mattered nothing once she had got a mistaken idea into her head.

With a kitchen knife I opened the packet and found it contained a gleaming eyepiece for a telescope and a letter from a Holborn optical supplier I had written to saying he was delighted that he had been able to locate this second-hand part for my Norbury and Poole instrument.

Normally I would have hurried up to Miss Constance's parlour immediately to fit it into her father's telescope, but this morning I had no interest in such trivia. I discarded the Amazing Free Offers and the Free Lucky Draws and was left with an envelope addressed in a hand that was vaguely familiar. Then I remembered *Notes on the Experiences of the Lawson Family* and realized that Henry Gotobed, who was in London for a few days, had written to me.

I read the short letter and let it drop to the table. I was so stunned that I just sat there like a fool, unable to come to terms with what it implied. Obviously Henry had no notion of the significance of what he had written, or the devastating effect it would have upon me.

As I write this account, separated by distance and time from Whispering Corner, I have the letter beside me. Reading it again still gives me a *frisson*. It says,

'Dear Jonathan,

'In between doing my research at the Reading Room at the British Library I have tried to discover more about the history of Whispering Corner. I approached this by concentrating on the unsavoury Sir Richard Elphick, and as a result I find that we have been labouring under an extraordinary misapprehension.

'To cut a long story short, Sir Richard never built Whispering Corner or lived in it. He did in fact build a house in a wood outside Lychett Minster!

'If you recall, the article in *The Gentleman's Companion* was headed *Notes on the Experiences of the Lawson Family in the House of Colonel Elphick in the Wood on the Edge of Lychett Village,* and I naturally concluded that it referred to our village as the description of the house fitted perfectly with Whispering Corner. *Mea culpa!*

'Looking into the matter further I found that the house built by Sir Richard was demolished about a hundred years ago and the wood in which it stood has long gone. Sad the way England has lost so much of her woodland.

'Of course I am sure that this news will not affect the novel for which you are using Mrs Lawson's "Narration" as a background. In a work of fiction it can hardly matter whether the events it is based upon took place in Lychett Matravers or a few miles away in Lychett

Minster. In fact it might be reassuring to know that your house was never haunted . . .'

* * *

When Henry Gotobed had written that letter he could have had no idea of the effect it would have upon me. The best way I can describe it is to say that I felt like the pilot of a light aircraft flying through heavy cloud who suddenly finds that his instruments have failed.

The implications were too great to absorb at once.

I had been forced to put aside the conviction of a lifetime by experiencing paranormal manifestations only to find that the basis for them was non-existent.

So what had I experienced? My first thoughts were that I was going insane, that everything that had happened at Whispering Corner had been a delusion triggered off by a fallacy. Then I sought to reassure myself with the thought that Ashley had shared some of the experiences with me. But supposing . . .

At that moment Warren walked in.

'You all right?' he asked. 'You look like you've seen a ghost.' Then he grinned at the connotations of his remark. 'Just in a manner of speaking. After the Reverend McAndrew's visit I expect this place is pretty well de-ghosted.'

'No wonder he was puzzled', I said. 'There haven't been any ghosts here.'

Warren sat down opposite me. 'What's all this about?'

I began to tell him, and what a relief it was. This young Australian was the most sympathetic and intelligent listener I could have chosen.

When I came to the end of the story I gestured to Henry's letter.

'Read that,' I said. 'You'll see that the murder and the disposal of the unwanted baby and everything that was described in Mary Lawson's "Narration" could have nothing to do with Whispering Corner. So what has been happening here?'

Warren read the letter carefully. 'But even if Henry made a mistake very bloody weird things have been happening here,' he said. 'I remember you telling me that when Hoddy went berserk in the cellar he got the idea that you were Sir Richard Elphick . . ." We sat in silence, the letter between us. 'Hang on a minute,' said Warren suddenly. 'I've got something that might throw some light on this.'

He went to this room and returned with a bookstore bag from which he produced a volume with a yellow dust jacket. In bold black type it had Colin Wilson as the name of the author and beneath it the title *POLTERGEIST! – a study in destructive haunting.*

'I first read it back in Sydney,' Warren said. 'When I saw that you hadn't got it among your occult reference books I bought this copy to

197

give you as a thank-you present before I take off.'

'Thanks,' I murmured automatically.

'Least I could do after so much hospitality,' he answered just as automatically as he ran his finger down the index. 'Here we are, page 215. Now listen to this.'

'In the early 1970s, members of the *Toronto Society for Psychical Research*, under the direction of A. R. G. Owen, decided to try to manufacture a ghost. For this purpose, they invented the case history of a man called Philip, a contemporary of Oliver Cromwell, who had an affair with a beautiful gypsy girl. When Philip's wife found out, she had the girl accused of witchcraft and burned at the stake, Philip committed suicide. 'Having elaborated this story and created a suitable background – an ancient manor house – they set about trying to conjure up the spirit of Philip. For several months there were no results. Then one evening, as they were relaxing and singing songs, there was a rap on the table. They used the usual code (one rap for yes, two for no), to question the "spirit", which claimed to be Philip, and repeated the story they had invented for him. At later séances, Philip made the table dance all around the room, and even made it levitate in front of TV cameras.

'Owen's group rightly regarded this "creation" of a ghost as something of a triumph, making the natural assumption that Philip was a product of their unconscious minds . . . '

Warren trailed off and his words seemed to hang in the air. Then he said, 'The novel you're writing, based on this house, brings in paranormal activity based on the "Narration", doesn't it?'

'Of course. And I see perfectly well what you're getting at. You think that as an author creating characters I created ghosts just as that group in Toronto created Philip.'

'That's how it seems to me.'

'Me too,' I admitted. 'But why? My other horror books haven't manufactured horrors.'

'Perhaps because you didn't write them in Whispering Corner. I told you it's a nodal point for ley lines. There must be something here that causes such things to happen, something that preserved the sound of whispering. And maybe it's something to do with you, a combination of you and Whispering Corner, and maybe if some other writer had come here it might not have happened. I remember sitting here and you talking to the vicar one night saying how your characters took on lives of their own and became like real people to you, and how in *Shadows and Mirrors* they actually worked out a different plot to what you'd had in mind. So when you began writing in this magical spot the process went further and the projections of your mind became reality . . .'

'It's all too fantastic!' I exploded. 'It's not as though I was even a believer in the paranormal.'

'It'd make a good theme for your next book,' Warren said with a laugh, which he bit back when he saw my expression. The fact remains, you read the "Narration" which you believed referred to this place, used the idea in the novel you were creating, and then things began to happen more or less as you described them in your book. Isn't that so?'

'Is is,' I admitted, and then added with short-lived triumph, 'But something happened before I had written it down. When I first came here I heard voices in my head which at the time I believed were caused by hypnagogsis but which later became part of the psychic phenomena – the point is I hadn't got into the book when it happened,'

'But the thought of whispering voices was in your mind,' Warren argued. 'When you met Henry and he told you the legend of the plague victims you were aware of them, especially as they were responsible for the name of your house. And at the time, did you think of using the legend in your novel?'

'It did occur to me.'

'There you are. The fact that you hadn't written it down didn't matter. The point was you had conceived it as part of your story in your mind.'

'I suppose you're right,' I said. Other thoughts were crowding in, about incidents I had put down to synchronicity, of what had been real and what had been extensions of my imagination.

'Did you have a scene in your novel about someone becoming possessed?'

'No.'

'So at least your fictional creations can have no bearing on what happened to Hoddy.'

'Oh, yes. We can say the hauntings came about in some mysterious way through me imagining them in my book, but as time went on an independence began to evolve just as it did in that experiment in Colin Wilson's book. The psychic researchers created a whole scenario for their ghost Philip, but he took on a persona of his own when he showed off his poltergeist-type abilities by making the table dance and so on. Once the ghosts in my book came to life – to put it paradoxically – they began to act more and more independently. Take the re-enactment of the murder. I didn't describe it in my novel until after I had experienced it.'

'I can see it's more complicated than I thought,' Warren admitted. 'If things happened here because they were projected in an author's mind that's not too difficult to follow, but you're saying that once they were created they took over . . . '

'Of course they did – or the power that they personified. And that power was evil because in my novel it went back to the wicked actions of Sir Richard Elphick. Once it had been activated it was free to influence us. And as time has passed it seems to have got steadily stronger. Perhaps it absorbed some sort of psychic energy from your ley system. It gave me a bad experience in the cellar once, but that was nothing compared to what it did to Hoddy. Luckily it didn't seem able to sustain its hold over him, but who knows what could happen if it became more powerful?'

'So what are you going to do now? You can hardly continue with *Whispering Corner* in the circumstances.'

'Of course I can. Whatever happens I've got to hand in a novel in a very short while.'

'But surely that'd be dangerous?'

'I don't know, but at least I'll try and make sure that the haunting can't continue. If fact has followed fiction, fiction can now follow fact. In my novel, Whispering Corner will be exorcised as it was in reality.'

The next few days were the most intensive I have ever known. Warren left reluctantly as he had promised to meet a like-minded friend with whom he had longstanding plans to visit Findhorn. He promised he would return to Whispering Corner 'to see how things were working out' as soon as he could, and as he left I got the impression from his almost exuberant admonitions to take care that he felt some anxiety about leaving me alone.

After I had driven him to Poole to catch his train I returned to Whispering Corner. The oppressive air, waiting for yet another thunderstorm to clear it, seemed to press down upon me as I stood in the centre of the lawn surveying my little domain. I was glad that I would be on my own for the next few days. Not even Henry's serious conversation would intrude on the working regime I planned for myself.

Despite everything, I still loved the house, and one of the positive things that had resulted from the revelation in Henry's letters was the knowledge that Whispering Corner was 'innocent'. No malign influences lurked in its fabric as I had feared. I had created the haunting and I would end it by fictionalizing the work of Dr McAndrew.

Of course there was a lot more to it than had been discussed with Warren. There was the aspect which I was only just daring to consider. It was epitomized by my memory of meeting Ashley, of driving through the rain and seeing her in my headlights and her car slewed in the ditch just as I had described it before I came to live at Whispering Corner. Perhaps it was the drowsy shadows of the trees, perhaps the Imp of the

Perverse had returned to tempt me from the chore of sitting at my laptop, but despite the stiffness that I still felt in my legs I decided to go for a walk in the woods.

Passing through the wicket gate into Church Walk I set off towards the village. Light through the leafy canopy above the path played like a hundred spotlights on the massive roots of the great tree which writhed squid-like over the bank. Everything was hushed. The occasional call of a bird only emphasized the heavy silence. I sat down on a spongy log half hidden by ferns and tried to absorb the tranquillity of the moment, tried to get my chaotic ideas into some order.

In this mood so many things seemed far away, otherworldly. Despite my yellowing bruises the memory of the wall collapsing like a brick-hued wave above me had become no more real than some old movie scene, it seemed impossible that less than a fortnight had passed since I had held Ashley in my arms. Moments of intimacy, such as our love-making on the midnight shore, had become transmuted into erotic nostalgia.

I do not know how long I sat there lost in a reverie. It was ended by the sound of voices as a couple came into sight along the path. She was small and fair-haired and wore the sort of cotton dress that is reserved for holidays, he had a camera slung on his shoulder and when he saw the array of roots he disengaged her hand to take a picture. They were smiling at each other, and there was a togetherness about them which I envied more than I have envied anything else.

Suddenly they saw me sitting in the shadow. The woman smiled and asked, 'Is this the whispering place?'

I nodded and climbed to my feet. The camera clicked. Their fingers linked again and they continued slowly through the trees. They – or what they seemed to represent – had broken my mood of introspection, and as I walked back down the path I was determined to bring Ashley back to Whispering Corner.

In the house I paused to put out a fresh bowl of milk in front of Mrs Foch, who lay in the old washing basket which Warren had made comfortable for her with a folded blanket. The cat was lethargic and merely opened her pink mouth in a silent mew when she saw me. Perhaps it was the tablets which I had to coax down her throat with sardines that had that effect upon her, but I thought it more likely that she was also a victim of the powers I had unwittingly animated.

It was warm and oppressive in my study, and even though I opened the window my hands were damp with perspiration as I switched on the Acer. I did not feel up to the physical strain of writing, but mentally I was on fire to continue with the novel, and the next few days proved to be a victory of mind over matter.

On several occasions fatigue overtook me, an I would wake up with my head on the table making painful indentations in my forehead, then I would sluice my face, have black coffee and get back to the story. When I felt hungry I would eat chocolate, and when that became too cloying I would revert to bacon sandwiches. And there were times when, had there been a packet of cigarettes in the house, I would have gone back into the habit I had broken a dozen years ago.

My first job was to complete the rift between Falco and Lorna, and this I did on the first night. Lorna left Whispering Corner as abruptly as Ashley had left me in Abu Sabbah, Although the situation and the locale was different, I found that Falco's sense of loss was akin to my own, and as I described it my eyes felt dangerously moist. As the night wore on I could not have said precisely whether I was writing about Falco or myself.

And no wonder. Thanks to what Warren termed the 'magic' of Whispering Corner my relationship with my characters must have been one of the strangest in the history of authorship. I created the fabric of their lives only to find it reflected in mine. As I sat in that sweltering room I remember how after I had described the arrival of Falco at the house he had inherited I had looked out and watched the scene re-enacted by Warren, then when I described the first time Falco made love to Lorna I had no idea that in a few days I would be reliving it with Ashley.

Figures of fact and fiction held hands in such a *danse macabre* that at times I really wondered if I was going insane. In retrospect I think there were times when I was. On one occasion I began to wonder if I had dreamed up everything, including Ashley, and would wake up in some aseptic room in a home for the bewildered. This thought obsessed me to a point when, shaky with fatigue, I had to go in search of clues to her existence. It was only finding some of her underwear thrown in the corner of the bedroom wardrobe that reassured me she had not been a succubus.

The curious thing was that as far as writing was concerned my mind was clear. I knew exactly what I had to write and I did it with precision. I typed until my fingers were cramped and my spine hurt from sitting so long in one position, yet I had no inclination to stop. If only I could have had such a burst of creative energy earlier on, I told myself, *Whispering Corner* would have been delivered to Jocasta Mount-William by now.

On the second morning of my new-found enthusiasm I saw the postman approaching over the grass, and when I went to meet him he gave me look of mingled curiosity and concern. I suppose I must have looked rather debauched in my dressing-gown with my hair uncombed and my face unshaven.

'Everything all right, then?' he asked.

I mumbled something about working late.

'Aye, there's work and work,' he said cryptically. 'Least you've got some interesting letters.'

He handed me four letters. Two were airmail – one with a New York postmark and the other embossed with the silver emblem of Abu Sabbah, while of the other two one bore my address in an unusual italic script which I recognized as Charles Nixon's favoured font on his computer.

Having commiserated with the postman on the unusual number of thunderstorms we were having this year, I went to the kitchen and laid the letters among the unwashed dishes on the kitchen table. While I drank my coffee I opened the least interesting-looking one, and found it to be ah official notification that the case to be brought against me by the Regent Bank would be heard before the Queen's Bench in London in three week' time – coincidentally the delivery date for *Whispering Corner.*

The news did not affect me as badly as it might have done. There is a certain relief in knowing the worst, and I consoled myself with the knowledge that if I could keep up the present impetus on *Whispering Corner* the novel would be completed before I faced the humiliation of having to admit in public that I could not pay the money I owed. If the story got picked up by a press agency I could imagine the pithy headings that would appear above the item.

I opened the letter from Pamela.

'Dear Jonathan,

'It was sweet of you to send your congratulations from Abu Sabbah (a place I had never heard of, why were you there?) but sadly I don't deserve them. The copy you read was not mine but the work of a baby-faced whizzkid a prodigy who roller-skates in Central Park and wears T-shirts with rude words on them, damn him! I just could not get the copy as the Feinstein account exec wanted it, and so I blew my chance and I feel like hell about it.

'Don't know what I am going to do. Doubt if I'll get another opportunity here but dread the thought of going back to London empty-handed. Feel such a failure and have suspicion that Liz is getting a bit peed off with having me here. She has given up sculpture for Aroma Therapy. Oh! Oh! What shall I do?

'Enough self-pity. I expect your novel is finished – were you recuperating after it in Abu S? Hope it goes even better than *Shadows and Mirrors.* At least one of us will be making it.

'I know that it's best for us both the way things have turned out etc. etc. but I must admit to missing you more than I expected. Been nice if things had been different. You'll think I'm saying that because

I'm rather blue over the Fleur de Lune disappointment, and perhaps you're right. Give Steve all my love when next you see him – he sent me a card of a topless bathing belle from Puerto Banus. Where has our little boy gone? Love to you too . . . P.'

I put the letter carefully back into its envelope and cursed the effort I had made to get a letter of congratulation written and posted while I was convalescent. What salt in the wound it must have been when she received it.

My first inclination was to rush off a letter of commiseration to Pam. Then I decided to leave it until I had time to consider the wording carefully. My initial disappointment and indignation on her behalf might only add to her depression.

The next letter was in Syed's handwriting, expressing the hope that I was fully recovered and saying that work had already started on rebuilding the college and he hoped that when it was completed I would still consider joining the staff. There was a PS from Jo hoping Ashley and I were in contact again with misunderstandings forgotten.

I held the last envelope in my fingers for a minute before I opened it. It was obviously Charles's belated reply to the angry letter I had sent him before I flew to Abu Sabbah, and I tried to guess the content. I remembered that one of his axioms was that the best form of defence was attack, and it was attack I found when I unfolded the heavy mock parchment with his name displayed across the top in viridian day-glo ink with the words 'Film and TV Producer' beneath it.

I shall not quote it verbatim here, it had been written with such venom and phoney outrage that it had the effect of making me feel physically ill, especially as it was because of this man that I would soon be in court. (When I recently found it again in my Regent Bank file, it had the same effect even though the whole business had come to its tragic conclusion.)

He began by saying how shocked he was at my letter, and how could I write in such a tone to someone who had done so much for me!

Without his effort and expertise my book *The Dancing Stones* would never have been filmed. But although he had never received his just financial reward for this dedicated work he had not minded because he was happy to give my career a helping hand. Since then he had devoted his time to endeavouring to get my last novel filmed. Surely even I must understand that he'd had to take living expenses (though not the thousand pounds a week he was entitled to as a producer) from the company during the two years he was labouring so hard on my behalf. It ill became me to 'demand' accounts as I had done. The implication I had made by doing so was such that he was considering putting the matter in the hands of his solicitor in order to protect his professional reputation.

He then went on to express his amazement that, as a best-selling and therefore highly paid author, I should be so reluctant to carry out my duty to Pleiades Films when for his part he had sacrificed so much of his valuable time in trying to promote another production for it. Alas, my ingratitude was the only reward for his sacrifice!

If I had played my part in the company, instead of hiding away in the country to evade my responsibilities, I would have been well aware of the company's financial state and the situation with the bank. Now that reality had caught up with me it seemed that I was going to place all the responsibility on him and this was something he was not going to allow. For the sake of his reputation he was going to inform my agent and publishers of my deviousness, and if I were to pressure him for money that I knew perfectly well he did not have – because of his lack of income due to his unrewarded effort on my behalf – he would fight me through the courts and demonstrate publicly what an ingrate I was. He added that he was glad I had written because it opened his eyes to the sort of man he had accepted as a partner and helped beyond the call of commercial duty. He now 'crossed me off his list'. In future if I had anything to communicate I should do it through his solicitor. Finally, although he never normally commented on anyone's private affairs, it was common knowledge that my wife had left me and gone to America, and if 'that lovely woman' had been forced to take such action it merely underlined the sort of person I was.

There was a postscript to say that he was sending a copy of this letter to his legal adviser.

He had not answered any of the points I had raised when I wrote to him, and when I had to turn over my Pleiades papers to my solicitor, he remarked after reading Charles's letter that self-righteousness is the standard defence of the conman.

And while there was something sick about receiving such a letter when one is about to lose one's house – a point Charles forgot to touch on – it was the reference to Pam coming immediately after her sad letter that incensed me. The opening line from Edgar Allan Poe's story *The Cask of Amontillado* once more came into my mind, 'The thousand injuries of Fortunate I had borne as I best could, but when he ventured upon insult, I vowed revenge.'

And suddenly I laughed aloud.

Charles Nixon would make the ideal model for the villain of *Whispering Corner,* the character who had been so shadowy that so far I had merely referred to him as XXXXX in my text. But now I had him – the medium who exploits Falco and Lorna in order to promote himself.

How well such a character as Charles would fit the role, with his glib pretence at being concerned for his victims, his ever-ready untruths and his overwhelming ego.

What should I call him?

Taking the hint from Poe the name Fortune seemed appropriate . . . William Fortune. That would do.

I left my letters with their diverse content amid the clutter of the kitchen table and hurried upstairs to my laptop.

Chapter 21

My first task was to write William Fortune into the story, beginning with the séance Falco had arranged after seeing the ghostly murder re-enactment. With a sort of bitter enthusiasm I described his pallid face and granny glasses. I decided that a formal charcoal suit would be more appropriate than the designer denims favoured by my model, but the flavour of his self-promoting conversation I retained, so that Fortune was constantly coming out with remarks such as, 'When someone very important asked me to hold a séance at Glamis Castle.'

As I worked through the day Fortune's motives became apparent. He sees Whispering Corner becoming another Borley Rectory, with him the master of mystical ceremonies. Keeping his intent from Falco, who hates the thought of any publicity connected with his new home, the medium arranges contracts for a serial in a Sunday newspaper and a book *The Whispering Ghost – the most amazing haunting this century* which will appear when the house reaches the apogee of its hype. Unbeknown to Falco, he also negotiates with a film company to cover the next séance.

In my mind I decided that as a young man Fortune was so presentable and confident that he did not think it necessary to become qualified at a trade or profession he was sure that a high position would come his way by right. It had not happened, and after a string of jobs such as demonstrating washing powder, touting insurance door to door and selling menswear – none of which occupations allowed him to prove his *real* ability – he decided that if he wanted acclaim and financial reward he must utilize his natural psychic gifts.

At the point where he enters the novel he has been quite successful as a medium and is looking for the opportunity to promote himself into a celebrity.

After the initial séance he spends a lot of time at Whispering Corner conducting an investigation. Here his hypocritical charm is used to calm the fears of its occupants, especially Lorna whom, with the tactics of Rasputin, he endeavours to draw under his influence after sensing that Falco is hard to manipulate.

This culminates in the quarrel between Lorna and Falco when, beginning to be suspicious of the medium's motives, Falco decides to call in an exorcist to get the house cleared of its supernatural inheritance once and for all – the very last thing that Fortune wants.

It was almost midnight when I sat back and stretched my cramped muscles with a feeling of weary satisfaction. I was very pleased with the character I had just incorporated into the novel. I had pondered over the villain for a long time – I did not want someone patently wicked – and with Fortune I could steadily develop his ambition into a menacing obsession, reinforced by the ancient evil surrounding the house.

To celebrate what I felt was a significant step forward in the storyline, I had a drink, then went to bed in a state of pleasant exhaustion.

Next morning I was about to start work when the postman brought me a letter addressed in the meticulous hand of Dr McAndrew. He hoped the exorcism he had performed had been effective, but he was still mystified that he had not sensed the discarnate entities I had described so graphically. If anything further happened would I please get in touch with him immediately.

Perhaps when the novel was finished I would explain to him that the entities of Whispering Corner had been the product of my own imagination, and by that time the haunting of the house would be over. If the ghosts had been created in my imagination then through my imagination they would be laid to rest. I planned to write a scene of exorcism conducted by an Anglican priest which would end the whole business.

The fact that the house appeared to be free of phenomena at present I put down to the fact that the force which activated them had been temporarily exhausted by the possession of Hoddy. I knew that each time it reappeared it had been more powerful, and I hoped that before it could manifest again I would have 'written it out'. But I had something more important to write in *Whispering Corner* first.

Looking back, I can only say I must have been in a most dangerous state of mind.

When I saw that the sky framed in the study window was darkening I was astonished at how the hours had passed. I had been too absorbed in the unfolding story to be aware of their passage. During those hours I had developed the role of William Fortune who, when he learns that Lorna has left Falco, hurries to Whispering Corner to play the part of the wise elder friend. He seizes the opportunity presented by Falco's lowered spirits to persuade him to agree to the setting up of a psychical experiment a few days hence. The intervening time is required covertly to arrange for media coverage.

Alone Falco is preoccupied – as I was – by the fact he is unable to find the whereabouts of his lover. He searches the house for her manuscript in the hope that it might contain the telephone number of an agent or the address of a publisher, but he finally accepts the futility of the hunt – as an author her manuscript would be the first thing she would think of taking with her.

It seems extraordinary to the young man that she could vanish so completely. It is almost as though she has been a figment of his imagination. The rooms where they had made love hold no trace of the emotion he had experienced. When he walks on the lawn there is nothing in the garden to confirm that a short while ago they had walked together by moonlight.

The only tangible evidence of their love affair comes that night when he collapses on to his bed and catches the faint redolence of her shampoo from the pillow next to his. This is so evocative that later that night, when he wakes dry-mouthed from too much alcohol, he believes he can hear her soft breathing beside him. He stretches out a hand but all that his fingers encounter is the fur of the cat who, also missing Lorna, has curled up on the side of the bed where she had slept.

Falco tries to assuage his sense of loss and anger by spending the day at his drawing board and drinking too much at night. He had such high hopes of starting a new life in Whispering Corner when he first saw the house, and now everything seems to have become a mockery of that hope.

It was at this point I stopped and realized that evening was drawing on. I went downstairs and had my first meal of the day, toast and a tin of Campbell's mushroom soup. I followed it by a very careful brandy – I was well aware that I had come to rely too much on the spirit, and tonight I wanted to be clear-headed. I was about to embark on the most important piece of prose I would ever write.

In the churchyard Falco leaned against the lichened wall and gazed pensively at the ancient yew with its grotesquely twisted trunk. Each time he had seen it in the past he had intended to draw it with the idea of using it in some future illustration. This morning he had felt too restless to remain indoors and the yew provided an excuse to leave his studio.

He took out his sketchbook and began to outline the trunk and branches. As he worked he thought how suitable it would have been as an illustration for one of Lorna's stories about an enchanted tree.

Why the hell did everything have to remind him of Lorna, he thought with a sudden surge of anger. If she had really loved him she wouldn't have gone off because of such a stupid quarrel. He had just bloody well misjudged the situation, and she had used it as an excuse to get away. Perhaps the haunting had affected her nerves more than he had realized, perhaps as she recovered from her accident she felt that she was making a mistake, that he was not the man for her after all. Perhaps she just got plain bored.

Whatever the reason, she had done what she had to do and all the brooding in the world would not alter that . . . 'Is that going to be the illustration for The Tree Prince?'

The sound of her voice behind him came as such a shock that he was unable to respond. His pencil point continued to shade in dark foliage.

209

He heard the iron gate creak, shoes on the gravel path.

'Hi,' he said as she came into his line of vision. She wore a navy polka dot shirt and slightly travel-soiled cream slacks, and at the sight of her Falco felt giddy in a way that he had not known since he was a child. Nevertheless, he managed to keep his pencil moving softly over the cartridge paper.

'Hi,' she responded with an equal show of coolness. She turned away, gazing at a distant smudge of stubble smoke as though it held exceptional interest for her. Then she swung round with an angry look.

'You really are a cold bastard,' she said. 'Is "Hi" all you want to say?'

'Sorry,' he said. 'Hi Lorna.'

'Very funny. Still, I suppose it was stupid of me to expect that you might be pleased to see me again.'

'Who says I wasn't pleased?'

'Your attitude. But, please, don't let me interrupt your drawing . . .'

Anger at his inability to respond as he had dreamed of doing in this situation and anger at her petulant words mingled and swamped him. Childishly he tore the page from the pad, clenched it into a ball and flung it on the grass.

'Oh, your lovely drawing,' cried Lorna. She dropped to her knees and began to unfold the paper and smooth it out. 'How could you do that!' She stood up with green stains on the knees of her slacks.

'I'm sorry,' Falco said. 'It was a stupid thing to do.'

'Yes, it was,' she agreed. 'But it broke the tension. When I came down Church Walk from Whispering Corner and saw you in the churchyard I thought I was going to be sick.'

'So that's the effect I have upon you.'

She gave a little laugh. 'You know what I mean, James. It may sound crazy to you but I was scared silly on the train, and it got even worse when I came in the taxi from Poole.'

'OK now?'

'Much better. Can I keep this drawing?'

'It's spoilt.'

'Not for me.'

They stood facing each other, not knowing what to say next. From behind the church drifted the smell of burning weeds.

'I'm not in the mood to see the vicar,' Falco said. 'Would you like a cup of tea or something?'

'The "or something" sounds best.'

Side by side they strolled up Church Walk, taking care that their hands should not touch in case it should give the wrong signal. When they reached the wicket gate Lorna asked if he would mind walking farther and he agreed. Neither was ready for the house in which they had shared so much. When they reached the bend over which the giant oak spread its branches Falco suddenly put his hand on Lorna's shoulder.

'Why the hell did you go off like that?'

'I was waiting for you to ask me that. All the way down I've been trying to think of an answer but I couldn't come up with one.'

'But after what had happened between us . . .'

'I know. All I can say is it was something to do with the house. Look how we had been getting on each other's nerves before we had that stupid, stupid quarrel.'

'It was fear of the ghosts?'

'I was scared of them, but it wasn't that that sent me running. There was something getting at me and some instinct made me want to run away. Self preservation? I don't know. But it wasn't because of the quarrel. That was only an outward and visible sign of something much deeper. Of course I was very angry when I left, but normally I would have got over it without doing anything drastic. I stayed in Highgate with a girlfriend I was at college with and all I know is that I was utterly miserable.'

'I didn't feel so wonderful myself.'

'Shall we walk through the wood?'

'If you like.'

They stepped off the path and soon were walking among the trees.

'I suppose there were times when Sir Richard's mistress felt like running away, especially when he bullied her . . .'

'I wonder,' murmured Falco. 'Some sort of possession might be next on the list.'

He was aware that she shivered. 'You mean those dead people might be trying to influence us, to make us feel what they felt.'

'It could be.'

'Did you get the exorcist to come?'

'His housekeeper told me on the telephone that he's out of the country on a case. He should be back in a week. I sent him a letter explaining everything for him to read on his return.'

'And William?'

'Our Mr Fortune wants to hold another séance, in the cellar this time. He believes that if he could locate the spot where the baby was buried and its bones could be given a proper burial everything would go back to normal.'

They walked on. Cobwebs hanging between tree trunks, still holding dew diamonds, sometimes clung to them, their footfalls sent a rabbit scurrying . . .

'. . . to Watership Down,' Falco laughed.

'How's the cat?'
'She missed you.'
'And you?'
'Need you ask?'

They came into a clearing no larger than the living-room at Whispering Corner, walled with willow herb and dappled with sunlight falling through the overhanging boughs.

'James, I'm back . . . if you want me.'
'Yes.'

They kissed, cautiously at first, then fiercely, and then, and neither would have been able to say afterwards how it happened – they were together in the long soft grass. Falco's fingers plucked at the buttons of her shirt while her hands unfastened his belt, and then they were making love more fiercely than ever before. It was their own exorcism of loneliness and mistrust, it was a celebration of their finding each other again, and Falco was filled with such sensual strength that it seemed he could ride her for ever – until she moaned her climax through clenched teeth and he shuddered and lay still on top of her, too spent to stir for a long moment.

When he made the effort to release her from his weight she traced the tips of her fingers across his face.

'Hello,' she murmured. 'I'm home again.'
'To stay?'

'Yes. Come the three corners of the world in arms and we shall shock them, my darling.'

I was exhausted as I pushed the Acer away.

I had written it. Its quality as a piece of prose did not matter. If I had unconsciously caused things to happen by creating them in my imagination and putting them down on the laptop, then I was now consciously using that power to influence events for my benefit.

In the past few weeks aspects of Ashley's life had mirrored the life of my fictitious heroine, her arrival in the storm, the love-making scene so accurate that she believed it had been written after the event – and now out of desperation I had depicted her return to Whispering Corner.

When I rose, having completed my chapter, and went to my bedroom I actually stumbled with exhaustion. Having sat in a cramped position all day and half the night my Abu Sabbah aches had returned remorselessly, but there was more to it than that. I was drained emotionally. I had lived the last scene I had written, in my fantasy it had been Ashley who had returned to me, and when my characters had made love among the trees it had been I who had taken Ashley in my arms.

Rather like my character William Fortune – I had to admit – I was trying to manipulate events through a recondite connection between the product of my imagination and reality. Of course when fact had followed fiction it was not exactly as I had envisaged it, it was as though once the process had been set in motion it could evolve independently, as my unwitting creation of the phantom Sir Richard Elphick proved.

Thus I did not expect Ashley to come back in exactly the same circumstances as those in which Lorna had returned to Whispering Corner, but I believed it was now likely that we would meet again. I was suddenly oppressed by the hazard of playing at God. As a novelist I was used to the game, creating characters and landscapes and situations at my whim to suit the needs of the story, but for the first time I was writing a scenario for a living individual. What right had I to do that? It could hardly be correct to treat Ashley as a character.

For one panicky minute I considered deleting what I had written, but then felt that any risk was worth taking if it gave us the opportunity of renewing our love affair.

It was fatigue which released me from the conflicting thoughts teasing my tired mind, I remember nothing more until I woke still fully dressed the next morning.

For the next two days I worked steadily on the build up to William Fortune's psychic experiment in the cellar. Falco and Lorna re-establish their old relationship unaware of how the medium plans to exploit Whispering Corner and in doing so put them all at risk. The words came well and I was encouraged, when I trekked to the village shop for coffee and a few groceries, to send a post card depicting St Mary's Church to my agent telling her that she could look forward to memory stick with the novel 'in the near future'.

On the morning of the next day I had an appointment in London to see the solicitor who was to represent me in court. As I shaved off several days' growth of beard, which I could have passed off as 'designer stubble' had I been half my age, I saw that the bruising had gone but I was definitely looking older. The laughter lines round my eyes were losing their sense of humour, and despite the tan I had gained from the Red Sea sunshine there was something unhealthy about my skin. Was this a reflection of the stress of the last few months? I had to admit that my intake of brandy probably had something to do with it.

When the novel and the court case were behind me I would get back into shape, I promised myself. Unfortunately I had made many such promises before, only to find that the time came and went and the circumstances of life somehow remained the same.

But this time I added, as hope sprung eternal, I would do it out of consideration for Ashley.

In London I had lunch with Paul Lincoln at the unlikely sounding Champagne Chinese Restaurant off Tottenham Court Road, and then we went on to see Swan, Floyd and Company. Here Mr Swan himself took notes and referred to papers with a comforting expression on his avuncular features which didn't change when he said, 'Oh dear, it does look as though the bank's going to screw you.'

I parroted my *cri de coeur*, 'But why just me? Why don't they go for Nixon?'

'They'll get judgement against him, but from the sound of things they won't take it further.'

'But that's not justice!'

Mr Swan's smile increased. 'When you get involved in litigation you soon see there's a difference between justice and the law,' he said drily. 'You have a house unencumbered by the claims of a spouse and children, so you are the natural target.'

'But I understand we can force Nixon to pay half,' Paul said.

'Oh, yes, but it's unlikely we could get an order for him to do so until after Mr Northrop has cleared the whole debt.'

'But couldn't we try?'

'Of course. I'll send him a very strong letter demanding that he honours his responsibility as managing director and major shareholder, etc., etc., and threatening all sorts of nasties if he doesn't. Perhaps it'll have some effect.'

I was depressed as I drove back to Dorset. The meeting had brought me back to the reality of my situation after several days of escape in the make-believe world of the author.

But the gloom vanished when I reached Whispering Corner. Ashley was waiting for me.

The reunion with Ashley was nothing like that between Falco and Lorna. There was no walk up the church path and no grappling in a woodland glade, I entered the house and found her curled up on the living-room sofa in front of the fireplace, and I remembered that she had a key. A book was open on the rug, one of my earlier novels which she had taken from the bookcase, and she was sound asleep.

I did not wake her, but went to the kitchen to make toast and a pot of tea. I needed time to calm the excitement of knowing that my experiment had worked – it had damn well worked!

A few minutes later I carried in the tea tray and touched her gently on the shoulder.

Tea, m'lady.'

Watching her open her eyes and begin to stretch lazily, it would have been easy to imagine that she had never been away from Whispering Corner.

Suddenly she became wide awake and swung herself into a sitting position.

'Hi,' she said.

'Can't you do better than that?'

'Hi, Jon.'

'Cup of tea?'

'Oh, great!'

It was banal. I suppose there should have been recriminations and explanations, protestations and declarations, but real life is more prosaic than prose and I simply poured her out a cup of tea.

'How's the novel coming?'

'Very well this last few days. There's a good chance I may still deliver on time.'

'Wonderful. You obviously work better when you're on your own.'

'And you? Been doing the round of theatrical agents?'

'No. I moved in with a couple of Kiwi girls in Fulham. I saw their ad in *Overseas Visitor.* It's just temporary, until I get a cheapo flight to Auckland. How's Mrs Foch?'

'She'll be in her basket in my study. She seems to like it best there. Hoddy cut her tail off.'

'What?'

'Poor chap had a brainstorm.'

'He never liked Mrs Foch. Can I go up and see her?'

'You don't have to ask, Ash.'

'Sorry. It all seems a bit unreal.'

When Ashley came down from visiting the cat her eyes looked suspiciously moist and I guessed it was not entirely on account of Mrs Foch.

'Perhaps you'd like to get out of this place for a bit,' I said. 'How about coming for a walk to the Chequers? We always intended to go for a drink there . . . '

'Jonathan, why the bloody hell can't you be human! Call me all the bitches under the sun if you want to, yell at me for running out on you! I can't take this let's pretend nothing happened – would you-like-another-cup-of-tea crap.' Her voice faltered. 'Or don't you care any more?'

'I care,' I said sombrely. 'I know you believed you had every reason to be angry, but why didn't you have it out with me?'

'Because I always run away,' Ashley answered with a sob. 'There's something about me that when things go wrong I just have to run. I ran away from New Zealand, I ran away from Sydney and I ran away from Abu Sabbah. I must have an escapist complex. I saw a psychotherapist about it once but I ran away from her. Anyway, you can't blame your parents for everything. You have to grow up some day!'

'But if you felt like that in Abu Sabbah, why are you here?'

I hoped the intensity of my interest in her reply did not show.

'It took a lot of courage-up-plucking. I felt dreadful when I got back to England, ashamed of myself for running yet again, furious with you for using our . . . our intimacy as copy for your bloody novel, and miserably lonely. I just wanted to get back to a life I could cope with, so I decided to go back home. Then yesterday I just knew I had to come and see you – and say goodbye to Whispering Corner. I tried to fight the idea but I felt that something was forcing me to make the journey. This morning I gave in, and here I am. I suppose I somehow wanted to clear the air before I left England. You see, I really did fall in love with you very deeply until I found that all the time you had been using me as a guinea-pig – almost to copying down the words I used, damn you! She was silent for a minute.

'In your line of literature you must have seen the movie *The Shining,*' she continued in a voice she was having trouble in keeping under control.

'I saw *The Shining.*'

'Good. Remember the scene where the wife looks at the novel her husband is supposed to be typing and realizes he's insane because he's just repeated the same phrase hundreds and hundreds of times? Well, I felt the same sort of shock when I looked at *your* novel. No wonder you hadn't wanted me to read it.'

'Ashley,' I said. 'I'll admit that after I'd met you, I changed my heroine's hair from long blond to short dark curls – that was meant as a sort of compliment to you – but the description which upset you so much was written before you came to Whispering Corner. The description of the motor accident which brought you I mean the heroine – into the story was actually first written when I was still living in London.'

'I know you're mad about coincidences, but you can't expect me to believe that. Why not be honest and admit that like most authors you borrow from life?'

'Because it's true. Something very strange has been happening here.'

'I agree there. At least I don't blame you for the haunting.'

'Perhaps that's just what you should blame me for.'

'Now it's riddle time?'

'Let me try to explain,' I said. 'Possibly it's something to do with the house. The fact is that since I've been here what I've written seems to come to pass, not exactly, of course, but near enough to be very, very scary. And I can prove it.'

I went on to remind her how I had used Mary Lawson's 'Narration' about events at Whispering Corner as the basis for the ghostly manifestations in my novel, only to find that these ghosts really were haunting Whispering Corner. 'Now,' I said, taking Henry Gotobed's letter from a drawer. 'Read this.'

She read it twice, frowning. 'Then Whispering Corner shouldn't have been haunted because Sir Richard Elphick had nothing to do with this place. Then what . . . ?'

'What we saw was the result of me thinking up those ghosts to put in the novel. In some way they became real.'

She looked thoughtful and read the letter again. 'OK, you write things and then they happen,' she said. 'I can't understand it, but then I don't understand how a television set works and I still see a picture. But for now I just want an answer to one question. Did you write a scene in your book in which your heroine comes back to Whispering Corner after running away?' I felt the words coming to deny it and then I choked them back. If there was to be any future with Ashley there could be no deceits. I knew I had to tell her the truth, even if it meant there was a danger of losing her again.

'Yes,' I said. 'Three nights ago I was missing you so badly that I wrote that scene in the hope that . . . '

I could not finish the sentence because Ashley flung her arms round my neck.

'Oh, I'm so glad,' she cried. 'It shows you still want me.'

Ashley had missed the paragraphs in the international news sections on the bomb outrage in Abu Sabbah, and this gave us something neutral to discuss. It was as though having talked about what had happened in the past – and I could not help wondering how much she believed my explanation – the future remained taboo. Having see her again in this familiar setting I wanted nothing more than to carry on where we had left off, but I had the sense to realize that it would not be as straightforward as I wished.

When the clock chimed twelve Ashley looked at me in mock dismay. 'Oh, dear, my carriage has turned into a pumpkin.'

'You weren't thinking of getting a train back to London tonight, were you?'

'I was originally, but . . .'

'Too late now.'

'I didn't realize how tempus was fugiting.'

'Anyway, you belong here,' I said impulsively.

Ashley drew a deep breath and looked up at me from the floor where she was sitting in the lotus position. 'I don't know how to say this without sounding stupid but . . . but do you mind if we don't sleep together tonight?'

'No,' I lied. 'I think it's difficult to take up where we left off immediately.'

'It's not that I don't want you. Believe me, I care for you as much as ever, only I'm still confused about everything. When we come together again I want it to be with no reservations. Oh, it's not you, Jonathan, it's bloody life.'

'Sure,' I said. 'Take your time. When you've been here a little while I'm sure you'll feel better.'

'Yes. Despite the ghosts I love this old place.'

I took her up to the spare bedroom, made sure she had everything she needed and kissed her goodnight.

On waking the next morning my mind immediately began to churn over the events of the previous day.

Remembering my visit to the solicitors I experienced a return of the old familiar panic about the debt to the bank, and to quell it I threw myself out of bed and began the routine of the day. Because of Ashley I shaved, combed my hair carefully and put on fresh clothing. By the time the aroma of coffee was in my nostrils the gloom and doom that can assail one on waking was starting to fade. I had work waiting for me in the study and at the moment it was of paramount importance.

Seeing Ashley, when I took a tray with toast and coffee into her room, further dispelled depression.

'How kind of you to bring breakfast,' she said between yawns. 'What time is it?'

'You should know that time stops ticking in the enchanted domain,' I said. 'Lie in for as long as you like and catch up on your rest.'

'And you?'

'I'll be in the study weaving the fates of my characters, like the Norns in Norse mythology.'

'As long as it's only your characters . . . I think I'll go for a walk in the woods later. It looks a lovely day outside.'

'Take a mac or an umbrella. This is a rare season for sudden thunderstorms.'

'Jonathan?'

'Yes?'

'Thanks for being understanding last night. I'm sure things will come right in a little while.'

Her words were reassuring and I left her on that note, not wishing to enter into a discussion on the psychology of our relationship. Too often one can talk things out of existence.

Upstairs I looked over the last few pages I had written to catch the flavour of the last scene, and then set to work. In their happiness at being together again Falco and Lorna remain unaware of the menace that is growing about them as a result of William Fortune's activities. While he protests that he is working to clear the house of its malign inheritance from Sir Richard Elphick, in reality he does all he can to encourage the paranormal manifestations, thereby endangering the occupants. Using his aggressive charm, and stressing how much *unpaid* time and effort he and his circle are devoting to the case, he tries to talk Falco into allowing him to hold a seance which will culminate with the excavation in the wine cellar.

At last I was approaching the part of the novel where I could give my imagination full fantastical rein. Up to this point I had worked hard at portraying my characters as people my readers could identify with. I had striven to suspend disbelief, as the buzz phrase has it, and if my technique had succeeded I had led them imperceptibly into the realm of the damned. Of course there had been periodic mini-climaxes of increasing intensity in order to hold the interest and whet the appetite, but now the time had come for madder music and stronger wine.

There was a renewed enthusiasm for the story burning within me, and I rubbed my hands in anticipation of what I was about to write. Just over an hour ago my mind had been in turmoil over my problems, but as my forefingers began to tap the keys they receded into limbo. Later that morning Ashley brought me a cup of tea before going for a stroll to the village – she had been shocked by the empty refrigerator – and during this break it struck me that what I was doing might possibly be dangerous. Was there a risk that the events I was about to describe in the fictitious *Whispering Corner* might reflect upon the house that was its model?

In the manic mood of the moment I did not care. After the disappointing sales of my last book and the patent hostility of Jocasta Mount-William, after abandoning one novel and wrestling with writer's block, it would be professional suicide to stop now or – worse! – water down the story.

Later, in more sober moments, I convinced myself that there was probably nothing to worry about. Since the visit of Dr McAndrew nothing abnormal had occurred and, I argued convincingly, should the border between fiction and reality be breached again it would hardly matter anyway. I would soon be quitting this house I loved, and the effects of its mysterious magic combined with my imagination would be ended.

The truth is that even if I had known there would be a psychic repercussion as a result of continuing with the story I would still have written it.

As I worked I got perverse pleasure out of building up the character of William Fortune. It was as though I was exacting revenge on Charles Nixon by casting him in the role of a sanctimonious crook.

My task was to portray the hold the medium was gaining over Falco and Lorna, and it became absorbing. As I typed I could almost hear his deep confident voice explaining, reassuring, cajoling and, at the psychologically right moment, bullying his victims. It was an equally demanding exercise to describe how their sense of independence deteriorated as he played upon their anxieties, especially in regard to Falco's love for Whispering Corner. I concluded the chapter with Lorna convincing Falco that Fortune should hold his séance.

'At least he's trying, James. And what's the alternative? You can't go on living here under threat . . .'

'You're right, of course,' Falco agreed. He swung round on his stool and took her hands. 'I'll go along with anything that gets this place back to normal so that you and I can just be happy here together. I'll even go along with Fortune.'

'Darling, you know that's all I want too. Just to be with the man I love . . .'

Wishful thinking!

Chapter 22

The next days were strange days. I felt mounting excitement as I worked towards the climax of *Whispering Corner*, and I congratulated myself that I had really got back to being an author again. As for the situation with Ashley, it remained in limbo. On the surface we talked easily enough on neutral topics, listened to music in the evenings and kissed goodnight before we went to our respective bedrooms.

Once I made an attempt to get back on the old footing. Ashley, suffering from a headache – a not infrequent complaint that was a worrying legacy from her motor crash – had gone to bed early and I had sat up with an old book on mediumship from my reference library.

Around midnight, bored with mediums and their inevitable Red Indian guides, the absurdity of the situation struck me like a revelation. I was sharing my house with a girl with whom I had explored the erotic passions of the heart from the floor of the room where I was now sitting alone to the tepid waters of the Red Sea, and with whom I had wanted to spend the rest of my life. It was artificial and perverse to be living like polite acquaintances. I went up to Ashley's room and sat on the edge of her bed.

'Jonathan . . ?' she murmured, coming out of her sleep.
'What?'

'Move over, Ash,' I said, lifting the duvet. 'This charade has gone on long enough.'

If I had hoped that my bold action would revive our old relationship and I would be welcomed into her loving arms I could not have been more mistaken.

Next morning we met at breakfast as though the incident had not happened. Ashley poured coffee, set down a saucer of Whiskas for Mrs Foch and chatted in her usual way. The tension was terrible and it came as a relief when, in the late afternoon, Warren arrived.

From the study window I saw him appear on the lawn by the great hornbeam just as he had when he had first arrived at Whispering Corner. I was pleased to see him, believing that the presence of the cheerful young Australian would ease the tension which now hung over us.

I had been working on a description of Fortune preparing for his séance, in which he plans to introduce an incognito Fleet Street journalist as a member of his circle, and I needed to get the paragraph completed before I broke the train of thought by going downstairs to welcome my friend. He could introduce himself to Ashley, and doubtless she would give him a cup of tea or a can of beer from the refrigerator.

My reluctance to break off reflected the fact that my work seemed to be going remarkably well – perhaps because it was an escape from the situation with Ashley. When I had come back to Whispering Corner after my visit to Abu Sabbah her absence had filled me with desperate loneliness, but now she had returned I was even more lonely. In some obscure way the girl I had fallen in love with had been replaced by a stranger. Several times I had tried to discuss the situation with her, and on each occasion she had said that she was sure our relationship would return to what it had been once she had 'sorted herself out'. She was unable, or reluctant, to explain what it was that she needed to sort out. I was oppressed by various dark speculations inspired by my fear that she still mistrusted me, and the only thing I was certain of was the fact that day by day we were drifting further apart.

The minutes went by and still I sought to get down another couple of lines of dialogue or another descriptive sentence before I abandoned the thread of the story. The result was that half an hour must have slipped by before I saw Warren, and then it was he who came through the door to see me.

'Sorry,' I said. 'I just wanted to finish this.'

'You seem to be in full cry. Don't let me interrupt.'

Although I was anxious to keep going, I gestured for him to sit down. 'Did you enjoy Findhorn?'

For a minute he extolled the mystical atmosphere of the place. 'You should go up there as soon as your novel is finished, Jonathan. A good dose of tranquillity is just what you need.'

'I won't argue with that,' I said.

'Has everything been all right?'

'All quiet since Dr McAndrew was here.'

'So it must be over.'

'Let's hope so.'

He stood silently for a moment.

'By the way, you're interested in coincidences,' he resumed. 'When I arrived I was knocked out to see Ashley Matheson here. I'd met her in Sydney. Small world. At least it is out there. Everybody seems to know everybody.'

I said something about the world becoming a village.

'If you fancy some chilli con carne tonight I'll go to the village for some mince.'

'Sounds great. Take Ashley with you. It'll be good for her to chat about the old stamping ground. She's been rather low-spirited lately.'

'OK. I won't hold up the creative flow any more. See you at supper.'

I nodded and returned to my imaginary world. By the time the sky turned to violet over the woods I had the dazed feeling that comes at the end of a day's intensive writing. I needed time to unwind before I joined Ashley and Warren, so I took the Norbury and Poole eyepiece from a drawer and went to Miss Constance's parlour.

The last rays of the setting sun reflected warmly on the brass of the telescope which, after Warren had worked on it during his first stay here, gleamed as it must have done when it first left the Liverpool factory a hundred years ago. The eyepiece snicked neatly into position and after a minute of adjustments I was scanning the treetops, amazed at the details of lacy foliage and birdlife that appeared in the lens.

Turning a wheel I raised the barrel to the sky and suddenly was lost in a fantastical world of pink-edged cloud sculpture. Were I an author of fantasy tales I would never be short of magical landscapes and citadels to describe with such an instrument.

I was euphoric when I went down to join Ashley and Warren and, helped by a few drinks, supper passed very well. The presence of a third party, especially someone she had met before, had made a difference to Ashley, and, while both of us were content to let Warren describe the Findhorn community at length, her eyes were bright and something of her old animation had returned.

With the climax of *Whispering Corner* approaching I decided to attempt a couple more pages before I turned in, and I was able to leave them chatting over a bottle of Macon without feeling guilty.

By midnight I had reached the point where Fortune's séance was about to begin under the lights of a camera crew. The story was winding up at last and I sensed that a stage in my own situation was close to an end as well. Unless a minor miracle happened the bank would take possession of Whispering Corner in a few days, and I had no idea of what I would do then or what the situation between Ashley and myself would be. But as I gratefully sank on to my bed all that mattered was to make my final chapter powerful enough to reinstate me as a popular author.

Next morning I had been at work for a couple of hours when Warren brought up several letters which had just arrived. One was addressed in an italic typeface.

'I was thinking of taking Ash to see the folly over at High Wood,' he said.

'Good idea,' I replied, my mind on Nixon's letter which I was fumbling to open.

It was a letter written in a rage, and I guessed it had been written immediately after Nixon had received the letter from my solicitor suggesting – quite strongly, I should imagine – that he pay his share of the company overdraft. Such was his anger when he composed it that words were misspelled, repeated and run together, but this only emphasized the manic effect.

He began by abusing me for 'setting' my solicitor on to him and continued with a series of 'how dare I's, such as how dare I demand money before the case had even come to court? And so on. The tone changed on the second page, becoming self-pitying. He claimed that he was broke and in debt, thanks to the fact that he had worked so long on my behalf without reward, his marriage was falling apart, and now I, whose mediocre book he had promoted into a film that had been seen around the world, had turned against him. He could never have believed I would have repaid him with such ingratitude. Well, he was wiser now, but the effect of my harassment was taking its toll on his health.

The final paragraphs were written in sorrow rather than anger. He wondered how I, who must be making huge sums out of my books, could think of demanding money from someone who had no regular income ('and at the moment cannot pay his telephone bill') and had got himself into this position through his efforts to get another film produced by *our* company. He added that thanks to me he was at the end of his tether and concluded, 'I fail to see how you can live with yourself – obviously others cannot!'

In his rhetoric he overlooked the fact that I knew he had recently worked as an independent producer, that I had never asked him to try and promote my work, and that it was Whispering Corner that was about to be sold, not his Richmond home.

Although I knew perfectly well that such bluff and moral outrage was part of his tactics for avoiding paying his share of the overdraft, there was an underlying warp of desperation about the letter that was almost physically repellent. Instead of throwing it into my wastepaper basket, I took it down to the garbage bin. As I did so I heard a door close and guessed that Warren and Ashley were on their way to see the tower, which had been originally built as a folly by Edward Drax at the end of the eighteenth century.

Back at the Acer, I re-entered the Whispering Corner of my imagination, where preparations were under way for Fortune's séance. Falco finds his house suddenly invaded by a film crew.

'They heard a rumour about my work here and just turned up, too late to send them away old chap.' Fortune lies.

The lighting cameraman and his assistant busy themselves setting up lights in the dining-room and the cellar while a sound mixer moves about with his Nagra recorder demanding hush while he checks his levels. Members of Fortune's group arrive in their different cars with the air of statesmen at an international conference, important and grave. One – who was not present at the first séance – takes a sympathetic interest in Lorna and gets into a deep discussion with her about her experiences since she arrived at the house. He is, of course, the Fleet

Street man.

Feeling almost a stranger in his own home and uneasy at the prospect of the séance now that there is media involvement, Falco strolls past the parked vehicles in the drive. He has almost reached the lane when an elderly dark green Morris 1100 cautiously noses between the old stone gateposts.

I wrote – *A man's head with a pink cherubic face and a shock of pure silver hair leaned through the driver's window.*

'I am looking for a house called Whispering Corner,' he said, tentatively.

'You've come to the right place,' said Falco. 'Have you come for tonight's meeting?'

'Actually, I've come to see Mr Falco.'

'That's me. You're .. . ?'

'Scott. Leslie Scott. I got back from Verona yesterday and having read your very graphic letter I thought I'd better come over as soon as possible.'

'But you're not . . .'

'Oh, that. I only wear a dog collar when ritual necessity demands it. It tends to chafe. But I'm a priest all right.'

'How kind of you to come. You can leave your car just inside the gateway. Sorry there's not a lot of room.'

'Have I come at an awkward time? It looks as if you're having a party.'

Falco shook his head. 'As a matter of fact, it's a séance.'

Abruptly the Reverend Scott pulled his head inside. The wheels of the Morris spun in the mould as he shot into the driveway to park.

'To hold a séance here is very unwise, if what you wrote to me is true,' said the clergyman, climbing out of his car.

'It's true enough,' said Falco. 'But I understand from the medium that through the séance he might discover the reason behind these manifestations . . .'

'Nonsense,' said the Reverend Scott briskly. 'Such things are snares and delusions. Like Saul, mediums trespass into forbidden territories, they make themselves prey to the minions of the evil one.'

'I must say I'm not completely happy about what's going to happen. It seems to be turning into a bit of a circus.'

'They're playing with things they don't understand. Can you stop it?'

'It'd be difficult,' said Falco. 'And rather embarrassing after I agreed to it.'

'Ye-es,' said the clergyman thoughtfully. 'Perhaps you could arrange for me to be present. No need for anyone to know who I am. At least I'll be able to give you protection if necessary.'

He took a small antique silver box from an inside pocket.

'Here I have the best possible defence against the dark power,' he said matter-of-factly. 'It contains a wafer of the Host, and with it there's a phial of holy water from the shrine at Walsingham.'

'Great' murmured Falco, whose instinct assured him of the Reverend Scott's sincerity but whose sense of logic balked at the accessories of exorcism. 'I'll introduce you as an old friend who has turned up unexpectedly.'

'Although your letter gave me a pretty good idea of the phenomena that have been occurring here, it would be helpful if you could give me the details of what's happened since you first found that there was something abnormal here.'

'It began with voices, whispering voices,' said Falco, as he led the Reverend Scott through the tunnel of trees towards the house.

I continued working through the morning, and I found that when William Fortune came into the story I described him and his actions with a bitter clarity that reflected my feelings about his archetype. It was as though Nixon's letter that morning had released an emotional adrenalin within me. I hated the man whose only response to my forthcoming loss of Whispering Corner was abuse and self-righteous indignation, and as I write this I have to admit to a feeling of such anger against another human being as I had never experienced before.

Edgar Allan Poe, exploited and embittered, must have known it too. The thousand injuries of Fortunato I had borne as I best could, but when he ventured upon insult . . .'

Poe bricked up Fortunato alive, for my William Fortune I reserved what to me was the ultimate horror.

It was after midday and I had reached the point in my chapter where the séance was about to begin when I decided to take a break for a snack and coffee before plunging on with the story and went down to the kitchen. Manx Mrs Foch regarded me with one green eye from her basket while I put a slice of bacon under the grill and switched on the electric kettle. Then, sandwich in one hand and a mug of coffee in the other, I went back up the stairs to Miss Constance's parlour. Before returning to work I wanted to relax my mind, and with this thought I decided to try out the telescope in bright daylight.

I opened the window and focused on the topmost branch of the hornbeam. I was amazed at the detail of its toothed leaves which appeared in the eyepiece. By carefully turning the brass adjusting wheels, I began an aerial exploration of the woods surrounding Whispering Corner.

For a few moments I was presented with a screen of leaves, and then I came to a gap in the foliage which afforded a glimpse into a natural clearing. For a moment the scene was blurred, but a touch on the focusing control brought sharpness. I saw the ground covered with dark ferns, a pair of brimstone butterflies waltzing through the air in search of blackthorn . . . and the forms of Ashley and Warren standing opposite each other in the centre of the tiny glade.

His hands were resting on her shoulders and, as I watched his lips moving and saw the expression of concentration on her face, *I knew*.

On one hand my act of unpremeditated voyeurism repelled me, on the other I found it impossible to take my eye away from the lens in which the two minuscule figures silently signalled the end of my hope that there could be a revival of what Ashley and I had shared before Abu Sabbah.

Warren's lips stopped moving.

For a long moment the two stood looking into each other's faces, then slowly – and, I could not help thinking, gracefully – Ashley inclined her head in a gesture of acquiescence. Warren lowered his hands and put his arms round her and she responded by putting hers round his neck. Then, their lips pressed hard together, they sank down on to the ferns. Ashley lay back, her eyes fixed on the sky while Warren raised himself up beside her and, with an air of gravity, carefully unbuttoned her shirt and unbuckled the belt of her jeans.

The telescope revolved on its tripod as I forced myself to thrust it away. At that moment it was not what was about to happen that sickened me but a perverse desire to watch further.

After I had met Ashley I had envisaged her as the heroine of *Whispering Corner*. Had I romantically come to think of myself as Falco? If so I was a fool. Warren was Falco.

I went back to my study and began to type again.

What else could I do?

It was late in the afternoon when there was a knock at my door and I heard Warren say, 'I'm sorry to interrupt, Jonathan, but I've got to talk to you.'

'Come in,' I said, and finished typing my sentence.

He came in, a study of mingled guilt and defiance, and – to my irritation – pity.

'It's about Ash,' he said. 'It's very difficult

'No need for it to be difficult,' I said. 'I know what's happened.'

'But how . . . ?'

'I may be a fool, but I'm not stupid.'

'But I've got to explain. You can't understand.'

'Oh, I don't think it's so difficult to understand. Betrayal, infidelity, romantic illusion, the need for a sexual work-out . . . there's nothing unusual in all that.'

'Don't talk like that. Forget you're a bloody writer for once, will you!'

I shrugged.

'Sorry,' he continued in a lower voice. 'I can guess how you must feel – I've been there myself, and with Ashley.'

'In Australia?'

'Yeah, in Australia.' He rubbed his hand across his face. 'You've every reason to think we're a right pair of bastards but I don't want to go away with you thinking I made a play for your girl while I was enjoying your hospitality.'

'What does it matter what I think?'

'You can say that, but it does matter to me. You've been bloody good to me – and anyway I admire your work. What I want you to understand is that Ash and I used to live together. In Sydney we had a flat in The Cross until . . .'

'Until one day she ran away?' I suggested.

'I guess you got some understanding of her. And you're right. Her problem has been that she wasn't able to sustain a relationship. She'd reach a point when something would snap and she'd just have to run.'

'So that's why you came to England. You were looking for her?'

'Not consciously. In fact I didn't know where she'd gone. At the time I thought it most likely she'd gone back home in New Zealand. But I was so restless I had to do something, and I'd always had an ambition to come to Europe and do a tour of mystical sites.'

'I can't get over what a coincidence it was that you should turn up at Whispering Corner, and Ashley should arrive a few days later.'

'Jonathan, that was no coincidence. Ash had told me so much about the place – you know, her dad used to tell the kids stories about it and their eccentric aunt. The name stuck in my mind, and when I came to England I thought it'd be interesting to see the old house. And when I saw that newspaper item and realized you were living here it was a bonus. The fact that I wanted to meet you because I'd seen *The Dancing Stones* was perfectly true.'

'All right. I accept what you're telling me.'

'I'm bloody sorry, Jonathan.'

'Kismet,' I said. 'What now?'

'We're going to try again.'

I said nothing. Perhaps I should have wished him good luck or said 'Bless you my children', but now I just wanted to be on my own. Further conversation would be bathetic.

'Ash just wasn't up to saying goodbye to you, so she's waiting for me in the village. We'll take the bus to Poole . . .' He went on, in his embarrassment giving me an itinerary.

I looked at my watch. 'The bus will be due soon.'

'Yeah. Better be on my way.'

He wanted to say something that, from his point of view, would make things right, make him feel that he could leave with a clear conscience because he had been honest with me. He made a movement as though he wanted to shake hands, but I pulled the laptop towards me. 'Good luck with the novel,' he said as he turned to the door.

'Good luck with Ashley,' I replied. The door closed and the two people who had shared so much with me at Whispering Corner were out of my life for ever.

'Lights, Jim love,' called Crispin Smythe, the young unit director, and the cellar leapt into harsh detail as two portable flood lamps were switched on. The camera tripod had been carefully mounted halfway up the steps so that the table which had been placed in front of the entrance to the wine cellar was in full view. On a stool at the bottom of the steps the sound man sat over his recorder with earphones that looked like oversized earmuffs.

'We can't waste film recording the whole evening,' Crispin Smythe whispered to the veteran cameraman. 'If anything interesting starts to happen I'll give you the word. Let's have a few zooms on the faces if they look shocked or startled, and I want a close-up of linked hands when they form the circle.'

'Whatever you say, Mr de Mille,' muttered the cameraman – the old cameraman's joke.

At the table William Fortune was arranging his group, while in a corner of the cellar, seated on an upturned pail, the Reverend Scott watched the proceedings with such a studied lack of expression that it advertised his disapproval rather than hid it. Only the journalist had recognized him, and had decided the evening might be more interesting than he had expected. Something must be afoot, but he was far too experienced to allow his interest to show.

Falco had introduced the exorcist as Scottie, an old friend who had come to visit him and was so fascinated by the proceedings that I told him it would be all right to watch from a distance.

William Fortune grunted acquiescence. He was tense with the knowledge that his chance to become a latter-day Harry Price was perhaps only minutes away. The one thing that did not worry him was the possibility that nothing might happen. After the last séance he was confident that there was enough latent psychic power in the house to produce a reasonable manifestation, what he had to concentrate on was stage-managing it to the best advantage.

'We're ready to begin,' he called to Crispin. 'Whatever happens, keep filming. You should get material tonight that will make you

famous.'

'And you,' said the cameraman.

'Fame is not something that interests me,' he said, taking up his position at the table.

Crispin tapped the sound man on the shoulder.

He pushed back one earmuff. *'Yes?'*

'You getting the words clearly?'

'I was.'

'Splendid, love. Mr Fortune, could you say that again – about not being interested in fame?'

'Fame is not something that interests me,' the medium declared. *'My work is to investigate the phenomena that link the visible world with the invisible, and in so doing to help others . . .'*

When he had finished his speech he called to Crispin, *'Would you like us to start with a prayer? Might help to get it next to a peak God slot.'*

'No harm,' Crispin replied. *'It would help with a Stateside network. We can always edit it out if it doesn't work.'*

Fortune bowed his head. *'Dear Heavenly Father . . .'*

Sitting across the table from Falco, Lorna caught his eye and hastily looked down as he grimaced his disapproval of Fortune's performance.

When he reached *'Amen'*, he said, *'Please hold hands in the usual manner and do not break the circle no matter what happens. We will now begin. Please sit quietly for a minute and clear your minds in order to be receptive.'*

The eight men and women seated round the table bowed their heads obediently. The only sound to disturb the silence of the cellar was the scrape of a match as the focus-puller lit a cigarette.

Fortune raised his head. *'Spirits from bygone times, tonight we earnestly seek to discover what it is that has brought you back to this house,'* his solemn voice intoned. *'Grant us a sign that you are with us . . .'*

At that instant Falco felt the table tremble. Then it rose several inches before dropping back to the floor.

'Did you get that?' hissed the director.

'I'm turning,' the cameraman hissed back. *'But the lights . . .*
'

At his words the floodlights dimmed, brightened, dimmed again.

'Answer one knock for yes, two for no,' cried Fortune, a faint flush on his pallid face reflecting his surprise at such a quick response. *'Are you the spirit of Sir Robert Elphick?'*

A knock, as though made by a clump hammer violently striking a plank, resounded through the cellar.

'Is it because of remorse that you return?'

Fortune's words were followed by a rataplan of knocks which echoed painfully in everyone's ears. The sound mixer hastily adjusted his controls while the blows went on and on in a rhythmic frenzy. When the medium attempted to say something they grew even louder as though to drown his words. Then the table began to dance.

First it rose, higher than before so that the sitters were forced to release their handclasps, then, freed from the circle, one end reared up while its weight rested on the legs at the opposite end. Thus balanced it began a parody of walking. Falco was reminded of a circus animal forced up on to its back legs to waddle after its trainer.

When it reached the centre of the cellar it crashed on to the stone flags. The knocking which had reached a deafening climax suddenly ceased, and the lights returned to their normal brilliance.

For a long moment there was silence.

Falco got to his feet.

'That's enough, Fortune,' he declared. 'You're making things worse . . .'

His voice trailed away as the lights faded to such a degree that the cellar was in semi-darkness.

'Jesus Christ!' muttered the cameraman, his eye to the viewfinder. It was not an oath but a prayer. The hitherto dark entrance to the wine cellar was filled with luminosity, rather as though a glowing mist was forming within its tunnel-like walls.

The Reverend Scott shouted something which no one heard, all eyes were on the opaque light in which – or so it seemed indefinable shapes moved. And from the cellar came the sound of voices softly whispering.

No one moved. No one spoke. The whispering grew louder, the words indistinct but their timbre increasingly urgent.

Lorna rose to her feet, her eyes fixed on the doorway. Falco tried to lean forward to seize her arm but it seemed as though all the strength had been short-circuited from his body. He could only stand and watch while Lorna walked forward into the unearthly light.

Suddenly she screamed. 'The baby! Where have you put the baby?'

She dropped to her knees and turned her head to look over her shoulder – and Falco gasped as he saw that the face of the frantic woman was no longer that of the girl he loved.

My fingers were stiff from typing and the glass of brandy and Perrier stood untouched beside the Acer. I had poured it out earlier to sustain my effort but as the final chapter of *Whispering Corner* had developed I had no need for it. I was caught up in the story and I was determined to bring it to the conclusion I had predetermined regardless of any qualms I might once have had. All that mattered in my world was to get the book finished.

The loss of Ashley and the forthcoming loss of my house had ceased to mean anything as I sat in the heat of my study with Mrs Foch curled up beside me. During those hours of concentration I had crossed the line between the everyday world and the reality of my imagination.

I wiped the sweat from my face, hoping that a thunderstorm would soon clear the stifling heat which brooded over the woods. No airs stirred, and far beyond the green sea of treetops a pale grey column rose perpendicular from a hidden stubble burn. I interlocked my fingers, cracked the joints and typed.

As her continuing scream rose above the disembodied voices, the girl began to scratch with her fingers at the earthen floor of the wine cellar.

It seemed that she would make little impression on the hard clay, but – as the cameraman who had zoomed in on the scene was the first to see – the floor itself was changing, loosening and moving of its own accord, spurting upwards in puffs of dirt, cracking and subsiding. It was as though some presence long entombed was stirring.

At the same time a smell, so revolting that it made the petrified watchers gag, issued from the wine cellar. The cameraman, who had done his stint on Third World wars, recognized it for what it was.

Then something *– something that nobody could properly describe afterwards, but Falco remembered as pallid and glistening – appeared in the seething earth to reach upwards towards the kneeling woman.*

'Begone, thou hideous demon . . . '

The Reverend Scott elbowed a path through the petrified spectators as though thrusting his way through a waxworks display. Holding the silver case containing the Host high above his head and intoning the words of exorcism, he entered the wine cellar. The whispering voices died away, the seething earth became still, the luminosity faded and in the main cellar the flood lamps returned to full power.

Falco was the first to move. He ran into the wine cellar, shouldering the clergyman to one side to lift the limp body of the young woman. Carrying her into the harsh glare of the lamps he turned her head to see with infinite relief that her blanched features were those of Lorna.

'Get her upstairs at once,' *ordered the Reverend Scott. About them people began exclaiming as they do after the shock of an accident. But before Falco could take a step with his burden, a cry of anguish filled the cellar.*

William Fortune, face contorted, mouth agape, sprang across the floor and hurled himself up the steps. He collided with the camera tripod. The Arriflex crashed to the floor below and burst open, film spilling out like black entrails.

Electric leads entangled Fortune's ankles. The cameraman tried to hold him, but with unnatural strength he tore himself free of the cables, plunging the cellar into darkness. The cameraman was hurled after his whirring camera and the medium was gone.

One of the crew produced an electric torch and a minute later everyone was safely in the hall. The door was slammed and bolted on the mephitic cellar.

As Falco laid Lorna on the sofa in the living-room the Reverend Scott said, 'The danger with exorcism is that when evil is cast out it sometimes enters another host. We must find that deluded man before it brings disaster upon him. The poor fool must have realized the risk he ran in order to promote himself. . .'

'Will Lorna be all right?' Falco interrupted.

'Put her to bed and when she wakes this ghastly business will have receded into the blurred memory of a nightmare. When you've done that we'll search for Mr Fortune.'

I briefly described the fruitless hunt for Fortune, who had taken to the woods, and the departure of the circle members and the film crew who, having got over their initial shock at the manifestations in the cellar, were cursing the destruction of what would have been a sensational film. Falco then sat beside the unconscious Lorna until dawn lightened the western sky.

There were only a few lines left to be written.

Outside it was dark, except for the occasional glimmer of sheet lightning, and suddenly I was utterly weary. The desperate need to finish the book had tapped some hidden reserve of energy, but now I was on the last page it had run dry. I drank the brandy and slowly began to describe how the exhausted Falco leaves Lorna sleeping normally. Treading carefully so as not to wake the Reverend Scott, who has spent the night in an adjoining bedroom, he goes downstairs to make himself coffee. Then, with the steaming mug in his hand, he walks into the garden to breathe the earth-scented air of the woodland.

Although his body ached with fatigue Falco felt at peace. He knew instinctively that Whispering Corner was cleansed and at last he and Lorna were free to get on with their lives.

He looked towards the ornamental urns flanking the stone steps up to the French windows, remembering how on his arrival he had planned to plant them with ivy and geraniums. Well, it was not too late. He turned to the nearest urn and uprooted dried weeds while his mind dwelt on the future.

Suddenly Falco froze.

In the glass of the French windows he could see a man hanging. For a moment he stood without moving, and then it struck him that the man might not yet be dead. The thought released him from the paralysis of shock, he took a step forwards and realized that he was looking at a reflection.

He turned and saw that at the corner of the garden, hanging by his tie from the lowest branch of the great hornbeam, William Fortune swayed ever so slightly in the breeze.

His face was blackened in death, his granny glasses had slipped down his nose and his unblinking eyes were fixed on the gargoyles perched above the house.

I typed THE END and went to bed.

When I opened my eyes I was puzzled by the pattern of the shadows in my bedroom, until I looked at my watch and realized that I had slept through until mid-afternoon. With this realization came memory. Yesterday I had finished my novel, this morning the case brought against me by the bank had gone before the court.

In less than ten minutes I was hurrying along Church Walk towards the village, trying to stop myself thinking about Ashley and Warren and what I was likely to hear when I rang the solicitor. It was foolish, but when I reached the phone box I was reluctant to dial the number of the law firm, it was as though the house would remain mine until I knew the inevitable result of the morning's proceedings. I delayed matters by ringing my agent.

'Just thought I'd let you know I finished *Whispering Corner* last night,' I told Sylvia Stone. 'I've brought it in on time after all.'

'I never thought you'd do it,' she said. 'How I'll enjoy sending it to the Mount-William. Is it any good?'

'You'll have to decide that.'

She said she was sure it was marvellous, asked the number of words and when would I get the memory stick to her, and ended up by saying I'd better start thinking about my next novel.

When she rang off I could no longer postpone the moment of truth. I dialled the solicitor.

'It went just as I expected,' Mr Swan said in a voice of professional gravity. 'The bank was given judgement against you. Unless you can clear the overdraft immediately I'm afraid the house will be put up for sale – probably by auction. I had a word with their solicitor afterwards, and the best I could do was get you a week's grace to remove your belongings.'

'Thanks,' I said dully. Then I felt anger suffuse me.

'And I suppose the bank isn't going to do anything about bloody Charles Nixon.'

'Well, in the circumstances, they hardly could even if they wanted to.'

'Sorry?'

'Then you don't know. Charles Nixon was found dead in Richmond Park this morning.'

'Suicide?' I said finally.

'Yes. He hanged himself.'

I replaced the receiver feeling I was a murderer.

I shall not go into my emotional state as I returned through the woods or the agony of guilt that frequently overwhelmed me. Suffice to say that when I entered the house I had made up my mind as to what had to be done.

For a while I sat on the sofa in the living-room, looking into the depths of my glass. Then as the twilight drew on I went to my study and brought down the print-out of my novel. I glanced at the first page, which seemed to have been written in another lifetime, *James Falco pushed his way down the overgrown path and suddenly beheld the house known as Whispering Corner.*

I had not dreamed of Ashley's existence when I wrote that. If I had not have hanged the character I based on Nixon, he might well still be alive. Had my anger against my old partner caused me to bring about his death in the way that some events had followed my fiction. Had I subconsciously arranged Charlie Nixon's death on my laptop in revenge for the loss of Whispering Corner?

I struck a match, lit one corner of the first page of the first page, watched the blue flame curl the edge and tossed it into the empty fireplace. Then page by page I burnt my novel. It was symbolic. The laptop still contained the work, but that would be deleted . . .

Sometimes I read a sentence before adding it to the pyre, here Falco heard the whisperings which were the prelude to the haunting, there he walked in the moonlit garden with Lorna. Once I paused too long reading a description of the woods that I had been particularly pleased with, and had to relight the fire. But when I came to a description of William Fortune I no longer dared to look at the typed lines. I turned the rest of the script over so that I could not see the writhing lines of the words as they burned.

I sat for a long time unable to focus my mind on what must be done next. How was I to break it to Sylvia that the novel she had been so supportive over was now nothing more than a mound of grey ash? I must have drunk quite a lot as I tried to dull the misery which welled up within me and shut out the recurring mental picture of a body dangling beneath a tree.

At midnight I climbed to my feet and mounted the stairs like a man twice my age. I just wanted oblivion, but for some reason I cannot explain I continued up the stairs to the third floor where brilliant moonlight shone through an open door. I approached and saw the telescope gleaming on its tripod, its barrel still askew as I had pushed it when I inadvertently spied on Warren and Ashley.

And I saw something else – the figure of a woman in a silken dress whose hem touched the floor, an old woman with a gentle face and white hair held by old-fashioned combs. Without a sound she crossed to the table in the centre of the room, laid her fingertips upon it and gave me a look – a look which seemed to me to be one of compassion. And then she was gone. No fading away – just no longer there.

I had finally seen the true spirit of Whispering Corner.

There was nothing frightening about the experience. It was as though Miss Constance, whose grief had moulded her life, had wanted to convey something to me in my hour of desperation.

'Miss Constance,' I called.

The only reply was a mewing from her cat who had followed me upstairs. Mrs Foch had sensed her presence.

I called again, but I knew there would be no answer.

Then I went to the table to see what her fingers had touched. There lay the poem written in her fiancé's hand. It was folded as before so that only the last verse was visible, an intimation of hope that transcended time to save my sanity.

And so like clouds above, all swiftly passing,
Our joy and sorrow comes alternately.
And over all I seem to hear this message,
Endure – take all that comes unwearily.
Something's calling,
Gladly calling,
Time will come when you will yet be free.

The next day I quit Whispering Corner.

EPILOGUE

Last night I finished my Narration.

This afternoon the dazzle of the sea is painful even through sunglasses as I sit on the terrace, Mrs Foch dozes in the same patch of shade and, like me, the heat has turned her into a creature of the night. After sundown she comes to life and chases stilt-legged crabs along the coral beach.

Palms rattle in the oven wind, in the bungalow the ululation of Radio Baghdad comes courtesy of Ashley's old radio, and I am drained now that I have completed my task of recording what actually happened during my occupancy of Whispering Corner.

On the table beside me is mail that was delivered after the last inbound flight seven days ago. During the long hours at my laptop I was too preoccupied to open it. Today I find that these letters have a remote quality about them, like messages in bottles which have drifted from another dimension.

When I left Whispering Corner I flew out to Abu Sabbah where some day – fundamentalist *plastiquers* permitting – I may possibly work at the Hamid IV College. Meanwhile I earn my keep, the beach house and basic necessities in a most agreeable way. I have become King Syed's *rawi*.

Once a week, in a state of painstaking sobriety, I visit the royal palace, and after we have dined it is my duty to entertain by story-telling. At first I read chapters from *Shadows and Mirrors* but latterly I have taken to improvising stories in the old Arabian vein which always begin with 'Know, O King . . . '

For these evenings I have discarded my M&S safari suit for a *rawi's* blue robe. Perhaps in a previous existence I sat in the dust outside a mosque telling wondrous tales of poor fishermen, flying unicorns, and lovelorn daughters of sultans for copper coins.

Apart from these weekly meetings with Syed, Jo sometimes rides her great black horse along the shore to my house for what she terms a 'talkfest', free from protocol. Over the weeks I have told her much of what I have written in my Narration, and to my own surprise more and more about my marriage.

'It may not be the love affair of the century,' she commented once, 'but it seems you two had friendship, and friendship counts for a lot in this tacky world. I guess when you found yourselves on your own as two people instead of parents you should have given each other a chance. If Pamela had stayed in London and you hadn't become the hermit of the woods you might have discovered new things about each other.'

'Too late now,' I said, and I said it with regret. Jo was right when she remarked that love can be instant real companionship only evolves with time and experience. And there comes a time when companionship becomes the most valuable emotional asset.

I have been thinking about Pamela a lot lately, perhaps because she is the only person I have corresponded with since I began my exile – apart from the Reverend Henry Gotobed to whom I send postcards of thanks for forwarding letters which still arrive at my house.

I say 'my house' because Whispering Corner still belongs to me. A couple of days before it was to be taken over officially by the Regent Bank a cable arrived from Y. S. Akkim, the Hollywood producer who made his name by filming Martin Winter's uneasy stories, offering a seemingly impossible sum for the rights to *Shadows and Mirrors.* The result was that I can clear the Pleiades debt and still have more in my new bank account than I previously thought possible.

Too much had happened for me to continue in Whispering Corner – redolent of lost love – with a calm mind. Nor could I rent it with a clear conscience for fear the latent power which turned my imagination into reality might equally menace the next tenant. Thus it stands empty. Its woodwork will decay, its windows will shatter to vandals' stones and the garden will revert to wilderness. In one of his letters Henry wrote that he had seen Hoddy prowling around it, but in all other respects the young man appears to have recovered from his ordeal.

Among the mail I read today was a card depicting the white sails of the Sydney Opera House, with no address and a few words in Warren's hand, 'All well. Married last week. Preparing for responsibilities of parenthood. Never forget you.'

Dear Sylvia Stone wrote asking if I could remember enough of my destroyed typescript to rewrite it. Clipper Press is desperate for a new novel from me since plans for the filming of *Shadows* have been announced with the usual hype. I shall reply that my writing days are over, for who knows what might happen if I portray more characters? My creative outlet will remain the verbal telling of Arabian fairy tales.

Other letters included an unexpectedly cheerful note, postmarked London, for my birthday from Pamela. Paul Lincoln sent me a complicated tax scheme and news about the winding up of Pleiades Films.

Which brings me to the late Charles Nixon.

Since I have been here I have regarded myself as responsible for his suicide. I had vengefully described it in fiction and it happened in fact, and I have wondered to what degree the malign forces which had been activated by my imagination had been taking possession of me during those last days when I was finishing *Whispering Corner.*

Ironically, I was blamed for the tragedy at the inquest, but for a totally different reason. Nixon's handsome actor friend accused me of harassing my ex-partner to death because of a stern letter from my solicitor that had been found in his pocket. It was a legal demand for a large sum of money he could not afford and it preyed on his mind. Indeed, I had hounded him to death – it was like a murder.

Now, for the first time, I am uncertain as to my guilt, thanks to a letter, redirected from Dorset to Abu Sabbah, from Olwen Nixon. It is brief, obviously written in quiet desperation, and intended out of her deep sense of fairness to reassure me after the accusation of harassment. She explained that the real reason her husband went into Richmond Park that night was because he had been informed that he had been infected by the latest plague to afflict mankind.

But still I wonder.

Although the exercise in catharsis has been successful in that I sleep without voices whispering in my dreams, there is still much to come to terms with – but that is for some day in the future. This evening I must obey a royal summons, and now the sun is balancing on the tawny hills and the first cool zephyr of evening is stirring Mrs Foch's silken fur. At nightfall the king's Rolls will come to take me to the airport.

Following the sabotage of Syed's college he made several concessions to the orthodox including the abandonment of mixed sex education. When the new college opens there will be segregated recreation areas and separate classes for boys and girls, taught by lecturers of the appropriate gender. Among the female lecturers required is one to act as my counterpart in the English department, and here Jo has shown her Machiavellian hand.

'We have found a person absolutely suitable to teach the girls English,' she wrote in a note brought by an army motorcyclist. 'She is arriving by this evening's flight to see if she could live happily in the kingdom, and we feel that you should be there to greet her in your official capacity. You can't miss her as you know her well.'

Pamela!

AUTHOR'S POSTSCRIPT

Sometimes it is of interest to speculate on how much of a novel's background is purely imaginary and how much based on fact. While the author of *Whispering Corner* is at pains to stress that the characters in this book are fictitious and bear no resemblance to any living persons, it must be admitted that the character of Andrew McAndrew was inspired by the late Reverend Dr Donald Omand who was one of the foremost practitioners of the Ministry of Exorcism in Britain.

The author had the honour to be both friend and biographer of Dr Omand, and has witnessed him performing exorcisms both at home and abroad. The method of exorcism described in the novel is based on these.

Although the house in the novel and its environs exist only in the author's imagination, there is a spot known as Whispering Corner close to the Parish Church of St Mary the Virgin outside the Dorset village of Lychett Matravers. According to local legend the name came about because indistinct voices of plague victims are heard there. In fields bordering the real Church Walk there are mounds thought to be foundations of dwellings which made up the abandoned pre-plague village.

Mary Lawson's 'Narration' in the novel owes much to a lady named Mary Ricketts who in 1770 resided in a Hampshire manor house known as Hinton Ampner.

Here she experienced both ghostly and poltergeist phenomena which grew in intensity until she was forced to leave in the August of the following year. She found the experience so remarkable that she described them in a Narration to be kept in her family. Many years later it was published in *The Gentleman's Magazine.*

After the Ricketts left Hinton Ampner it was let to a family named Lawrence who immediately experienced paranormal happenings and left abruptly. After this the house remained empty until it became derelict and had to be demolished.

The exploding glass may be an extreme manifestation of a poltergeist in conjunction with haunted premises, but it is known outside the pages of fiction. In October, 1985, Mark Jordan of Capital Radio visited the King's Arms in Peckham Rye, South London, in search of material for a Hallowe'en programme. The pub is reputed to be haunted by the ghosts of air raid victims from the Second World War when it was struck by a bomb.

Mark Jordan had been interviewing the landlord and his wife for several minutes when he asked them if they had ever considered having the place exorcised. At that moment a glass on the bar by him literally exploded and the sound of this followed by cries of alarm and the clatter of fleeing feet were caught on tape and heard by millions of radio listeners.

The poem quoted in *Whispering Corner* as being written by Miss Constance's fiancé actually appeared in *A Soldier's Poems,* published during the First World War, by R. E. Alexander who served with the Seventh Queen's Own Hussars.

Finally it should be explained that the kingdom of Abu Sabbah is so small that it is only to be found on the most imaginative maps.

Marc Alexander - London